LOOK BEHIND YOU

BARRY MORGAN

For Ryan,
who set up a fan club in NZ

More Evil Reading
for Eon Griselda

LOOK BEHIND YOU

Barry Morgan

Look Behind You

Published by The Conrad Press Ltd. in the United Kingdom 2022

Tel: +44(0)1227 472 874

www.theconradpress.com

info@theconradpress.com

ISBN 978-1-914913-56-3

Typesetting and Cover Design by: Charlotte Mouncey, www.bookstyle.co.uk

The Conrad Press logo was designed by Maria Priestley.

Printed and bound in Great Britain by Clays Ltd, Elcograf S.p.A.

CHAPTER 1

The rain was pounding down, not quite at monsoon level yet, but getting very close to it in intensity. It bounced off the passing cars that were in such a hurry to get home, giving them an illusionary halo, making them look almost soft in the darkness. Their lights dancing off the ever growing puddles were beginning to resemble small lakes in the unseasonable weather.

Thunder rumbled overhead and the whole town was illuminated for a few seconds by a brilliant flash of lightning that turned everything an intense white, with highlights of bright blue and purple.

However, the aesthetics of the scene were completely lost on the young girl huddled in the entrance of the club doorway. She didn't care how amazing the pyrotechnics looked, all she knew it was a hopeless task trying to get home in weather like this.

Her brain, totally addled with drink, simply didn't have the capacity or imagination to come up with anything better than to just sit down heavily on the concrete step of the club and review her options. Staring up at the menacing clouds, she realised just how wet she would get if she moved from this spot. At best she would be utterly soaked, verging on at least totally drenched and possibly close to drowned.

Was it really worth trying to get home at this point in time? But then she was already getting splashed and wet through as it was, by just sitting in the doorway. She was going to get bloody wet, whatever option she took. 'Fuck it! No buses this late now, and there would be no bloody taxis out in this lot.' She looked back at the club in anger.

'Another crap evening. sodding typical,' she muttered to herself as the rain started to penetrate her jacket. She pulled it up around her head in a vain attempt to keep dry. Scowling at the sky she uttered, 'Bloody funny, now how do I get home in his lot? The evening hasn't exactly been a success has it? And like, this is really the icing on the cake. Bloody thanks.'

Scowling at her inner thoughts, she thought her mother had been right again, and her annoying words haunted her now.

'Try and say something without swearing,' she had said earlier that evening, 'It always gets you noticed if you're nice, and you could even smile from time to time. Now, that would really get you noticed.' The girl had laughed at that, she didn't need a smile to get noticed. There were plenty of good-looking guys out there, and she knew she acted like a magnet to them, even at seventeen. A grin spread across her face, she knew what to do to get noticed, and a smile was a long way down the list.

'No swearing, now there was a novelty', she thought. 'Fuck that, everyone swears', but then she had just smirked at her mother and simply said, 'OK I'll give it a try,' as she flounced out of the tiny terraced house in Maidstone, knowing it was a promise she wouldn't be able to remotely keep once she began drinking. As she walked out she pulled her short dress down tight against her long legs, so it looked as if it had been vacuum formed on her, rather than just put on. Besides, the whole point of an evening out with the girls, wasn't to be nice, it was to get totally ratted, and if possible, laid in the deal.

Anything to escape the crippling restrictions of home, and her parents. She wasn't sure who was worse, her dead loss mother who had driven her father away with her nagging, or her bloody step father who she had picked up to replace him. Not so much of a father either, he was usually pissed most evenings, and had a habit of lashing out when it got the better of him. In fact, she thought, anything to escape her bloody sad life in general. And she had such a boring, mind numbing job to cope with, on top of everything else. Of course they had rubbed that in by saying that was her own fault, she should have done better at school, got a few GCSEs, and found some meaningful employment.

But then she had discovered boys instead, and they were far more fun. Besides if she played her cards right, her looks might land someone with a bit of cash to splash. Sod the bloody supermarket then if she did. Sod everyone including her parents. Sod them all. But there was the whole weekend to enjoy now, starting with the club in town tonight. She could have walked in from her home to save a bit of cash, but the bus was reasonably cheap and at least it was warm. Besides, her feet would give her enough grief after a night on the dance floor in heels. 'Save your energy girl,' she muttered.

But that night the local talent were all complete tossers, and only interested in one thing, which she didn't feel like sharing with these losers. All estate boys, no class or cash there. So she stayed with her friends and stuck to the drink, stating, 'I'll give the guys a miss tonight. There's always Saturday. And I'll really make up for it tomorrow. These bastards thought just a vodka chaser would get them a quick shag. No chance! I ain't that cheap!'

She could hold her drink, or so she thought, but without realising just how drunk she had become, her behaviour went from bad to worse, and she had sworn at the barman once too often. As a result, she was politely, but firmly ejected from the nightclub a little before quarter to midnight. Her friends, all as plastered as she, had just laughed at her plight, abandoned her, and gone back into the club to continue drinking and eying the talent. Although she really wanted a confrontation with the security guards, she thought the better of it, and reluctantly knew she would eventually have to set off in search of a cab already on the road to take her home, as there were no buses at this time of night.

But there were no taxis anywhere to be seen, they were still dealing with the more lucrative late night rail commuters, eager to finally get home, and the taxis wouldn't bother with the clubs until well after one am. The rain didn't help either. People out for a drink, meal or returning from the cinema had already picked off all the cabs in town. Did she stay at the club and hope a cab might turn up, or walk back in the rain? 'No brainer,' she thought. 'Might as well start, if I take the footpath by the river, it will get me back quicker. Sod the rain.' She stuck her tongue out at the sky, for all the good it did.

An unsound decision, she knew, walking back at this time of night, but she wasn't that far from home and the drink had given her enough bravado to think she could do anything. She was invincible, she could do what she wanted, what did she care about the whole stupid, fucking world. So she unsteadily staggered off, swearing at the unlit cabs as they swept by, and no way was she going to ask her stepdad for a lift, she had her pride, and he couldn't care less anyway, she wasn't his child, and he would probably be pissed at this time of night.

Tottering about on her heels, she slowly made her way home. After fifteen minutes she could just about see the houses of the estate come into view. She was soaked through, but who cared, she could shower and fall into bed when she got in. The rain had started to ease now, and she was so much happier that she wouldn't get much wetter. Cursing the local council for switching off the street lights in yet another cost cutting exercise, she swayed along the footpath in the dark, only pausing to be sick. 'All that drink gone to waste.' Looking down at the vomit, she managed a hollow laugh.

She thought it was a good job there was no one about at this late hour, and in this foul weather, to see the state she was in, and she laughed out loud this time at the thought. She was still feeling sick and bent over to heave again, but she lurched back onto the footpath and was nearly run over by a cyclist racing down the footpath. 'Bloody drunk,' he shouted at her. She returned his insult with a raised index finger and a mouthful of foul insults.

Standing, just, she watched as he disappeared from sight. 'Last I'll see of him,' she said, and laughed out loud. 'No balls to even have a fight. Fucking wanker!' And she staggered back on the path. But the cyclist had other thoughts, he was furious at the near collision and the insults, he had braked hard to swing round to chase back after the girl. 'Think she needs a good slapping to give her some manners,' he said under his breath.

Giggling at her triumph, she was totally unaware of the cyclist bearing down on her, and she certainly didn't expect the well-aimed punch to the side of the head as he rode past. The pain didn't even have time to register, she had no idea what had hit her and she collapsed onto the wet grass like a sack of coal. There was no way she heard the cyclist's shout of glee as he jumped off his bike and ran back to the prone figure.

She was sprawled, face down on the grass. Grabbing her and kneeling on her back to stop her moving, he just saw red, and he started to hit her head as if it was a punch bag. Blood went everywhere, covering his top and shorts. Angrily he pressed her face into the mud with one hand, whilst wrestling with her clothing with his other. She couldn't have fought him off even if she had been sober, he was far too strong to resist. Her short skirt didn't offer him much of a challenge, and his hand soon found her pants. Almost in a frenzy, he started to pull them down, which enabled him to feel her soft, warm body. This was what he was after. The frustration he felt, suddenly lifted. Rubbing his hand up and down the top of her legs, he felt for the delights that were his for the taking. She couldn't resist him. She was his. Lying face down, she hadn't uttered a sound. It was at this point that he realised she had stopped struggling and he thought she might just let him have his way without the violence, without resisting him.

'Wise choice girl,' he whispered, 'I could really hurt you, and I know you'll enjoy this. This is what you really want, whore!' Rolling her over, he realised there was no resistance from the girl, she was silent and limp. Her eyes were wide open in fright, but they were unblinking. Her face was smeared in mud, her mascara wiped all over her face. Thinking she had fainted, or was in shock, he slapped her face, but got no reaction, she was not moving, just staring into space. A this point he realised she wasn't breathing either, he had accidently suffocated her, killed her, murdered her.

'No, you can't be dead' he muttered to himself, 'Bloody hell, no, I didn't mean that to happen, I was just going to give you a good slapping, put you in your place, you pig ignorant slut. Teach you not to insult me. Now I have to get away. I didn't mean this to happen, it was an accident, but no one will believe me, not after the others. Need to get away from you, you stupid cow, look what you made me do.'

Fleeing in a blind panic, he remounted his bike and rode away as fast as humanly possible, leaving the lifeless body next to the footpath without a care or a second look. She didn't matter, got what she deserved, she didn't count. He was more concerned that someone might have seen him, but he didn't even glance back to check for witnesses. For all his previous bravado, he was scared that he would be caught and held to account. Escape was the only thing on his mind.

The heavy rain started again, and he was reassured that hardly anyone would have been out in this weather, he would be soaked by the time he got back, but it would help disguise the scene of the crime and even clean up his riding gear. He arrived back at his lodgings ten minutes later, totally soaked. The rain began to wash the blood and mud from the girl's face, before starting to form puddles around the body. There was a huge flash of lightning immediately followed by an ear splitting clap of thunder. People in town jumped in fright, all except the figure laying on the footpath, she would never move again. Lightning reflected in the puddles, and there was more thunder but further away now, then silence except for the rain softly falling on the body.

CHAPTER 2

There had to be absolutely no trace of the killing, he had to quickly eliminate every trace of evidence, and permanently, without making it obvious. 'No clues. No clues. Nothing to lead them here,' he muttered under his breath.

Striping off in the yard behind the house, he had crept in to the kitchen in just his underpants. Shivering in the cold, the bloody T-shirt was quickly rammed into the washing machine, along with the Lycra cycling suit. After careful rearrangement they were hidden amongst a normal dark wash that was already half filling the drum, so they wouldn't look out of place. Preparing the machine with powder and stain remover, he felt a slight sense of relief now.

'Soon be gone, no evidence, no evidence,' he muttered over and over again. Sitting on the floor, he sat there just watching the drum rotate, washing the blood away. Thinking of his actions tonight, his brain was working overtime on how to find a solution to cover his tracks, and more importantly, to make sure he wasn't discovered or tracked down. 'Breathe deep' he said. 'Slow down, don't panic, it will be OK.'

After a few minutes he was feeling slightly more in control of the situation. But his composure was suddenly utterly shattered by a blast of hot alcohol sodden breath on the side of his face and a harsh whisper in his ear. 'Make sure you sort everything out properly this time, prat'. Her voice so close to his ear, it made him jump. He hadn't heard her creep up behind him, and he couldn't help but recoil at the intrusion into his space and thoughts. She had a habit of doing that recently, creeping up on him, thought it funny to keep him on edge, to be unpredictable as well as bloody rude. But she could, couldn't she, it was her house, she could do what she wanted.

Still finding it amusing, she pushed his face away with her hand and simply laughed at him. 'You're a useless bastard aren't you. Can't even be trusted to do the washing properly. Bloody mess you made of it last week. And just look at you, run out of clothes have you, or were you feeling lucky? Fat chance there, eh?' Looking down at her tenant, she roared with laughter and then sneered, 'Bloody funny creeping up on you and making you jump, you didn't think I was in did you? I was going out with the girls tonight, going to have a bloody good drink, but the weather was so foul, I stayed here with my friend,' she said waving a near empty vodka bottle at him. 'So you can sort the place out while I'm catching upon my beauty sleep, you freeloader.'

With that she only just managed to turn around without falling over, and unsteadily headed upstairs and her bedroom door. 'Hope you break your bloody neck,' he said, but not so loud that she heard, he couldn't risk her picking on him again. 'Beauty sleep, you arsehole? You'd need to be in a fucking coma for years for your face to improve,' he said with real hatred.

His angry thoughts turned back to his current plight. This bloody relationship had turned into a nightmare. Got to get out of this place. But how? I've lost everything once, can't risk losing it all over again. I've got no proper job, no money, no prospects and no home, except here. She needs a fatal 'accident' to cure this relationship, but not until I've cleaned her out.

Anger welled up inside and there was a loud metallic bang as he slammed his fist into the front of the washing machine in

13

sheer frustration. Then sinking back to his knees, he rested his forehead against the vibrating machine as if in deep thought. But he hadn't got a clue how to resolve the situation he had got himself into, so he simply shook his head as if to clear it, and then like some scolded dog, did as he was told, and headed off to clear up, the fight completely knocked out of him. Nursing bruised knuckles, he retraced his way back into the dark living room of the old shabby house, where he picked up the empty cups and dirty plates they had used whilst watching some brainless TV programme earlier. Lazy bitch hadn't even picked them up. But he hadn't either, he was just interested in getting out of this shit hole and venting his anger in a ride, even in the rain.

Looking around at the threadbare carpet, the scruffy sofa, clothes strewn everywhere, it resembled a doss house. In a way it was, he just dossed down in the place, and it was a complete mess, but it served as home for the moment. But then he had nowhere else to go, so it had to do. The dishes and cups were taken back to the kitchen and he filled the bowl to wash them.

Deep in thought he would have a lot to contemplate tonight and he knew sleep would be utterly impossible, his brain would be hot-wired in bed and he would be awake for hours. Jesus what a cock up, he had destroyed everything tonight. His whole life was a total mess, and everything seemed so pointless now. But then he had gone too far tonight. Much too far.

Heading upstairs he stared at the messy room, who cared if the place looked like a shit hole. Well actually he did, his army training subconsciously took over and he reluctantly began to put things in their place, and tidy up. Do as you're told, don't argue, follow orders, he was well used to that, well most of the time.

CHAPTER 3

It was well after two o'clock in the morning when the girl's body was found by an insomniac dog walker. His young dog wouldn't settle and he thought a walk across the park might help tire it out. The dog had been let off its lead, allowing it to run free, and it shot off to the other side of the park. He just stood there in the hope it might run off some energy and sleep when he eventually got it home. It was dark and the park's lights were all switched off now preventing him from seeing where the bloody dog had run off to.

Now he couldn't even see the stupid animal, but he could hear it. Bark, bark, bark, what was the matter with it now. The barking continued from the same location and he assumed it had cornered some animal. Bark, bark, bark. Bloody animal. It was only the barking of the dog that had alerted him to the presence of the girl. Up until then he hadn't been taking any notice of his surroundings, just concentrating on keeping his hood up to prevent the rain from pouring down his neck. 'Bloody dog' he shouted at the errant animal 'Too bloody wet to play, come here stupid.'

But the dog had no intention of returning, and he was forced to walk over the sodden grass to put it back on a lead to take it home. It was only then that he spotted the girl surrounded by a pool of water. The excited dog running around the prone figure. Bark, bark, bark. Shooing the dog away, he knelt down beside her. He reached down to shake her, thinking she had passed out through drink, like so many kids did these days. Tramp!

It was only then he realised she was cold to his touch, and her face was unblinking, just staring into space. She had not just passed out, this was far more serious. Feeling for a pulse, he couldn't find one, she looked dead. The dog was still scampering round the body as he rang 999 on his mobile for the police and ambulance. The police were there in ten minutes and after the inevitable questions, the police believed his story and checked an ambulance was on route, although it was a pointless gesture for her now.

By the time it arrived, the dog had been caught, leashed and the pair of them stood a little way from the body, both shivering from the cold. The ambulance crew confirmed the girl was dead at the scene and that this was a suspicious death. Obviously the body couldn't be moved until the forensics team had investigated, so the police taped off the area, covered the body and departed the scene, leaving just a solitary policeman to guard the body whilst they awaited the forensics van.

A white van, emblazoned with that role, arrived within the hour and carefully erected a tent over the body to protect the scene of the crime. Now shrouded in secret, the body was carefully photographed, as was the surrounding area, before the body was eventually allowed to be taken away to the mortuary for further examination.

The dog realised play time was over and was led away by his owner, who would spend the rest of the night explaining to his wife what had happened. The rain had now stopped, but thunder sounded weakly in the distance, as if it knew all the excitement was over, and it shouldn't make such a fuss.

The tent was left in place, surrounded by a barrier of blue

and white police tape, plus the same the solitary young PC who had obviously drawn the short straw down at the station that evening. The scene would be re-photographed in the morning, the tent removed, the tape thrown in the bin, and the park returned to its normal muddy state as if nothing had happened.

CHAPTER 4

Back in his dismal room, he was thinking. Everything used to be so planned, so perfect, so organised. But then his life had actually been organised for him in the army, he didn't have to think too hard, he was perfectly institutionalised. Just follow orders, do as you are told. Just as well really, as he had been told on many occasions that he wasn't exactly the sharpest knife in the draw, he wasn't capable of rational, or for that matter, any sort of imaginative thought.

But he was thinking hard now, lost in his own thoughts, walking around on automatic, staring into space, where had it all gone so wrong. If he thought about it, it really was a case of bad to worse recently. And it was really, really bad now. 'Use your brain man,' had been shouted at him so often in the army, now he really had to use it in earnest. And that was so bloody hard for him. But what was new, life just wasn't fair, you played the hand you were given, he just seemed to get crap hands.

When he looked back at his life, it wasn't anything to boast about was it. He had a shit homelife, he hadn't done well at school either as a result. Years later he found he had ADHD which had made learning so hard for him then, but in those days he was just labelled as slow and stupid. In the end, after years of being bullied by teachers who just wrote him off, he found they couldn't give a shit and he wasn't qualified in anything. He only escaped with the poorest of marks in his GCSEs, so it was a case of crime or the armed forces. He had watched mates get involved in drugs, sure there was big money to be made, but they all turned into fucking unthinking zombies, all zoned out and useless. Most of them ended up inside, as they hadn't got the brains to stay out of trouble. He might push his luck for a while dealing, but he knew that he would get caught at some point. Luckily the army suited him fine, no need to work things out, that was the job of the officers. He wanted to fight, to be a killing machine, nothing more, nothing less. Somewhere to vent his anger at how life had short changed him.

The army channelled his anger, and he was the perfect cannon fodder they needed to keep the rest of the world in check. Don't think, just follow orders. It became his life, simply because he didn't know anything else, and he didn't have to work things out. Unlike now.

After years in the army and tours all over the world, he had slowly risen through the ranks, turned a desire into a career, his whole life was centred around the army, in fact it was his whole life. Although he married a local girl, he spent more time on tour than he did at home. He didn't mind, the army gave him a cheap house to live in, he had sex on tap when he returned, and the tours kept him occupied. It wasn't exactly a dream existence, but it was better than anything he known before. It all seemed close to perfect for him, he trained hard, got promoted, which gave him a bit more money in his pocket and he was pretty happy. But after the last tour, he had a total breakdown, he couldn't cope, he really doubted his ability as a soldier, screwed things up, got things wrong which endangered others, it was the start of a downhill struggle he couldn't control, and his life started to fall apart as a result.

Post-traumatic stress disorder they called it. Sounded almost innocent to most people, but to him, it was hell on earth. It started innocently enough, just with constant inconvenient flashbacks. Then he would find himself totally out of kilter with the outside world, in situations he couldn't explain, so emotional he would break down in tears for no reason. He would think he could smell the desert, or something would act as a trigger point to make him think he could smell it. A combination of hot dust, human waste, rotting vegetables, explosives, even diesel, depending on where he was. It was like some subconscious alarm bell that he would have reacted to when on duty.

Although he was in a safe environment, his mind sent out protective messages that took over his body, a weird self-preservation mechanism set off by an innocent memory that was misinterpreted. The feeling of confusion was often coupled with a feeling of isolation. Fragments of memory, dark incomplete pieces of past experiences, that led to an emotional overload.

These were bad enough, but they started to join together into a surreal and inaccurate vision of events. They were almost daydreams at first, a shutdown of his memory replaced with what he thought had occurred. He couldn't rest with everything whirling around in his head, he found it close to impossible to sleep, and when he did, he dreamed, dreams that became nightmares, and he would awake disorientated and exhausted. Then the dreams would start all over again, and soon they became constant nightmares. Nightmares every bloody night. Him shouting, over reacting to the dreams. His screams, the constant flashbacks. So real he could smell, hear and even taste his dreams. They were exhausting and confusing.

PTSD. It took over his life. Killed his career. It crippled his work, destroyed his life, and not being able to cope with even the simplest tasks, take or issue orders, he was immediately taken out of the front line, assessed and flown home. Home? The army was his home, his life was consumed by the army.

It was a disaster, he had gone to pieces, woken in the middle of every night in a cold sweat at what he had seen. Those evil dreams. They became a regular occurrence, they came every night, night after bloody night, and the screams. So real, and they were his screams in the dreams, because he had something to scream about. And he could do nothing about it. He became a head case, avoided by his team who realised he couldn't command now, he was a liability, a danger to them, he just wasn't stable or reliable any more.

Because of this, he had lost his life, his dreams, his desires, his family and home, and worst of all his career, the army. His whole focus in life, the only thing that had meant anything to him, the one thing that had kept him going. And now he had absolutely nothing, this was all he had, just this bloody house, where he could see himself aimlessly walking about, just collecting up the debris without conscious thought, he was simply moving one piece of crap to another location, an exercise in rearranging the deck chairs on the Titanic, and he was miles away now, literally, thinking hard, sweat pouring down his face.

He was back in the desert now, he was on his last tour, peacekeeping they called it. Not for him. No, he just thought of it as a chance to put the ragheads in their place at last, back where they belonged. Sub humans living a century or more in the past. Religious nutters all of them. With thoughts like that he was always hostile, always looking for a fight and it was little wonder the locals resented those like him.

The room around him faded, and darkness took over, he was far, far away, imagining he was back in that bloody armoured personnel carrier again. Hot, cramped, dark, claustrophobic. Remembering his smart arse reaction to a piece of advice not to go down a certain route, but he of course he knew better, changing everything to look for trouble, looking for a fight, and then running into the ambush. Oh, he found plenty of trouble that day.

Sitting inside the baking metal interior of that giant armoured tin can, laughing with the other squaddies, thinking he was invincible, before that incredible flash of light that blinded him, an impact that knocked him senseless. Then the explosion, a nanosecond later, that ear-splitting noise, the heat of the blast, the flames, the smoke.

Then silence, he couldn't see or hear for a few seconds, then the panic set in. Was he dead, no he couldn't die here, he was in charge, and it wasn't his time. The APV had slewed across the dirt road and ground to a halt. The engine still running but they were going nowhere. Shit, he knew they were a sitting target for a second killing shot, he had to get out before that happened. Can't get killed here, can't cop a shot now. In the confusion the rear doors had already been swung open and he could just about make out soldiers struggling and stumbling out of the back of the vehicle in a cloud of dust and smoke. They were already crouching down looking for cover, weapons raised to fight back, and he couldn't wait to join them. 'That's it lads, give it back to them, I'm coming, I'm coming.'

But inside it was complete and utter chaos, and he was

trapped, his survival training kicked in but he knew he had to get out and take cover fast. Just survive for now, get out of this death trap. Fire back ASAP, take some of them with him at least.

'Fucking kill someone for this,' but the soldier next to him was pinning him down, trapping him, what was the matter with him, he didn't move. He shook him. 'Get out, get out, take cover, move it man,' he shouted at the still figure. 'Move it' and he violently shook him again.

The other soldier just slumped on to him and he realised he was now covered in blood. They both were. Who's blood? The other soldier was obviously dead, the rocket propelled grenade had exploded beside him and he must have taken virtually the full brunt of the explosion. As he pushed him off, he realised he was plastered not just with blood, but with human remains, guts and brain. The soldier had dissolved into an unrecognisable bloody mess and it poured onto him. His screams echoed around in the APV as he fought to shake himself free. After several frantic minutes he was free and standing outside the APV. He was shaking, he had lost his helmet and weapon, and had to be hauled to the ground by the other members of his troop to prevent himself becoming a target.

Smoke was pouring from the vehicle now and the troop moved away quickly to avoid any impending explosion. Flames erupted from the vacated interior enveloping the body of the dead soldier. As he looked back at the doomed carrier he could see him silhouetted by the flames. Flames that would soon consume his body. He seemed to be dancing in the fire. Dead but in torment. Burn, watch him burn, watch him dance, watch the flames reduce him to ash, watch his face burn away, a macabre smile still on his face, watch the flames burn through the uniform, the flesh catch fire, see the bones exposed. It all seemed to happen in slow motion.

Watching in horror, that could have been him, he was the lucky one, not that poor sod! It was an image that haunted him. Over and over again. His fault, his fault, his bloody fault. And night after night he was visited by the spectre of that same poor sod. A solder in full desert battledress. They were both sitting side by side in the armoured carrier. 'I saved your life', it would say to him, and he looked perfectly normal, to then turn round, and his face would be just blood and gore. A hole where an eye should be, his jaw blown away, the brain exposed. The spectre would reach out for him, to then fall to pieces and cover him in blood and flesh. He couldn't stand it. There were flames and that body in the APV. Now he couldn't stand the feel of flesh, couldn't cope with even the smallest splash of blood on him.

The scene played back to him countless times. Every night the nightmares grew worse, and he was removed from front line duties, and flown back to the UK, where they treated him for shock. They said he had been so very lucky, that poor sod next to him really had saved his life.

But it was no good, he was traumatised, couldn't cope, useless to the army. Couldn't even do a desk job, let alone carry out field service. They tried training duties, but every time he handled a weapon, his hands shook so badly he became a danger to those around him. The army clearly had no use for him.

Obviously he was debriefed after the incident and fingers were pointed at why he had changed his orders. He had no answer. Blamed for a death, destruction of the APV, disobeying orders, it became easy to start the process to discharge him, he was threatened with a court martial which could eventually blame him for everything. As a result they used this as an excuse to then stop his treatment, referring him to an NHS service rather than specialist counselling. On top of this, his personal life started to come apart. His wife simply couldn't cope with his mood swings, she just didn't understand what he had been through, and his marriage slowly unravelled before it eventually totally disintegrated. She went back to her mother and he lost his married quarters as a result, and then suddenly his life was gone.

If this wasn't bad enough, he was found guilty of misconduct and causing the death of a serviceman and eventually discharged and sent packing. A hopeless case. After he was discharged from the army, everything he valued, had evaporated before his eyes. He had nothing, nowhere to go, no family, no life. Where the hell did he go now? There was little help out there. He felt isolated and deeply disappointed with everything in life and he became depressed and withdrawn.

Friends put him up for a short time, sleeping on sofas, floors, even a car at times. But that proved too much for most of his friends, and he soon stopped asking for help. When he didn't have a bed, he slept rough, and some times, if he was lucky, there was a hostel available. His army pension kept him alive, but it was used for one purpose. Drinking. Drinking to drown his sorrows became a regular feature in his life, but one night, he bumped into Tracey in a bar. They were both the worse for wear, and when he blurted out his sorry tale over a drink, she took pity on him and said she had a sofa he could use that night.

One thing led to another and he stayed. Tracey was no looker but said she could do with a man in her life. He was too pissed to disagree and took up her offer. Then what real option did he have, he had nothing better to do, and nowhere else to go, so he became that man. They got along OK, and he pushed his luck a bit further. It worked and they soon became lovers, but even that had its drawbacks, and everything seemed to conspire against him again. Sex was very hit and mix. The more he tried to please her, the more anxious he became, and the more often he failed. He simply wasn't up to the mark, she said.

Often he failed to even get an erection, sometimes he became flaccid during the very act. Every time he failed in bed, she would poke fun at him. Soon the fun went out of the insults and they just became insults. This just made things worse and eventually he became impotent. For both of them that was a disaster. Tracey really needed sex in her life, she saw it as the only reason men existed. And he had become redundant on that front. Desperate to remain her lover, he tried all the harder, as it was his only real hold over her. His only real hope of starting life again, and he so needed that. But his failures only made things worse.

It didn't matter what medication he was prescribed, what advice and counselling he took, nothing seemed to work. The trauma of the explosion haunted him, ruined his life, even destroyed his sex life. OK, so he wasn't that great in bed, but they couldn't sleep together. Tracey couldn't stand the screams, being woken every time he had a nightmare. As their sex life disappeared, she became cruel in her treatment of him. She started to taunt him, said he was only half a man, useless to her, that he should leave, but it never quite got to that stage.

She never got around to that, there were other ways to hurt him. She knew this threat terrified him, she knew he couldn't lose his home again. And then where the hell would he go? He was trapped.

Slowly he began to despise her, another woman who had let him down when he needed help, some understanding. But he kept those feelings to himself, buried deep within him, where they festered. Bloody women, wanted it all, kicked him out when it suited. Tracey was the worst of all. She let him stay in the house but they didn't even sleep together now, he just cleared up the house and she would go out enjoy herself. To make matters untenable, every now and then she would come back with some guy to make sure she added insult to injury, and he knew all about that. That was agony, hearing the laughter, the giggles, the bed, the sounds of her making love, so loud, so intentionally loud, and she knew it upset him. She wanted it to. Useless bastard, he was useful for just one thing – now he couldn't even do that. She knew what she wanted and she would go out of her way to find it if he couldn't provide it.

And then there were the tears, he would often be in tears as she climaxed, gritting his teeth in the frustration of knowing it should be him, but he was a useless bastard, he couldn't perform for her. It was all her fault. He had been reduced to a eunuch because of her. Bloody, bloody, fucking woman. Damn all women. They were all as bad as each other. Those thoughts built up in him, becoming a hatred for all women.

She was always mocking him, walking away to find a new lover, leaving him to fend for himself. She was enjoying herself tonight, and hearing her groan over and over again through the thin walls, was just too much for him, he vowed to have his revenge. But it was revenge against all women, not just Tracey, she could wait, he wanted something special for her, a perfect revenge was waiting at some point. There are others who would bear the brunt of his hatred for now.

And his hatred became just that, a wave of revenge attacks against women. Simple acts at first, just enough for him to feel he was superior to them. Something to flatter his ego. Not on his doorstep though, always in the next town or somewhere where he was working. Arguments in clubs and bars was a good place to start. A slap or punch would be satisfying enough to put some mouthy woman in her place. But sometimes that wasn't enough for him, and he took to stalking, following women, frightening them when they didn't expect it. If it was dark all the better. He wanted to be the monster hiding in the shadows.

It took many forms, barging in to them when walking, pushing them over in the street, swearing at them, he saw all women as the enemy now. Something to be loathed, beneath him, to be treated with contempt. But he was careful for a while, nothing too violent, nothing that would get him noticed, but the simple random acts began to lose their appeal, lose their impact and satisfaction for him, and he began to feel the need for something more forceful.

It always fascinated him that women had become so much more brash, a new generation who thought they were equal, if not better than men. They need to be taught their proper place in society again. But how? The need to take some sort of action that would fulfil his needs always alluded him because he wasn't really a thinker, he acted on instinct rather than planning things out properly.

Sometimes it all became too much for him, and he would descend into a deep depression and contemplate what his life had degenerated into, but that simply made him feel resentful and bitter. It was always someone else's fault, he couldn't see what he was becoming, couldn't even contemplate seeking help any more. That had been tried with the army but they didn't want to know, couldn't help him, hadn't really tried had they, just written him off. He wasn't in the wrong, they were, all of them.

The Medway Towns were a good target for him. There were a lot of squaddies there, so he had a chance to drink with a few of the lads, but he found he was older than most of them and they regarded him as a bit of a has-been when he started to regale his tour exploits.

But the Towns were big, a quarter of a million people there, a place to easily hide in, to get lost in, operate in secret from. A place for revenge, an operational base for him. What he hadn't realised was his odd random attacks had started to be recorded, to be noticed as they grew in number. They weren't associated at this point, they were just statistics, annoying numbers that made the Towns look like a trouble spot. A Saturday night drinking trouble spot.

However, there was a large immigrant population in the Towns as well, which made them an irresistible target for him. As he walked down the High Street, there seemed to be headscarves on many of the women. This always infuriated him and he often wondered what he could do about it. This was his country, what were they doing here. More bloody ragheads here than in Iraq. His misogynistic feelings were so mixed with his xenophobic fears, that they completely expelled any logical thought he might have had in his head. Foreign woman became the centre of his hate campaign and he began to think of ways to intimidate them.

Saturday night was too obvious for an attack and Muslim women didn't drink, they would return for prayers that night. Sitting in the pub that evening, he contemplated his plans whilst he got more and more inebriated. In the end he was so pissed that night, he fell asleep on a bench in the bus station after missing his bus home.

Waking with a shattering hangover, he was in no mood to face any nonsense that morning, and it was pure bad luck for the young woman on her way to pick up a Sunday paper, simply because she was wearing a headscarf, a symbol of his hatred. It was like waving a red flag to him and he pushed her out of his way. She swore at him, and his response was a punch to her face, and as she fell, a series of kicks followed that rendered her unconscious. This was his first proper entry on the police database, and his first real mistake. His criminal psychology profile was about to be started.

CHAPTER 5

Although this was regarded as a hate crime and recorded as such, it didn't match other assault crimes he had committed. It remained as a single entry on the crime sheet, unrelated to anything else. It was lucky for him that those other records were computerised into so many categories, and scattered over most of the county on different databases that were rarely shared, let alone collated.

There was no doubt he was on record already, but no one had simply put all the attacks together, they were not only in different stations, but filed under all sorts of headings. They simply weren't related as far as the system was concerned. But as the attacks grew and more reports were made, people began to look at the figures simply because they made the force look inept. Was it worth allocating a bit of manpower to perhaps see what was behind the spike in the statistics?

Juniors were in deed allocated to hunting for connections, and they examined a lot of unsolved cases. Modus operandi were eventually compared, records re-examined, emails sent out for cross referencing. Eventually patterns were found, forces co-ordinated and scenes of crimes mapped. Computers can be very useful at times, especially when operated by a generation who are not frightened by them. By broadening the search and more effectively asking the right questions, the similarities began to appear. Once reports were filed, conclusions and assumptions made, it became obvious there might well be a connection, and that they could solve a lot of cases if they could find and convict this lone attacker.

A final report was compiled, all the attacks collated and the final conclusion dumped on the desks of each divisional commander, which was of course, eventually delegated down the line to someone low enough in rank to take notice of it. One such file had dropped on Robert's desk weeks earlier and he had ignored it for the most part, giving it just a cursory glance, just to make sure he wasn't caught out if asked about it, but he had enough on his plate as it was, without taking this on as well.

When he did get round to reading though, it did make interesting reading, this guy could be responsible for a lot of minor stuff, a nuisance criminal Robert called him. But there was not enough factual matter to take it too much further, and Robert knew he would have to wait for more information, or another attack, for him to take it really seriously or allocate any time to. There would definitely be another attack, he knew it, it was all too common, he was a serial attacker, and sooner or later he would strike again. Robert wasn't too concerned, it was all minor stuff and anyway it was a waiting game for the time being, any new info, any new clues, anything at all, and then he could apply some logic to the case.

The file was put back into his in tray, off of his desk, hopefully to await his attention at some later point in the future, when he had enough time to read it properly, or when the attacker struck again. Just not at the moment, he was busy enough, he was always bloody busy and under duress. But the gods have a wicked sense of humour and Robert got his wish for more information the next morning. His workload was about to expedientially expand to breaking point.

CHAPTER 6

'Sorry to call you in on a weekend Robert, but your sex attacker has overstepped the mark this time it seems. We have a murder on our hands now, and I need you to take over the case. This one is right on our doorstep as well. If it is the same guy it appears he has joined the next league now. All the previous attacks have all been fairly low level attacks on women as you know, threatening assaults, except that last one in Chatham,' said the chief superintendent. 'I know you haven't had much of a chance to look in any detail at the files that were sent to you, but do we have any leads at all on this maniac?'

'Not much at the moment, I'm afraid,' said Robert guiltily grimacing as he picked up the case notes some junior officer had compiled and dumped on his desk earlier. 'Apart from the GBH attack, all the other cases have been fairly low key and we aren't even sure yet that they are the same person, they just have MO similarities,' Robert picked up and glanced at the file again, playing for more time.

Superintendent Robert Steele had transferred to the Kent police from the Met the previous year, primarily to look after his aging mother who lived in Wateringbury near Maidstone. He missed London, he missed his old manor, he knew the criminals, the gangs and his team. Kent was a bit too quiet for him, and he would never have thought of moving except for one twist of fate when he had used his personal knowledge of a local friend to solve a series of murders. He grew to like the county during his work on the case and thought that perhaps

Kent might offer him some excitement after all, although the pace of life was a lot slower, but so was he now.

Robert had never married, he never really had the opportunity, or time he said sometimes, too married to the job. As a consequence there was no partner, no siblings, and his mother was the only family he now had. In his late 50s, he could have taken early retirement and spent all his time with his mother, but he needed to keep his hand in, and she would have driven him mad. Police work had always been his life, he craved it. It was in his blood. No, early retirement was out of the question at the moment. Still a few useful years of policing in him yet, he hoped. And you never know, he thought, there might just be a chance of meeting that special someone, but he wasn't holding his breath.

His thoughts returned to the matter in front of him. If he could catch this bastard, then his dedication to the force would have been worth it. Flicking through the thin file it didn't take him long to finish it again, then look up to meet an enquiring look from his superior. 'OK, so what have we got then?'

'Sod all really' Robert replied wearily. He looked at his file as if to check his information. 'Well we have a fairly detailed description at least from the previous attacks, especially the Chatham attack. He is definitely white, somewhere between 5'8 and 5'10. Fairly light build, scrawny even, but wiry, very strong, not someone you'd want to pick a fight with by all accounts. None of the victims seem to be able to pin his age down. Definitely not a teenager, nor someone too old, but he could be anywhere between late twenties to late forties. All of the eight previous victims, assuming they are attacks by the same person, have a reasonably similar MO. They are all attacks late at night, single women, secluded locations. All have been sexually motivated but strangely none have resulted in rape. He always stops short of the act, but sounds as if that is the initial motive of the attack. All of the attacks have been violent, but no weapon used, the attacker relies on his own strength. All are ambushes, the attacker hides and waits for a victim. That's a dangerous strategy as he could be seen hiding or discovered whilst in waiting. So he is a risk taker, someone happy to take on a challenge.'

'OK where does that take us?' asked his boss. 'That reduces the number of suspects to just about 12 million by the sounds of it.' Robert saw the humour in this, 'Not quite sir. We know he is English. He has occasionally uttered something during the attacks, and when he has, he doesn't have a foreign accent, in fact his victims all agree he is a local man. So excluding the 11% of foreign and immigrants in the country, that would reduce it down to about 10 million, and if we jump to the assumption he is a local man because of the accent, then we have no more than 2 million people to interview.'

'Hmm, piece of cake then. I'll expect him in custody by the end of the week then, Robert?' 'I wish,' said Robert. 'The guy is no fool. He hasn't left any clues yet. I don't know about last night, they haven't finished examining the crime scene as yet. His attacks are always from behind, and he doesn't appear to wear a disguise, so he is very sure of his own abilities. Almost a professional approach. Could be ex-forces, sounds like military training. Long shot that though. Security guard, body builder, someone very sure of themselves. The lack of disguise makes me think these are almost opportunistic attacks, but they are very random in timescale and over an area of hundreds of square miles.'

Robert stood up and walked over to the incident board, which had a large map at its centre. 'If you use geographical profiling, then we have a problem in that the Thames distorts the attack area. If you look at the locations of the attacks, they started six months ago at Harrietsham, just the other side of Canterbury. The next one was soon after, just two weeks later in fact. This time, actually in Canterbury. A river walk along the Stour. A young foreign student walking back to digs from an evening class. A certain amount of daring in that, as it was a populated area. He must have been confident to do that one. Nothing for over a month, then an attack in Hoo, north of Rochester, and one in Tonbridge a day later. Both violent. Then a two month pause and an attack in Dartford, a week later, one in Gravesend, and another a day later in Strood on the outskirts of Rochester again. There are lots of minor incidents to consider as well that could well be him as well. And then the two recent attacks in Medway and finally Maidstone last night, the last one a fatality.'

Robert looked at his superior and said, 'We need to do a lot of legwork here. CCTV tapes to look at for the girl. Plus someone try and make a detailed profile on this maniac as well. I'll need to have a small squad of officers that are good on the computer sir, to help me narrow this down. And a good sidekick, someone to do a lot of coordinating, and a lot of my legwork.'

'You can pick your foot soldiers Robert, but I've someone I really want you to team up with, I'll get her here for Monday morning, you can sort the rest of your team and have them assembled so you can give them all a good briefing on Monday.'

Robert looked quizzical, 'Her, sir? You said her?' 'That's right

Robert, a young lady I want to put on this case. Bright young thing, someone being fast tracked through the ranks. You could use a woman's point of view on this I think,' he paused to let that sink in before continuing. 'The press need to know about this, can I leave you to prepare the usual statement, with as little information as possible for the first one. Just say body of a young girl etc, etc. Police not releasing details until family has been contacted. You know the drill. You will need to fill in more information when the family have been contacted. That is happening as we speak, so you will be able to release her name for the evening news bulletin and put in an appeal for witnesses. I'll send you all the details over by email later this morning.' Leaving Robert to ponder over those last crucial sentences, he turned and left.

Sat in the now empty office, surrounded by files, notes and a pad on which to make further notes, Robert could only ponder what had been dropped on him from a great height. 'Shit,' he muttered, 'Another bloody needle in a haystack job. OK Mr detective, where do you want to start with this? Bugger it, You've even got to play nursemaid to some college graduate. A bloody woman as well, Just hope she is of some good, never did understand the creatures.' His mind was working out how to start the general press statement without it sounding too bland, but without giving too much away. If that wasn't bad enough, he then had to do the same again later, but releasing details of the victim - that one would hurt.

At that moment his thoughts were elsewhere, he had a team to pick, although he didn't have much choice with one member. Shaking his head at that thought, he put down half a dozen names he could work with, although they weren't all based here, but scattered all over the county. There would be a couple of subtle secondments to be made. The note pad came out again and a few scribbled notes were made. After about ten minutes, he transferred those thoughts to the computer as he prepared the press release. It made sad reading. A young life reduced to half a page of A4, not even that when he re-read it.

CHAPTER 7

Not far away there was a troubled soul who was tired of wandering around the house in a nightmare, he had gone back to the kitchen, to think things through. The washing machine was still on, with the incriminating evidence hopefully now destroyed in the process. Standing watching the machine, he slid down the wall and ended up sitting on the floor watching the last few minutes of the spin cycle come to an end. His mind spinning aimlessly like the washing he was watching, as he contemplated what he had done that evening.

Hours earlier, he had cycled home in a panic, the events of the evening still ran around and around in his head. This had been a disaster, he hadn't meant to kill her, it was an accident. But who would believe that? Just that he was strong, she was so weak and she had it coming, insulting him like that. Who did she think she was? Drunken cow, she needed teaching a lesson anyway. She just happened to be in the wrong place at the wrong time. And I was the right person to teach her the right way. But it had all gone so wrong, he had lost his temper again, this wasn't planned, he preferred to hunt down his victims, so much more satisfying. That was why he loved the army, the hunt, then the kill.

But this was pure opportunism, he had lost his control and she had paid the price. Served her right. World would be a better place without women like that. Thought she was so clever, I taught her who was the boss, who was the strongest sex. She should have known I was so much better than her. Did

I leave any clues though, didn't cover my tracks this time did I, bloody disaster all that blood, needed that clearing away quick.

Bloody Tracey again, she had been behind me riding off like that. At least she didn't see what I'd put in the machine when I came back. Always going out with her mates. Bringing that bloke back, making sure I heard everything. Had to take my frustration out somehow. I could either hit her or blow off enough steam with the cycle to calm down and forget my problems, or with luck I would find a victim to prove I was still superior, I was better than any woman. Got both tonight and he smiled at that thought.

The act of ambushing women and humiliating them was so good for him. Remarkably he was finding his libido was starting to return, but he still couldn't complete the act - not yet, but he was sure it would all return to normal soon. He was still the master. But it was never going to happen with Tracey was it. This was the only way out, sex with anyone but her.

Arriving back from the attack he had opened the back gate, and carefully taken the bike around to the back of the house before securely locking it and finally protecting it with a water-proof cover. It was the only thing that mattered in his life. His last treasured possession. It kept him fit, kept him strong, kept him ahead of the rest of the human race. He just had to outlast some of these morons and everything would come right again, he was better than this, he deserved more, he was still a winner.

Stripping off and sneaking in quietly, so as to not alert Tracey, he realised he needn't have bothered. She was either drunk and passed out or out with a few girlfriends in some bar. Another arsehole who had ruined his life, she would get what was coming to her as well.

Had to pick his time and place, and he knew there would be an opportunity at some time soon, and she would be at his mercy then. Teach her to mock him, insult him, taunt him, knowing that he couldn't do anything about it. His teeth were so clenched at the thought of revenge on Tracey, he had to make a concerted effort to relax and think positively.

Revenge? And just how would he do that? She was the main breadwinner, he only had menial agency work on a part time basis to fund himself, and most of that went on bills and food. More cash, he had to get hold of more money to carry out any plan. There was money stashed away in Tracey's accounts, but he needed the account numbers for a start. Still fuming at how Tracey had belittled him, he had been put in his place again tonight and relegated to clearing up the house.

The Lycra suit was in the washing machine which was destroying the evidence and it would go in the tumble drier and come out spotless. She was well out of it and he could hear her snoring now so he decided to have a shower to get rid of any evidence of the attack.

Thinking back to the girl in the park, it felt good, it washed away the memories of the night's attack. Stupid cow, taught her a real lesson and I left her behind, a brainless twat and there were so many like her, and still plenty more out there for me to dominate. But the smile on his face slowly disappeared as it began to dawn on him just what he had done. This wasn't an attack, it was murder, he had killed someone this time. Pausing, he shrugged his shoulders as if it didn't matter. She deserved it anyway, he thought as he dried himself and walked back to the kitchen to make a sandwich, and then he would try and get some sleep.

CHAPTER 8

It was 7am and the WPC looked nervous as she stood on the door step of the run-down ex-council house. Although she was accompanied by a male colleague, she felt duty bound to break this bad news. People took it so much better from a woman. She knocked on the door, preparing herself for this horrible task, one she had performed before, but not one she was ever able to perform without apprehension. Eventually the door opened and an unshaven man appeared, he stared at the two policemen, but before they could speak, he asked 'OK what's she done now? I presume she's got herself arrested last night.'

'Sorry? Mr Brookes?' the WPC said. 'No, Hardcastle,' he replied. 'Brookes is Sally's surname. I'm her stepfather.'

'Ah' said the WPC, 'Can we come in? Is your wife, Sally's mum here. We've got some bad news I'm afraid.

A mousey woman ran to the door already in tears. 'Bad news? Not about my Sally, please.' 'Mrs Hardcastle can we come in? I think this is best not discussed on the doorstep.' 'Of course, of course,' she said and ushered them into the front room. 'Bill go and make some tea please.' The man left them alone, mumbling under his breath all the way to the kitchen. 'I'm sorry Mrs Hardcastle. I think I've some very bad news concerning your daughter.'

There was a pause and the WPC could see the terror in the woman's eyes as she prepared to receive the news. The WPC emptied a small plastic bag onto the coffee table in front of them. Amongst the items was a photo travel card. She picked it up and asked, 'Is this Sally's?' The woman nodded, tears now streaming down her face.

'Then I'm really sorry Mrs Hardcastle, but Sally was killed last night. Her body was found not far from here and taken to the hospital. I'm afraid I will have to ask you or member of your family to identify the body at some point, to confirm it is Sally.'

The man appeared at the door with a teapot. 'We'll both go,' and he sat down looking shocked. 'I can't ask Lois to do that on her own. We'll both go.' Ten minutes later, the two policemen, and the couple left the house and drove to the hospital for the formal identification. An hour later they were driven back, totally shattered and left to grieve in private, with the two policemen returning to their station.

The WPC was visually upset by the task and turned to her companion. 'It's bad enough when you have to inform someone of a death. That tends to be a road accident or a heart attack. Something that can be explained logically. But a murder, especially of a young woman is so bloody different. So hard to cope with, the loss of a life. The deliberate act of taking a life. Something I can never get over.' She hung her coat in the locker and headed off to the canteen very aware that there were two people, who's lives that had just been destroyed by her visit.

CHAPTER 9

'That was the end of the national news. Over to Peter for a roundup of the national weather.' A large map appeared on the screen, it was covered in symbols that were supposed to explain the dreadful weather they had been experiencing. Finally, the presenter finished and a voice off screen said, 'And now the local news for those in the South East.' The screen image changed and Robert saw the local newsreader appear. 'Police in Maidstone have just released the news that a young woman's body was found near the town centre last night. They say they won't release any further details until the next of kin have been contacted.'

Robert knew this had already been completed, but it gave him a little more time to prepare the public for the next stage. The newsreader looked up at the autocue again. 'Police say the cause of death has yet to be established but they are treating the death as unexplained at the moment.' The papers on the desk were shuffled and she began a new story. 'Commuters in the south east have complained....'

Robert switched off the TV and thought, no doubt that will give the shoppers something to talk about this morning, and he set about writing the next news bulletin. A task he didn't want to do, but it was the first step in unravelling the case. Perhaps the appeal might lead to a breakthrough, a missing clue, a witness even. A sad way to start any day, and he knew it would get worse before it got better. He had already begun work on the follow up press statement, and he wasn't looking forward to compiling that one, as it would entail a public statement with him as the centre of attraction.

CHAPTER 10

She was a stunner, and she knew it. At 5'9 she was well above the height of most woman, but at a size 8, she was on the other hand, much smaller. Her naturally long blond hair, beautiful fashion sense, high heels and assured nature, made her very noticeable as she made her entrance. Knowing she would turn every head in the office when she walked in, it gave her great pleasure to know she could have any man there, but she had no interest in any of them. Boring egoistical louts, everyone. A culture bypass every time.

She wanted to look down her nose at her admirers because she knew they all had one thing on their minds. It was what made the male mind so easy to manipulate, and she could almost hear them drool as she walked by. Sorry boys, I'm out of your league, well out of it, she thought. She smiled at them. Most of you don't even come close to being interesting, let alone vaguely attractive. She strode through the investigations room, straight into Robert Stone's office with just a cursory knock on his door.

'Katrina Jaeger, sir. You were expecting me I believe?' Robert's first impression was one of pleasure, but he was strangely apprehensive of his new assistant. She was very sure of herself, and he was not sure if she was going to fit in with the rest of this team. She was a lot prettier than they were for a start!

'Well yes, and no,' said Robert. 'All I know was that a female officer had been seconded to me, to assist with catching our sex attacker. They haven't told me anything about you, your specialities, your background or your police work to date. I'm afraid your personnel records haven't caught up with you yet.' Robert had been watching her face, and noticed her grimace at the mention of the sex attacker.

'Can you fill me in on your background a little please before I introduce you to the rest of the team,' he said. 'What would like to know?' came the instant reply. There was a seductive note to her voice, almost playful, it was slightly deeper now, and Robert instantly recognised that he was dealing with someone who knew how to use her sex to her advantage, and he only hoped she wouldn't cause too much of a stir amongst his sex crazed staff. 'Your police history would be a good place to start. I'm intrigued to see why our superiors thought you would be a good match for this investigation.'

'I spent three years at Birmingham University studying Criminal Psychology, sir. I was very tempted to go on to a Masters or PhD there, but decided to apply for the police instead. I was accepted by the Met and I've worked for them for the past three years.' She paused, which made Robert curious, 'And then? Why the move to Kent? What made you change forces? A lot quieter here, and nowhere near as many cases of that sort or calibre here.'

'Personal reasons sir. I'd prefer not to discuss them, if that is all right with you, sir? Let's say I needed a change of scene and company sir.' Robert made a mental record to make some enquiries into that enigma. She was obviously not going to divulge any personal secrets to him at the moment.

'Why Criminal Psychology? Not a very ladylike subject.' Robert realised he had unintentionally said completely the wrong thing. Oops, that wasn't very PC, he thought. She was instantly on the defensive, 'Sorry sir, not very ladylike? Do you think that being a woman excludes me from some subjects?'

'Not at all,' replied Robert. 'Badly put. I should have said it was an unusual subject to study, especially for a woman. It's not exactly a nice subject is it?'

Robert quietly thought to himself that he was digging an ever deeper hole and that he needed to climb out of it instantly, and re-establish control of the conversation. 'Sorry, that sounded very chauvinistic, and I apologise. I'm not used to graduates, especially clever female ones. Most of the team came straight into the police from school. You are somewhat different to what I was expecting. I need to get used to some professional help.'

She smiled, 'I'll take that as a compliment.' Robert thought, I bet you will. You look as if you love a bit of praise.

'Birmingham?' he asked. 'I know, doesn't carry the kudos of Cambridge or Oxford does it? But it is the oldest centre for Criminal Psychology and rated as one of the best courses in the country. I was lucky to get a place. It's is a very hard course to get on to,' she answered.

Robert had been jotting down some notes during the conversation. Without looking up, he asked 'That's a German name I presume.'

She replied, 'German no, Dutch actually, means hunter. My grandparents were refugees in the second world war. My grandfather saw what was happening in other countries in Europe and realised his family were at risk. Jaeger is a Jewish name you see. He came to Britain late in 1938, just in time, with his new bride and my mother was born here some years later, as I was, in case you were wondering if you had a European migrant on your hands.'

'Would it matter?' said Robert.

'I suppose not, but not everyone likes foreigners and you are soon singled out if you are different. I sound foreign, even Katrina is awkward with some people. I'm always getting called Katherine,' she answered with a stiff smile on her face.

'You obviously have an interest in the criminal mind. What made you study it?' he asked.

'My older brother was murdered when I was a teenager. I needed to find out what would drive someone to commit such a dreadful crime. I'm still trying to find out. You want to catch this man, and I think I can help you.' She smiled and sat down on the chair in his office and read the file notes which were handily placed on the edge of his desk.

Robert was left with no doubt he now had a woman on a mission within his team. Woe be his sex attacker if he was confronted by her. This would be interesting when he did the joint introductions later this morning. Jaeger finished reading the file, looked up at Robert, smiled a very confident smile at him whilst returning the file to his desk. She rose, excused herself and went out into the main office to look at the incident board. Every eye in the office was focussed on her and she was loving it. Robert hastily gathered his notes and his thoughts and headed out to give a briefing and an introduction. Well let's see how they like each other.

CHAPTER 11

He pretended to be asleep when Tracey eventually lumbered out of her room late the next morning. She was still totally pissed and he could hear her bouncing off the walls downstairs, he knew in this state she wasn't able to even remotely stand upright. She was on her own this time. No male friend to torment him this time. No groans and squeaking bed last night. Rolling over in bed, he tried to ignore the noise and drunken giggles as she staggered back up the stairs. To his surprise, the door to the spare bedroom opened and she fell into the cramped space, landing on his bed.

Jesus, what does the drunk cow want now? he thought. She struggled under the duvet fully clothed and he felt her wet mouth on his ear. She still stank of booze and stale cigarettes. 'Oi lover boy, want to try again? Shall we see if you can rise to the occasion? Ha, ha. Could do with some action today, no one would come home with me. Just the bottle for company.' A cold hand slid down his naked body, resting on the side of his leg just above his groin. This made him shudder as it was particularly sensitive area. After being frozen out of her life for so long, he couldn't believe she would even contemplate taking him back as a lover.

She snuggled up to him, enjoying the warmth of his body. Her hand slid round to his stomach and began teasing the hair on his body. And then the hand began to go lower, slowly twisting his pubic hair gently as it did. He tensed, was he up to this? He could feel himself stir, but he wasn't sure if he could go the whole way, as he was repulsed and excited by her at the same time. The hand moved down to his penis as she began to rub it and he definitely stiffened this time, the excitement earlier had stimulated him for sure, and the realisation that he could control her again, made him harden in her hand.

'Well, there's a difference from your previous performance. You are a big boy now.' She said and laughed. She threw back the duvet and attempted to pull off her clothes. He went to help her and managed to get her top and bra off, which enabled him to fondle her breasts at the same time, he gently pinched her nipples from behind, making them harden. Finally shedding her tights and pants, she fell back into the bed and rolled over on top of him. She began stroking him, but it was no good, he wasn't going to be able to get hard enough to perform in time.

After several frustrating minutes, Tracey rolled off him disappointed. 'Bloody useless bastard.' she sneered at him. 'Good for nothing. Again.' She slumped back onto the bed and rolled away from him. He tried to cuddle up and gently stoke her but she shrugged away from his touch.

'Useless, useless bastard, you have to go, you have to leave,' she muttered again, but she no longer tried to pull away from him. Trying to caress her gently, and in the act, stimulate himself, he found his efforts were in vain, as he could now hear the snores of a very drunk ex-lover echo through the room. Bloody women, they spoil everything, he thought to himself. I wasn't expecting her to come on to me like that. I wasn't prepared, couldn't get it right. It has to be perfect, everything just right. She had spoilt it again. Stifling a groan, he could have cried at the frustration of the situation. So, so close! It had nearly been right, perhaps the attacks were helping prove who was boss. Perhaps the next victim would help him go the whole way again, he would be sure of it then.

CHAPTER 12

It was eight am and Robert had the team assembled in front of him. Katrina stood beside him so he could introduce her to the case officers. Collecting his file notes he waited for the noise to die down naturally before he cleared his throat and began. 'Gentlemen, I would like to introduce you to DS Jaeger who will head up the team and report directly to me. I have asked for you all, simply because you have all worked with me before, and you all have experience on murder cases. In other words, you know how the system works, and what I need you to do.'

Letting this information sink in, he watched their faces intently, the fact they were all working under a female DS would be a novelty for all of them, and he was interested in how they would react. Equally he was keen to see if she was prepared for any sexual incorrectness from his team. After a few seconds, when both parties had a chance to eye each other up, Robert broke the ice.

'In front of you are the case notes to date. I have allocated each of you various tasks and I will expect you to work in the pairs I've indicated. DS Jaeger will collate your findings along with her own enquiries, and I will try to make sense of everything each day, so that I can brief you each morning.'

Pausing to let the detectives look through the notes, Robert stepped back and introduced Katrina again. 'Gentlemen, I'll hand over to DS Jaeger for her input and summary of where we are so far.' Katrina didn't hesitate once, she must have memorised everything in the file in just a few minutes, thought Robert. She went through the attacks, the time scales, the locations, MO, Robert's and her own thoughts on the type of person they were hunting, and then asked for questions and suggestions.

Like schoolchildren, several hands were raised. 'The distances are pretty big for these attacks and they seem totally random. Any thoughts on why they are so far apart?' asked one DC.

'Several theories, one is these are totally random attacks, it could be more than one person, the attacker is mobile and able to pick his targets as he pleases, in which case we have to look at profiling and narrowing down a huge amount of information to catch him. It will be more about him making a mistake, than us catching him.' said Katrina.

'Another is that he moves around with his job. Could be a traveller, mobile sales rep, someone who does part time or agency work. All of the attacks have a railway station reasonably close by, so one of the first tasks is to see if CCTV is still available for the dates. See if anyone crops up twice on any film. One team will tackle that aspect. Another group will check all the job agencies to see if we can match anyone to the dates and locations more than once. The third team will go through the sex offenders list to see if a name or a face turns up to the other two lists. The boss has allocated those tasks to separate groups already.' She paused and looked at them. The pause was really to let the team know who had done the leg work already, and make sure they knew she hadn't tried to steal the glory for Robert's hard work. She had now neatly set the hierarchy of the team. Robert at the top, she definitely in the middle, but directly reporting to him, and everyone else at the bottom of the pile. It wasn't a big team, but if they needed more bodies, the pecking order had already been established with new members firmly under everyone else.

She continued, 'Whilst I'm waiting for your information to come in, I'm going to see if I can enhance the profile of this character, see what makes him tick, why he sexually attacks women, but doesn't rape. Why the victims are so random, and why he has turned to murder, but still not raped. Gentlemen, you all have your tasks, can I ask you start to narrow down the field for me. Thank you.' She turned to Robert, 'Anything to add sir? Anything I missed?' Robert almost felt inferior to this whirlwind, and could only answer with a simple, 'No, perfectly explained. Well done.'

Satisfied she had made a good impression and stamped her authority on the case, she asked if she could discuss the case in private with Robert, and after he nodded, she followed him into his office. 'Sir, I hope you are happy with the situation. I know I must have been a surprise when I was seconded to your team, but I hope I have something special to add. A woman's perspective, if nothing else.'

'OK' said Robert, 'So what makes you so special that I can't get the same results from my usual team?' 'You are hunting a woman hater, an extreme misogynist obviously,' she replied. 'Obviously?' asked Robert.

'Yes, he has to intimidate them, show them who's boss, prove this mastery over them. Why are they are attacks and not rapes is slightly odd though. If he has gone that far, why not complete the deed. Is he scared of leaving sperm or DNA?'

'I think there is another reason,' said Robert. 'That he is not capable of completing the act, he may be impotent and this is his way of regaining his manhood, by intimidating his victims. But after six months I don't think it has worked if that is the case.'

She pondered the thought, 'Is that likely? Would a man take this course of action?'

Robert almost laughed, but replied with a straight face as he didn't think she would appreciate his thoughts. 'Well that's where you might find me useful. I can give the man's point of view here. And yes, if previous cases are anything to go by, losing your libido has been known to provoke attacks. Blame transference. You are the physiologist, you're the expert on male behaviour. You put a few scenarios on the table and we will look at them, alongside mine.' Robert paused, he could see he had put her nose out of joint.

'We are looking at this all wrong. There is a missing link here. We are profiling the attacker already, when we ought to be looking at his victims as well. What have they got in common? That's where we must begin.'

Katrina immediately disagreed, 'No I'm sorry but we must start looking at the attacker. Get inside his mind.'

Robert interrupted her. 'No we don't know enough about him to waste that amount of time and energy building up a profile which will need amending later. No, there is something in common with all these attacks. That is what I want you to do first. Go and interview the parents of Sally Brookes now. Find out where she had gone that night. Ask them for a modern photograph that we can use on information posters as well. Find out the names of her friends and their contact details so we can build up a picture of her movements. If you can find out where she was in Maidstone, go there, interview them and get information on her movements. If I am wrong and there is nothing to link the victims, I'll eat humble pie and we concentrate on the attacker.'

Robert could see she wasn't enjoying being bossed about, but she had her notepad out and was making notes instead of arguing with him. That would come later no doubt. 'Next track down and interview all the other girls who have been attacked. You have their contact details in your notes. I am particularly interested in where they were going and where they had been. Don't rely on these notes. I want an in-depth interview with each. Confirm the description of the attack, the time, the tiniest of details. You were right in your brief this morning. He is the one who will make the mistake. He will provide the clues to track him down.'

Robert smiled at her, 'Right girl, off you go, and bring me back lots of info in the morning.' Katrina, closed her notebook, scowled at Robert, in the nicest of ways of course, but he recognised the look of a pissed off policewoman straight away. She went out to secure a desk and get her computer on line.

'Watch out boy,' he said to himself, 'She'll have your job one day, and won't even blink in the process.' Returning to the files on his desk, he pondered if the attacker would make a mistake soon, or lay low after he had killed his last victim. Deliberate or accident? It would have been something to make him think. He had a feeling there would be a lull in the attacks now. Robert was tempted to research the history of his new assistant but thought better of it. That was almost voyeurism, it would wait. She seemed efficient, that would be enough for the moment.

Hardly any of the task force came back to the office that night. Most had phoned in with progress reports which Robert was processing, and adding to the case boards that surrounded three walls of the office. On the central board was the map with each of the attack locations. Leading out from each red dot was a marker pen rule leading to a photograph of the victim. Underneath each photo was a name, date and time of the attack, occupation of the victim and a short description of the attack.

On the left hand board was the start of the profile of the attacker. Height, weight, build, age, descriptions of attack, MO, and possible occupations. Speech, accent, in fact all the little clues he had already left behind. Definitely a local man, or someone who now lives locally. Had to be. On the right hand board were possible CCTV sites with ticks or comments alongside denoting what was available, what had been seen and what was unavailable. A good start, thought Robert as he switched off the lights and went home.

Back in his boring suburban semi he turned on the TV in time for the nine am local news. It was a little early and he had to watch the weather report first. The screen changed and the local newsreader appeared. She looked up to read the article on the autocue. 'Police have now released further details of the body found this morning in Maidstone.' A photograph filled the screen as the voice continued, 'It has been confirmed it is the body of seventeen year old Sally Brookes, a Maidstone resident who had been out with friends at a local nightclub on Friday evening. Police have confirmed that they have begun a murder investigation and are appealing for witnesses for anyone that may have seen Sally on Friday evening.'

A contact number was added to the screen and Robert thought, well that's as far as I can take it tonight. Swallowing the remains of his now warm scotch and his TV dinner, he went up for an early night but couldn't sleep, there were too many thoughts running around in his head. Where to go now, was at the top of his list.

CHAPTER 13

Close by there was someone intent on cleaning his bike. He wasn't taking much care in the task as he was still furious, with himself more than anything. In fact furious didn't really begin to describe his feelings, he was still seething at his own failure with Tracey. To have triumphed in the bedroom last night would have helped restore his standing in the house. No longer would he have been relegated to the cramped lonely spare room on his own. He would have been her lover, an equal once more. He so needed to be a man again, to be complete, to be normal. But Tracey had wrecked all that, caught him out, again, found him unprepared, again, and he had not been able to perform, again, let alone satisfy her. Tonight she would go on the hunt once more, leave him in that shitty house, and come back with another man to humiliate him, again.

When he had finished outside he made his way back to his room to clean up. Looking in through her half open door, he could see she was still asleep, sprawled half in and half out of the bed, snoring loudly, as she always did when she had been drinking. 'Sod her' he thought and crept away so's not to wake her. 'I don't need the confrontation, the arguments or the humiliation, this morning.'

He went downstairs for something to eat and was in the act of pouring milk on his cereal when the phone rang. It made him jump and the milk went everywhere bar the bowl. 'Bugger,' he muttered under his breath as he tried to mop up the milk, and answer the phone at the same time. It was just before 6am and he knew it would be an offer of some part time work first thing on a Monday.

'That Carter Rogers?' said a squeaky voice from the damp mobile. 'That's me,' he replied. 'Good. Atlas Agency here. Got two days work in Rochester, fruit packing if you are interested? Starting 7.30am today.'

'Yeah, I'm up for it, text me the address and contact details on the mobile, and I'll be there. I'll grab the bike, should be able to make six fifteen train and be there in plenty of time.' The line went dead allowing him to shovel down the remainder of the cereal, before grabbing his coat and free his beloved bike for a quick sprint across town.

Luckily Tracey's home was close to the station and he managed to get the train with ease. Carrying the lightweight racing bike onto the train, he had little consideration for the other travellers. Their disgust became apparent when he wedged it across one of the sliding doors in the carriage making it close to impossible to alight there. Looking at the crowd, he gave the evil eye to several commuters, who now thought it wiser to ignore this thug, rather than remonstrate with him. Satisfied that they weren't going to give him any grief, he grabbed a window seat for the short journey to Rochester.

After a few minutes, the woman sitting opposite Carter began to get worried as she watched him wrestling with his thoughts. He was obviously angry with something, she could see that look on his face, watch as he subconsciously clenched his fists. His whole body seemed to twitch, as if he was subconsciously fighting some imaginary enemy. She thought of moving away but realised it would only draw attention to her, so she quickly buried her face in her paperback. Every now and then, she caught him looking at her, or rather straight through her, for he was obviously far away, and definitely not in the carriage with the rest of the sweaty crowd. Much to her relief he got off at Rochester and the last she saw of him was as he reached into his pocket to retrieve his mobile and read the messages.

Glancing up as the train started to roll out of the station, he saw her looking at him, and gave her one of the most evil grins she had ever seen, before picking up his bike and marching off down the platform. 'Stupid cow, she'll be thinking of me all day,' he said to no one in particular.

Carter was deep in thought as he rode to the pointless menial job on the industrial estate. His mood had swung from anger to self pity in a matter of minutes. It was a state of mind that was totally confusing to him, and he was finding it almost impossible to come to terms with, let alone cope with. Why had his life been so fucking hard? He dreamed of life in the fast lane, but all he did now, was plunge headlong into the oncoming traffic. He was an accident just waiting to happen. There seemed to be no fairness in life, no love, no meaning to anything he had ever been involved in. The one thing that meant anything to him, had been taken away.

His mind became a jumble of confused memories, of past resentments, and disappointments. His home life with a demanding and cruel father, who always wanted better. A man who tried to live his failed life through his inadequate son, and when his son failed to live up to his expectations, resorted to the belt and a beating, especially when he was drunk. His mother cowering in the corner of the kitchen, terrified of her husband, knowing if she tried to intervene to save her son, the belt would be used on her. Recalling how she had finally run away from them both, and he was left to fend for himself in a house of hate. His miserable surroundings, the cramped dirty house, that bloody awful school where he was bullied for being stupid. The uncaring teachers, the poor marks, always being at the bottom of the pile. The canings. Eventually he had grown big enough not to be intimidated but his father just argued and made life hell anyway. And then the chance to escape, to get away from everything. The army. How he had enjoyed being able to take out his anger on the enemy, it didn't matter who they were, it was all legit. How he had a proper family at last, the tours of Bosnia, the middle east, the killings. But the smile on his face faded as he remembered the attack on the troop carrier, the blood, the death of his friend. His breakdown, losing his place in the world, and the only thing that mattered to him, the only thing that gave him purpose.

He could feel the anger returning as he remembered his wife leaving him, the loss of his house, his job, everything. Carter had thought that his new start with Tracey might be his salvation, but even that had gone so horribly wrong. Now he had no idea of the direction his life would take, not that it mattered, it was bound to be a disaster. Someone would throw a spanner in the works pretty soon, they always did. Recently it felt as if a whole box of them had been emptied into his life. It didn't matter, life had always gone wrong for him. His life now was one of lurching from one disaster to another again.

Feeling sorry for himself, he wasn't really paying much attention to the other road users, and accidentally strayed into the path of an impatient motorist coming up fast behind him. The harsh warning blast of the car horn made him jump and he lost control of the bike, clipping the car's nearside mirror, folding it back against the door with a bang. No damage, but he received an obscene gesture from the furious car driver as he drove off in a hurry. 'Ignorant pig,' Carter shouted after the car and gestured back.

The car driver saw the gesture in his mirror and slammed on his brakes. The car was hurriedly thrown into reverse by the driver, who had decided Carter needed a lesson, and he was definitely the best person to give it to him. The car gathered speed and Carter suddenly realised it was being deliberately aimed at him. A thought flashed across his brain as he stood transfixed to the spot 'Christ I don't need another nutter in my life just now.' Mounting the bike in a vain attempt to cycle away, he realised he had nowhere to go and he was just moments from being crushed. Pushing off with all his strength, he knew he couldn't escape and he closed his eyes and waited for the impact.

At the last moment he heard a screech of brakes expecting the car to smash into him and crush him, but the impact wasn't a crushing one, just hard enough to knock him over and send his precious bike flying.

Carter was still laying on the ground stunned as the car driver raced over and grabbed the front of his Lycra riding suit. His right hand already in a fist and raised to strike Carter in the face. His subconscious army training must have clicked in and he instantly blocked the blow and grabbed the man's arm. Using this as a fulcrum, he used all his force to pull the man closer, totally unbalancing him in the process. As he fell towards him, Carter raised his head and caught him beautifully across the bridge of his nose with the top of the cycle helmet.

The car driver fell to the pavement with a noise like a stuck pig being kicked, and lay there senseless.

Struggling to his feet Carter bent over to inspect his fallen foe. 'Arsehole' he muttered, 'Just because you've got a car, doesn't mean you can throw your weight about.' Grinning at his enemy Carter delivered an almighty kick straight into the man's face. There was a satisfying crunch as he felt the man's nose break. The sight of blood, set Carter off and he delivered a second kick into his mouth, shattering several teeth in the process.

It was a cold, vicious attack, delivered with no feeling except one of extreme anger. He had no time for scum like this. Rolling the man over to examine the damage he had inflicted. He had certainly rearranged the man's features. But it wasn't enough and he stamped down onto his face with all his might. 'A wonderful sound,' he thought and he stomped down again. And again. And again. A red mist moment where revenge and anger overtook reason, before he eventually stepped back from the body.

'Enough,' he thought, and calmly picked up his bike. After inspecting it for damage, he mounted it and rode off as if nothing had happened. 'Now where was this factory' he muttered to himself. The car driver was erased from his thoughts as if nothing had happened.

CHAPTER 14

'OK, what have we got so far?' asked Robert. 'Hours of CCTV from the rail stations,' said one voice at the back of the briefing room. 'Well that is going to be a sifting job for one of you in the office. Make sure that you only pick images from the days of the attacks, that should narrow it down for a start,' said Robert.

'Scan through and take out all the irrelevant images and record everyone else in the approximate age group. We know his height, or close enough to disregard the short and the very tall, the old and the young, any obvious ethic groups, and the ladies of course.' There was a ripple of laughter as the team looked directly at Katrina.

Looking at the DC he scowled, 'Enough. I want you to take two random railway stations each and compare every face, frame by frame to see if a face crops up on both. This guy has to get about somehow. I don't think a car is involved as we've already gone back through the videos and there isn't a single vehicle that appears twice on any of the tapes. That means the guy is either using public transport or something else. A long shot I know but if he does use trains, we look for that face again at the other stations. If we get a third sighting, it's a fair chance we will have our man.'

Katrina butted in, 'We also need to check on CCTV from around the areas of the attacks, is that available?' Robert nodded, 'Not much as most of the attacks were at night and in secluded spots. However, the tapes have all been copied and are on file in each of the individual report boxes. We need a volunteer to go backwards in time on those tapes, before the attacks, and see if we can pick out any familiar faces that might possibly match up with faces from the stations. Banks you can do that when you have finished with the station videos.' There was an audible groan from the hapless DC.

'DS Jaeger, are there any other snippets of information we might pursue? asked Robert. Katrina looked down at her notes. 'As we have no DNA, no photos and as yet no profile, not much. We have a rough description and we know his approximate age. We know he is white and strong, wiry is the description everyone uses. Not at big man in build, but someone who is very fit. There is a good possibility he is a military or ex-military man, probably ex, guessing by his age.'

She paused to let the sheer lack of information on the attacker sink into the team's brains. 'As a start I want someone to go through all the Armed Forces discharges for the past nine months. That is three months prior to the first attack. Saunders, that's one for you.' Another groan from the back of the room, but his colleague cut the joke protest short, 'Guv, we have a lot of information from agencies using part time or contract employees. There are literally hundreds of them including masses of stuff on the web.'

Katrina held up her hand to stop the DC, 'For a start, investigate just the traditional agencies. I don't think this guy has a permanent job and just does casual work. Because he attacks in the evening, it would appear he has been doing something else during the day. That should cut down your workload. Investigate every agency, but just on the days of the attacks. Then ask them to widen the search to three days prior to the attack. We need a common name here. We have very little to go on, so I'm starting a physiological profile on this man. I've put what details we do have on the incident board.'

She dismissed the team and turned to Robert, 'There is another line of enquiry I think we ought to investigate sir. This man is violent. It might be that he has a temper or got into a fight or even has a record. Might be worth going through the records to investigate all attacks in the last nine months. Might just get a cross match somewhere.'

'Good idea,' said Robert. 'Dread to think how many people that might involve. Put a report of the most likely attacks in that period, and keep a record of all new all serious attacks that occur from now on. How have you got on with a report on each of his victims?'

She quickly answered, 'I've been able to borrow a couple of WPCs to compile a history on the girl's movements. I have made a report for you in outline. Most of them were on their way home having worked late, or had been out on the town celebrating. I think our attacker goes on the hunt in the evening, which makes me think he is on shift work, or in a relationship where the partner wouldn't notice irregular movements, or he just lives on his own.'

'Thanks,' said Robert as he turned away and returned to his office. 'Christ, this is even worse than a needle in a haystack.' and he settled down in front of a mountain of paperwork to make his own notes. 'We are missing something here,' he muttered to himself. 'But you will make that mistake sooner or later, and I will have you.'

CHAPTER 15

It had been the usual brain numbing experience for Carter. But he didn't need to think much in the menial job the agency had found for him. It was just cold, miserable work that would pay the rent. Just needed to do as he was told. Yes sir, no sir, three bags full sir. Keep quiet and collect his money at the end of the day. Packing fruit, what sort of job is that? he thought to himself. Carter had been in a foul mood all day, testosterone had coursed through his body since the attack on the motorist earlier, and it needed an outlet. His thoughts went back to the motorist. His foot involuntary twitched as he remembered the final kick that broke the motorist's teeth.

'Stupid arsehole', Carter muttered under his breath as he smiled at the memory of the pool of blood he had left the man in. Unfortunately it was loud enough for the foreman to hear as he walked past. 'What was that?' the foreman said. 'Nothing,' said Carter. 'Just thinking out loud about something else. Nothing to do with you.'

'It has everything to do with me. I suggest you shut your mouth if you want to work here. Plenty of Poles and Latvians who would love this job. You cause me any problems and you can fuck off now, and with no pay.' The foreman glared at Carter, 'Got it sonny? In fact I don't want to see you again. Collect your money at the end of the shift and bugger off to your hole, and don't come back. I'll phone the agency and ask them to supply someone new tomorrow, someone without attitude.'

Turning away Carter could hear him laugh as he walked off. 'Another arsehole. Another little Hitler the world would be better off without.' The look of hate Carter gave the foreman as he disappeared into his shabby little office was enough to wither any mortal. But the foreman was obviously not human, some machine, some jobsworth who was promoted way above this abilities, thought Carter. Scum of the earth. An hour later, the shift ended and Carter went into the office to collect his meagre pay. The foreman was there to gloat. 'Well sonny, you got what you deserved,' he smirked. Carter said nothing but he was thinking hard. He simply looked at him and gave him a sinister smile. 'Your loss arsehole. Shit job I could do without, so you can stuff it.'

Turning on his heels he walked out of the factory with his money. Not that he went far, just to the edge of the carpark where he hid the bike and waited in the shadows for the foreman to emerge. The foreman appeared some ten minutes later after shutting down the factory and switching off the lights. He was illuminated by a single security light which went off as he crossed the car park. Carter knew he had the right vehicle as all the other cars had departed, leaving the solitary car in isolation at the edge of the park. The bushes around the edge of the tarmac would provide all the cover he would need. Having already let down the front offside tyre, he was now positioned for the perfect ambush. The foreman was fumbling with the ignition keys in the dark when he noticed the flat tyre.

'Bastard,' but he had barely muttered it as Carter crept up behind him, and in complete silence, slammed his head into the roof of the car. The foreman slid down the side of the door unconscious. Carter gave him a good kick before pulling the wallet out of the foreman's pocket. Stuffing all the notes into his own pocket, he threw the empty wallet on the ground next to the body. But not before he had carefully wiped it to leave no fingerprints. 'Felling good now. Time for the hunt to begin,' he said and headed off into town on his bike.

CHAPTER 16

'OK people, what have we got so far?' said Robert as be stood in front of his team at eight am, three days later. He gestured with outstretched arms for silence. The room slowly quietened down and all attention was focused towards Robert. Katrina stood beside him with a sheaf of notes. The expression on her face showed boredom and contempt for the obviously restless detectives who sat facing her. 'DS Jaeger, I believe you have collated everything to date, would you be so kind as to put us all in the picture. I believe we have some leads and fresh information to share?'

Glancing at her notes, she said, 'Some interesting evidence has come to light. The forensic evidence from our attack and murder scene in Maidstone has produced something I think we should investigate further. There are bike tyre tracks at the scene, enough to take a good impression. There are also footprints of bike shoes around the attack scene, so we can identify those, and hopefully track down records of the shop they might have come from. So we are looking for someone who takes cycling seriously. To date none of the other attacks have mentioned a cyclist, so this could be a one off, but I have a feeling it is connected to all the other attacks,' she said and paused for a few seconds to let that information be absorbed. 'This isn't some sort of hunch, it actually ties in with CCTV that you have managed to get from the stations. Because of the long time scale involved, only about a quarter of the stations had records we could examine. Most of that was either poor or of no use. But after the clues left behind on the latest attack, I looked at what taped evidence we did have, but this time looking for people carrying bikes on the trains. Loads of them as you will have guessed. The field could be cut down by only looking for someone who fits our descriptions given by witnesses so far. That still produced scores of possibilities, so I asked you to print off all the identifiable faces to see if any cropped up more than once. They did, we had about 60 regular bike riders but obviously not all of them rode racing bikes. That cut the list down to about 40 from local stations.

Next we had to cross reference those with dates that the attacks took place. Evidence became very thin then as the attacker can't have used the bike on every occasion. However, because the attacks took place over such a wide area it would seem either this guy wasn't in full time work and working casually, doing agency work or had other means of support.'

Again she paused, watching their faces for the next surprise. 'There are thousands of people working for agencies and it has been a long process narrowing down the employees to fit our attacker. We specifically asked about employees who roughly fitted our description, that narrowed it down further. Then you guys cross referenced that with names on the previous list with those who were employed on the days of the attacks, that at least cut the list in half again. Taking another angle we asked about those who had a history in the armed forces, security, even the police.'

That raised a laugh from her audience which she quickly quashed with a raised hand. 'Enough, it has been known, so don't rule it out, we must look at all possibilities at the moment. And if you go down that avenue first we might just hit on our target. All of the records have photographs of applicants and addresses. Because of Data Protection we had to obtain a court order to gain access to these records before the documents could be copied,' she quietly said with a definite smile on her face. There was silence now as her audience realised this might just have produced a suspect. When we ran a face recognition programme against images gleaned from the CCTV - and Bingo.'

CHAPTER 17

Carter hadn't succeeded in intimidating any new victims after his attack on the foreman. There was a fear that the police would put two and two together and point the finger straight at him, he needed to play it safe this time. So he rode around for an hour and then decided that discretion was the best part of valour, and he would give hunting a miss that night. Slowly he rode back to the station and waited for the train. Well that was his intention, but at the last minute he thought that it might be better to put some distance between him and the attack. Then he wouldn't be recorded on CCTV at the station, which would mean he wouldn't have to explain why he was still on the scene so long after being dismissed after his last job.

As he cycled away he wondered how many clues he had left at the scene of any of his attacks. There was a smile on his face when he thought back and remembered each case. Quite a few now because he enjoyed the hunt, the fear in their eyes and the violence. Yes he enjoyed the violence best of all. Teach woman their place in life, he thought.

Thinking back hard, he couldn't think of anything too obvious. Sure he would have been recorded on CCTV, but he was always careful to not carry out his attacks close to his place of employment, or near where the agencies sent him. Sometimes he got lifts, he had hitched, travelled by train, bus and gone by bike, the mode of transport was varied and he tried to make journeys as different as possible, just to make tracking him difficult. Recognition, no, he always disguised or hid his face and attacked from behind. They might have guessed his height and weight, but nothing more. Were his attacks even linked together? He doubted that as well, they occurred over too large an area. No, he was in the clear, he was sure.

CHAPTER 18

'Bingo?' Jaeger repeated, but as a question this time. 'No, that would have been too easy, and I would have come in here to announce we had our man in the cells already. No.' The detectives in the room became restless, they knew they were about to have their workload greatly increased. 'OK, it was a good start but we haven't got enough detail to narrow down the suspects yet, so they all go back into the melting pot again, and we widen our search.'

There was no hesitation in her presentation as she was determined to get this right, prove her point and most of all prove her worth. A woman in a man's world, only she needed to be better than them, she always had, she had so much more to prove.

'We will look at this from another angle and instead of looking for historic ties we will concentrate on the latest attack only. The attacker must have been a cyclist. That is confirmed by the tyre tracks and the footprints. Forensics should, with a little legwork from you, be able to match the make of tyre, and with luck the bike shoe,' she said.

'We have to make an assumption that the attacker is fairly local, you don't go riding any distance at night in the rain, so we will concentrate on a 5 mile radius to start with, to track those two items down. That is about sixty five square miles. I want every bike shop and sports shop visited to see if they stock either of the two items. If so, can we work out from the wear on the impressions how old the items might be, that might give us a link as to when they were purchased. We can then search records for card transactions and possible CCTV records, we might just get lucky there. Identify and search gentlemen, Identify and search. Now that will take two of the team out of the equation. I want two more to have a detailed look at the attacks starting with the most recent, in particular any that are in the local vicinity. The rest of you have been assigned tasks that I have detailed here.' With that she handed out individual work sheets to the remaining team.

'We have had two days so far to sort this, with little progress, because we hoped there would be an easy solution, a cross reference, a face recognition that would make life easy. It didn't happen so we are back to doing it the hard way. But we will get there. This man will make mistakes, he has made a huge one already because of a spontaneous act, we have to find him.' Robert had been watching and listening from his office, he had already been briefed, so he knew what was coming. He had hoped there would have been more progress, but that was life. When the briefing was over he called Jaeger into his office and shut the door.

'I'd like to put out another press statement about the last attack. An appeal for witnesses, we have an accurate time of death so we can narrow down the time slot we are looking at. I want as many details of the bike and the clothing released to see if any one recognises the bike rider. I then want a team member to keep an eye on new sales of similar tyres and footwear in the town. We might just panic him into changing both. If he does, the card transactions it will be available as would CCTV. Worth a try on both counts,' he said.

Jaeger nodded, 'I'll get on to it now.' she turned and walked out of Robert's office. Robert just sat there with his own notes, deep in thought as to how he was going to prepare the press conference to make it look as if he was making some sort of progress. Right, need details of the bike he thought, see if forensics could shed any light there. Would the team strike it lucky, would there be a lucky break, a careless clue, the bike tracks had been a huge careless mistake and Robert realised his prey was both human and fallible. In this case it must have been an impulse attack and not planned, someone with a short fuse for sure.

Later that day the phone rang in Robert's office. The voice at the other end said 'We have identified the tyre and it is a Continental Grand Prix 4000S II Folding Road Tyre. A serious choice for serious road cycling, fits a decent racing bike. There were loads of stockists locally and they were widely available on the web. You are not going to have too much luck with the shoes either, Muddyfox, we think a TRI 100. Again widely available on the High Street, places like Sports Direct and all over the web. The shoes won't show much wear so we have no idea how old they were, but the tyres are almost brand new, so a recent purchase or they haven't been used much, no more than a month at the most.'

Robert put the phone down. Better than nothing he thought. OK at least that gives me something else to put in the appeal tonight. At five pm Robert sat in front of cameras again, and reading from his script he announced that they had some important new developments in the killing in Maidstone earlier in the week. Reiterating the name of the victim, her place of demise and the approximate time of her death, Robert almost casually dropped in that they were looking for a dedicated cyclist and they had identified the type of bike from the tyre tracks and even the type of shoe the killer was wearing.

The contact numbers were flashed on the screen and Robert repeated them slowly, twice before the police logo faded in. Robert knew he was overplaying his role by giving such important evidence to the public, but it might just jog people's mind and point a few fingers. I bet we have a flurry of suspects and nutters on the answerphone in the morning, he thought.

CHAPTER 19

Carter sat in front of the TV screen with his mouth open, he had just realised that for all his clever tactics to cover his tracks, he had just made one bloody great mistake. His first thought was to find the new shoes he had purchased and dump them instantly and as far away as possible. Did he still have his old ones? Scurrying about his room in panic he found them in a box under his bed. Immediately he swapped them for his new ones and took them down to the passage way by the front door so they were obvious. Hiding his new shoes in a carrier bag, he poked them under his clothes at the bottom of the ancient wardrobe that dominated his room. To be disposed of later, he thought, but only when it was safe to do so. Bloody waste.

'Fuck, what about the bike, the tyres man,' he mumbled to himself. Luckily the bike had quick release wheels and he rushed downstairs to remove both entire wheels. Could he replace the tyres before she came home, he would have to be bloody quick. There were always spares in his room in case of punctures or damage, and changing a tyre was second nature to him. The front one was a piece of cake, and he had that changed in minutes and back on the bike. Admiring his handiwork he was taken by surprise as he heard a key in the front door, his smirk turning to a look of panic in just those few seconds.

There was a lot of fumbling before it opened, giving him time to flick the light off quickly, and then quietly, rush upstairs and push everything under the bed with just seconds to spare. Laying under the duvet, Carter heard her slam the front door and unsteadily climb the stairs in the dark. She was pissed as usual, but at least she didn't have anyone with her this time. No confrontations, no arguments, well not until the morning at least.

The creaking floorboards on the landing indicated which way she was heading, luckily it wasn't in his direction and slowly her muttered oaths about every sin on earth, and how everyone was out to get her, diminished as she staggered into her own room, eventually collapsing noisily onto her bed. More swearing, then silence. Heavy snoring a few minutes later clearly indicated she was dead to the world. It would give him time to quietly remove the other tyre just using the light from the window. Couldn't risk switching a light on, she was bound to be woken by it and that would lead to questions and arguments, at worse she would start nosing around his room and see the tyres.

Creeping about the room, he selected the tools he needed, but it was awkward in such poor light, and he was acutely aware of any noise he made, might wake her. It was slow work but eventually he managed to get the new tyre on. The wheel was gently propped against the wall, so he could fit it in the morning as he dare not try and put it on that night. Slowly calming down, he took a deep breath and started to relax.

The curtains were now drawn, plunging the room into darkness. Calm, deep breath, he had to have a quiet dark room to sleep, light disturbed him. Although his brain was racing, he was tired and for once it didn't take long for him to fall into a fitful sleep. To an outside observer Carter was still in torment, he was definitely restless, tossing in the bed, the duvet sliding to the floor as he wrestled with his inner demons. And they were real demons to Carter.

It was his demon soldier with his face blown away that he was wrestling with him. Carter was covered in warm blood and entrails, he was drowning in blood, it was everywhere, and he couldn't breathe because of the clouds of choking dust and smoke as well. Although he struggled as hard as he could, he couldn't get away, he was pinned down, couldn't move, no matter how hard he tried. He simply couldn't get away.

In his nightmare he could see the soldier move his head towards him, he could see the mouth open to say something, to accuse him. But he was dead, Carter knew he was dead, but he was still able to talk to him. This terrified him more than anything, dead but not dead. How many others would come back from the dead to haunt him. Would they never die? In his dreams the soldier now faced him and hissed 'You killed me. You changed the plans, took a different route. Clever bastard weren't you, but you knew best didn't you? But you killed me!' A blood soaked hand reached out for Carter and he felt himself try to scream.

There was a crash outside his room, a light came on in the passageway waking him. Carter thought he must have screamed and woken the landlady, but she just wanted the toilet. Pulling the duvet back on the bed, Carter was sweating so hard that the bed felt damp. Turning away from the light, he waited until she flushed the toilet and staggered back to her room before he tried to go back to sleep. His eyes closed and he was soon asleep, and back in the desert just waiting for his nemesis to appear. And he did.

CHAPTER 20

Robert was in early the next morning, knowing he would be facing the wrath of his team. They would be facing a barrage of messages left after the appeal. It was not a pleasant task and hours of valuable time would be wasted sorting this out. There would be the usual nutters, and those who had a grievance to air, anything to get an enemy or a neighbour dropped in it. These were the people who knew everything had to be investigated, and who knows, the police might actually find something, or at least make them suspicious of something else. Robert hated these messages, it demonstrated a malignant side of a society he loathed, the nasty evil underbelly of society that had nothing better to do, than to stir up hatred of others who didn't conform to their views. The curtain twitchers of old, but in a digital age, where communications were so much more effective and dangerous. There would be mistaken identities, there would be those who had the time and locations wrong, to be gleaned out first. The task was endless, but he hoped at the bottom of all this there might be that one clue, that one nugget of information that would give them the edge to catching this murderer.

As he entered the briefing room, he was pleased to see the team assembled already. Jaeger already had a sheaf of notes at the ready. 'Morning Boss,' she said. There was no emotion on her face, an absolutely professional approach Robert thought. Joining her on the platform at the front of the room he saw that extra snippets of information had already been added to the incident board behind their heads.

Holding up his hand for silence, he sat down and gestured to Jaeger to continue. Knowing she had already been busy, he was curious to see if anything new had turned up. 'We are missing three of the team this morning,' she said. 'They, along with myself, spent hours last night starting to process the calls that came in. They are going to get a few hours of rest this morning before resuming.' Robert was impressed at her enthusiasm, but he knew she had an ulterior motive.

'I'm tired,' she continued, 'But we have broken the back of most of the messages left, sorted the loonies out, well most of them I hope, and the obvious malicious calls. There is still a lot to do.' With that she handed out sheets to the remaining crew, stifled a yawn and simply added,' All yours, I'll be back after lunch with the other guys to help you out if that is OK with you, but you have a huge list to check, plus you have some of the team checking the sports outlets a well.'

She turned on her heels, and headed to Robert's office with a single sheet which she handed to him. 'Done the best I could in the time we had, sure the guys can reduce the suspects down even more, but these six look as if they might be worth a follow up, sir. Hope you don't mind if I cram in a few hours of sleep before I do another late one.'

'I do,' said Robert. 'Get some proper shuteye, come back when you feel up to it and it's normal hours for the rest of the day, no over doing it please. That was really good work last night and I appreciate the effort, but you don't have to impress me, I can see your qualities and that you will go far. But don't overdo it, the guys are beginning to see you as a detective, a good detective, not an Amazon. Put things into perspective, but keep up the good work.' Smiling at her, he hoped she would at least smile back, but no. She simply nodded at the sheet on his desk and left. Silly cow he thought. She is bloody clever but she has such a massive chip on her shoulder that will over balance her one of these days. Picking up the single sheet with the six names, and their addresses, he wondered why they should be visited.

CHAPTER 21

Robert and Jaeger weren't the only ones up early that morning. Carter had silently crept down to his precious bike, and was busily reassembling the rear wheel. The snores from the back room confirmed his landlady was still sleeping it off, and that he hadn't woken her, nor was he likely to. The bike was disguised and he could ride it about without suspicion now. Back in his room his rucksack was packed with the cycle shoes and the tyres which he had folded and tied up ready for transport to a place of disposal. Knowing they had to be destroyed not dumped, he had also packed a can of lighter fuel and a disposable lighter. Just ride off into the woods somewhere, burn them and bury the ashes just to make sure.

It was still early and he had no work booked for today, so he made a pot of tea in the kitchen taking it through to the tatty living room intending to watch the news for any developments. His mobile rang making him jump. It was the agency, who were pissed off with him after being fired from his previous job. Carter tried to explain it wasn't his fault but they said the floor manager had been attacked and he had pointed a finger squarely at Carter. There was a good chance the police would be involved now. Even if he was innocent, they didn't want him on their books, and there would be no further offers of work for him in the circumstances.

Carter swore loudly, it was the only reaction he was left with that meant anything to him. In his anger he felt like punching something or someone. That arsehole had it coming anyway he thought, but I'll have to try a few of the other agencies now or he'd have no money to pay the old ratbag upstairs. Turning on the TV he caught the end of a report for the local police saying they were overwhelmed by the response about the cycle murder. He heard the phrase 'Cycle murderer' used and suddenly thought this is getting too close for comfort.

'Good name for you,' said his landlady softly into his ear.' 'Fuck you,' yelled Carter as he jumped up off the sofa, spilling the tea in the process. 'Why do you creep up on people like that?' Staring into her bloodshot eyes, he realised it was a look of pure malice.

'Well soldier boy I think that title fits you down to the ground. I know you've killed in the past. You are violent for sure, I've seen your temper in action and I've got my suspicions about you now. And after all, you do have a bike.' Carter sat down on the sofa, he wasn't sure if she was joking, winding him up, or if she knew something. He would have to be so bloody careful with her.

'Just because I own a bike doesn't make me a killer, you stupid prat.' His words were spat out, but he said everything too hurriedly and he tried to stay calm, not to look guilty, not to sound unconvincing. He hoped his face hadn't give too much away, or he hadn't blushed, as he knew he was a hopeless liar.

'OK, calm down, it was only meant as a bloody joke,' she answered. 'Can't have you getting so upset can we. After all you haven't got anything to hide have you?' With that she gave him an almighty poke in the chest just to emphasise her comment and laughed at him. Carter really didn't know how to take that. She didn't usually joke with him, perhaps she did suspect something, she might just phone up the police, have them come round, have their suspicions aroused. Could be the thin edge of the wedge, an excuse to get rid of him, to make life just plain awkward. Trouble is he couldn't take the chance now. Knowing that he had no alibi for any of his actions, they would delve into his movements, look at dates and certainly put two and two together. Too many coincidences to avoid the finger being pointed.

CHAPTER 22

The foot soldiers had been out all day checking on the suspects on Katrina's list. Several had been at work and would need a second visit in the evening. Out of the remaining four, three had supported alibis and were removed from the list. One wasn't at the address they were supplied with, and he immediately became the prime suspect for the moment. As the evening wore on, both of the absent suspects were eliminated after a visit, one of them became extremely upset that his name was on any list, let alone one as a murder suspect. It was taken off immediately to placate him.

The outstanding suspect was cross referenced against his national security records, DWP records, police records, electoral role, driving records, national insurance, in fact just about anything and everything that might help locate him. Nothing. His house had been repossessed and his whereabouts were unknown. 'Could be our man,' said Katrina when she appeared the next morning. 'Has anyone cross referenced his employment records? To see if was working nearby any of the attacks.' 'Doing it now,' said a voice from the back of the office. 'Have his employment and NI records on screen as we speak.'

A silence descended on the office, an air of expectancy hovered over everyone for several minutes until the same voice disappointedly said, 'No, can't be him. He was a sales rep for a local manufacturer and he was out of the country on at least four of the attacks. Company went into liquidation recently and left him high and dry. Seems he had an expensive lifestyle, lots of debts and no means of paying for anything. Cross him off as well.' 'Bugger,' was all Katrina heard from Robert's office behind her.

'OK,' Katrina said, 'Let's look at this from another angle and start cross referencing. We know all the women attacked had nothing in common. They were just unfortunately in the wrong place at the wrong time. They are all different ages, professions, ethnic groups, they couldn't be more diverse. Attacks have a similar MO, but that's all. We have dates of the attacks and locations which is our starting point again. Someone will need a lot of alibis to avoid this getting them pinned on them. We need to start working on the agencies again. We have a basic description of the assailant which is really helpful as we can eliminate many of the suspects that might be dropped into the frame. It will also help if we start getting suspects to investigate from other sources. If we start profiling this guy he know has a violent nature but he is cunning which suggests planning. To me that still suggests a military or security connection, so have to start looking at old discharge records. From his suggested age I don't think he is a serving soldier. To get some idea of the numbers involved in people coming out of the services I looked up the figures for medical discharges last year. I've looked at medical discharges instead of dishonourable discharges, just as a starting point. For the navy four hundred and forty six, the RAF it was one hundred and forty eight and here is the frightening one, army one thousand, nine hundred and thirty two. These are just medical discharges. This guy is very active so I don't think he was discharged for a physical injury, but a mental or trauma reason, if at all. I need someone to start looking into this, Stuart this is one for you.' She paused, 'OK it's a long shot but it might cross reference nicely somewhere down the line. Start on those in the county, sure that will give us a big list anyway without going outside Kent. I'm sure he is a local man from reports of his accent.'

She looked around the room for signs of dissent, but she had their complete attention simply because they now knew this was going to mean a lot more work than they thought. Alright we know he is a bike rider, but that is incidental, might be a nice connecting point somewhere down the line. Anyone on the suspects list will head to the top, if he is a bike rider. There is going to be a lot of computer input and correlation on this one, I think we are going to need a couple more bodies to help on that front.'

She stopped and waited for a response, but they were already thinking how to narrow this field down. Behind her Robert interrupted with a single comment, 'There is another possible avenue we could also look at. We know this man is violent, if we go back to when the attacks started and have a look at GBH and assault records we might get another cross reference. DS Jaeger and I will look through these before sending you guys out to follow up.'

Robert turned and went back into his office, Jaeger followed closely. 'OK, we have lots of strands of enquiry, time to narrow them down. We had little success with the station CCTV but we do have a lot of common faces, we need to narrow those down to possible cross referenced attacks, so we need to find the nearest station to each of the attacks, run through the tapes to see if a face appears more than once,' said Robert.

Frustrated he sat down in his office and said to Jaeger, 'Christ this is worse than looking for a needle in a haystack. There are too many avenues to investigate. Our only hope is he will make a mistake somewhere down the line, but I'm not going to bank on it. To make matters worse I've suggested yet another area we might delve into. I just know this is not going to be easy, we need that lucky break, a connection, a clue, that one little piece of information that will point us in the right direction.' Without smiling, he ushered her out of his office so he could think clearly.

CHAPTER 23

The young WPC sat next to the badly bruised patient in the hospital bed and said, 'Do you think you can give me a description of the attacker?' The man slowly nodded, he could, and painfully gestured for something to write with. The nurse accompanying him looked at the WPC and whispered, 'He can't speak. The attack has severely damaged his jaw, broken his nose and most of his teeth. He was lucky not to lose an eye, especially as the eye socket has been destroyed. He will only be able to write his answers. Please keep it as short as possible as he has suffered major trauma and is finding it hard to cope with, and I don't want to distress him any more than necessary.'

The WPC offered her note book to write in. 'Was the attacker on foot, or in a car?' The man shook his head and began to draw something on the pad, a crude cycle. She looked at it puzzled. 'Can you confirm the attacker was a cyclist, not a motor cyclist' she said. He nodded. 'Do you remember anything about him, his height, his race, his looks, what he was riding, colour of the bike, anything. The notebook was quickly snatched back and he began to write at speed, anxious to impart as much as possible to locate his attacker, and get some sort of revenge. After a few minutes he handed the note pad back, and slumped back on the bed.

'Can I ask you to leave please,' said the nurse, this is proving tiring for him. He is going to be prepared for an operation shortly and won't be able to communicate for at least a day. I don't want him distressed before surgery.' The WPC just took the notepad back, she had others to see still, and knew this would be a long boring day. The WPC spent the rest of the day interviewing the other attack victims, a few were in hospital, most were at home recovering, and few had gone back to work. Most were the result of drunk brawls, work disagreements, domestic fights and by the end of the day she had a note pad of names and descriptions to type up for the computer to cross reference.

She had no idea she was carrying vital evidence. It just seemed a very mundane investigation, as she hadn't been given any background information, just a task to complete. It hadn't been deemed important to inform the workers what they were collecting. The next morning she started to type up her reports. She had managed to do seven interviews, and it would take several hours to file all of them. The description of the cyclist attack would go unnoticed until the following day as a result.

Another WPC, one of four assigned to attack interviews was also completing a similar task. She had the other vital clue, the attack on the foreman, this time with a name attached. At this stage these were just random incidents and it would take a stroke of luck to tie them together amongst the plethora of information. A little bit of clever joined up thinking was all it needed.

That wouldn't occur for days. The work force was far too busy with the traditional methods of investigation to sift through peripherally gathered material that cluttered up their thought processes. There was a danger that they had spread the net too wide and gathered too much information to be collated efficiently. Cross referencing would take a long time and a lot of man power to put two and two together to make four.

The answer to their problems lay within arms-reach - if only someone would look carefully. In fact it took two more days before someone thought there might be a new avenue to investigate.

One of the team looked at the info on his screen and he thought it was worth looking at. Jaeger was called over, 'Here guv, this of any use. Two attacks on the same day. First one by a vicious cyclist, which is who we might be looking for, and he seems to have got the better of a motorist after an argument. And in the same town, on the same day, an attack on a night shift manager. Nothing proved, but we have a name and address - not been followed up by the looks of things. We missed it because there were no sex attacks that day. Could be a coincidence. Worth a look?' She wasn't really convinced, 'Just two attacks, are they connected to our case? They don't tie in with attacks on women, wrong dates. But it's still a slim possibility. Drop it downstairs, let uniform have a look, if they have time.'

Had he been in the room, Carter would have breathed a sigh of relief that no connection had been made, and he still wasn't in the picture for the murder. The case notes were passed on to uniform who admitted neither case had been followed up, they were still in the pending file because of manpower shortages. They made a couple of excuses to justify their lack of enthusiasm. One because the witness was still in hospital, the other because it hadn't been prioritised properly. With some embarrassment the notes were accepted back with a promise of a foot solder to be put on the case immediately.

It was a busy day for the station and eventually a squad car ended up at the factory to take a statement from the foreman about his attack. Couldn't have happened to a nicer person thought the PC who interviewed the angry foreman. Eventually he admitted that he had been attacked from behind and robbed, but he hadn't actually seen the attacker. Insistent that he knew the attacker, well at least he had his suspicions, but was reluctant to make too much fuss just in case he was wrong. He didn't need a legal case on top of everything else.

However, when he made a full statement and provided a name and address of a temporary worker he had sacked earlier, the PC realised he might be worth talking to. A bike rider, and possibly a violent one. Putting in a radio request for a follow up, which was granted, the officers set off to investigate the lead. The first piece of the jigsaw was about to drop in to place.

CHAPTER 24

Carter saw the squad car pull up outside his house, he had been expecting this and he wondered why it had taken the foreman so long to make his complaint, or were the police just slow. His story was ready, he knew nothing could be proved, he had gone home after the sacking, and he knew he wasn't on any CCTV, this would be a case of sour grapes by someone who wanted to point an aggrieved finger at him, just to drop him in it.

When the knock at the door came, he waited until the second knock and then opened it confidently to the two officers, who politely said they were making enquiries into a case, and could they come in and have a chat. 'Of course,' he said and showed them into the living room with an offer of tea which was politely declined.

They said they were interested in agency workers in relation to an attack, it was just one line of enquiry to be investigated. His name had come up because he was on the books of the factory where the attack took place. They asked him to confirm his identity, where he worked in the past, and were immediately interested in the fact he was solely an agency worker. Everything was noted. Carter waited for the next question, he had it all worked out what to say, he had an answer for everything but there was no accusation.

'So you get to see a lot of the county I suppose,' asked one officer. 'Inside of factories mostly,' answered Carter. 'It's really the only work I seem to get after my discharge, suffered from

PTSD after my service.' 'Sorry to hear that,' said the officer, but he made a quick note of the facts, 'And which agencies do you work for?' 'Loads of them,' he replied with a smile, hoping to make life difficult and confuse the issue for the time being. 'Like a list of them if you wouldn't mind sir. It would help eliminate you from our enquiries.'

Carter knew he had to comply, he remembered a few of them but deliberately missed out some of his major employers so that they would have a harder job to correlate a connection between the attacks. The other officer had just sat quietly making notes up until that point but suddenly realised there was also another strand of enquiry to be followed up on. Looking through the file of the attack by the cyclist, he realised Carter fitted the description given by the motorist, but said nothing.

However, when they left he spotted the cycle at the far end of the hall and discretely took a photo on his mobile when Carter wasn't looking. He had a hunch they would be returning, he didn't believe in coincidences. Hiding his phone behind his files, he also managed to take several shots of Carter. Without making Carter suspicious, they thanked him and made their way back to the car. It wasn't until they pulled away that either of them spoke.

'I think we need to go and have a chat to CID when we get back. That guy fits a description of one of the attacks and he has a great motive for the second one after getting fired. I'm not sure what CID are looking for but I have a feeling we might have some useful info here,' said the driver. 'Agreed,' replied the other officer, 'Didn't want to spook him, but I think there is enough to pay him a second visit soon.' They returned to the station and immediately went up to the CID incident room where they found a very sympathetic ear in the form of Katrina Jaeger. She called Robert out of his office and explained what the officers had found.

One officer said, 'We probably had enough to bring him in on suspicion of the attack, but we know you are working on something bigger and though it would be best to check with you first, as I have a feeling he might be able to help you with that.' 'Well if I am correct, we have an agency worker. We can check with his employers to see if he cross references with any of the locations of the attacks. He is ex forces, with a medical discharge. He is a cyclist, thank you for the photo of the bike, it won't admissible in court, but I bet if you show this to the motorist who was attacked, it will prove a match. And I see you snuck a photo of our man in question, just discretely show that to the motorist. From his description and your photo, I think we have our man for the two attacks at least.

However, whether he is the cycle murderer is another matter. Well done you two and thank you for bringing your observations to our attention. Brilliant.'

Jaeger quickly brushed past the two uniforms and out into the main office. 'Drop everything, we have a suspect we need to cross reference immediately.' She turned back to the two officers, 'Can you go and see the motorist who was attacked, show him a photo of the bike first and then show him the photo of Carter to see if he can identify either. I'll clear it with downstairs. Then lose those photos - they were taken illegally, but not before they are downloaded onto my data file.' She smiled and added, 'Radio back the results please, we may ask you to pay a further visit to our friend here.'

She almost ran back into the incident room. 'Right who's

checking the agencies - we have a name, see if he is on their books and when and where he was employed. Who has the CCTV cross reference job - we have a photo now, see if you can spot him on any of the tapes, especially with that bike.' She turned back to Robert and smiled again. 'I think the Gods may have just smiled on us today.' Robert had to agree, but they had taken a bloody long time to do it through. She smiled at him, turned and strode back into the main office to shout at the detectives, 'Come on, come on, I need a result guys.'

CHAPTER 25

Carter was unhappy with the visit. The police hadn't asked what he thought they would. Surely they would be more interested in the attack at the factory. This didn't ring right. They were too polite and he was sure they would be back. He wasn't sure if they would be able to prove anything, but he was not going to take the chance. He knew he fitted the frame for the attack all too well. They had gone back to check something, he knew it, it was a gut feeling. Taking two steps at a time, he ran up the stairs into his room and started to pack. Stay one step in front if you can, he thought.

There wasn't much to pack, he always travelled light. An old army trait that had served him well. Searching through his meagre belongings, he then realised the tyre and cycle shoes still need to be disposed of. 'Shit, they can't be found,' he muttered to himself and they were hurriedly packed into a small rucksack. There was lighter fluid on the bedside table which would make sure they would burn and there was a lighter to hand to make sure of the job. The rucksack was grabbed and he was downstairs and onto the bike in seconds. There were plenty of remote spots he could destroy the offending items, but it had to be quick.

In his hurry to get out of the house he had forgotten that his bag was packed and in full view in his room. If she spots it, she is going to put two and two together and make five. Am I going to flee, why? It was too late to go back, he would have to think why the bag was packed, taking stuff to the charity shop perhaps.

Didn't matter now. No time to think, there were plenty of bins on the industrial estate nearby, the shoes and tyre were dumped in one, along with the cleaning fluid and a lit match. There was a satisfying whump and plenty of smoke. Evidence destroyed. Now what?

CHAPTER 26

The team in CID were working flat out. Every member had been allocated an employment agency to contact. Not all complied but when threatened with a search warrant, wasting police time, obstruction and no end of illegal gestures, they all complied without further protest. Carter seemed to have worked for just about every agency in the county. As they produced hit after hit with dates and locations, Katrina pulled a team member off to help her check if any of them coincided with the dates and locations of the attacks. It didn't take long to get a cross reference, then another and another.

Katrina looked at her boss, 'We've got him! Bastard! She pointed to two members of the team, downstairs now, grab a uniform car and a couple bodies for backup on the way. Quick before he gets away.' She turned and grinned at her boss, 'You want to be in on this sir? But Robert waved her away, 'Your shout, go and get him. Just bring him back safely please. Everything by the book, no balls ups, he has a lot to answer for, and I want to make sure he is charged with everything, we need to throw the book at him.'

With the noise of feet pounding down the stairs receding, Robert went over to the window to see a squad car and an unmarked car with his crew, hurl out of the car park and head off at high speed. Hopefully there would be a call from them requesting a van to take the prisoner into custody. A nice thought, and a feeling of relief and satisfaction swept over Robert. He realised he was feeling old and perhaps it was time to let some of the new up and coming blood to take over. After all she had done most of the work on this case. Good call K.

The police crew weren't exactly subtle and the blues and twos were excessively used on the journey. It was only when they were close to the suspect's house were they switched off. But it was ironic that it was that very noise that pre-warned Carter that something was up. Carter could hear the noise as he was returning on his bike, he pulled up in the next road with the pretence of grabbing fish and chips, leaving his bike chained up outside. For once he wasn't in his Lycra suit, just ordinary clothes, so he blended in.

Remaining as calm as possible, he left the bike, took his fish and chips and walked towards his house. Carter had a feeling the police cars would be parked outside, he was right. As he turned the corner, he could see them surrounding his home about four hundred yards away. Staying back with the now gathering crowd, he felt safe and unobserved. Safety in numbers he thought as he ate a mouthful of chips. Much to his amazement, the front door was opened when they hammered on it. His landlady had returned. Tracey let them in with little protest and they swept into the house, all except a tall elegant woman who remained to question the landlady.

They both went in eventually. After about forty minutes the entire crew came out, holding large poly bags with his possessions in. Bugger, Carter thought to himself, that's all my gear gone, will have to buy some more. As he continued to eat the chips as if nothing was the matter, he realised he had virtually nothing in savings and life was going to get very hard for him to survive without it. The police cars were eventually driven away and the crowd dispersed.

Throwing his paper in the bin, he started to walk back to the bike. Carter stopped, it was rather a big giveaway and they would be looking for it after discovering it wasn't at the house. They would have an all points out for him now, and he needed to go to ground, but where?

CHAPTER 27

'Shit, shit, shit,' shouted Katrina as she slammed the door to the incident room. 'OK, so we missed him, he can't be far away. I want his picture in every squad car - now. Guv, can we organise a press conference at short notice to get his name and photo out there quickly. I'll get onto the radio stations. We need flyers done. We need to act fast, he can't get away, not when we are so close.' She looked at the bags of evidence, 'I'll get this checked for prints, cross check them and bag it up as evidence for when we do catch him. 'She turned to her team, 'Everybody, look for that bike, we have a photo of that as well. That's a dead giveaway.'

She turned to Robert, 'You heard I suppose?' 'Sort of guessed when the van wasn't called out. One of those bloody things. OK, we know who he is, we are pretty sure he's our man and he will know by now he is being chased. So we have a manhunt on our hands. Inform all the ports, France is easy to reach and far too big to search. Get flyers out in all the rail and bus stations. I'll sort the TV, you do the radio. I suppose you are a whizz at social media - you can spread the word around that way as well.'

Returning to his office Robert rang through to his superiors to update them, then the TV stations to organise a hasty press conference. Sketching out what he wanted to say to camera on a notepad, Robert tweaked a few words before putting it down satisfied. 'OK, think where will he go, how does a soldier's mind work? Does he have army friends, will he need medication, does he have close relatives, will he go on the run or stay put. Can't imagine he will hang about, too well known, he would soon get caught if he hangs about. Need to go back to his house and search it. Sure his landlady will be the key to this. She knows him better than anyone.'

CHAPTER 28

Carter had exactly the same thoughts. His house and landlady were the solution to everything. Despite the danger, he needed to get back in there. It would be the last place they would expect him to go in the long term. It was his safe haven, except for her, but he had plans for Tracey, and he needed her money.

The light was fading when he approached the house carefully, crossing to the opposite side of the road, he was wearing a woolly hat pulled down tight as if to keep the cold out, and he shuffled along with his hands jammed into his pockets.

There were plenty of alleys and low garden walls to make his way home easily enough, without being caught after a recce.

Trying to be as casual as possible, he managed to walk past the front of the house without being noticed, but he had seen the strange car outside and noticed the light in his room as he glanced up. That's it being searched again he thought. Damn and blast. The drizzle didn't help his mood and he pulled up his collar to keep out the cold. Walking past the house he went into a local pub on the corner to waste some time and think out what he was going to do next. Luckily the pub was a good old fashioned one and didn't have a TV, just as well, as his name and face were starting to be splashed across the media just as he was innocently sipping his pint. From his vantage point at the bar he could easily glance across the road and check for progress. After a slowly sipped pint he could see the car had gone and everything seemed to be peaceful again. Time to go.

Quietly walking out, he walked back past his home with the intension of going into town. The car had definitely gone. The lights were out. She had gone to bed, he knew she would have taken a large drink with her. Give her another ten minutes and she would be snoring, and dead to the world, perfect timing, just give it a bit more time. Stretching his legs he easily covered several blocks before returning to his street.

She would not be expecting him to come back, that would be the last thing she would think off. Eventually when he was feeling brave enough, Carter went back, silently took his keys out and selected the right one. There was no noise as he slid the key in and opened the door. Silence was of the essence and he needed to be a silent as possible to catch her by surprise.

But as soon as he pushed open the door, he was confronted by Tracey who let out a huge scream. There was flash in the streetlight as she lunged forward, and he felt the blade as it went through his coat and into his ribs. The pain was excruciating and he fell to the floor. In the pale light he could see his howling landlady about to go for the coup de grace, the blade held aloft for the strike. Kicking out he managed to knock her off her feet before she could strike again. She went over backwards, heavily hitting her head on the floor. Although it was nigh on impossible to stand properly after the attack, he knew he had to immobilise her quickly, and he collapsed on top of her, using his dead weight to pin her to the floor. His hands instantly went round her throat and she didn't utter a sound after that.

CHAPTER 29

There was plenty of action in the incident room. Robert wasn't sure how much of it was productive though. They had identified their suspect, they had enough incidental evidence to almost certainly tie him into the attacks, and with luck, the murder at Maidstone. By sheer bad luck and poor timing they had missed their man. But he had the gut feeling that Carter wasn't too far away, he may have fled the scene but how far could he have got. Carter had gone to ground and would be biding his time to make good his escape. But where?

'Jaeger, my office please,' he shouted out to his junior. She obliged, pleased to leave the chaos of the incident room. 'Thank you,' muttered Robert. 'We need to move fast. He is still in the area, I just know it. I want the area swamped with uniform, unmarked cars, the lot. I want him found. Look for that bike. I know it will feature in all this. I want someone back to his house, we can start from there. Question his landlady again. She might well be sheltering or hiding him. There is more to their relationship than meets the eye, I just know it. I need to do another press conference, get him in the public eye, make the people out there into our eyes, if needs be, offer a reward.' Looking up he noticed the expression on his subordinates face was one of anger. 'Look, I'm just as pissed off as you are that we missed him. We were too bloody enthusiastic in our approach, we should have been more subtle. Easy to say with hindsight I know, but we have made a lot of work for ourselves and we need to put it right, quickly! Organise the team into groups, investigate his past, look into his friends, old army contacts, his work records, anything that would give us a hint of where he has gone. Keep checking every port and airport to keep an eye open for him. OK you are on the case, do it.' and with a wave of his hand she was dismissed. Furious, Jaeger turned and left the office.

CHAPTER 30

Carter was bleeding heavily and he knew he needed medical attention quickly, but he now had to deal with Tracey as well. Propping himself up on his elbows, he felt for a pulse. It was faint but still there. 'Good, she is still alive,' he said to himself. 'Thought I might have strangled her, no great loss if I had, but she will need immobilising until I can think things through. She was bloody lucky, and for that matter so was I.'

There was a tow rope in her car, that would do the trick for now. Leaving the prone body, he made a super human effort to stagger out to her car parked in the garage. Luckily the car keys were still hanging up where she normally kept them in the kitchen, and the rope was in the boot. Staggering back, he knew he had to keep her alive and quiet, until he could empty her account, he needed her money until he could get away. Leaving her in the hallway he slowly tied her up, but every pull on the rope hurt him. Eventually he was satisfied she wouldn't be able to escape easily, but just to make sure, he used some duct tape from his room to tape her mouth and keep her quiet.

When he had finished, he dragged her in to the dining room and left her out of sight behind the sofa. Looking down he knew from the ever growing red stain on his shirt, he also needed urgent attention. Carter was exhausted and the room started to look a different colour, he felt faint and he knew he was going to pass out if he didn't do something about his wound quickly.

There was a first aid box in the kitchen, that would have to do for the moment. Luckily there were some large dressings in the box and he used these to do a makeshift bandage to stem the blood before he keeled over. Slumped on the floor, breathing heavily, his strength gone, he knew he was in a bad way, but luckily his army field training had taught him enough to prevent him dying, for the moment at least. Feeling horribly sick, he found that the room was now closing in on him, it was like looking down a tunnel that was getting darker, and he collapsed in a dead faint in the kitchen. Carter would remain in this position for some time, unaware that the police were just minutes away. He missed the cars scream to a halt outside, he missed the heavy banging on the door, and he missed the two beady eyes that peered through the letterbox.

'Can' t see a bloody thing from here,' said a remote voice from the road. With that the letterbox snapped shut. Jaeger looked at her colleague, 'Go around the back and see if anyone is about or if there is an open window or door we can gain entry through. A few minutes later the officer returned shaking his head. 'Nothing guv. Can't see a thing through the windows, everything is locked up tight. We'll need a warrant if you intend breaking in legally.' She nodded and turned back to the car. She knew the rules.

In the kitchen Carter had come to, he knew Tracey was hidden behind the sofa and out of sight, but he was in full view if someone looked in properly, it was pure luck that he had fallen down in front of the sink. When he heard the letterbox snap too, he crawled into the passageway and jammed himself up against the front door as quickly and quietly as he could. Every movement was intensely painful but he had to listen to

112

the conversation outside. As soon as he heard the word warrant, he knew he was in deep trouble. Neither of them could be found in the house, this had to be his safe haven, for a few weeks at least. At best, he had a few hours before they would be back. The pain in his chest was becoming too much for him to bear, what had that cow done to him?

Pressing his ear against the door he could hear car doors being slammed, engines started up and eventually quietness. Plucking up the courage to carefully look through the letterbox, he confirmed that the coast was clear and he was in no immediate danger. Except from that bloody knife wound. Staggering back to the kitchen he grabbed the first aid box to patch himself up again. It would be dark soon, he could get away, let them search the place and then he could come back.

CHAPTER 31

Robert confronted Jaeger as soon as she walked back in the office. 'Don't bother asking, I've already applied for the warrant, I've got more friends than you have, and I couldn't sit here doing nothing.' A smile enveloped his face as he knew it was something she couldn't have organised at such short notice. Theoretically they didn't need a warrant, but because Carter hadn't officially been arrested and the house didn't belong to him, Robert was taking no chances on creating a stupid technicality that might well get the case thrown out if Carter was later charged. As the house appeared to be empty they had no real claim to enter the premises apart from searching for Carter.

Robert knew the procedure inside out and had already phoned ahead to ask for an available magistrate. He had been given a time and was already on route to the court with his evidence file when he heard that the house was empty with no visible sign of entry without using force. If the landlady had been helping Carter, then he would need the warrant to force an entry or allow him access to enter without a fuss. To the magistrate it was a formality, and he promised Robert the warrant would be back on his desk ASAP, a couple of hours at most. Robert had shown due cause in his application, presented his evidence and knew that the case would be reviewed, and then reviewed again before it was issued. Patience was a virtue here.

Looking at Jaeger who was impatiently pacing the office floor, Robert could understand her frustration, she was young, impatient and all too eager to show what she was made of. However, the use of the blues and twos on route to arrest Carter had shown she didn't always think first, must get them all focussed.

He shouted out from his office, 'Have you found that bloody bike yet, have you even bothered to look for it, you lazy bastards. That is evidence, and I want it found. Remember to look for it when you go back.'

The warrant arrived after a couple of hours and was immediately pounced upon. The team couldn't wait to get back to the house again, and give it a thorough investigation. Jaeger knew they had taken everything of value from the house already, but it hadn't thrown up any clues at all. Had they missed something? The bag on the bed seized earlier, indicated Carter was aware that he was being hunted. They must have missed him by minutes before. Shit, a stupid mistake or bad luck?

She knew her boss had out guessed Carter once and known he would go back to the house. Could he do it again? Was the landlady in on this? She seemed hostile when questioned earlier. It was academic now they could gain entry. They had a tame locksmith on call for such visits, Robert had no reason to break in when it would take a few minutes to enter without a complaint being made against him later, especially if they found nothing. He would meet them at the scene but stay in his car out of sight.

The team were assembled, given their instructions, told to be careful this time and not to warn Carter of their approach. On this occasion Robert was in the lead car, determined to stamp his authority on the situation, and make sure it was done by the book. With no noise, no lights, and no undue speed, the two cars sedately left the yard and headed out on the first stage of the manhunt.

CHAPTER 32

Carter felt dreadful, but he knew his time was extremely limited, and he made a frantic effort to get out of the house without collapsing. The room swam in front of him. Every few minutes he had to pause and get his breath and think how to escape, but now with the added problem of Tracey to deal with. There had to be a stop gap solution until he had a proper plan. Her car offered the easy solution of escape but the police must have clocked it on the original search, and would certainly be looking for it in the future if it disappeared now. It was unusable at the moment. She would have to be hidden before leaving, but where for Christ's sake?

Carter knew the house had a long garden and joined several others. Could he hide her in the garden, if they brought a dog with them it would only take seconds to find them both. It was dark so he could move about outside without being spotted now. There were no lights switched on, so no one knew he was there. Looking around he had a lightbulb moment. It was a long shot but if he heaved her into the neighbour's garden and joined her to make sure she didn't make any noise, the car could be used at some future date, and the police would assume they had both fled by some other means.

Had he got enough strength to get her in the garden and then over the fence? This was going to really test him. Carter opened the garden door and dragged Tracey from behind the sofa and into the garden, it took all his strength to pull her outside. Luckily there was no moon and it was pitch black outside. Carter pulled her along the path so as to leave no trail on the grass. The lawn was seventy foot long, far enough away from the house as to feel safe. It was as much as Carter could do to lean against the rubbish propped up against the fence at the bottom of the garden.

A feeling of despair swept over him as he realised he couldn't possibly carry her over the fence, and he felt close to tears in sheer frustration. Tracey was now conscious and struggling against the ropes. Carter kicked her hard and then knelt down to whisper in her ear. 'Make a noise and it will be your last, especially after stabbing me, you stupid cow.'

Leaning back against the fence, he discovered the wood panel moved. God, they just slide into the concrete posts. Scrambling around the base, he managed to get his fingers under the base of the panel. Pulling the earth and debris away from the fence he managed to lift the panel up enough to roll Tracey under it and into the next garden.

Lock up the house was his next thought. Time was getting short now. When he staggered back to the house he had an idea and took the chance of going upstairs although this drained him of any of his remaining energy. Dragging a suitcase down from Tracey's wardrobe he filled it with her clothes and scattered underwear on the bed. It gave the impression she had fled in a hurry, and had been implicit in Carter's escape. It would send them on a wild goose chase.

Carter had to hang on to the banister for all he was worth, as he nearly fell down the stairs. Looking around the kitchen he realised it was covered in blood and bandages and there was blood trailing back to the front door. Grabbing a plastic carrier he threw everything in, it could be disposed of later on. Blood by the door? Mop it up man, kitchen roll, be quick.

Just as he finished a poor job of clearing up, he heard the first car pull up and instructions yelled by Robert. 'Right you lot, get the locksmith over here, you two round the back now and check, the rest of you with me.' Carter knew he couldn't out run them and limped out the back. Christ, lock the door moron, and he limped away as the gate opened, and two officers strode into the garden.

Carter froze, fearing the worse before he realised they were looking the wrong way. They hadn't seen him yet, but they soon will, how long would his luck last? Very slowly dropping to his knees he edged over to the side of the garden and inched his way silently towards the rear where the panel had been raised. His army training had come in useful again tonight. It took him a couple of minutes to reach the panel. The real problem was how to raise it silently. There was nothing for it, he had to wait.

Suddenly all the lights in the house went on, beautifully illuminating the garden. Carter was lying on the ground against the panel, not daring to move. Staying as still as possible he gently felt for the edge of the panel, but waited for the right time to move, hoping it would be soon, he just hoped no one would come out into the garden in the meantime. The light in the kitchen that was illuminating the garden was turned off and Carter knew he had to move fast. His fingers were already under the edge of the panel and he pushed it enough to roll under. Holding the panel with his other hand, he raked some of the leaves back against the panel to disguise the fact it had been moved.

Tracey was on the other side, looking frightened. Perfect Carter thought. She knows what's good for her. In a wave of pain, he stood up enough to be able to drag her further up the neighbour's garden and behind a small shed and out of sight. It was bloody cold and damp in the garden and Carter curled up around Tracey for some warmth although he realised later he was almost certainly keeping her warmer than him.

Several times during the next hours, detectives came out into the garden, torches were waved around, including one over the fence into the garden they were hiding in. But they were well hidden and eventually the squad left. When it was quiet, Carter took a chance and stood on a barrel at the end of the garden to see if the coast was clear. It appeared to be. There were no lights, no voices, all seemed quiet, now what?

The sky was lightening to the east, he would have little choice but to move soon, whatever the risk, or he would be discovered and there would have been no point in trying to escape. Leaving Tracey in the neighbour's garden, he pushed the fence panel up enough to roll under. His chest hurt terribly so he slowly made his way down the garden to the gate at the side of the house. Unlatching it quietly, he opened it without a squeak and peered around the front of the house. Bugger, there was a uniform left on duty. Were they expecting him back?

Creeping back to the gate, he made sure he made no noise to attract attention. Working his way round to the back door he was positive there was no one in the house. Searching his pockets for the backdoor key, he was going to sneak in and watch from inside, but the key was gone. His pockets were empty, he must of dropped it rolling about in the garden. Christ, this all he needed.

Wobbling back to end of the garden he knew he wouldn't be seen, but he needed to get Tracey back into the house before light. The panel was lifted and he rolled back under. He dragged Tracy back to the panel, the sky was grey now, no longer was it the protective black to hide them. Again the panel was lifted and Tracey pushed through, he followed close behind.

With handfuls of leaves Carter covered her body to ensure she wasn't easily seen. As he went to go back to the house he stopped dead in his tracks as a thought hit him. Key, bloody key moron, find the key! In despair he turned back to panel and a search of the neighbour's garden. Sod it this is all going wrong.

CHAPTER 33

'So what conclusion have you come to Jaeger?' said Robert. 'I know what I'm thinking, be interesting to see what you're thinking after that visit.'

Jaeger looked down at her feet. 'I don't know if we are being led up the garden path or what to believe at the moment. The house was empty except for that suitcase of her stuff scattered about. Did he come back? Did she go with him? If so, was it peacefully or by force? The car is still there, why wasn't that taken, we're they spooked, panicked and left? But how, on foot, taxi, another car? I'm sure they have done a runner but they must have had an alternative means of escape. Did she go with him, is she part of all this, protecting him, protecting her lover perhaps? There is more to this than meets the eye.' She sighed, 'What do you think sir?'

Twiddling his pen, Robert was in no hurry to give an answer. 'Hmm, let's see what we've got then. We have our suspect, have him banged to rights, but he has escaped. Best we can do is put out an all points with as much info on him. He's ex-military so he knows how to go to ground. She on the other hand doesn't have anywhere to go, she has no family we can find, so the chances are she will surface sooner or later and we have no idea where of course. So just what was their relationship?'

The pen was laid down and Robert looked up at his junior. 'Not much to go on is it. I would be inclined to assume they are an item. Doesn't make much difference if she went along willingly or by force, they are both missing. They must have taken another car, a hire car or stolen, you can check those both out. Now have they have gone to ground, locally, far away, abroad possibly. Whatever, they are going to take some finding. OK starting point, all ports and airports notified, car hire companies, stolen cars.' Robert paused, 'Go on then.' and she was waved away to begin her search.

It proved in vain. There were only a few stolen cars over the past few days and they had either been found abandoned or burnt out. There were no hire cars that couldn't be accounted for. She spread her search to the neighbouring towns with the same result. So how did they escape? The only conclusion was they didn't, they were still here, someone is hiding them. Hotels and guest houses had to be investigated, Jesus there were dozens of them. This was going to be a long day. She called the team together 'Right team we have a job to do. I'm going back to the house, something isn't right here.

CHAPTER 34

Carter had spent hours going through the two gardens before he found the key. The pain in his ribs was killing him, there was blood seeping through his dressing and he knew he was slowly dying, he had to stop and rest. Leaving Tracey covered in leaves at the bottom of the garden, he staggered to the back door and slid the key in. Painkillers, he needed painkillers, and a stiff drink to crush the pain.

There were a few tablets in the bathroom cabinet which he quickly swallowed. There was vodka in her room which subsequently disappeared, to be followed by two more tablets. Feeling giddy, but that was more to do with the vodka than anything, Carter managed to get down the steep stairs, out the back door and reach the back of the garden before collapsing.

Katrina had just pulled up outside the house but Carter was utterly unaware of that fact as he was slumped out of sight, slowly bleeding to death. Using the keys that the locksmith had made, she let herself in the house. It looked the same, she could see nothing out of place. Upstairs she looked in desperation for something, anything that might give her a clue as to where Carter had fled to. And had the landlady gone with him?

She was intrigued as to the whereabouts of the bike, she could only surmise Carter had taken it with him. Back of a car perhaps? She had no idea it was around the corner tied up outside a shop. Having spent an hour looking around the house she came to the conclusion there was nothing new to be gleaned from the house and left, unaware her solution was laying comatose just yards away from her. Back to the office then. Blast and damn, she thought to herself, I was so sure there was something in that house.

By rights, Carter should have died by now, but he was made of tougher stuff. Decades of army life and extreme living conditions had made his body resilient and used to neglect. As he slowly opened his eyes again, he had no idea how close he had come to being caught. But he was in imminent danger now, and he knew how he had to take some drastic action, he needed to get both of them inside and hide. It was his only safe haven now, hide and then escape. Escape, but that was something he could think about later.

Summoning the remnants of his strength, he uncovered Tracey and started to drag her back to the house. It was a slow, painful exercise and one he nearly didn't complete. It took him over an hour to get to the back door and just managed to push her into the kitchen before he sunk to his knees. She was still tied up and Carter knew she couldn't escape, she was dragged back to the lounge and hidden behind the sofa out of sight.

To make sure he didn't fall over, he leant on the walls back to the kitchen and locked the door before he slumped onto the hard tiles. Consciousness left him again, and his head hit the ground with a nasty thump that would leave him with a impressive bruise later, but at the moment that was the least of his worries as blood started to pool around his chest. His life was draining away and the option of dying was becoming a really strong possibility now.

CHAPTER 35

There was a conference in the incident room when Robert returned after lunch. Jaeger was in full swing and he stood at the back of the room to hear what she was going to do. Listening carefully, he could hear her frustration, she had no leads, no ideas and nowhere to go. She asked the team for suggestions and ideas, there were a few offered, but none offered any real substance. Robert strode into the room and waved his hand for silence.

'OK, we have searched the house three times now. We've taken everything we can out of the dwelling, and we have no clues. We disturbed him by the looks of the half packed bag on his bed the first time. We went back and it looks like she was going to join him. Why would she? He left in a hurry, was she not ready? Or did he go back for her, was she a willing partner or taken. Why the half packed bag? No, that is a red herring, I'm sure of it. That bag should have been packed and taken. There was no way she could have got out of the house in the time we pulled up and entered, she wasn't disturbed. We had the place surrounded. That was a set up. I think she was an unwilling partner. But why? What did she know, what hold does she have over him? Robert paused to think before turning to the incident board. 'Neither of them seemed to have many friends, I presume we have phone books, address books, mobile numbers so we can do a run down on friends and make sure they haven't been innocently put up somewhere. The car is still there, so they didn't use that, they didn't use a hire car or a stolen one or even a taxi. So they walked away? I don't think so somehow. They are still in the vicinity, I just know it, our job is to find out where they are hiding. Carter had access to a lot of warehouses, factories, storage depots. I wouldn't mind betting he has a bolt hole he has found somewhere and he has simply jumped on a train and walked there.'

There was a silence in the room in which a dropped pin could have been heard, before Robert continued. 'Assuming this is a possibility, she has joined him willingly, otherwise there is no way he would have got her out of the house. Right back to square one, we have a list of his employers, split yourselves into teams, sort the companies into geographical areas, Jaeger will take control of that. Go and look, go and investigate, find something. If not, make sure you eliminate every possibility, and then warn all these companies to be on the lookout, to constantly check all their buildings. I just know he is nearby, waiting for a chance to escape. Right get to it.'

Robert couldn't have imagined just how close Carter was. The trouble was he had to out-guess him quickly, but he hadn't managed that. Most criminals weren't that clever, they made mistakes, and they were impatient. Patience was something he had a lot of. It would take time to track Carter down, but he would. Everything comes to he who waits he thought.

Jaeger came back into his office and he looked up at the intrusion. The look on his face must have said everything, and she was quiet. 'Well? said Robert, 'Anything else? We don't have much to go on. Have you got anything else to add to this? I just know they haven't got far. You agree or not?' She just nodded, 'I thought the house might just have offered another clue, but they haven't been back, everything is still in place, they haven't left anything I could use. So I agree with everything you said. She is with him, they planned a getaway, possibly got a friend to drop them somewhere. But they could easily be in London by now, anywhere in fact. They are going to need money, so a check on both their accounts would be a start. But I'd suggest we leave that for a week or so to see if they are used, if so we have a location.' Robert smiled at that.

CHAPTER 36

Carter came to, his fingers felt the blood on the floor, it was warm and sticky and it shocked him, he hadn't realised that he was bleeding so much. Now he finally realised he was in real trouble. Bugger. Where had he thrown the first aid box in his hurry, he remembered the carrier bag, where the hell was that. The wheelie bin in the garden! Propping himself up on one elbow, Carter felt for the handles on the cupboards in the hope they were strong enough to take his weight as he hauled himself up. They were, and he used the cupboards to lean on to get to the back door and outside. The carrier was in the bin and he managed to retrieve it without too much trouble.

Back in the house he took the contents into the lounge to take own blood sodden dressing off, he was horrified to find he was still bleeding, the wound hadn't closed up at all. This was a job for stitches, but he couldn't ask for a doctor or go into hospital. This he would have to do himself. There was a sewing box in one of the draws in the bureau, had he got enough courage to sew himself up? Didn't have much bloody choice did he.

On the table were bulldog clips, no he thought, too silly. Once he had managed to grab the sewing basket, he found it almost impossible to thread any of the needles, and he knew this was a lost cause. There were a lot of large plasters in the first aid box. Cleaning up the wound as best he could, Carter peeled the backing off the largest plaster he could find and applied it across the wound, pulling the skin together as hard as he could. It held. A second and third plasters were applied before the first one pinged off. Fuck he thought, not going to be as easy as I thought. Pushing the first plaster back in place he knew it would come loose at any moment. There was still the duct tape in the kitchen that might do. It would be clumsy but it would hold everything together. Carter stumbled out to the kitchen and brought the tape and a pair of scissors back to the sofa.

A large dressing was placed over the first plaster and a strip of duct tape hastily applied over that. It held. It wasn't pretty but it worked. Carter continued until the stab wound was closed and dressed. A wave of nausea swept over him and he grasped for air. The room closed in on him again, and he collapsed on the sofa and then onto the floor.

Tracey heard him fall, and she squirmed round to the edge of the sofa to be faced with his not quite closed, but very glazed eyes. She spotted the scissors that lay amongst the debris Carter had produced, Tracey thought there was a chance of escape if she could reach them. Carter was wheezing badly and Tracey knew he was going to be out for some time, so she had to hurry. She wriggled across the room as best she could, the bonds Carter had tied her up with were very effective, and made movement close to impossible. Eventually she reached the scissors and rolled over, with her fingers searching for the blades.

It was frustrating as she could only move the scissors a small distance at a time, but she could feel the edge bite into the rope. The sheer thickness of the rope made progress very slow but she could feel it part a small section at a time. It took nearly an hour for the rope to break and she had managed to free the section that held her feet to her hands.

She could stand if nothing else. Because she had been tied for so long there was no feeling in her legs, and it took what seemed like ages before she could stand properly. Her feet were still bound as were her hands behind her back. She could hop at least and took a few tentative moves to the front door. Don't fall over she thought to herself.

Get to the door, you can turn round and pull the latch even if your hands are tied behind you. It wasn't easy to get along the passage to the door, but eventually she reached it, and turned around to feel for the latch. Finding it, she pulled hard and there was a sigh of relief as she felt the door open. It swung back on her and she had to hop out of the way and then hop back around the front and on to the front step. Freedom.

CHAPTER 37

Jaeger realised this was going to be a long job and one she had to organise properly. Her team had gone through Tracey's address book and discovered there were few friends listed, and those contacted, admitted they hadn't heard from her in a long time. It seems she had lost contact with most of her friends. She had only a couple of members of family, and they were far flung, and then only received Christmas cards if they were lucky.

It looked as if she was a lonely person and had taken up with Carter some time over the past year and may have eventually run off with him? Did she know about his crimes, was she part of them even? She wouldn't have gone willingly if she knew about his darker side surely, no, he must have some sort of hold over her, sexual perhaps?

The search teams were being efficient and had visited most of the listed companies where Carter had been employed. Sure there were hiding places in all of them, but nothing that could be used long term. Most sites were modern, well run, either fenced or secure at night. It was unlikely that any of them would provide a hideaway for long. All the companies had been warned prior to the visit, and had already searched their sites for possible hiding places. Nothing so far, and Jaeger was beginning to think they were definitely exploring a dead end. Shit, now what? Where do they go from here? Her mind raced, if this didn't pan out, then they were back to square one and a long waiting game. Waiting for a mistake, she had only one avenue to explore now, money withdrawals. Track them from the cash point. A long shot but it was all she could come up with at the moment. Striding into Robert's office after taking yet another call on a negative search, Jaeger looked at him and said, 'This isn't working, wrong idea, we need a new avenue of investigation, something to outguess him.'

CHAPTER 38

Tracey couldn't believe her luck as she fell through the door and on to the doorstep. She was free, but couldn't shout for help as she still had her mouth taped. Laying helplessly on the step she looked out into the street hoping to attract attention from anyone, but there was no one about at this time of night. As she struggled to stand upright a hand grabbed her ankle and pulled her forcefully back into the house. Carter had heard her noisy exit, come to enough to realise she was trying to make her escape via the front door. Knowing that if she escaped, he would have to make an unplanned and very hasty escape, and all his plans would go out of the window, he would almost certainly be caught if that happened. Summoning all his strength Carter stumbled to the front door to stop her escaping, he could see she had the door open and had managed to get outside. But watching her fall over made him think there was a chance after all to stop all his plans coming apart, and he made a desperate grab for her ankle. Lucky for him, she was helpless, he had her by the ankle now and she realised it, she could feel his strength in his hold and she knew her escape plan had come to nothing.

Pulling her quickly inside, Carter used his foot to push the door to, and then collapsed on top of her to stop her moving again. It would be some minutes before he had his breath back and could move properly. Eventually he was able to stand up over her prone body. Laughing at her, he dragged her back into the lounge, dropping her in a heap on the floor before him.

Grinning through his pain he looked at Tracey and almost spat out his words, 'OK if you are going to try to escape, I'll have to secure you a bit better than this.' Carter had a sinister grin on his face and he punched her in the face in his anger, and then in the stomach, which took all the wind out of Tracey, and she couldn't resist him, there was no fight left in her and he knew he would kill her if she resisted. Carter reached down and untied her feet and then pulled off her trousers and pants leaving her naked from the waist down. She looked terrified, but Carter simply stood her up and marched her to the downstairs toilet and sat her down on the pan.

'We are going to stay here for a couple of days, weeks possibly, so get used to it. Taking the frayed end of the rope he started to tie her to the toilet and then the cistern. The pipes and plumbing were substantial and provided a good secure anchor for the binding. The rope was supplemented with a generous lengths of duct tape, making escape almost impossible. Carter stood over her, admiring his work but holding onto the wall to steady himself. Feeling light headed, he had to rest, but not before he had laughed at Tracey tied up in front of him. Satisfied she couldn't escape, he leant against the wall as a spasm of pain hit him, he stood still waiting for it to pass before returning to the sofa and a drink. After a large gulp of vodka he slowly searched the house for painkillers and more sprits, but had to be careful not to turn on the light to see what he was doing. After half an hour he had found enough of both to settle himself down and rest. Curled up on the sofa, he swallowed a handful of painkillers that were washed down with another very large mouthful of vodka. Thinking it would be better to stay downstairs out of sight, as it also served to be in the right place, if she tried to escape again. Not that she was able to do that now.

Ramming a couple of cushions under his head and pulling the tatty throw over him, he was asleep in seconds. Tracey sat immobilised on the toilet shivering in the cold wondering what this madman was going to do to her. She genuinely feared for her life, especially as she had failed to kill him, he would certainly want his revenge on her now. In the next room Carter was indeed dreaming of violence and a weak smile crossed his face as he slept. It would be some time for him to regain consciousness again. Tracey would have to wait to learn of her fate until morning, and she silently wept.

CHAPTER 39

The CID team were in bright and early the next morning. They looked subdued, knowing that they had all drawn a blank in the search. For once Robert took the lead in the briefing. 'OK, that was a long shot, but still a good idea. I still think he has gone to ground locally. The car wasn't used, so they used some other sort of transport. Have we checked the railway CCTV? They could have just walked away and caught a train. I don't think anything will show, as he will know he is being watched. Local buses might be the answer, they also have CCTV. I need someone to check the local routes and then track down the vehicles used that night. But I fear this will also draw a blank.'

Looking around the room Robert noticed no one had made a noise for several minutes, they were all looking for a new avenue of enquire, a new lead, something new to investigate. 'Alright, we've searched the house several times now, nothing to go on there. There is no obvious trail, no obvious escape route or means of transport which says to me that this was done in a hurry. I really don't feel they have gone far. God knows how many estate agents there are in town, but they are all on the web and they always state if a house has vacant possession. I need another couple of bods to search through every site on the web and look for empty houses. I think he may be holed up in one of those. He may well be posing as a new house owner to any unsuspecting neighbour. I will be back on TV this evening to highlight who we are looking for and why they are wanted.

There will be a reward offered, which no doubt will bring in a whole bunch of crank calls again. So be prepared for some extra work tomorrow sorting out that. OK off you go. DS Jaeger will sort your rotas.' Waving a hand in dismissal, he walked to his office to write the script for the press conference.

CHAPTER 40

Carter slowly awoke as the weak sunlight managed to finally illuminate the room. Everything was still grey this early, and he felt around for the vodka bottle as he couldn't see it in the poor light. Clumsily falling off the sofa and onto the floor, he landed on the half full bottle, and although he felt sick, he eagerly unscrewed the top for a much needed drink.

The splitting headache he was suffering from, took second place to the excruciating pain in his chest. Have to do something about that today he thought. Taking another handful of pain-killers wasn't a good idea he knew, but he washed them down with the vodka anyway. Carter didn't really care, he hurt and this would help. His brain was fuzzy and his thinking muddled. So far he had been lucky, apart from getting stabbed. Knowing the police had been through the house several times it was unlikely that they would ever think of looking there again. The car had to remain in place, although he intended to use it to escape at some point in time. In fact it would be a good source of money if he played his cards right. Money, that was what need to be sorted, if he was to escape this mess. Tracey was the key to this, and he went in to the toilet to speak with his captive. She heard him coming and wondered if he was going to kill her this time.

Carter stood in the doorway and looked down at her. Drawing closer he lowered his head to whisper in her ear. 'I need money to get away. I need your money, I need your card numbers, your online banking codes, everything to help me escape. Only when you give me that, will I let you go. Do you understand, nod if you do. If you don't give me the information I will kill you, as I will have no use for you.' She nodded, but in her heart she knew her days were numbered, as soon as he had the information, she would be killed, it was a dead cert. Just play for time girl and hope.

Carter knew what she was thinking as said, 'I need to hole up here for a couple of weeks, change my identity, get some money and paperwork together, but I need to do this slowly. I will then take you to a remote spot and set you free, I don't need your murder hanging round my neck as well. If I'm ever caught there will be enough to jail me for years, but I will get out. With your murder, I won't. Understand me? I'll make it inconvenient for you to contact anyone, but you will be alive.' Tracey didn't believe a word of it, but would go along for the moment, hoping there would be a chance to escape later.

Carter knew he had to put a lot of things in place before he left the house, and he would be spending a lot of time on the computer soon to try and raise some funds. First he needed to sort himself out. Sitting on the sofa, he found the room was beginning to spin, and he realised the combination of drink and drugs was not a good one. At least the pain was subsiding, he smiled at that thought before he slumped over, out for the count again. Tracey could hear him snoring even in the next room. She had to think how to prolong her existence and realised she would have to go along with Carter's plans for the time being. Struggling against the rope and tape, it soon became apparent that she was firmly restrained and had no chance of escaping for the moment. She began to cry in frustration. In the neighbouring room Carter slept a drug induced sleep, and he would be unconscious for the best part of the day, leaving Tracey to think what to do next. She had to escape, he was out cold so she had a slim chance of getting away if she could break her bonds. Pushing with all her might she managed to pull some of the tape away, but most of it was wound firmly around the pipework. Her legs were simply taped around the bottom of the toilet pedestal and she concentrated on freeing them. It took nearly an hour before the tape gave way.

CHAPTER 41

'Nothing,' said Jaeger. There were just thirty two vacant houses on the local estate agents books, and everyone had been visited without a sign of the fugitives. There were no break ins and the estate agents have double checked every suspect house. She looked at Robert and went to speak again, but he stopped her. 'Not surprised, another long shot, but it had to be checked. 'Did we get any response from the press conference?'

'The guys are checking through them now, nothing of any use so far,' she replied. 'So where do we go from here? They have just vanished into thin air. I don't understand how they could escape and leave no trace. There has been no movement on either bank account so they must have money in cash or some other means of funding this, that I haven't discovered.'

'We are waiting for a mistake, that's how we caught him out last time,' Robert replied. 'Nobody is perfect, we all make mistakes, and he will slip up at some point. So it is just a waiting game. Go and help the guys follow up any leads from the phone calls. You never know we might get lucky, but don't hold your breath.'

Jaeger left the office and joined the team in the incident room. Her mind was buzzing, she was more intelligent than Carter, but he was street wise and lucky. So where to go? Where to even start? Would he try and leave the country? No, too easy to pick him up at the airports or cross channel routes but she renewed her alerts to all passport controls. Ireland would be the easiest to escape to, especially as a trip to Ulster didn't require a passport and a short drive south would see them in Eire, a different country. She gathered some of the team to explain her theory, they would be looking at all passenger lists across the Irish Sea. She needed to contact the Garde in Southern Ireland for help and alert them to keep their eyes open. Back to the computer and a plethora of emails.

CHAPTER 42

Money, the key to everything thought Carter. Still nursing a sore head, he had woken up in the afternoon and sat pondering how to get anything out of Tracey. Checking up on her a few minutes earlier, he hadn't seen that she had loosened some of her bonds. His head wasn't clear enough yet to focus on the minutiae of life, and she was still tied up. Tracey however, sat on the toilet very quietly, she dare not move, he needed her for the moment, bide your time she thought, don't upset him.

But Carter had other things on his mind, he was wedged in front of Tracey's computer in her bedroom, doing his research. Credit cards would be a good start, he didn't own one at the moment and wondered if he would even be eligible. It would give him access to a lot of instant cash, as well as not leaving an obvious trail. These cards would all be new and no one except himself would know about them. There were dozens of them on the web. All had huge APRs but he would be maxing them out as soon as possible, so who cared. Applying for every one he could, he was amazed at how few checks he needed to go through to obtain a card. They would arrive in the post in a few days.

Bank account now. There was a real need for a new one, but he couldn't just walk into the nearest bank and set one up, too many checks, could it be done on line? Google came up trumps again, there were loads of companies that would set up an account without checks, this was unexpected, all too easy. Application after application was filled in and he was immediately accepted for most of them, with the added bonus that they all came with debit cards. Those that wanted awkward information were rejected. All he had to do now was wait for the cards to come in the post. It would give him limited funds in the short term.

Could he do it with Tracey, having a credit card, and bank account for her would be dead handy. Bloody hell even that could be done on line. There were loads of people offering loans on line, they were easy to apply for as well. This was looking better and better, but Tracey was still the key to his problems, and he needed to convince her to part with her banking information. Everything else would be short term.

Her car was another source of cash but he would need it at some point, but he could sell it easily enough when he had got away. It was all too easily traced to go roaring around the country in it. He needed the registration papers and a transfer into his name before he could do anything.

The pain in his chest suggested that he deal with the wound first, and he abandoned the computer for the first aid box and the sofa. Carefully taking the bandage off, he was pleased to see the wound was no longer bleeding but it was incredibly tender. It appeared to be healing slowly so all he could do was replace the dressing and hope for the best. Even the dressings were running low and he knew that at some point he would have to replace them if he was to recover.

Clearing up the old dressings and putting them in the large bin in the kitchen, Carter thought about changing his appearance. Hair colouring? Be easier to shave it all off and go bald. Grow a beard as well, not a bad idea. He'd have to get a change of clothes, the police hadn't left him much to change into, but there were a few things in the wash.

Searching through Tracey's belongings he eventually found the car documents, old cheque books which gave all her account details and a small amount of cash in a draw, more in her handbag and various bits of change all over the house. Not much to go with he thought, but if he could slip away just before closing time, he could grab some bread, milk and bandages from the supermarket close by. It was a chance he would have to take. Tracey wasn't going anywhere, but he needed to check on her.

She was too busy trying to free herself to hear Carter sneak up to the toilet door. She was struggling with the tape and was caught by complete surprise when he rushed into the room. 'Naughty, naughty,' was all he shouted as he hit her hard. She didn't remember anything after that. Carter looked at the bindings, he needed something more effective to stop Tracey from escaping otherwise he would get no sleep and she would be able to slip away if he wasn't careful. Rearranging the ties, he freed up the rope and made a sliding noose out of one end. The other end he threw over the old fashioned cistern above her head. Pushing her head back so she leaned against the wall, he placed the noose around her neck and pulled the rope tight, but not enough to choke her. She would not be able to escape without strangling herself.

Satisfied he could leave the house now, he gathered up the cash, put a woolly hat on and found a plain pair of Tracey's glasses to complete the disguise. He just hoped they wouldn't be looking for him in Boots and Tesco.

Slipping out the back door and locking it after him, he

climbed over the low wall into the alley beside the house. Tucking the carrier bag under his arm he looked very ordinary. Walking into town he took as many side streets as possible and got to Boots just before they closed. It helped that it was getting dark and he felt fairly safe. Boots had a great collection of dressings and bandages for his wound, plus painkillers which he paid for with cash as he couldn't use Tracey's contactless card. Everything was dropped into the carrier. Hurrying along to the supermarket, Carter grabbed a trolley and tried to do his shopping without attracting too much attention. Picking up essentials such as milk and bread, he topped it up with tins of soup, tuna, microwave meals, cold meats, more painkillers and a bottle of cheap scotch which was also paid for in cash. It was dark now and he felt safe walking back to the house. Remembering he had the car registration form in his pocket, he dropped the letter into the post box in the High Street.

That was so bloody easy he thought, I can go out if I'm careful and not get caught. But the smile was wiped off his face when he spotted the police car outside his house. Damn, now what? He had to think fast now, just don't panic.

Walking slowly on the other side of the road he could see the policeman talking into his radio. When the officer had finished talking, he walked up to the front door, knocked several times and when there was no response, looked through the letter box. Convinced there was no one in residence, he walked through the side door and into the garden to check the back door. Luckily there was a convenient bus stop close by and Carter stood in it and watched, feeling relieved he had remembered to lock the door. The officer returned a few minutes later and resumed his conversation to his boss over the radio.

Carter could only hear parts of the conversation and strained to listen in without being obvious. Turning his back to read the ads helped disguise his real aim. He could just make out, 'It's OK Sarge, I've checked it front and back and it's empty and locked up. No lights, all the doors locked and the car is still in the garage. I'll do this again tomorrow as part of my regular patrol shall I?' There was a muted reply and the officer nodded to himself, got back in the car and drove off. Far from being put out, Carter now knew they would check on the house every day and that if he took the car he would only have a few hours before the police realised it was missing. Walking into the adjoining road, he dodged down the alley and climbed over the wall into his garden. The key slid into the back door and he quietly entered the house, putting the carrier on the sofa. Before he unpacked it, Carter checked on Tracey to see her reaction to the noose. She glowered at him and he could see the rope was tight around her neck, he loosened it off. 'Good isn't it,' he smiled at her, 'Stop you escaping again Houdini.' Walking back into the other room he was looking forward to enjoying a large Scotch and the cold meat sandwich he had promised himself. She could wait, he couldn't.

CHAPTER 43

In the CID office, things had slowed down. It looked as if the pair had escaped, simply because there were no new leads, no financial movement, no new attacks, no sightings and nothing from the ports and airports. Jaeger was frustrated beyond belief, she was beginning to lose her team as they were reassigned different duties because there was nothing new for them to do, and manpower was always short.

Eventually both she and Robert were given new cases to examine on top of their case load, as reluctantly neither of them could justify what was beginning to look like a cold case. Checking every day on the accounts, the house and the car, she had to admit it was looking unlikely they would ever get that fatal mistake Robert was so convinced would happen. Days turned into weeks and eventually the case was deemed just pending and the team disbanded. Jaeger took up other duties and was regarded as just part of the group now, but this case annoyed her, because she was more than ever determined to bring it to a positive conclusion. Little did she realise that the answer to her problem was just a couple of miles away, and also playing a waiting game.

Those couple of miles had become a slim but brilliantly convenient safety barrier for Carter, and he still couldn't believe the police just relied on a drive by car check. They had just assumed they had escaped. All very well but he was becoming ever more frustrated as well. It had been weeks since he used the house as a haven. And although the police visits had now all but ceased, he knew it was time to move, simply because he couldn't hide here for the rest of his life. Feeling like a creature of the dark, he wasn't even able to switch on a light. And then there was the small matter of Tracey - but he had a solution to that as well.

His cards had arrived, his accounts were activated, the loans in place and in new bank accounts, the car was in his name and he had already arranged by phone with a dealer at Newark on the A1 to sell the car for cash, which he intended to buy a van with. Something he could sleep in if needed, something he could dump without financial loss at some point in the future. There were plenty of dealers in Newark he could pick up a cheap van from.

Now the big problem, Tracey, and parting her from her money. Carter had kept Tracey alive with just soup and things he could liquidise, which was easy to feed her with. Sitting her on the toilet meant he had no problems with soiling. She was growing weaker as her confinement and limited diet started to affect her health. The noose had worked perfectly and given him freedom of movement, which in turn stopped him going stir crazy, but had done nothing for her mental health.

Carter had managed several visits to the town, usually at night, to stock up on essentials. His wound had healed, not perfectly, but enough to move around without too much pain. Although it was a wound to his chest, his ribs had saved him, the knife hadn't penetrated any vital organ, missed his heart and hadn't punctured his lung. His appearance had dramatically changed, he now sported a beard, his hair had been cropped with the aid of clippers he purchased in Boots, he was thinner as well.

Long hours confined to the house, hiding from view during the day had given Carter plenty of time to plan things, provide an escape plan and secure a future where he couldn't be found. It was all planned out. Now was the time to put it all in into action. Tracey needed to be persuaded to give him access to her online bank account. How to convince her to part with the information? He had his charm offensive lined up, now let's see if she falls for it.

The soup he had prepared was placed in a bowl which he carried into the toilet. This ritual had taken place for several weeks now and Tracey was prepared for her only meal of the day, and Carter knew she would be receptive. Kneeling next to her, he took the gag off and started to feed her. For once he smiled at her. 'I am going to escape to Ireland shortly, do you want to come with me?' She stopped eating and looked at him incredulously. 'I need money, I've managed to get a couple of thousand together but I need access to your savings to pull this off.' She almost spat at him, 'Do you think I'm going to fall for that? As soon as I give you the codes I'm dead. There is nothing to stop you killing me, just like that girl.'

'You know that was an accident, I can kill you now, I can leave you tied up here and you will slowly starve. or you can come with me and start again. If you come with me we can escape to Ireland. I know how. You have no life here and the police think you are helping me anyway. Your choice.' Carter was watching her face as he got up, turned and started to walk to the kitchen. 'Wait, I can't trust you, how can I even remotely trust you after you have treated me like this? she shouted at him.

'You can't but I'll set you free tonight, you sleep with me overnight, and tomorrow morning before the crack of dawn, we drive off and I'll explain all on route. Considering you nearly killed me, I think that is a pretty good offer. We used to be lovers once, remember.' Carter just smiled and turned around and took the soup back to the kitchen. She would be hungry later and want to talk. He had left the gag off, let's see if she shouts out. There was silence but he knew he was beginning the path to success. He looked in at her. 'I have enough money to get away for the moment and you can come with me, and we can sort the money out as we go along. If you can help me, you are free.'

CHAPTER 44

The day had drawn to a close and Jaeger had drawn another blank. She had done the usual checks, the house was still locked, the lights were off, the car was in the garage and the accounts were untouched. Same as every day, same as it would be tomorrow. No movement. Nothing. Where the bloody hell had they gone, and worse, why can't we find them. If they had fled the country, the normal checks hadn't picked them up leaving. False passports? No. Were they even still alive? The thought of a suicide, a mutual pact or a murder and suicide hadn't crossed her mind until then. It was a macabre possibility! If that was the case then the bodies were bloody well hidden somewhere. They might never be found in that case.

Looking around the office, she noticed the file on Carter was still open, was it an omen? An open case still? It would have to be until they found them - dead or alive. The file was closed and replaced on her desk. She switched off the office lights and left the office. The thought of an unsolved case annoyed her, but she knew there were a lot of other unsolved cases in that office, and many would remain unsolved for ever.

Jaeger was thinking hard all the way to her car. To solve his bloody case needed some tangential thinking. Turning on her heel, she went back to the office and picked up the file again. This was going home with her tonight. They had missed something, something obvious, some little clue, something that would blow the case wide open and she hoped she would spot it tonight. Driving away she decided to go past the house, just for her own piece of mind. But her thoughts were far away and she even failed to notice Carter's bike, still locked up outside the fish and chip shop.

CHAPTER 45

Carter had been planning for most of the day. Keeping his word, he had freed Tracey from the toilet and she had slept in the same bed as him that evening, although tied to him so he was aware of any movement or attempt to escape. They were up just after ten as he wanted to get a head start on the police. Carter knew once they realised the car was gone, the hunt would be on, with him as the prey. They would have broken cover, so their escape plan had to be perfect and fast.

Carter watched for the police check and it came and went without incident. They were travelling light, just a case each. Carter had already tried the car and it started after a couple of attempts. In went Tracey's laptop, the cases and nothing else. Carter made sure Tracey was dressed but had tied her hands together and then tied them to the door handle to make sure she couldn't run or even reach the car horn. She complied and sat quietly, whilst he relocked the house to give nothing obvious away. It had to look undisturbed for the night.

Just before midnight, Carter pushed the car out onto the drive silently, shut the garage doors and drove quietly away.

Talking about his escape plans, he explained he was going to get them to Ireland if she wanted to come with him, or she could be set free in Cambridge which was on route if he went via the M11. Whatever option he took, he wanted her bank codes beforehand and would be stopping at the Lakeside services the other side of QE bridge on the M25 to log on to their internet. She had the option of being killed there, being free, or coming with him to Ireland.

She said nothing, she knew she had little chance of escaping without giving him the bank codes. As they travelled on the M25 she spoke softly to him. 'I don't think there is much chance of us escaping together, you stand a better chance on your own. I don't think I want to be with you after the past few weeks, I want to be free again.'

'OK,' replied Carter, 'But if you don't give me he codes, you won't be leaving Lakeside alive. And I mean that. If I can get some money transferred, I'll drive you to the outskirts of Cambridge and set you free. It's remote enough to give me a couple of hours head start to get on the ferry.' She nodded in agreement, just give him the money and try and escape, if they caught him, she'd get it back anyway.

The car crossed under the Thames at Dartford and Carter took the road off to the services where he parked as close as possible to the service building. Sitting in the car, she agreed to his demands and gave him all the information he needed and Carter logged on to Tracey's account and emptied it into several of his new accounts. What little money he had in his account was also transferred. He checked the money had been moved, she sat meekly waiting for the death blow she knew was coming. To her surprise he just looked pleased and said, 'OK that's worked, but we go to Cambridge first, and then part company and go our separate ways.'

Knowing the car would have been logged on the toll cameras, the drive to Cambridge was a bit faster than usual and he turned off just over an hour later on to the A14. Traffic was light as he drove up to the bridge over the Cam.

Carter slowed and waited until the sole car on the road had passed before he put the hazard lights on and pulled over above the centre span. It just looked as if he had broken down and wouldn't attract any attention. Tracey didn't really believe he would keep his word, and she was prepared to make a run for it if possible. It would be better to hit by a car than be killed by Carter. Pulling the passenger door open Tracey saw he had a knife in his hand, and she flinched back into the seat, but Carter simply sliced the rope which held her to the door handle. With her hand still tied she was yanked out of the car and pushed against the crash barrier. Tracey pushed him away and he fell backwards. Seizing her chance, she started to run knowing she had little chance of surviving a knife attack.

Carter caught up with her in seconds and knocked her to the ground. 'Hope you can swim,' he shouted in her ear as he picked her up by the arms, and propped her against the safety rail. Bending down, Carter grabbed her legs by the ankles and lifted her up in one go and then pushed her backwards over the edge of the bridge. Carter lent over the barrier to watch her end. Watching her fall, he thought it seemed to take ages before there was a satisfying splash as she went under. She didn't reappear. Carter smiled and threw her case into the water without a second thought. One less problem to take care of, he thought as he drove away. There was no remorse, her death just made life easier for him now.

Carter had the rest of the day planned out long ago, he knew his route and how he must implement it quickly, before the police realised he had got away. However, he made a quick stop in a convenient layby. The bank accounts were already set up and he began by transferring much of Tracey's money into different accounts to confuse the trail further.

To ensure it would work, he stopped at every petrol station, village and shop with a cash machine to with draw the maximum £300 from each. The credit cards were also maxed out on each stop. Turning on to the A1 Carter went on to Peterborough and did the same exercise with different accounts. It was now 5.30 am and he need to be at Grantham by 8.30 for his appointment with the garage who were interested in Tracey's car.

Carter arrived with a hour to spare and finished transferring Tracey's money into his new accounts, which were then transferred again to confuse the trail. Every time he made a note of where the money was, and how much he transferred to each. The police might well see her account was empty but it would take them an age to trace everything again. By then be would have been able to have taken tens of thousands out in cash, plus have the cash from her car. Just in case they could stop his cash flow, he had to be as cash rich as possible.

As the deal had already been agreed on the phone for the car, there was no problem completing that transaction with Carter simply handing over his new V11 in exchange for the money, and he was on his way in less than a quarter of an hour.

There was a lot of casual chat in the salesman's office and Carter deliberately said he was going over to Ireland to work on a long term project and hoped to move there. Until then he would be staying with a friend who was also working on the same project. There was a promise of a company van and he wouldn't be needing the old car. His friend was collecting him in town later on in the day. The salesman didn't care, he was only interested in the profit he could see sitting on his forecourt and he was happy to pay for the Volvo. A money transfer was made, which Carter moved later that morning.

It was short walk from the salesroom to the station where Carter caught a train to Doncaster. On route to the station he had detoured via the high street shops where he purchased a small backpack, and a cheap jacket to complete his deception, which was hidden in the pack. The journey to Doncaster was uneventful but it gave him a chance to shave off his beard in the toilet, dump his old coat in the holdall along with the money he had collected. Once completed, he put on his new jacket and sat in a different seat on the train so that he wouldn't be recognised, and alighted a completely different looking person to confuse any CCTV.

More money was transferred in Doncaster where he purchased a small cheap van from a used car lot, and a tent for cash from a camping shop in the shopping centre. Carter then treated himself to a decent breakfast on the industrial estate where he brought the van, and he felt at ease at last. Transport that couldn't be traced, money in his pocket, Tracey was out of his life at last. There were resources scattered all over the place he could tap into, and not all of them could be traced.

Time for a new life, and here the trail would go cold and he would vanish. They would be looking for him in Ireland, he would be in Europe, but first he had to get to Newcastle to put the next stage of his plan into action. There was enough cash with him to make sure he didn't need to use a cash machine again for a while. The was always the danger the police would be able to trace the accounts and block them. That would take the co-operation of the banks and possibly a court order, he would have another day at least to empty the accounts or at least drain a good percentage of them and keep moving the remainder. Even if he lost the cash in them, he still had access to other accounts that hadn't been transferred into yet. These were his loan accounts and they were his back up. Life was good, he felt free at last. Carter smiled at the thought, yes, life was good, very good and he was back in control. He smiled again.

CHAPTER 46

It was well into the day before Jaeger went through her Carter routine. She had other case work to sort first and that took several hours to organise and get what was left of her team working. She had read through the box file several times the previous night, there was nothing new in it and she knew she had missed nothing obvious. So where to go now? It remained at the bottom of her to do list for the time being.

Just out of routine, rather than curiosity, she checked on Tracey's account expecting to see the same result she had seen for weeks. She stared at the screen in disbelief. Jesus, the account was empty. When had that happened? How had they managed that? The account had been emptied remotely, but where from? Could it be traced and where had the money gone. More importantly who had control of it? She needed an answer quickly.

Rushing into Robert's office she blurted out, 'They are on the move, the money has been emptied from Tracey's account. They are alive and on the move, sir.' Robert smiled, 'Knew he was hiding somewhere, get someone down to the house, they might have been there and left clues, check for the car, if it is still there, then they have used other transport, if not check all the local road cameras and see if we can track it somewhere. Get down to the bank, demand their help to track where the money has gone. Put an all points report out and alert the ports and airports, they will want to get out of the country fast.'

Robert sat back at his desk. The hunt is back on, he thought to himself, now let's see if we can outthink him for once. Watching through the glass of his office he watched Jaeger fly round the office organising her team. When she stopped he beckoned her back into his office and said, 'OK get your coat, you and I are going to spearhead this. Phone the bank and say we are coming down to pick their brains after we have been to the house. Still got your keys? OK let's move, we need to act fast on this, get your team to phone in any progress.'

They were in the car when a report came through from the local squad car that Tracey's car had indeed gone. 'They have been back to the house,' said Robert. 'OK there first, get someone to phone the bank to ask for their help, we will be there in an hour. Jaeger get the team to check the ANPR cameras to see where he is heading, we will see if any withdrawals he made coincide with any camera results.'

They arrived at the house within 15 minutes, the squad car was still there, and the officer reported that the house was still secure, locked with no break ins. Before they could get into the house, there was a continuous stream of phone calls to Jaeger reporting on the progress of the car. It had been tracked on the M20, M25, the services at Lakeside where it apparently stopped for a brief period of time, they were still checking the internal cameras to see if they went inside, that at least would confirm or deny whether there were working together, M11, A14 and A1 as far at Grantham, nothing after that.

'Right he has either dumped the car, or he has holed up there, get the local police on the case, look for that car, check the hotels, motels and B&Bs get their photos out immediately. They think they have got a head start on us. Carter is working to some sort of plan, why is he heading north? Get an alert out to all the ports on the East coast, he is still going to try and escape to Europe I'm sure.'

Jaeger produced the keys and they entered the house. It was obvious from the state of the place that it had been lived in for some time. 'Damn' said Robert as soon as he entered the house. 'They have been hiding here all along. Right under our bloody noses. Damn, damn, damn, why didn't we check the house out?'

'We did, there was no sign of them, I came down here again to check, nothing had changed, we assumed they had fled. There was no sign of them, the house was checked by patrol every day, nothing,' she said defensively. 'He's been very clever and she has to have been in on this.' Robert and Jaeger examined the house and realised they had been completely fooled. It was time to put things right and hunt them down, and they drove to the bank in silence.

Robert and Jaeger got their interview, but the bank couldn't help that much. Yes they could confirm the money had been transferred. Online banking was easy now. All they could do was say where the money had been transferred to, but all they actually had were account numbers, no other information. As the accounts weren't with their bank they couldn't even supply who had the money as there was no reference, and no name, just a number. But they could see where withdrawals had been made, so they had a location and route if nothing else.

Robert swore under his breath when he realised he had been so easily out manoeuvred again. Carter must have known he could confuse the money issue very easily. The bank said it was more than they could offer help on, they would need to go to central clearing as they didn't have the expertise or authority to track the accounts. They did run off a list of the accounts that Tracey's money had been transferred into as a consolation. 'We need a court order to block those accounts,' said Robert, 'Can you get on to that please,' Jaeger nodded and took the list.

Looking at Jaeger, Robert said, 'OK we know he is in Grantham, we need that car. Find that and we hopefully find him. Contact the police there and see if we can get any leads. You are going to heading north otherwise to try and sort this, or at least until we get a new lead on Carter.'

The air of despondency was palatable when he got back in the car. On their way back to the station Robert said, 'Get the forensics team down to the house, see it they can come up with anything new. I still can't believe they were bloody holed up in Tracey's house all that time, so bloody, bloody obvious, why didn't we cotton on?' Jaeger became immediately defensive and angrily turned on her boss, 'We checked it three times, we then checked it every day, we didn't miss anything, they understood how we worked and used it against us, we need to out think him now.'

CHAPTER 47

Carter had already assumed the accounts would be blocked and as this was a second day according to banking hours, those accounts were transferred remotely and the maximum emptied at an ATM in Doncaster just in case. Any cash left in other accounts was redistributed around the new accounts he had set up, knowing the new accounts would require a new search and a blocking order. It was easy to stay that one step ahead and move the cash around electronically and take money at will in cash whenever he could.

Keeping his hat on at the ATMs to make sure any security cameras didn't pick up his new look, Carter emptied everything he could, and made his way back to the van he had brought in the morning. It took a few seconds to be on his way, to the public he looked ordinary, and so did the van. No one took a blind bit of notice of him. Carter headed north again.

The signposts now said Hull, and on the back roads he was using, they were less likely to have ANPR cameras and squad cars to worry about, even if they realised he was in a van. In the back of his mind he had an idea that a trip to Newcastle might not necessary, and he wanted to try something out before trekking all the way north. Carter knew there would be an alert out for him but he had all his documentation in his own name so a quick exit would be out of the question as it would mean he would soon be identified and consequentially caught.

His plan was to see if he could get a job on a ship, possibly one of the ferries out of Newcastle, but of course there was

Hull in between as a trial run. Worth sussing out to see if what was possible if nothing else. A quick run up the M18 and M62 found him in Hull, and he headed for the docks looking for shipping offices. However, whenever he made an enquiry about signing on, the answer was the same, they only wanted experienced seamen with certified papers. Damn, but Carter wasn't really phased, this just saved himself a long drive, but it did mean he also couldn't go to Ireland as he had so cleverly mentioned that to the car salesman. His red herring had back fired on him. So a change of plan, a change of ID was needed, and time to properly rethink how he was going to get away. Not just get away, but have a new life where no one would find him.

After he had driven away, he headed south again, pulling into services on the M1 where after a half decent meal, he fell asleep in the van for the night, exceeding the four hour waiting limited by several hours, just for the fun of it.

CHAPTER 48

It was late in the same day when the Grantham police tracked down the car. Luckily for them the car salesman had washed and valeted the car and placed it in the prime location at the front of the lot, where a passing squad car had spotted it. It was immediately impounded and driven away for forensic examination, with its capture immediately phoned through to very pleased Jaeger. Robert could see the smile on her face from his office and knew she would burst into his room with what was obviously a lead. She got as far as 'We've got the car, unfortunately not Carter yet. Grantham are doing a search for us of hotels, pubs, motels, campsites – the lot.'

Already on his feet, Robert had his coat in his hand as he knew this heralded a visit. 'OK spill the beans, but tell me in the car, we are going for a ride.' Before they left, the team were given a myriad of tasks that would keep them busy until they returned. They used Robert's car, a rather impressive unmarked black BMW and they were soon heading for the QE2 bridge and the M25 motorway. 'The car is in Grantham, which has been impounded. We have a really good description of his appearance now, and he is on their internal CCTV. No sign of her though,' said Jaeger. 'This is all too easy,' said Robert, 'Where did they find the car?' 'Car lot,' replied Jaeger.

'Damn,' he replied, 'So he has dumped the car. He won't be in Grantham, he has gone to ground. We need the bank to see what has happened to those accounts and if money has been transferred and to what, and if so, gain the new numbers so they can be blocked as well.'

They made good progress along the A1, using the blues and twos, with Jaeger on the phone to her team for virtually the entire trip. By the time she had finished, her mobile started to ring with answers to the first of her enquiries. Robert could see her nodding out of the corner of his eye, and he saw her start to write numbers down in her note book.

After a few calls she turned to Robert to relay the results of her enquiries. 'OK we know the money has continued to be transferred. Those original accounts have been emptied, so there is not much point in closing those down. However, we do know the numbers of the new accounts, but it's too late to have those blocked, we will have to have those blocked first thing in the morning. We have CCTV from the car lot in Grantham so we have a good description of him we can distribute You never know, we might get lucky and someone might recognise him.'

'Doubt it somehow,' answered Robert, 'He's not just one step ahead of us, but two, or possibly three at the moment. OK we know roughly where he is. If he has dumped the car it's one of two reasons, he is short of money or he has other means of transport. Could be he is short of cash, which I doubt judging by the number of withdrawals he has made, or perhaps he just wants to confuse the trail. Get the Grantham force to check on other car sales in the area, they now have a decent picture of the guy. He may just have purchased a different car to make his getaway. Let's hope so.'

Their car entered the outskirts of Grantham where they soon made contact with the police handling the case. There was little to add to what they already knew. Frustrated, Jaeger found a local hotel with a couple of free rooms, and they made themselves at home to compare notes and plan a new strategy in the hope that the trail wouldn't be too cold in the morning.

CHAPTER 49

The next morning Carter had realised he had made a mistake taking money out in Doncaster as it had given his location away, but he thought he could confuse the issue by returning to the town again, where he managed to empty the secondary accounts from a different set of ATMs in the town. Leaving the van down a side street, Carter took everything in cash, not transferring anything this time. The trail had to go cold here.

Those transactions would be picked up in the morning and they would think he had either stayed there or he was still heading north. It didn't matter much, as he knew that the accounts couldn't be closed down immediately, and he had at least another day before the new accounts were closed down. Most of the money now was in cash, and there was all the loan money in untraceable accounts, and under company names with no connection to him. Wandering around the town he collected a few new items, had a good lunch and thought how to get around the ID problem.

It was late now and he needed a place to rest up. Picking a quiet layby on the A1 this time, he settled down in his new sleeping bag. Carter knew he needed a decent night's sleep as he need to visit a whole range of new banks, shops and supermarkets in the morning to take the last of his money and then head south for this escape. Even with the noise of heavy traffic passing all night, Carter woke refreshed and started his tour of the town to empty the remaining cash from the known cashpoints. The ATMs were in garages, shops, anywhere but in town. The car was always left out of sight and he retraced his steps to make sure the car wouldn't appear on CCTV and give a way how he was travelling. Go south young man, he thought to himself.

CHAPTER 50

Jaeger and Robert each sat around a coffee on a table covered in paperwork. She had been on the phone for hours now and the notebook in front of her was filled with numbers and comments.

Jaeger looked up at Robert. 'Well he really is still one step ahead of us. He has cash from the car, he has cash from the ATMs in Grantham and we know he was heading to Ireland according to the car salesman. Since then we know he has taken money out in Doncaster yesterday, and again this morning. So he is mobile. Car or Train? Car would be my bet some of these locations are in the middle of nowhere, but the force there have already checked all the garages and confirmed all the sales. Nothing, a couple of sales from the regular dealers, all on personal contract. The used car lots have had a visit, but they came up blank as well. They were few and far between, half a dozen sales between them, none to anyone answering our man's description, so he went out by public transport or train. We need to check the station CCTV to see if he left that way. I'll do that as I presume you want to go up to Doncaster to check things there. I've contacted the station there and they are expecting one of us his morning. I can get about using the police here, they say I can borrow a couple of bodies and a car until you are finished and you can pick me up later. I'll use the guys here to check the accounts, and see if we can track and block those.'

Robert smiled and said, 'OK you seem to have it all under control. I'll leave you here in the tender care of the guys, you liaise with the team at home to do your leg work, I'll see what I can find in Doncaster and I'll pick you up from the station here at about six so we can get back to Kent tonight.' Robert left and picked up the car outside to head to Doncaster. It would be a bloody long day again he thought.

CHAPTER 51

Carter was going in the opposite direction, he had cleared out the accounts. That was his last traceable connection, everything that tied him to Tracey was gone, she was gone, he was free. Carter let that sink in, he was free, untraceable, he had got away with it. Now escape and enjoy life. Still smiling at that thought, he re-joined the A1 and headed towards London, unaware that events were about to take a U turn for him.

Carter would be unaware of those events for quite some time yet. There was his plan to put into place, and he was eager to do it. There was far too much cash in the van now. That needed to go into the business accounts, so he stopped at Lichfield and again at St Albans to put money into those accounts. Carter had set up standing orders through one of his business accounts, to repay the absolute minimum amount back to the loan companies, so he didn't default and the accounts would be safe in the short term. It would take the police a while to figure out where the money had gone.

There was one problem remaining. What he needed now was a suitable victim to swap IDs with. An ID that would require stealing, and by force if necessary. Time to go hunting again, something he was good at, all he needed was a suitable hunting ground and he was pretty sure he knew just the place. Carter smiled to himself, was he going to follow the long-winded procedure from the 'Day of the Jackal', no, that would take weeks, he needed something much more immediate. Carter knew he would need to make this perfect and fool proof, as there would be no second chances. If he got it wrong, he would be caught, and he couldn't risk that.

Knowing he had been lucky so far, Carter had to plan things a lot better now. His resources were limited as were his methods of escape. With his present ID he wouldn't get far, it would only be a matter of time until he was tracked down. His only real option was, he had to hide, bide his time and escape by some unlikely method, that no one would think about. Ireland was out, exit by a major port or airport was out of the question, although Europe would be his final destination. Staying in the UK was out of the equation, and why would he stay here, there was nothing to keep him here.

CHAPTER 52

It was a cold, drizzly morning. It was a totally overcast, cheerless sort of day for the Police in Cambridge who had just recovered Tracey's body from the Cam in the early hours, after a report of a possible suicide. They were now in the process of identifying the body. Unfortunately, in the university city, suicides were not uncommon, and bodies in the Cam were just another sad reflection of the negative pressures of modern life. There was no real urgency in the recovery process, the boat had pushed the body into the bank where it could be hauled out without so much effort. An ambulance stood by to take the hapless victim away.

It wasn't until the body was dragged from the water, that the police realised her hands were bound. This suicide immediately became a murder case, and it became a matter of more importance rather than just another pointless death. The body was taken to the morgue at Addenbrookes to await a post mortem, although it was fairly obvious she had been drowned. That was confirmed later in the afternoon, and a criminal file opened by the police. It was confirmed she was alive when she went into the water, so it was a deliberate drowning, no accident, and no suicide.

The police went through her clothes, nothing, they went through the missing persons list, again without success. It was pure luck that the police had recovered a bag at the same time, they simply assumed they were connected and it arrived with the body for examination. One of the officers finally got round to opening the case and there was a single item of clothing with a name on it. A track suit top had been identified with a hand scrawled name in indelible ink. The body had a name now, possibly. Back to the missing persons list, negative there, but a confirmation on the persons of interest list.

A short time later, a phone call confirmed the police were looking for Tracey in relation to a murder in Maidstone. 'Well strike her from the wanted list,' said the officer. 'She's become a victim. Can you inform the Kent station dealing with this and tell them she is a definite murder victim. They have a second murder to deal with, can they give us as many details as possible and we will start a search at this end, just in case he is still in the local area, but I wouldn't hold my breath, I suspect he is long gone.' Carter was in fact much closer than they ever imagined.

CHAPTER 53

Both Jaeger and Robert had drawn blanks on their respective visits, so they were on their way back to Kent that evening. The only positive note had been the tracing and blocking of Carter's accounts, but there was nothing in any of them anyway. A bit of good old fashioned detective work with the CCTV revealed Carter had indeed taken the train out of Grantham but there was no record of where he had alighted. His new appearance had been too good for the observers to pick him out of the crowds. They had to assume he had picked up a car somewhere, but where and what was it?

They knew he had money and wanted to get out of the country, possibly to Ireland, but they also had an alert out at all the ports just in case. They knew what he looked like from the description from the car salesman - but that could be changed. In effect they needed to distribute his old photo and his new photofit and hope that might produce a lead.

Jaeger's phone rang. 'What? Say that again please,' said Jaeger in disbelief. The message was repeated and she put the mobile down. Jaeger looked at Robert. 'Pull over we need to talk, this changes everything.' Robert found a safe place a few miles further on and brought the car to a halt as gently as possible, as he was expecting bad news. 'OK, what's wrong? You look like you've seen a ghost.' 'They've found Tracey, well her body at least. She's been murdered, drowned at Cambridge.'

The news of Tracey's body being discovered had thrown a large spanner into the works. They were now looking for just one person - that meant Carter was much more of a loose cannon, he had no ties, he could go where he liked. Robert knew he was a lot more dangerous, and a bloody sight harder to catch now.

'Alright, where's the body, we need to start again from there. We are going around in circles at the moment, we need to completely rethink this now. Carter is guilty of two murders now, he has nothing to lose so he can hide better. He has out thought us, got away, murdered his accomplice, emptied her account, stolen her money, changed his ID, got transport and put us back to square one. Get the team to set up a press conference for the morning, whilst we see the body, get the facts there on that, and go home.'

Jaeger phoned the hospital to warn them they would need to see the body and identify it formally. An hour later they had identified the body and ended up speaking to the local force to see if they could throw any light on matters. They could only guess where she had entered the water, but thought the A14 bridge upstream was the most likely choice. Apart from that there was nothing new to add to the case and the pair resumed their journey back to Kent in silence.

Robert only muttered a muted farewell when they arrived, he had confirmed the press conference had been set up for ten am the next morning by phone on the journey back. There was an urgent need to prepare his notes for the morning, to explain there was a man hunt on now, and he needed all the help he could muster from the public. It was a vain hope, but he had to start somewhere. It would keep him awake for most of the night on how to put this together for a decent impact. Not so for Carter, who had found a nice little B&B in Watford rather than a motel. No questions, all cash, untraceable. There was a distinct difference in their attitudes to life. Carter had no real worries now, it was all going his way, he was in the driving seat, and as a consequence he slept like a baby that night. Robert was up all night, as he needed all the help he could get at the moment. At two am he had his conference notes in order and he retired to bed as well, but it was a troubled sleep.

CHAPTER 54

At 9.15 Carter had left the B&B after an excellent breakfast, paid his bill in cash and headed towards St Pancras. The car was parked at Hatch End, and a train taken to Central London. Carter was on the hunt. Hunting for a very specific prey, a doppelganger.

In Kent, Robert was preparing to address the TV crews at ten am. Settling uncomfortably behind a desk, he adjusted the microphones in front of him, made sure the photos of Carter were projected behind him on the screen when needed, and he shuffled his notes, as the press, note books and cameras at the ready, filed in.

The landlady at the B&B was clearing away, the morning news still on the TV behind her in the dining room. She wasn't really watching it, it was on for the benefit of the guests really, so she switched it off just before Robert started his conference. She was far too busy to watch the news on Sky, she had to wash up, make the beds and go shopping now. She missed the plea for help, she missed the photos of Carter by seconds. She certainly would have been interested and somewhat horrified to have known she had just entertained a double murderer that morning. But purchasing a new supply of bacon, sausages and eggs was more important than the news, she could catch up later on, before the new customers arrived that evening.

Carter's bed was stripped and remade, the carrier bags grabbed and she was away to Tesco. Don't forget the bread as well, she thought to herself.

In Kent Robert finished his conference and questions from the press after eight minutes. Carter had arrived in London about the same time and was now on the tube, on the hunt, and feeling confident.

The landlady was now in the car, half listening to the radio, they were playing a lot of her favourites, but she missed the news at 11, as she had just pulled into Tesco and was looking for a parking place. The engine switched off a few seconds before news of the hunt for a vicious mass murderer came on. Sausages, now they were in isle two she thought to herself.

CHAPTER 55

Robert knew he would be facing another plethora of calls now. But it was better than no leads at all. Having spent ages answering questions, he felt there was little extra he could do for the moment. His attempts to follow Carter's money had drawn a blank, the accounts had been emptied. There was no help on locating his transport, whatever it was at the moment. As for his location, they had no idea at all, Carter had well and truly given them the slip again.

Wait for the mistake, Robert had said earlier, it was his only hope at the moment, because Carter had completely outsmarted him up until now. But he couldn't be lucky all the time. Robert knew Carter wanted to leave the country, that would be his first concern. The police in Europe wouldn't be too bothered chasing a British criminal, so he would be a lot safer on the continent. Obvious route to go. That was covered, so he was still in the country, somewhere.

Thinking back to the press conference he was pleased at the job the guys in the office had done on the ID photos. Using existing photographs of Carter, they had shown how he looked a few months ago, how he looked a few days ago from the description from the car salesman, and how he might look in several other guises.

The phone rang within minutes, first of the crank calls, but they had to check them all. Amazingly several were almost certainly right as they matched the time and locations where they could place Carter through the ATM withdrawals. The positive responses were matched to one of the photofits so they could try and see what he looked like at any one time. At the end of the day Robert felt he might be making something of a breakthrough. But it wasn't until after six that evening that the landlady looked at the TV as she waited for the first of her guests to arrive. She recognised Carter at once and phoned the Kent number on the screen.

'The man you are looking for, stayed here last night, paid in cash, and I took a note of his car number for you, is that of any use? He said he was going into London, don't know if he meant driving in.' Robert was watching his team answering the calls when an arm was raised and a frantic wave to Robert to come over and take the call. 'I think that will be most useful madam, can I just hand you over to my superintendent as I think he would love to talk to you in person, please hold.' The phone was gleefully handed over to a very interested superintendent who proceeded to listen extremely carefully and take down as much information as humanly possible. 'Madam that is excellent news, you have helped us immensely, my thanks. Please don't mention this to anyone, as we would like to take him by surprise if possible.' There was a huge grin on Robert's face when he handed the phone back.

'Jaeger my office quickly, we need to set up a search and snatch team. We have a location for last night. It looks as if he has come full circle back to London, just a guess, a hunch if you like. I'm sure he won't have taken the car into town, he will be on foot or using public transport, much easier to hide. Why has he come all this way, where is he going? Could he be heading for Europe on the train? Get the Met to swamp the station at St Pancras, we need to get teams out looking for that van.

Distribute that number to the local police see if they can locate it. Concentrate on station car parks on all the lines going into London from the Watford area. Fingers bloody crossed now.'

At bloody last, Robert thought. At bloody last, a break. Don't lose him now son, out think him. Why is he here, has he gone into London? Don't scare him off. Think man, think. What is he up to? Sitting back behind his desk, he watched Jaeger carry out his orders. It's a waiting game now, set the trap and wait for the prey. Within the next hour, Jaeger had the Met all over the station, and she had every squad car in London out searching for the van.

CHAPTER 56

Carter was indeed at the station, he had been there for most of the day looking for a suitable victim. A traveller from the continent, someone who wouldn't be missed for a while. But so far no one suitable. Carter felt safe however, having changed his appearance again, he now had dark glasses hiding his face, and a flat cap to finish the job, and he just looked normal, a visitor or tourist. He was very much at ease, but this had been a pointless exercise today, perhaps tomorrow it would be better. But as he prepared to leave, he noticed that police had started to arrive en masse, Carter didn't like the look of this.

Sitting in the sandwich bar watching arrivals from the Eurostar, he had been scouring the crowds for someone about his build, but what he was really looking for was a victim for his ID swap. Today hadn't been a success, no one seemed to fit his looks or build, he would have to try and find someone tomorrow. More police arrived, Carter viewed this with trepidation, probably nothing to do with him but there was no reason to test the theory. Leaving a half drunk coffee, he made his way to the underground, picking up an Evening Standard on route.

His Oyster card purchased earlier that day made sure he made a hasty retreat into the bowels of London, The tube wasn't too busy and he found a seat without too much trouble, settling down to read the paper, pretending to be yet another bored commuter, the paper hiding most of his face. It wasn't until he started to read the paper that he saw his own likeness. It was all over page 5, along with several photofits. Christ, he thought, if I don't get recognised now it will be amazing. I need to get out of London again and hide for a while. Paranoia and panic started to set in and he spent the next thirty minutes wishing the train would go faster so he could collect the van and get out of London.

Almost running out of the station he headed straight for the van. Need to get away, out of London at least, certainly not back to Watford, the opposite direction, the coast, yes, head south, nearer the continent. As he drove off, a local squad car entered the street. The officer radioed in '451 reporting, Hatch End Station checked, negative, where do you want me to go next?'

Carter had a sat nav he had purchased earlier, stuck to the windscreen. It was just on, it wasn't programmed for anything specific, but it enabled him to use as many back roads as possible without getting picked up by traffic cameras. It was a slow almost painful journey across London to then be confronted by a choice of where to go next, of how he could hide and ultimately how to escape. Choosing a route out of the capital near Lewisham, he roughly followed the course of the A20 towards the coast. It took hours not using the main routes and eventually he had to pull in near Maidstone, take a nap and collect his thoughts.

In fact he slept far longer than he wanted too and woke as it was getting light about 5am. Carter realised he was close to home at this point and decided to tempt fate and drive past the house, just to check on what the police were up to. When he arrived and drove slowly past, there was nothing to see. However, at the bottom of the road he spotted his precious bike still locked up outside the local shops. Utterly amazed no one had stolen it, and purely on impulse, he pulled up, unlocked the bike and threw it in the back of the van as quickly as possible. At that time of the morning no one spotted him. With the bike safely ensconced in the back, Carter began to smile to himself. It was a smile that soon grew and soon had him laughing out loud, he thought they hadn't even found the bike, let alone him, bloody useless morons, and he drove off still laughing. With no real idea of where he was going, he headed in the general direction of Folkestone.

With a desperate need to get organised now, he found a local garage that had just opened with a decent cafe attached, but what attracted him was a sign in the window, free wi-fi. Parking around the back of the cafe after filling the car with fuel, he ordered a bacon sandwich and a coffee, and sat down in a corner with the laptop. Although his brain was racing, he tried to as stay calm as possible and think straight. Where to go? B&Bs and hotels were out of the question, too much public contact. Camping? But he was always in view to the general public as well, no he needed something a bit more private. Holiday homes, no, too many details to be filled in. As he went through the sites he came across caravans, no he didn't want to buy one, but could he hire one on a short-term lease? Bloody right he could, and all done over the web as well, money paid from one of the company accounts, just pick up the keys when he arrived. Wonderful and easy.

The site near Dymchurch wasn't up market, but it was busy and he could hide out here easily, loads of passing public and multitudes of holiday makers to hide amongst who didn't give a shit of who he was. A quick visit to a local supermarket on route for food and drink, meant he arrived about half past twelve. The site office was busy, excellent, he was quick, just staying long enough to confirm his booking, give a false name, pay in cash, and collect his keys and car pass, and as he left, he breathed a sigh of relief, he was safe again.

The car was hidden behind the caravan for safety. The caravan was fully equipped and he dumped the food and drink in the kitchen, falling asleep on the king size bed with no effort at all. When he awoke, the television was switched on so he could watch the evening news. Was he still wanted, but how big was the man hunt? But when the news, and then the regional news finished, he was almost disappointed that he wasn't mentioned on either at all. Well that didn't last long did it, police have given up already, he thought to himself, time for a celebration and he reached for the scotch he purchased earlier. There was a smile on his face again.

Thinking hard now, he needed a fool proof method of how to get away. Something different, not obvious, something that would work. His mind tried to cope with it all, but he was tired and the drink didn't help. He had nothing to eat for hours now and his body was having none of it. A quick sandwich followed by a drink solved that problem. Dozing off again, he wouldn't wake until long into the following morning, it had been a long eventful day and he was sure he was safe for the time being. He slept deeply and for once it was a dreamless sleep, the demons of the past were quiet for once.

CHAPTER 57

Far from abandoning their search, the police were intensifying their efforts. They knew what Carter looked like now, they knew what he was driving, they had a rough idea where he might be going, and that was out of the country. There was now a very tight inspection of all individuals leaving the country, especially in the south east. That meant from London right round to Southampton, the Irish routes and all up the east coast. So far, the search for the van had proved negative, it hadn't appeared on any of the traffic or ANPR cameras. No squad car had picked it up, it had vanished off the face of the earth along with its driver. They could only guess where it had been hidden or disposed of.

Robert was convinced he would try and get across at Dover or Folkestone. It seemed obvious, perhaps too obvious. Knowing Carter was street wise but not necessary the sharpest knife in the draw, helped Robert come to terms with the fact that he had avoided capture so far. It would just be a question of time before he made another mistake or his luck ran out.

All the hotels and B&Bs were being checked out, pubs with rooms, motels, AirBNB, campsites, holiday homes, caravans, there must be tens of thousands of hiding places. And there was the van, they must be able to find that surely, but it could be anywhere in hundreds of square miles of countryside, in a car park, burnt out somewhere, scrapped, any number of endings for the vehicle. But the chances are the vehicle was still in use somewhere. But where?

Robert assumed the conversation about going to Ireland was a red herring, but had made sure that all the Irish crossings had been alerted - just in case, it might had been a deliberate attempt to mislead him and then actually attempt the crossing. Robert returned to his office, sat down and muttered, 'Bastard, I know you are out there, but I can wait.'

CHAPTER 58

So could Carter, he had slept the sleep of the dead, and was only woken by the sound of kids discovering they could use the side of his caravan as a goal. His dishevelled appearance outside put an immediate stop to the football game and he went back inside to rustle up some breakfast, which proved to be a toasted bacon sandwich made with the aid of the microwave, it was as much as he could cope with, as he was still so tired. His brain was not functioning properly and he was confused on how to get onto the continent without being caught.

Leaning against the cushions in the dining area, he dozed off again, his brain awash with half ideas, part plans and incomplete escape routes. Eventually he came too, his brain had finally clicked into gear and he picked up the iPad to see if the escape plan he had dreamt up in his sleep, could be put into action. Go via the Isle of Wight? As it soon proved, you can't, that plan was dropped. Where next? There were direct routes from Portsmouth and Southampton to Dieppe and Caen, no they were bound to be watched. Bournemouth, Weymouth, Plymouth? No, they were all direct routes, they will be watched as well. Fly? Boat? Ferry or private? Something short and sweet so police had little chance of reacting. That would be fly, but not direct.

Continuing the search Carter found he could get from Southampton to Guernsey in 45 minutes at short notice by air from Southampton. All UK, no passports. Dare he risk going to France with his own passport? Changing his ID would be risky and the police would soon cotton on to a stolen passport, but if he made the French shore, he could soon lose himself. It was big country and he knew how to go to ground. There was a ferry from Guernsey to Dialette in France. Dialette? Never heard of it and hopefully neither had anyone else, but there would be customs at both ends, so a proper ID had to be in order.

OK, he needed to steal an ID. A foreign ID, from where? Foreigners coming into the country did so at Dover. How to get to Dover? The van was too obvious and would almost certainly be picked up. A short search revealed there was a bus service right outside the site, even had the times they left. Alright, grab a sandwich and look for a victim.

Sitting on the bus, Carter was lost in thought. If he stole a passport then he would have to move really fast and be on the plane to Guernsey that same day as it would be reported almost instantly. There had to be a plan to make sure it wasn't. Easier said than done, he thought about the options, most of them didn't bode well for the chosen victim.

Arriving in Dover, Carter watched several ferries disgorge their cargo of cars, caravans, lorries and eventually people, who wandered off in the town to catch a coach or train into town. Chances were they would have booked a room to overnight and go in the next day. The ferries arrived all afternoon without Carter finding a suitable victim, but as he was about to give up and go back, he spotted someone who would do very nicely. Same sort of build, same height or near enough, age didn't matter that much, within 10 years or so. You sunshine, thought Carter, will do very nicely.

The proposed victim only had a large back pack with him, which was helpful, it could be grabbed and made off with. Carter watched him from the other side of the road, waited for him to pass and set off to follow. Hopefully he hadn't made plans to leave straight away. Luck was on Carter's side tonight as the victim walked into the Best Western near the marina. The hotel was well known in Dover. It had a brilliant position on the front. A big shopping complex was directly behind and a marina behind that. What Carter liked was it had a decent bar and was open to the public. It would have cameras which would prove a problem later, as it would place him in the hotel at a specific time, but he would have to chance that.

Watching his victim go up to the desk, Carter made a note of the man's name and his room number before asking if there were room available in a fortnight's time and at what price, to avoid suspicion from the clerk. Watching out of the corner of his eye, Carter saw the man head for the bar. Following a few seconds later he watched what he ordered and followed suite. Turning to the man he said, 'Snap' to the other. 'Sorry', was the response, followed by a curious look at Carter.

'Apologies', said Carter, 'It's what we say in this country if there are two things the same. It comes from a children's card game, players take turns in putting a card down and if they are the same, they shout Snap! Anyway Skal!' and he smiled at the newcomer. 'In my country it's Proost', and he clinked glasses with Carter. 'Proost', replied Carter and he smiled. 'Good to see the Dutch like this country still.' That raised a smile and started a conversation with the Dutch man that went on for hours, and eventually an invitation from Carter to join him for dinner which was gratefully accepted.

Carter only left the meal for a short time, on route he managed to obtain a pack of Paracetamol from reception and bottle of Vodka from the bar. The bottle went into the deep pocket of his jacket, he had plans for that later. Returning to the table Carter realised the Dutchman was now far from sober. Carter knew he would make his excuses and leave soon, so he had to be prepared. Paying the bill he said 'The drinks are bloody expensive here, but I'm still thirsty. 'Have you got a room here, because I've got a bottle of Vodka if you've got some mixers in your fridge!' he laughed hoping the thought of a free drink would be tempting enough to get into his room. The Dutchman grinned, 'Staying here for a couple of days, so if you want to say a couple more Proosts, then I am in agreement.

They went up in the lift and the bottle of vodka was produced for inspection. Walking along the corridor, Carter had the bottle ready in his hand, but he was holding it by the neck. As they went into the room Carter swung the bottle with all his might at the back of the unsuspecting head in front of him. The Dutchman crashed to the floor and Carter was utterly amazed he hadn't smashed the bottle in the process. The door was quickly closed to hide the prone body. Propping the Dutchman up against the bed, Carter went to work.

Crushing the Paracetamol up in a glass, he poured in some vodka to dissolve the powder. Pushing the head of the victim back against the bed, Carter managed to open his mouth and pour the mixture in. Getting him to swallow was another matter. Holding his nose, Carter stroked his throat and it worked. The rest of the bottle of Vodka eventually followed. It took the best part of an hour and it was dark when the last of the sprit went down. It was joined by every miniature sprit in the fridge.

Carter was quite sober now, but the Dutchman was having problems breathing and there was a good chance he would not survive the night. It didn't matter, so what, he thought. Grabbing the backpack, he checked it had all the things he needed, passport, wallet, travel documents. That will do nicely, he thought, and he left the Dutchman to rot. The do not disturb sign was attached to the door handle on the way out, and Carter was out of the hotel in minutes. Time was of the essence now, as he had to get back to the van, collect his belongings, and his money to get away. Keep it simple, keep it quick, he thought.

A taxi was hailed to get him back to the camp and the caravan. Once inside, Carter just grabbed his bag that he used at Tracey's house, there wasn't a great deal in it and he just needed to transfer the Dutch documents into his bag. As he felt round the backpack he discovered the bottom was loose. Pulling it away Carter found he was looking at plastic bags filled with white powder. Sticking his finger through one of the bags to check, he realised it was coke. 'Fuck, he was a bloody drugs runner, 'No wonder he was travelling light. He must have had a meet at Dover to hand over the goods. Christ I hope no one thinks I've killed him and stolen them.'

Carter rammed the Dutch clothes back in the backpack. But there was coke everywhere from the open pack. He was badly shaken, he didn't need to get involved in this. He knew he would have to dump the drugs somewhere. Running outside, the powder was tipped out but in his haste enough of it went everywhere with some of it ending up back inside the van.

Everything went in his bag and he decided he would look the part if he rode off on his precious bike, the exercise would do him good and clear his mind.

Inside the hour he was back in Dover, ready for an early departure on the ferry, much simpler this way. Easy man, easy. It would be a long time before he police got lucky, thought Carter and I'll be long gone by then. There was a cafe in town and he went in ordered breakfast. Carter went into the toilet cubical to transfer the documents and sort the bags out. Taking out the wallet he pocketed the cash, and any useful ID he could use. The passport was in there as well, the picture wasn't that brilliant but he could just about get away with passing himself off as the Dutchman, provided they didn't look too closely. Carter was now Aldert Frank. His few clothes were rammed in his case. Ignoring his discomfort at the drugs find, he sat down and ate breakfast slowly, before pushing the bike back along the beach to the hotel bar. Sitting down he ordered a coffee and slipped the Dutch bag, minus the drugs under the table. Now needing to change his appearance, he walked into town and purchased riding gear, a back pack and a helmet. In a bus stop on the front he bundled his clothes and money into the new backpack and left his bag next to the bin there.

Wheeling the bike to the ferry reception, he purchased a single ticket to Calais, went through customs without more than a glance and sat down in the restaurant to await the arrival of the ship in the French port. Before they docked, a change of clothes was needed. Disembarking in his new guise, he was waved through, and he was away, to get lost quickly.

CHAPTER 59

Clearing up in the Dover hotel began in earnest straight after breakfast and the maid ignored the Dutchman's room after seeing the 'Do not disturb' sign, but was slightly suspicious when the sign was still there in the afternoon, and still not turned over at two pm when she finished her shift. She knocked softly but got no reply. She didn't want to use the master key, but reported it to reception instead, who ignored it, guests can lie in, she was told. 'Your problem,' she thought then, and went home.

However, action was eventually forced when the Dutchman had a visitor late in the afternoon. He was told his friend was still in his room, and they couldn't raise him on the internal phone. The visitor was insistent that they contact his friend as he had an important meeting to attend, and eventually the receptionist asked security to open the door and just check if everything was in order.

The security guard quietly opened the door after knocking, looking in sheepishly, at first he could make out a shoe and then a leg. Pushing the door open he could see their man was in, but laying on the floor. It took him a few seconds to realise it was a body on the floor, he definitely wasn't breathing, and by the glazed look in his eyes, he hadn't breathed in some time. A vodka bottle lay close by, and the security guard put two and two together and made five, thinking he had overdone it with the vodka. Radioing down to reception, he reported the situation, and said unfortunately they had a death to deal with.

The police and ambulance were there in minutes and the room sealed off so the authorities could investigate the death. Everyone assumed it was just a careless accident and took their time in the examination. In the meantime, the visitor was quietly asked to stay put and fill in details of who the friend was, and to answer a few questions. He was grilled for a few minutes, but insisted he only knew the victim by an internet enquiry. And was meeting up for the first time to discuss a possible business link up to import entertainment products from Holland. Satisfied the police eventually turned their attention back to the body as it was moved to the ambulance, and without anyone noticing, the 'visitor' quietly slipped away to the car park door. He was already on his mobile as he walked back to his car.

The Dutchman's bag wasn't found until later and was put into lost property at reception. It wasn't until the body was examined later that day, that the police found they had a murder, and not an accident, on their hands, as the victim had a fractured skull and the toxicology results revealed an overdose for good measure. Only then did they take the matter seriously, and descended on the hotel for a second time, but this time with a full forensics team. Everything in the room was bagged up and taken away for examination. The inspector was curious as to why there was no luggage and asked in reception if anyone had seen him come in with a bag. A barman said he had a backpack when he arrived. At the mention of a bag, the receptionist turned around and produced the bag that had been handed in that evening. 'I think this might be what you are looking for.'

It contained nothing but a few clothes which were shaken out on the counter along with a little white powder which was instantly recognised. 'Seems our friend here was doing a little extra work on the side, where's his so called business partner?' But he was nowhere to be seen, and they now knew an opportunity had been lost to break into a drug ring.

The police identified the Dutchman from his credit card payment at reception, but could find no passport or ID. Staff were called, and one by one they added little snippets of information the dead man. The receptionist gave the police an accurate description of the man's arrival and other staff filled in the evening's movements in the bar and restaurant.

Intrigued by the ever clearer picture being painted the inspector asked, 'I presume you have CCTV in the hotel, I'd like to see it so we can identify this third party.' When the tapes were played back, they confirmed Carter had been with Frank most of the evening. 'He looks familiar, sure I've seen his face recently. We will need the tape please.' The sale of the bottle of vodka and request for the Paracetamol from his new friend were all captured on tape, which raised an alarm with the inspector. This proved the death was pre-planned. Clear mugshots of Carter were taken from the tapes and broadcast to other forces to see if he was wanted elsewhere. It wouldn't be until the morning that Jaeger would spot the email with the connection and the manhunt would start all over again. Dover police had to do all the paperwork first before a smile would be put back on her face for the first time in weeks. Although it would be a very big smile.

When the photo of Carter was transmitted to her station, Jaeger couldn't believe her luck and rushed in to Robert's office to say he had been spotted. 'This might be good news and bad new sir. Carter was in Dover yesterday, he has become part of a suspected murder and possible drugs running. There is no sign of him now and it is possible he has taken on the guise of the Dutch victim, as his ID and passport are all missing.'

'Christ, I bet he is already in France,' said Robert. 'Get the name of the Dutch victim see if he boarded either ferry or Eurostar under that name. Quickly, then alert the French police to be aware that Carter is on their patch under one of the two names, and get hold of the investigating officer at Dover ASAP please. Warn the ferry companies and customs I will need CCTV of passengers boarding the ferries this morning. You and I are going to the coast to track him down, Jaeger.'

Inside the hour they were in Dover viewing CCTV footage. It took most of the morning to find Carter. As guessed he had boarded an early morning ferry under the name of Frank which meant they were only searching one ship thank goodness. They searched the tapes for hours before they spotted him in his new disguise, but at least they knew where he was, and what he looked like now. Robert hoped that on a bike he wouldn't get too far ahead of them at least.

The murder enquiry at Dover had managed to track down a taxi, which led to the caravan and van along with a mass of fingerprints and drugs which definitely tied him to the Dutchman. This meant a European Arrest warrant could be issued and the French police could be alerted. Robert thought to himself, OK you are on the run once more, but you made a big mistake killing again, and especially getting involved in drugs, time for a bit of publicity old son.

CHAPTER 60

Carter was on a real high. The getaway proved to be so easy. There were no witnesses, the new ID had got him across to Europe where he knew he could hide much easier than in England. Tracey's money and his own were safe and untraceable, and even better, most of it in his bag. And she was gone, out of the picture for good. Silly cow, did she really think I'd let her go. His ribs still hurt and he rubbed the stab wound as if to justify his actions.

And then there was the pleasure of outsmarting the police to relish as well. Life was good, but he needed to change his appearance again. Sooner or later the police would piece together what had happened, would track him down by CCTV if they ever got their act together, eventually they might manage that. Assuming they would, he had to stay one or more steps ahead of them. The latex suit had to go for the moment and a more ordinary appearance adopted.

Of course he now had the French police to contend with as well, would that be a challenge? Don't presume they wouldn't be efficient, he had to be on his toes and plan well ahead. OK, so I'm in France, he thought, now what? The money wouldn't last for ever, eventually he would need to find work or turn to crime to support his way of life. Neither really appealed to him.

The latter was more attractive but he knew that there was a fair chance he would eventually get caught and the French police carried guns. Even if he was convicted in France there would be an international arrest warrant out for him, and he would be whisked back to England to face life behind bars. Work didn't need to be considered at the moment, but he had to admit it had a few advantages, such as shelter and money. Sitting down at a coffee bar he just thought, that's for later, just enjoy the taste of freedom for now.

CHAPTER 61

Robert summoned Jaeger into his office. 'I've been thinking. Carter thinks he has got away, I know he thinks he has outsmarted us. I'm not sure what the drugs angle is just yet, but it won't help him as the courier is now dead, murdered, and he most certainly had a hand in that. Whatever the courier was carrying has gone, and there is no money or ID either, so we have to assume Carter is carrying them.'

Pausing for a moment, he looked up and smiled, 'We need some hard-hitting publicity to flush him out, and to put a little pressure on him for the French police, and more importantly, the drugs cartel.' Handing her a sheaf of papers he said, 'Have a read through this and tell me what you think.'

Intrigued she started to read the script, and she smiled, 'You sure you can release this? It's pretty detailed and tells Carter exactly how much we know.' The penny dropped and she grinned at Robert over the paper. 'And it points the drugs cartel straight to him as well.'

Robert smiled, 'Exactly. As much as I think the French police will do a great job, Carter isn't really their problem, he's ours, and they will expect us to do most of the leg work. However, I know it's unethical but I feel a little help from the underworld wouldn't go amiss at the moment. I want photos of every guise Carter has taken to date. I am going to release these, along with both identities, full names. I am also going to totally rubbish him, paint him in the darkest terms, a thoughtless psychopathic, and multiple killer that people won't protect under any circumstance. I will also release the drug connection to ensure criminal ears prick up, say that he has double crossed and killed their courier and run off with goods. That should get a few extra pairs of eyes on the continent working. It might get me a bollocking from higher up, sod it. It's worth a try.'

The press release went out that evening. Robert was as good as his word. Labelling Carter as a mass killer who had killed three times, had a trail of sex attacks and was on the run with tens of thousands of pounds of illegal drugs. It was watched with interest in a pub in the East End showing Sky News, a mobile was reached for, and the man relayed the news report to a third party. There was a response from the other end that was met with just a nod from the caller. Finishing his drink, the man went out to his car to drive home where he packed a small case and his passport. Checking his wallet and credit cards were all in place, he strode out to his car and proceeded to Dover. He thought to himself OK, this arsehole has a head start, but he wouldn't be too hard to track down, and I have an awful lot of contacts I can use over there.

Three hours later his car was in France. The mobile was put to good use, a contact was informed and the car sped off. There was a plan to be discussed, informants to be put into action, police to be encouraged to spill a little information. Yes it shouldn't be too long before he was located, the drugs recovered and this scumbag rubbed out, painfully and slowly. Smiling to himself he arrived at his destination and turned into the driveway of a pretty town house on the edge of town, just off the road that led to Boulogne. A case was recovered from the back seat and the man disappeared into the house, eager to track down his prey.

If Robert had known what he had unleashed he might had felt guilty, but he had hardened over the years, and really couldn't care less what happened to Carter now. Robert had no time for low lives dealing in drugs, especially those that dealt in murder along the way. This guy needed bringing to justice, one way or another. He might get lucky and get caught by the police rather than the cartel. We'll see, Karma time.

Robert had gone back to his office after the press release. Feeling happy with himself, he realised he had overstepped the mark somewhat, but he was sure it would produce results, if it didn't, it would give Carter something else to worry about. Tough shit, he was too old to worry, he would be retiring soon, he hoped. There were his own informants to check up on in this country. Feelers were put out in the drugs world by his team, to see if there were any connections in the UK that would help track down the Dutch connection.

Several names were put forward to investigate at a later date, but any information would be passed to the French police first. Although it was his and Jaeger's case, the French would do all the chasing from this point. All he had to do was just make sure the wheels turned, and he oiled them from time to time. Info was shared and the French took it as a matter of pride to make sure Carter was caught. It was almost as if to prove they were better than the English, who had failed to catch this evil master criminal. Robert couldn't care less, his ego could cope with it, he just wanted Carter removed from his life. Why? So he could rest easy then, his guilt cleared for letting him get away in the first place.

CHAPTER 62

Carter was unaware that he was being hunted on three fronts, he knew he had to be clever now though. Here he was in France, that was the easy part, now where would he go? North? Holland, Belgium, Germany? No, he didn't think he would find any work, he didn't know the countries, didn't speak the language, No, it would be better to go south, warmer if nothing else. There was plenty of casual work at this time of year, farmers always appreciated an extra pair of hands, especially if they were cheap and paid in cash, no questions asked. Grape picking? Not a bad idea but he would have to get to the Loire at least. It would be better to get to Bordeaux and the wine areas in the south, plenty of ex-pats, always find a friend, loads of ex-forces retired in the area. Eventually he would like to get to Spain, easy to lose himself amongst the Brits there. But that was all a pipe dream at the moment.

Get out of Calais as soon as possible then, get on the train, go south, the railway line meandered down the coast, that was one option. Considering this way he decided no, if they twigged that he had taken the quickest route out, he could be trapped very easily. No go the most unlikely way. Mounting the bike he peddled off into the old town, it was a good bike and he thought he would make Boulogne easily but he obviously couldn't use the A16, he would have to go by all the back roads. It would double the distance but so what. Pausing for a moment, he almost took the coast road along the cliffs, but that was the obvious alternative, no, just back roads, let's see how many miles could be covered on the bike first, he could always break the journey and go on the train at some point, that would confuse matters and make his journey much more unpredictable.

Boulogne was easily reached by late afternoon and Carter thought he needed to find a place to stay. The French had caught onto the idea of bread and breakfast or chambre d'hôte during the previous decade, an English idea with some merit for once. As farms were taken over by bigger companies, those who didn't want to move to the cities had to find other income, and letting rooms to tourists proved very successful and profitable. Carter was on the lookout for an old tatty chambre where no questions would be asked. It didn't take him too long to find one and he booked in with no formalities after waving a handful of Euros about, that he had changed on the ferry. The bike was propped in the yard, and he was shown his room. They both spoke enough of each other's language to get by. Between Carter and his new host, they worked out that he could purchase a basic meal with wine that evening, and there would be a decent breakfast at the chambre from seven am onwards.

Carter was more than happy with the arrangements and drank as much as possible with his cold meats and bread that evening. He talked a lot more than he should have done due to the drink. Feeling the worse for wear, he finally crashed out just after midnight and slept like a baby knowing he wouldn't be found, he was safe and enjoying life.

In fact it was nearer to eight thirty when he came to, his head hurt, and his eyesight was still blurry from the copious amounts of cheap wine he had consumed the evening before.

The quilt lay crumpled on the floor as a result of a restless night. He couldn't remember dreaming but he felt tired, so there was a good chance memories of the desert had come back to haunt him during the night. But a clean T-shirt was found in the backpack along with some shorts which he hauled on prior to joining his hosts downstairs, in time for a new day.

The strange looks he received from them were explained when they said he had been very noisy that night. Carter thought they meant when drinking the wine, no they replied, in bed, when they thought he had been asleep. Carter tried his best to explain but failed. His basic French was totally inadequate to explain his circumstances. Luckily there was an old French/English dictionary in the bookcase which Carter half explained his past to them with the aid of this, but the couple still viewed him with some suspicion. However, the promised breakfast appeared, continental of course, but the madame of the house also provided him with hard boiled eggs and cold meats which were readily washed down with plenty of black coffee.

Carter wanted to be pleasant so that he could sow a few false leads for anyone following him or hoping to get an insight into his plans. Although he knew where he was going, he made up a very convincing story of some old army friends in Paris he could stay with, then he was hoping to travel down to the Loire for the wine harvest to find casual work there, and then travel back to England for the winter, where he would look at work in the security trade to make use of his army skills.

The old couple took in every word and believed him. In the end they even felt sorry for his plight when he explained he needed this year away to combat his demons. It proved a long, slow explanation, often aided by the dictionary. In the end it was close to eleven when he left them. They waved him off as they watched him cycle away to catch the train to Paris, when he was actually going in the opposite direction to Rouen.

CHAPTER 63

The media picked up on the Carter story with a vengeance. His face was plastered all over the TV and the tabloid end of the market and even made it page seven of both the Mail and Express in the UK. However, English papers tend to find their way on to the continent at least a day later than in the UK, so the chamber landlady didn't spot his face until a visit to the local market later the next day. She bought the paper but could understand little of the background story. It looked serious so she took it home to see if her husband could make any sense of it. An hour later her husband was on the phone to the police who consequently arrived at their house to two cars, all lights flashing.

They took the sighting very seriously, made copious notes before one car departed to the train station at Boulogne to confirm Carter's travel arrangements, whilst the other obtained as much information about Carter's stay as possible. Descriptions of his bike, clothing, destination were all reported back to their office, and an all points alert put out for Carter. No one at Boulogne station remembered seeing Carter the previous day, CCTV was checked and confirmed that he hadn't left from there, so they presumed his whole story about travelling to Paris was false. Was he still travelling by bike? If so, an area of 70km around Boulogne would be cordoned off with random traffic checks.

In fact Carter hadn't bothered cycling as far as Boulogne, he stopped at the local station at Hesdigneul and had caught the train to Abbeville. Once there he looked for an old van again, rather than cycle or use the train everywhere. It gave him a lot more flexibility. Cycling around the town it didn't take him long to find an old battered Citroen van with a stupidly low price tag in the window, which wasn't surprising when he attempted to drive it. If it lasted the week he would be surprised. Haggling over the price eventually got Carter his van, and he set off with the bike jammed in the back, in the general direction of Normandy, a place he had always intended to visit, but he wanted to go via Dieppe. They were both places of invasion, one a disaster, the other a huge success on the whole. As a military man they meant a lot to him to see them first hand. Dieppe was just over seventy km away, about an hour and a half in this crate he thought, if he was lucky.

CHAPTER 64

Jaeger's file from the Met had arrived weeks before but Robert had never had the time or inclination to study it. In the lull whilst he waited for news from the French authorities, he reluctantly opened it and started reading. The first half showed her qualifications, her courses, achievements her progress in the Met and then bang, it all halts with a recommendation for transfer. Intrigued Robert read on but could find no reason for the transfer. Remembering when she arrived, she had just cited personal reasons and was unwilling to discuss it any more. Robert called her into his office to explain more before he decided the role she would be playing in the Carter case.

'Sit down. I've been going through your record from the Met, all very clever, all very fast track and then it all halts and you are transferred. When you came here you said it was for personal reasons – care to elaborate?' 'Not really sir, private reasons, clash of personalities', she replied and actually blushed. 'OK' said Robert. 'I won't probe, I'm not that nosey. I just wanted to know how many languages you spoke and did you fancy a secondment to France, so I had a presence on both sides of the water?' She smiled at that, 'That's rather a silly question to ask, I'd love to go to France and help, if they would have me. And three is the answer, English, French and Dutch.'

They looked at each other for a moment before Jaeger broke the silence. 'You know I was being fast tracked. I was promoted above people with longer service records. There were some nasty accusations about me sleeping around to get promoted.

All untrue.' She stopped, her head dropped and she whispered, 'Except one, a senior ranker came on to me and he was a good looker, and I thought why not. His wife caught us and said she would blow the whole thing up publicly and prove that was exactly why I was being promoted. She knew a lot of the senior Met wives, and was prepared to risk her husband's career in revenge on both of us. At worst he would be retired early with a fat pension and no fuss on health grounds, at worst a scandal and he would be sacked. I did the honourable thing and jumped before I was pushed, and took a transfer, and here I am.'

'And here you will stay, you've been a bloody good officer and I intend to keep you, if you'll stay. We all make mistakes and as far as I'm concerned this goes no further than my office. Now go home, pack, bring your passport and we will sort your expenses, travel and your secondment. Now let's see if we can't get this right, as we need to catch this monster.' Jaeger turned and left, but not before she had smiled at Robert and thanked him.

But Robert however, had another card up his sleeve, the drug cartel connection, he had been quietly working with his own informants and feeding various other departments in the force with information, in the hope they would lead to a breakthrough and arrests that would enable him to tap into the French side of the trade. And it had worked, using his information, a dawn raid in London caught several wanted criminals, and Robert knew all would be involved in his case. Hours spent interviewing behind two way mirrors finally revealed a name and that a hitman was already hunting Carter on French soil. Bloody hell thought Robert, nothing like complicating things.

First things first, research through the databases to identify him and if possible track him across the channel. Then warn Jaeger ASAP, that she wasn't alone in her hunt.

CHAPTER 65

The hitman, aka Joe Marche was an old school criminal, if you took something that wasn't yours, you paid for it, one way or another. Carter had screwed up an operation that had run smoothly for the best part of a year. It was an operation Joe had personally helped organise, and he was annoyed that some idiot had interrupted it. Luckily for the cartel no money had been lost from their end but a considerable amount of drugs had been, and the Dutch connection had doubts about the claims that an outsider had disrupted the flow, and taken the consignment. Either way he needed to find the truth, recover the drugs, or make sure that whoever had interfered in their business, wouldn't do it again, ever.

Marche was a man of connections, he had insiders in many gangs and police forces that could be bribed, blackmailed or simply worked for him. They kept him informed of police operations, imminent raids and when things were getting too hot to handle. The French police were no different, his contacts had followed up the story of Carter going to Paris and he realised it was a red herring. Marche needed to visit the old couple's lodging house and get some more information. From police contacts he already had their address and paid them a visit soon after the police had.

Unfortunately arriving in an English registered car immediately raised their suspicions and Marche had to explain he was a special investigator working with English police on drugs cases. Fabricating a story that he wasn't so much concerned with catching Carter, that was the job of the police, but investigating how he could disrupt the drug barons who were polluting modern society and killing youngsters across Europe. Marche wanted to them to think hard about everything he had said that evening, anything at all. They said he was looking to work on the farms, to go south eventually and pick grapes, be a handyman and fit into the local community. Marche thanked them profusely and left them thinking they had helped society no end.

Marche was confused at why the French police hadn't tracked Carter at the railway and it was only when he was on the way to Boulogne that he realised there were so many local stations on the line. A short investigation and a photo of Carter shown around along with a description of the bike yielded a result and one of the staff said he had bought a ticket to Abbeville. Marche smiled, he was one step ahead of the police now. It was going to be guesswork from Abbeville. Carter was ex-army which meant he would regard himself as logical, Marche just regarded him as conditioned, he would work to a set of parameters that would seem imaginative to him but straightforward to anybody else.

If he had mentioned fruit picking then the choice was Normandy to the west and southwest. He would stay off the main roads which meant travelling along the coast. If that was the case there would be a good chance he would be unable to resist the D Day landing sites or any of the famous battle scenes. Marche had his direction, his agenda and it was simply a case of tracking down his prey. Dieppe was closer and Mache thought there was a good chance he would visit there first. Worth a detour at least.

Jaeger wasn't finding life quite so smooth, having been assured she would be integrated into the enquiry to hunt down

Carter, she found she was simply surplus to requirements, a passenger to the main enquiry. After protests, the French police provided her with a car and driver, provided she radio in anything that might help with the main enquiry. She already knew that Carter had not used the main station at Boulogne and mused at how he was moving about. The French enquiries had just logged the interview with the B&B, and she thought that would be a good place to start. The couple were feeling harassed when Jaeger started her interview. They explained they given all the facts to the police and then the special investigator from England and now Jaeger. Special investigator? Who the hell was that? she thought.

When she returned to the car the driver informed her that they must return to HQ as there was important information from England for her, concerning Carter. They were back in the office within half an hour, where a dossier had been emailed across with a photo of Marche, his description, photo, MO, car, channel crossing time and the fact that he was a bloody dangerous criminal to deal with. Jaeger passed the information on to the French investigators and then added her dealings with the couple earlier in the day. At least she knew who the special investigator was.

This put a whole new light on the proceedings and a general meeting was called to discuss strategy. The fact that there was a professional criminal hunting Carter meant they had to catch him as well as Carter now. Jaeger produced her information and the traffic department managed to track his car from Calais to Boulogne and then down to Abbeville and then on to Dieppe where he appears to have stopped for the moment. Jaeger suddenly realised that not only was Marche on the hunt but he had information that she didn't possess, what the hell could it be?

'Quick', she shouted, 'I know what he is looking for, can you get the Dieppe police to track Marche's car and arrest him if possible. Carter doesn't realise we are tracking him, and certainly doesn't realise he has Marche on his tail. Carter is an ex-military man, he is going sight-seeing the great battles of WW2 because he doesn't think he is in any danger, and has all the time in the world.'

Marche was indeed in Dieppe and mingling with the locals and tourists. He knew what Carter looked like, and he thought he had a good chance of finding him in the town or on one of the vantage points overlooking the town and sea approaches. Marche knew it was a long way round of finding someone but he had other options including searching hotels, camp sites and the like, later in the day, he could quietly dispose of his quarry then. Jaeger was on route to Dieppe, she had radioed ahead and the local police were searching for Marche's car. It would take several hours for her to catch up, and she hoped they would still be in time. Having already spent several hours on a fruitless search, Marche was beginning his second sweep of the town when he spotted Carter going into the tourist office. Pure good timing, he didn't want a approach him in such a public place, but waited for him a short distance away, where he could observe without being noticed.

Marche was also being hunted, and the local police had little difficulty in finding the expensive English registered car. They were lying in wait discretely for Marche to return. This was all being relayed to Jaeger who was now entering the town. As she approached Dieppe, so Marche started his approach to Carter as he left the office. It took him about fifty yards to position himself behind him, and then gently push a gun into his back.

'Mr Carter, I have some friends back in London who would like to have a word with you about a small matter of a murdered courier, and a large consignment of drugs that have gone missing. I won't shoot you here, unless you make life difficult, but my car is very close by, and I think it would be helpful if you discussed matters there.' Carter had little option but to obey, he realised he knew he could almost certainly overpower the gunman, he'd had enough training in the army in that subject. It would be unlikely he would be shot in a public place, so the car park would be the obvious place to make a break for it, and if possible ram that gun down this guy's throat and find out what was going on. There was no point in panicking, be logical, his time would come, and he was sure he could overpower this thug.

Marche was thinking much the same, he knew Carter would be extremely well trained, and was equally dangerous, and he concentrated on making sure he didn't make any untoward moves. Neither of them spotted the police slowly advancing towards them in the car park. Carter saw the uniforms first and said nothing, he realised the situation they were about to walk into, and was already summing up the situation to his advantage. He was thinking about how he could turn things on their head. Had they clocked him or the hit man? Who was the target? Who had they cottoned on to? Marche was more intent in getting Carter in to the car, finding the drugs and then killing him as compensation for screwing up his operation. He had totally failed to spot the advancing police.

As they approached the car and Carter reached for the

car handle, a voice shouted, 'Put your hands up, drop your weapons, and get on your knees. The instructions were repeated in French. Marche realised they were aimed at him, and he instinctly ducked. Carter saw his chance and rolled into Marche as he ducked. Marche bounced off the car and lost his gun in the process. They both scrambled for it with Marche winning, he half crouched as he turned to take aim at Carter, it was enough of a target for one of the French police to realise Marche was armed and about to shoot. A single shot into Marche's back killed him instantly. Carter couldn't believe his luck, both Marche and the gun fell at his feet. Rolling backwards with the gun, he couldn't be seen by the police and he crawled as fast as he could past several cars to get out of their line of fire. By now he was on the edge of the car park, he slowly stood up behind a camper van. Peeking around the edge of the van he could see the police slowly advance on Marche's body. They were obviously expecting to find him on the floor as well. Carter took his chance and rolled across the park wall and jumped over it. There was a shout as he was instantly seen, but by then he was heading into the crowds that were watching from the shops. Carter knew the police wouldn't fire at him because of all the tourists. Bowling into the first shop and pushing everyone out of the way, he found himself in the stock room with no way out. Above his head and well out of reach was a small window. Throwing everything he could reach into a pile, he managed to clamber up to the window. It didn't open, it was fixed.

'Bugger, it would be,' he raised the gun and smashed it with the butt, knocking out as much of the glass as he could. There were shouts behind him in the shop as the police decided they needed to corner Carter quickly. As he turned, he saw a helmeted head come round the door and a gun being raised. Carter had no option but to fire first if he was to escape. The noise was deafening in the confined space and Carter saw his bullet hit the wall just beside the policeman's face, he ducked back into the hallway for his own safety. It gave Carter just enough time to escape.

There were shouts in French behind him as he jumped up and threw himself through the hole, broken glass in the frame cut him in several places as he fell through. There was no one behind the row of shops, as it opened in to a loading bay car park. All too bloody open for his liking, a perfect killing ground, hide man, quickly, he thought. There was an open loading bay at the end of the row and he ran for it before he could be seen. As he went to jump up he spotted a young boy stacking boxes that had been delivered earlier. Carter raised the gun at the boy, who dropped the box in fright. As he ran up the steps he put his finger to his lips as if to say, keep quiet. The boy just backed away and pressed himself against the wall terrified. Carter pulled the shutter down and bolted it so it couldn't be opened from outside. Not a moment too soon.

The police realising that it was too dangerous to follow through the window had flooded into the loading area and were now searching every nook and cranny. Carter grabbed the boy and pushed him to the front of the shop. Looking out he could see the police appeared to have abandoned the car park except for one unit which was manned by one policeman and a rather elegant woman that Carter had seen the night they had raided his flat in the UK. She would recognise him for sure, so he needed to stay hidden for a while. The shop owner eventually came through to be confronted by Carter holding a gun to the boy's head.

'Shut the shop, put a closed sign on the door and come back here, or I will kill the boy' said Carter. 'Don't make any signs to anyone outside, don't pull down the shutters, just do it quietly.'

The man nodded, he couldn't risk this madman hurting him or his son. He did as he was told and came back to comfort his son who was in tears. All three hid in the stockroom for well over two hours. Carter found racks of tape in the back room and taped them together back to back with numerous wraps. A single strip was taped over their mouths to ensure there was no cry for help. Jaeger was still stomping around the car park. An ambulance had collected Marche's body and the majority of police cars had been moved away from the scene. The shops had started to close up now and put their roller shutters down. The crowds had thought it too dangerous to stay, and observe the chase, and had either gone of their own accord or been cleared by the police. Carter was still armed and decided to bluff it out. Taking the shop owners coat and a hat from the shop, he walked out, turned around as if to lock the door and proceeded to wind down the shutters. The car park was full still as people hadn't been able to collect their cars. Carter's van was still at the end of the park and Marche's was next to the police car. Carter took his time locking up and started to walk away from the car park, he was sure if he went down enough side streets he would eventually come back to his end of the car park and retrieve his vehicle and bike.

Wandering off slowly he waved to a couple of people in greeting, who in turn wondered if he were some old friend they had forgotten about. There was a small supermarket he discovered on his travels and he bought some first aid products and a bottle of whisky, along with some snacks he could eat in the van. Camping would be the preferred option tonight, but not too far away. When he finally got back to the car park, a lot of the vehicles had gone, and there was only the one police car as far as he could see. It was taking a chance to drive off but there were several exits, so he waited until the English policewoman was looking the other way, and drove off.

Jaeger was on the phone to her boss to explain that somehow Carter had escaped yet again and she had no idea where he would go. She said her only guess would be the D day landing beaches after all he had stopped at Dieppe as she had guessed. The police had said she could continue her search but they couldn't spare a car and driver. So she was going to book into a hotel for the night, take Marche's car as he wouldn't have any further use for it, and to avoid any extra expenses. Robert said that wasn't really in the rule book, but you could claim the car was impounded as evidence.

She had all of Marche's possessions including his car keys from an earlier search of the body. She started the car and went in search of the nicest looking hotel in Dieppe to assess the day's events, formulate a plan of action, and get a good night's sleep in the bargain.

Carter was just outside town in a farm campsite in a small two man tent, eating sandwiches and dressing the wounds caused by the cut glass from the window. Feeling sorry for himself. He wondered how the hell the gunman had found him, and if they would send anyone else. At least he wouldn't have to look out for the flash black Jag now. The tent had been pitched in a corner, away from others on the site as, he had a feeling his nemesis might well pay him a visit tonight. The whiskey bottle was opened and a generous portion disappeared down Carter's throat to help him sleep and ease his pain.

Early the next morning he was woken by a hand shaking his foot. It was a shock and he jumped not expecting anyone to come close to his tent. 'Sorry mate, didn't mean to wake you, but you seemed in a bit of a state, just checking to see if you were OK. I heard screams.' 'It's OK,' replied Carter, Just nightmares, I'm OK.' 'No shit man, that was some nightmare,' said the Australian voice. Carter could now see a rather lovely female face to go with the voice and he smiled, 'No honestly, I'm OK, just tired after that dream. Don't worry I'm OK.' She now had her face inside the tent, 'The hell you are, there is blood everywhere, what have you done to yourself? Here let me see I'm a nurse.'

Carter looked down and saw he was indeed covered in blood from his flight through the window. Thinking hard he said 'Oh that was an argument in town and I got pushed into one of those fish tanks you see in all the restaurants. I'm afraid I had to leg it – I didn't realise I'd cut myself. How did you know I was English? She smiled again, 'You scream in English so I made that assumption. Let me clean this up please, looks nasty. I'm Susan by the way, just arrived this morning.' Carter didn't protest, 'There is some first aid stuff in the bag behind you that might be of use.' She gently crawled into the tent and sorted Carter in minutes. None of the wounds were serious, they just seemed to bleed a lot, they were more superficial than anything he was pleased to hear. Carter was cleaned up easily and found at the end of the session, he was being embraced. Bugger, thought Carter my luck might just be in for once.

CHAPTER 66

Jaeger didn't quite get the sleep she thought she would get. There were emails all through the night to help her enquiries. The first one concerned the shop where Carter had held the owner and his son captive. When they didn't return home and the wife heard about the shooting she feared the worse, and informed the police while she made her way to the shop. Although shaken, both victims were able to give a good description of Carter even down to the stolen hat and coat. Jaeger then seconded all the CCTV of the car park and shops during the night. Finally she found Carter in the disguise as described by the shop keeper. She watched him walk away from the shop into town and an hour later walk back and drive off.

The van was too far away from a camera to pick up the registration but at least she knew what she was looking for, a white 2CV van. God, the French must have made millions of these bloody horrible vehicles. There were fewer on the road nowadays as tastes have changed and most have rusted away, but there were plenty still about. Jaeger put out an alert to stop and search any such vans in both the Dieppe and Caen areas for next few days. It was then a logistical exercise to see how Carter would get from one place to the other, provided they had out guessed him, and the D Day landing beaches were still his destination. Jaeger was convinced they were.

OK, Carter has one big disadvantage here, she thought, the Seine. There was no way he would risk the toll at Honfleur or the bridge at Tancarville as they were easy to seal off. That left him Rouen or Rives. Either one could be monitored, and he would have to come south to go through Caen, which was virtually the only way to the beaches. She had a feeling that he would avoid the motorways as they were too easy to close off with no way of escape except on foot. This was making a lot of assumptions and Jaeger had a feeling Carter wouldn't show for several days, time to let things cool down so he could slip in unnoticed. Once past Caen, the countryside was criss-crossed with small country roads that led to the beaches that were spread over 15 miles of the Normandy coast.

She had done all she could for now, grab a breakfast and try a few of the routes, and basically lay in wait for him. She had the other problem to solve, where was he staying? All the hotels and guest houses were meant to fill in questionnaires as to occupancy, but if it was a cash transaction, these weren't always completed. The French don't like paying income tax any more than the rest of the world. Every town had a camp site and there were caravan sites that took in passing trade as well. The list was endless. It was alright to ask the local police to check, but it was a little short of impossible.

She had an inkling that Carter would still keep to his agenda, but it was a long shot and an awfully large area to cover. After breakfast she headed for Bayeux, down what she thought were logical but obscure routes, the Jaguar ate up the miles in pure comfort. Must put in for one of these when I get back, bloody nice motor, she thought. She arrived at 'Gold' beach long before Carter ever would. She drove the full length of the landing sites before it dawned on her just what a colossal task policing the area would be. Let's hope the Gods smile on me soon, I could do with a bit of luck.

CHAPTER 67

Carter was fast asleep, the previous day had taken it out of him. Amazingly he had met up with this stunning nurse who had sorted him and then made herself at home in his tent. It was bigger than hers, but she had better sleeping bags and they were swapped for Carter's which would be washed out in the morning. Although he was snuggled up, it didn't stop his dreams of the dessert returning and he thrashed about in the tent during the night. Suddenly he was restrained and woken by Susan. 'It's OK, I'm here now, calm down, breathe slowly. Want to talk this through now?'

Carter knew it would be useless, it had been tried so many times, but he thought it he better to explain what had happened as she would have an idea what he was going through now. 'Obvious PTSD, has no one done anything about this?' she said. 'Nothing they could do about it' he replied 'When I didn't respond, I just got removed from service and dismissed as incurable. Not their problem any more'. 'That's bloody stupid and not right at all. Have to sort this out.' And she cuddled up to him.

A hand went down his side and started to gently rub his hip, it started to move across to his groin and he placed his hand on hers.

'That's another part of the problem, not sure you'll get much response there, haven't been able to react for months and that has led to all sorts of personal problems that have left me impotent', he said. 'Don't believe that for a moment,' Susan whispered in his ear. 'Perhaps I could start the treatment early' and her hand moved further across his body. 'My, you are a big boy,' she giggled as began stroking him with one hand and fondling his balls with the other hand.

Much to his amazement he began to stiffen and soon Susan was holding an erect penis, she continued rubbing to make sure the erection maintained, then leant across and began to suck him. It was a pleasure Carter hadn't known for a very long time. She was getting faster and Carter knew he would come quickly if she continued, and he placed his hand on her lips to slow her down. She laughed and withdrew, 'See you've been getting the wrong sort of treatment.'

Carter reached across and tweaked her nipples, taking one into his mouth, as he did so his hand reached down, past her pubic hair to find her very wet. His fingers went straight inside and then started to rub her clitoris. She moaned and started to writhe with every stroke. She moved towards him and then on top of him. Pushing his hand aside she guided him inside her and slid his full length into her body. They made love for close on fifteen minutes, she climaxed several times but moved slowly enough so that Carter retained his erection without coming. It was a huge release for Carter. Never had he experienced sex like that before. Susan collapsed on top of him and waited until he became flaccid before moving away.

'See, I am a bloody good nurse, and I know how to treat my patients. We will have another session shortly, when you are up to it,' with that she grabbed his penis and gently began to stoke it again. It had the desired effect and for once, Carter knew he would sleep well, and a dreamless sleep for once. Not that he was going to get much sleep at this rate.

The dreams were always going to be there, but tonight they were buried deep. Carter was exhausted, but other memories circulated around in his head. The sex attacks, the Muslim woman in Chatham, the girl who upset him whilst he was cycling, she set this all off, and Tracey. Oh yes, Tracey, but she deserved everything she got, he smiled in his sleep remembering her imprisonment, her demise on the bridge. And then there was the escape and that stupid Dutchman, bloody drug runner, he deserved to die. They all got mixed up and confused in the end, and his mind just ignored them as he was so tired. The soldier in the APV would wait for another troubled night, he had all the time in the world.

CHAPTER 68

Jaeger was not going to get much rest, she had been busy making sure the press got the right angle on her hunt, she had made herself available during the evening for press interviews and gave several papers he full inside story on the shooting and Carter's history in the UK, the three murders, the series of sex attacks and the drugs link up to date. The fact that he had escaped to France bringing his violence with him, that had led to the death of one of the drug's gang in Dieppe and the kidnapping of the shopkeeper and his son at gunpoint was not ignored. She painted him as a dangerous psychopath who would stop at nothing to escape from justice, including murder. She asked the public to be on the lookout or the 2CV van, although she knew that was a worthless request, however she did ask them to keep an eye out for the racing bike.

There were photos of Carter past and present that were distributed, and the end result was that Carter made the headline news both in France and England. There was extensive TV coverage in both countries, and Jaeger was also now well known in both countries. She said nothing about him visiting the D Day sites theory, as she hoped to catch him by surprise there. All this was relayed back to Robert who felt the net must be closing in on Carter, he had been so incredibly lucky to escape so far, it was only a matter of time now, surely. He would have dearly loved to have been in France, swapping places with Jaeger, who was heading up the case, basking in the limelight, taking the credit, and then when Carter was caught, moving on, being fast tracked once more, whilst in reality he just looked forward to an empty retirement.

His mother wouldn't last for ever and then life really wouldn't have much direction for him. There was no family, no sons or daughters to carry on the family name, he didn't even have a hobby or passion in life he could look forward to. It seemed he had handed over the reins far too early. Robert so wanted to go out in a blaze of glory, but it wasn't going to happen was it. Putting the phone down after a long conversation with Jaeger, discussing their battle plans and strategies, Robert felt tired, whilst Jaeger sounded on top of the world.

In Bayeux, Jaeger knew she was winning the battle, Carter couldn't escape for ever. At the moment he hadn't resurfaced but Jaeger knew it would be a waiting game, with the odds stacked on her side. She was in position and she was waiting to apply the coup de grace when the opportunity presented itself.

There were no doubts in her mind it would lead to her career taking off again, and nothing this time, could happen to stop that. All the leg work had been done by her, it was her case and the credit would be hers. She felt sorry for Robert, he had been a good boss and given her the chance to crack this case, but he was old and would be left behind again, stuck in that bloody horrible office in a dead end job, awaiting his pension. Poor sod, but that's not my problem, Carter is. She gathered her notes and headed for another night in a hotel at the government's expense. Funny how things turn out some times, with her career seemingly to have gone full circle again.

Robert was doing much the same thing, he gave his mother his mandatory phone call to make sure she was OK and didn't need anything. His mother was fine but wanted to know all about the Carter case. Eventually Robert managed to get her off the phone and went home to his cold unwelcoming house. Sod this for a game of soldiers, he thought to himself as he turned the key in the front door to his home. There must be more to life than this. Dumping everything by the door, he made himself a sandwich from anything he could find in the fridge, poured himself a stiff drink as compensation, and fell asleep in front of the TV, as usual. It seemed pointless to get excited about a case he had no control over.

CHAPTER 69

Carter had a problem, he couldn't understand how the drugs shooter had found him, nor could he comprehend how the police had found both of them after that. What sort of clue had he left behind? How had they both out guessed him? It made no sense at the moment. Desperately thinking back, he started to reconstruct his movements to find where he gone wrong. The Dutchman must have been the start, he must have been identified with him somehow. Stupid sod! His face had to be all over the hotel CCTV. OK so they know who I am, they know who's identity I have taken. Damn, the old couple in the B&B would have identified him if there was any publicity. What the hell did I say to them? I was so pleased with myself that I got a bit pissed and gobbed off. Did I say where I was going? Must have. Idiot.

Susan rolled over next to him and gave him a hug whilst still asleep. Grinning to himself, he was distracted for a moment, nice one son, he thought, you were at fault, you left a trail a mile wide. You're an army man, why are you heading this way? To see the war sites. So bloody obvious. Couldn't resist Dieppe could you? Well the D Day stuff will have to wait, do it another day, because you are making it all too easy for them.

I remember saying I was going apple picking, that puts me squarely in Normandy, so the beaches are well and truly out. The Loire perhaps, do a bit of grape picking. Nowhere too big, he remembered visiting Amboise long ago when he was on NATO manoeuvres, going to the castle and being impressed with the Da Vinci exhibits. Remember he was very impressed with their local wine Vouvey, especially the sparkling variety which they didn't export. As good as Champagne he was told, but a lot cheaper and more powerful. The later was all he was interested in, and when he found it was less than a fiver, he became a fan of it. That was a good place to start then. Throw them off his trail. Stay away from the beaches and head south. Don't let them get the drop on you, don't do the obvious, think man, for once, throw them off your trail.

The trouble now was he was wide awake, the sky was lightening, so it was about 4am, he gently rolled over and closed his eyes and tried to sleep, but the dreams were there. 'Screwed it up again, didn't you?' the voice sounded off in his head. 'You are so bloody stupid, you didn't just kill me, you've been on a real killing spree haven't you?' The dead guardsman and Carter were back in the APV and he was speaking to Carter through that shattered face. Drops of blood fell on Carter as he spoke, but Carter couldn't move. 'So what are you going to do now? The police are hunting you down, it will only be a matter of time before you are caught. And you, the criminal mastermind, have only been on the run for a couple of days.' The soldier laughed at Carter before disintegrating, covering him in blood and brains.

'Bloody hell man, were you ever dreaming. What the hell sparked that dream off?' said Susan. You were screaming the place down. What's the matter?' Carter was sitting up, he was wringing wet with sweat. His ghost had gone, but everything he had said to him stuck in his brain. Carter knew he wasn't clever, he would get caught somewhere down the line, and he would get put behind bars for the rest of his life. A free spirit they called him, he wouldn't be able to cope with a life sentence, locked away forever. Struggling to get out of the tent, he stood outside naked, breathing heavily. The cold air cooling him quickly. Must get away, lose himself again. A hand grabbed his ankle. 'Oi, come back for some treatment please, I'll kiss it better.'

CHAPTER 70

Jaeger had spread a wide net to catch Carter, time to start pulling it in. She personally manned the route along the D Day beaches, stopping every now and then to check the skyline for Carter's van. Convinced he was unable to resist visiting, she was in danger of not pursuing other clues. All of the hotels, B&Bs and campsites around Caen, Bayeux, Saint-Lo and Honfleur were regularly checked, rechecked and checked again - nothing. It was hard to understand, where the hell was he? Where was he hiding. Where was that bloody silly car?

She felt like scaling the search down when nothing of Carter was reported, but she knew he was out there, she felt it. OK, now rethink what he would do, think like him, not a policeman. If he isn't here, where is Carter? Back to the last sighting at Dieppe. Where had he gone from there? Jesus, that's it! He's still there, the very thing he pulled on us at Tracey's house, he hasn't moved at all. Cheeky bastard. Pulling over she radioed her thoughts back to HQ, where they were taken seriously and a promise of a new search was made. Turning the Jaguar around she headed back down the lonely coast road towards Caen, then Le Harve and then back to Dieppe to start again. It was nightfall before she got back, it was a long drive, the best part or seventy miles with toll roads just to be difficult and slow you down further. Traffic was heavy, especially at Honfleur, which just made the journey tiring. Although a new plan had been agreed, there had been no time to implement it that evening, it would be action stations the next morning. It was frustrating for Jaeger and she poured out that frustration to Robert during the evening. She could almost hear him nodding at the other end. She sighed loud enough for him to hear it down the phone. 'Think you're right, do it,' was all she got from Robert before he put the phone down.

CHAPTER 71

Carter had actually moved from Dieppe, not far, but in the opposite direction to the D Day beaches. They would have to wait, he felt there was a definite danger there, if the shooter and the police had out guessed him at Dieppe, then they would assume he was still heading for the landing beaches. Not now. New plan, he explained to Susan, he had changed his mind and thought she wouldn't want to see old battle sites. Susan understood and was actually relieved. But she didn't want to be far from the sea. To placate her, they went along the coast and pulled up near Le Treport, about 10 miles to the east, where there was a huge beach.

It wasn't long before they ended up in the surf, after finding a parking place in the dunes. They both started off with costumes, but she was intent in losing hers, and with a smile it came off in seconds. She grabbed it with one hand and ran her hands down his front, then down inside his trunks and started to fondle him. She kissed him on the mouth and then started to kiss him on his chest and stomach. Carter was definitely stirring now and he was very erect when she pulled down his trunks and took him in her mouth. Carter was in heaven and placed his hands on her shoulders. She frequently disappeared under the waves as she sucked him. The evil side of Carter came to the fore and he imagined holding her under the water, drowning her, making it look like an accident, letting the body float in with the tide days later. Another drunk tourist who was out of their depth. Another witness gone from his life.

The red mist cleared, his mind came back into focus and he simply massaged her hair while she made him climax. She kissed him again while he started to stroke her. She moved slowly against him as his fingers entered her and she soon groaned as he brought her to a climax as well. After their adventure in the surf, they dried off and got back in the van to look for somewhere to pitch up for the night. They ended up camping on a farm where they were welcomed after spending a few Euros on eggs. Carter asked if they could pitch the tent there to save looking for an official campsite. After a few more Euros were spent on food and a small 'fee' they were found a spot to sleep for the night.

A couple of bottles of local cider were purchased and they settled down for the evening. But Carter had another restless night and was exhausted the next morning. Susan understood and left him dozing in the tent, whilst she walked into town. She wanted to bring back some hot croissants, and if she was lucky, find a decent coffee. The shops were opening up as she reached the outskirts of town, the bakers always one of the first, and she ordered up breakfast. A little cafe was putting out ashtrays on the tables outside to prove it was open, and she went over for a grande cafe au lait. The newsagents next door had English papers on show, they would be a day old at least, but she bought one anyway. It remained rolled up on the table whilst she drank the wonderful coffee. She never got round to reading the paper but took it, along with the croissants, back to the farm.

Carter was still asleep in the tent and she him hit with the rolled up newspaper before waving the hot croissants under his nose. Carter stirred, pushed the paper aside, and grabbed breakfast off of her. The paper remained at the back of the tent while they thought about what to do with the rest of the day. Again they ended up on the beach before heading back to the farm and an early night. They sat consuming the eggs and all the local delights the farmer's wife could find. Susan packed up the backpacks ready for the morning, but more to make a bit of space in the tent. Carter seemed so tired still, and fell asleep almost instantly, much to Susan's disappointment and annoyance.

She wasn't ready for sleep and gave him a sharp prod, but he was already in deep sleep and she sat up in the tent thinking what to do, as it was still light. Grabbing the paper in frustration, she wacked his bare arse in the hope he would join her, but he barely stirred. She threw it out of the tent in annoyance where it fluttered in the breeze. It started to flap around in the wind and she knew she would have to gather it up, to stop it annoying her. As she picked the paper up, Carter's face appeared on just about every page, she couldn't believe it, why was he in the papers? She read the articles in disbelief, murders, sex attacks, drug running, Christ what had she got herself into? Susan panicked, it was obvious she was in danger, huge danger. Could she get away without waking him? Le Trepot wasn't far away, she could get there quickly. It wasn't very big, did it have a police station even? It was no good getting into town and finding out there was no one to help her, but she had to take the chance, she had to get away.

The newspaper was strewn everywhere now, she grabbed a page so she could easily explain to the police who she was running from. Her backpack was outside the tent but she dare not take it, it would slow her down. Her T-shirt and shorts were within easy reach and were quietly slid on, her shoes were picked up and carried with her to avoid any noise. The country road into town was fairly poor quality and had a lot of loose material on the surface, not exactly ideal for walking on in the dark, but she had to get away.

Not that she had any intention of walking. She started out walking but that became a trot and soon she was running in blind panic. There was a chance Carter would wake at any time, especially if he had that nightmare and he could use the van to hunt her down. It took her about fifteen minutes to reach the town, but it was in complete darkness and she panicked again as she looked around at the complete desolation. She was shivering with fright after reading the newspaper report, because she now realised just what he was capable of, and she wasn't sure how she hadn't become one of his victims. The man was truly possessed.

The train station was deserted and locked up and she couldn't see a gendarme, or for that matter, any living soul on the street. There had to be a bar, anything that was still open, they would help her. She listened carefully, music, and down a side street there was indeed a bar, and every head turned towards her as she burst in. 'Aide moi,' she screamed, 'aide moi'. She pulled out the newspaper and repeatedly pointed at the photo of Carter and tried to explain he was only a few kilometres down the road. Finally someone put her story together and a gendarme was quickly summoned arriving a few minutes later.

Sitting Susan down with a large brandy, the gendarme managed to get the gist of the story out of her. Once he had established what had happened, and that an infamous criminal was hiding just down the road, he immediately radioed in for support. Alarm bells went off at police HQ, and because Jaeger was on the support list, she was one of the first to get the call to say that Carter had been spotted, and he was right on her doorstep, just as she thought. She was dressed and out of the door in minutes. She already had the location of the bar from the report and arrived long before any police back up.

Jaeger had the farm location out of the girl in seconds, and grabbed the gendarme to help arrest Carter now. He protested that they must wait for reinforcements, but she was determined that speed was of the essence, and she knew he would escape again if they didn't move quickly. And she so wanted the glory of the arrest, it would help her career no end, she could see the headlines now. Mass murderer arrested by lone police heroine. Leaving Susan behind in the bar to explain what had happened, and where they had gone, Jaeger and the gendarme jumped into the Jaguar, and sped off to the farm, back down the country road, the wheels spinning on the loose gravel.

Back at the farm Carter had indeed woken from his dreams, he was still groggy after his encounters from his desert nightmare, to then fail to find an expected warm body to comfort him, it left him feeling uneasy. Something fluttered into his eyesight as he sat in the tent entrance, the paper she had bought earlier and not read. As he picked it up, he then saw the newspaper headline, headlines about him, they hit him in the face, she must have fled after reading this. Bugger, get in the van and go - now. You have been rumbled, and she has gone, but be bloody quick, you need to go.

Carter wasn't to know that Susan had already alerted the police and Jaeger was just moments away, determined to capture him. However, the Jaguar wasn't the quietest of cars when pushed, and Carter heard it coming as he prepared to pack and escape. When he looked out of the tent flap, he saw the dreaded black Jaguar screech through the farm gates, and he thought the drugs cartel had caught up with him again. It couldn't be the police, there were no blue lights. The car skidded to a halt just a few yards away from the tent and illuminated Carter in its powerful headlights, he felt like a startled rabbit but at least he could react. But the car door flew open, and Jaeger threw herself out of the car straight at him.

'Give yourself up Carter....' That was the last thing she uttered as Carter had already reached into his bag and produced the gun taken in the fight at Dieppe. He thought she must be armed and instinctly fired to make sure he got the first shot in. Hitting her square in the chest, she collapsed in front of him. Shots were now being fired back at him by the gendarme, who had also bailed out of the car, but was now sheltering behind a stone wall for his own safety.

Carter was faster and already out of the tent and running to the van, he returned fire, not at the gendarme, but at the Jaguar to immobilise it. Judging by the loud bang and subsequent hiss, he managed to hit one of the tyres. Sprinting to get away from car's headlights, he made it to his van and roared off down the lane knowing he couldn't be pursued. Everything he needed was already packed in the van, the tent would be abandoned along with Susan, wherever she was - sad bitch. Carter had no real thoughts for her or Jaeger who lay still on the damp grass, her white blouse slowly turning red as her life seeped away. Unable to move, she lay on her back looking up at the stars, thinking how beautiful they looked, it was the last thing she saw. Her eyes closed as she took her final breath feeling no pain as she died.

The gendarme called out, but there was no reply, the man had got away, he could safely emerge from behind the wall. It was only then that he saw his companion, dead, the result of the gunfight he had so ineffectual in. A brief, frantic radio message back to HQ, resulted in a belated police backup and a few minutes later, an ambulance for her assistance, but far too late. He had his story all worked out, he would be the hero in a fire fight, he had tried to save her but the English criminal was far too clever for them, ambushing them in the dark, She wasn't careful and he thought she had warned Carter by her reckless approach. He had been put in danger by her but he had managed to fire back and he might have wounded Carter but he wasn't sure. It was bad luck the car had been damaged, otherwise he would have pursued and caught him. He was in the clear, his story stacked up. A hero in the making, he would have his photo in the papers and admired by his comrades.

The Jaguar was taken away by low loader, the ambulance departed with the body, the cars dispersed leaving an empty field. Above, a solitary owl hooted, almost as a comment on the proceedings. News of Jaeger's death didn't reach Robert at his home until the early hours of the next morning. At first disbelief overwhelmed him, and he sat down in shock. In all his years in the police force, he had never lost an officer on duty. This was tragic, as he had sent her to her death, it was his fault, she had died because of him. Robert had such faith in her, he was sure she would triumph over Carter. Thought she would come back with his scalp, instead she came back in a body bag. This was all wrong, and he still couldn't believe it.

Walking to the kitchen in a daze to make himself a cup of tea and gather his thoughts, he found he was crying. What he done? The tea was never made, he just wept. Robert didn't sleep at all that night, he just gathered up his notes on the case that Jaeger had phoned through to him earlier. Feeling helpless and after two hours of uselessly moping around his house, he realised there was nothing more he could do, and packed a bag for his journey to France. There was going to be a row about him going to France to pick up the pieces of Jaeger's case. But it was his case now, and he would resign before giving it up. He needed revenge and close this case once and for all.

After phoning for a taxi, he waited by the front door with his suitcase, he had no intention of taking his car, he needed something faster. The taxi dropped him off at police HQ and he went in to gather his own notes on Carter and confront his superiors. There was no one in the CID office this early, just the uniform coppers on their night shift. The silence suited Robert perfectly, a little peace in which to collect his thoughts and files, whilst he prepared to face an uphill battle.

News of Jaeger's death was on the early morning news, and there was an air of sadness that pervaded the CID office as the officers came on duty. It was noticed by everyone when they came into the station, but Robert ignored everyone, he was on a mission, he was out for revenge now, and woe betide anyone who stood in his way. The door to his office remained closed for several hours as he consulted the web to see if he could charter a plane to Dieppe to get him to France in a hurry, whether the higher ups agreed or not. He had emailed several of his superiors to make his intentions clear, by nine am he was in a meeting with them.

There was indeed a row over Robert leaving his team behind, especially as he had lost his second in command. His superiors were not happy and put every possible obstruction in his way, but Robert insisted on taking up the case, nothing was going to stop him. He said his team could take on other cases or be reassigned, eventually his superiors gave in, and Robert was allowed to go to France to chase down Carter. The charter flight had already been provisionally arranged, the French police informed, and Robert went out to his team to explain what was happening.

'We have lost one of our team, she died needlessly because she believed in justice more than her own safety. I will be away for several weeks and won't return until Carter is behind bars or dead. The latter is an option only because both he and the French police are armed, and both are prepared to use weapons. I would prefer to see him behind bars because I know it would destroy him, but that's just my opinion. I have appointed one of you as my liaison officer, simply so the records are kept at this end and procedure followed. I will see that Jaeger did not die in vain. I will catch him, he will be brought to justice. That is all.'

Picking up his case, Robert left, his driver already assigned and happy to get his boss to the airport ASAP. Robert didn't speak at all on route and couldn't wait to be on his way as soon as the car stopped. His flight from the local Headcorn airfield was uneventful and he landed at the small airfield at Dieppe to be greeted by the French police Commissioner. The cartel's Jaguar had been repaired and was presented to Robert for his use, complete with new radio communications. Robert didn't speak a lot of French, just enough to get by, so he was allocated a French/English speaking liaison officer at the headquarters, where they went through the case to date. Robert made it clear that he thought the French police had done a marvellous job, and that Jaeger's death had nothing to do with them, there was no blame there.

After reading the gendarme's report, it was clear Jaeger had rushed into a situation unprepared, and her death was caused by her impatience. A moment of bravado that misfired. For the moment he asked that they intensify their search for Carter's van, that they issue a new public appeal along with ID photos and stress just how dangerous Carter could be. For his part, Robert would coordinate the search and put his personal knowledge to good use. He said he would not interfere in the French search, that was a French job, on French soil, even if Carter was a British citizen. The killing of Jaeger was on French soil and therefore a French crime to be investigated by the French.

All of this was appreciated by the French police Commissioner who had a great deal of sympathy for Robert, as well as understanding the importance of him being personally involved in the case. Robert was given his own small office where his liaison officer would operate from. Robert had no intention of being there unless necessary. Where to start? Interview with Susan who had blown the whistle on Carter. See if she could shed any new light on the case. Robert listened intently to every word she said. After a long interview, a new press release and TV broadcast were prepared with translation. All the media were interested, Carter and Robert would be all over the news for days now. Might help, Robert thought. Carter your days are numbered, and he walked out of the office to his car.

CHAPTER 72

Carter was in hiding, there was no way he could get far that night. By pure luck Susan had packed up the bags the night before, and he had thrown his in the van. The money was concealed in the van from the time he had brought it. In his panic that night, he fled as far away as he thought was safe. Or at least as far as he could go safely, just to gather his thoughts. France has a lot of woodland and just south of Dieppe is an extensive forest area. It was easy to hide the van down a track and throw a few branches over it to keep it safe from prying eyes.

Sitting next to the van Carter had time to reflect on what had happened. Good job he had the gun, those drugs guys would have cut his throat if they had caught him. That bloody car had scared the shit out of him, didn't expect to see that again. It wasn't until sometime later that he put two and two together. Why had that woman tried to apprehend him? Where had he seen her before, she was familiar. Oh shit, she was the one who raided his house, and she was with the police in Dieppe, not the drugs guys, he had shot a bloody policewoman, now all hell would break loose.

And Susan? Had she realised who he was from the paper and fled, had she informed the police? If his face was plastered all over the papers already, they would now have a field day after the shooting of the policewoman. Bugger, now the hunt for him would really heat up, where the hell would he go now? It had to be somewhere they wouldn't even think of looking for him. Think man, so far you have said you are going to the D day beaches, apple picking in Normandy, grape picking in the Loire around Amboise, where haven't you mentioned. Wherever it is, it has to be a bloody long way from here. Go south, go by back roads, do I go to English areas like the Dordogne and the Lot, and become a handyman or something. Have to change appearance again and take that chance. Bloody van would have been reported by now and that need to be disguised or changed. Paint it would be easier.

Dare he risk moving the van again? Only at night. Alright then, disguise the van. Best place to get materials would be Rouen. Get the bike out and the back pack and come back with paint, maybe something else to help change its appearance. No too much like hard work, just drive in, lose it in traffic. Carter had enough food in the van to make sure he didn't starve that evening and when it became dark he moved the van into Rouen so he could drive around to look for a DIY store, which were rare in France, or find a suitably large supermarket that sold everything.

It took him an hour to drive into Rouen, and about as long to find what he wanted. Crossing the river to the south side of the city, which avoided the one way system, he moved into the Jardin des Plantes area to find himself looking at a Carrefour City. Perfect he thought, but they don't open until seven am, so he would have to hide the car and be back early in the morning. Looking at the map Carter realised there was a huge area of woodland to the west of the city. Getting there was the big problem, as the city lies in a double loop of the Seine, go south and there is no obvious crossing, go north and you end up in the old city, a maze of small streets. Looking harder

Carter found there was a tunnel under the river, near Sahurs that would lead straight into the forest. The route from where he was, to the forest ran through the industrial areas and main rail lines and marshalling sidings at Sotteville on the minor road D18.

It wasn't until he cleared the main town and moved into the suburbs that he found he was running alongside a wooded area. A roundabout took him directly into the Foret du Rouvray. Bloody marvellous he thought. Much quicker. The woodland was criss-crossed with tracks, and he had no problem hiding the van until the morning. 'No bloody sleeping bag,' he said to himself, 'Have to pick one of those up as well in the morning. After an uncomfortable night Carter was back in front of the supermarket at seven am. Hiding the van behind the supermarket trolley shelter, he was ready as soon as the doors opened, taking a trolley into the supermarket almost at a run.

Throwing in sandwiches, drinks, a bottle of scotch, which the French seemed to like far more than brandy, paint, sleeping bag, brushes, a beret, and a cheap sat nav. Stopping at one display he spotted some stencils. That's not a bad idea he thought, and he went back to the paint brushes for a small brush. 'Bit of signwriting this evening I think,' he said.

A few other odds and ends went into the trolley and he was at the cashpoint and away before anyone recognised him. Throwing everything into the van and reclaiming his Euro from the trolley took about a minute, and he was away. Carter was thinking hard, did he stay in the area and disguise the van or get away as soon as possible. He chose the latter, get away, get far, far away. Before he programmed the sat nav in, he had a look at the map. The A28 toll was the motorway to the south, last route he would take. Stay off the motorways, especially the toll roads, far too well monitored. The countryside as he left Rouen was hilly but soon became as flat as a pancake and pretty open, so finding a hiding place was going to be one of luck.

Crossing over the motorway that led to Paris, he had no real option but take the N154 to Evreux, and he hammered the van down the road, before people would really be awake and hopefully the gendarmes would still be tucked up asleep. Bypassing Evreux he was soon heading for Dreux which at least looked as if it had a wood or forest to the north of the town. That would do. There was no need to go into the town, he found a lane which went into the woods. Same procedure, go in deep, camouflage, eat, and tonight paint.

It was well after eight pm when he finished painting it in gloss green. It would be dry in the morning, and he could add a fictitious mobile number on the side to complete the disguise if he had time. When all said and done, it looked naff, but it looked different, it would do for now. It was now getting dark, and he wanted to get to Chartres and heading south as soon as possible.

CHAPTER 73

Robert thought to himself, promises are all very well, now you have to keep them if you are ever going to catch this monster and your credibility is to remain intact. His own mind was still in turmoil, Carter had given everyone the slip, he always seemed to be one step ahead. There was a plan somewhere in the man's head, he had to break in to his way of thinking, outguess him, or use his logic to out think him for once.

Robert's first stop after the press conference was the farm house, where the couple were as helpful as possible, and Robert treated them with respect. They were still in shock and had no idea Carter was so dangerous. They told Robert in great detail, everything Carter and Susan had said whilst staying on their site. Robert made copious notes and sat at their kitchen table pondering where Carter might go, what he might do, how he would hide, what was his master plan, and did he even have one, or was everything done on a whim with no logic, no plan. No he didn't believe that, Carter was too conditioned, he reacted, he wasn't proactive, he wasn't that organised. Like most criminals he was still a creature of habit. So where was he heading?

Normandy was out, he wouldn't go there, and he didn't believe he would go further west, too easily trapped in Brittany unless he got on a boat and fled the country, always an option but the passports would be instantly spotted. Robert didn't think he would go back up the coast to Calais or into Holland.

Paris was definitely out, he would stand out like a sore thumb, he would have to find a flat, lots of paperwork, no he was not going to go with that, and how would he support himself? That left two options, east to Germany? No what would he do? That left south. There were over a million ex pats in France, he would either lose himself there, or go into Spain, plenty of villains hiding on the Costas still, he would fit in easily.

Robert decided almost on a gut feeling, he would concentrate on routes south. A totally non logical feeling maybe, but it felt right, it offered Carter his best chances of escape and hiding in a British community, especially if he was useful and he became helpful. Gaining the trust of the gullible wasn't that hard, especially older people who could be very protective as well. If things got too hot, Carter could escape to Spain, Italy or even north Africa, where it would be almost impossible to get at him. South it is then.

Robert thanked the couple for all their hard work and patience, he reassured them that they had done absolutely nothing wrong, the exact opposite in fact, and they looked relieved. For Robert, looking at the map of France he realised just how bloody huge it was, twice the size of Britain and with less people. An impossible task he thought, just look at what he was up against. There are massive areas of countryside, millions of small roads that Carter could use. Where the hell did he start?

Back to good old police work and out came the note book to put ideas and thoughts down for future reference. Travel came top of the list, that bloody van should be easy to spot, but Carter would never use main roads and it would be impossible to police every lane. He knew from holiday experience you could travel all day on country roads and never see anyone. But using small roads greatly limited Carter's speed and he would almost certainly travel by night not day, Robert guessed. And only about a hundred miles a day, because Carter would be cautious.

Robert guessed the south of France around Cahors would be a good starting point to aim for, that would be about five hundred miles with an overnight stay each night. That seems very logical to him, and hopefully to Carter as well. It would be a safe option with plenty of diversions that could be taken along the route. OK, time to outguess Carter, Robert thought, and he started to divide a possible route into hundred mile segments. Where would he have stayed last night and where will he be tonight. Set the trap and see if it produces the right prey. Hundred mile stints thought Robert, let's look at the map.

Drawing an arc on the map with his finger, the first big city south from Dieppe would be Rouen, which was almost impossible to avoid because of the Seine, then south to Chartres, also bloody hard to avoid because all roads seemed to descend on the city. All the tourists and locals went on the two motorways, there was no way Carter would do that. Robert looked at the map, if he was making for the border, then there was an obvious route through Chateaudun, Vendome, Blois and Chateauoux that would avoid the major roads, along with by passing Le Mans, Paris, Tours and Orleans.

Was it too obvious? Would Carter stay put where ever he was hiding at the moment? Robert didn't think so, it was too close to the scene of the crime, he just knew Carter would go south as there were so many options that would open up for him, so many places he could hide, even a choice of countries. Carter must go south, it's the only way open to him, and he must have realised that. The trouble is, he must know that as well, it is the only logical option, and that we will figure this out, and he must take evasive action on route to stay undetected.

Robert pondered over the map. Carter didn't think we could read him like a book with the D Day and Dieppe visits. Now there is nothing so obvious, this is pure cat and mouse. A horrible thought crossed Robert's mind as he sat there. Christ! If he goes far enough south, he has a choice of continents even, it would be so easy to get to North Africa. That would be a nightmare if he did, there would be no way to bring him back to England. It suddenly occurred to Robert that Carter was a soldier, it would take so little effort for him to become a mercenary, just about every country in north Africa was involved in a fight against terrorism, civil war or dissent. Carter would fit right in, get lost in the warring factions, he would get paid and probably enjoy himself in to the deal.

If it wasn't in his original plan, it will eventually dawn on Carter that Africa would be an attractive final destination. Robert shared his thoughts with the French co-ordinator who said it was a feasible plan but stressed that France was such a big country it would be impossible to search and monitor all the small roads in the country. There was limited CCTV on the major roads and absolutely none on the minor roads.

The police could at best, keep an eye out for the van, but they didn't even have a registration for the vehicle and to stop every 2CV in the country would be impossible. They agreed that to flee to Spain would be a great objective for Carter and it was a huge border, well over three hundred miles with tiny unmonitored mountain roads everywhere. Carter could always enter Andorra where he could be harboured and escape the long arm of the law, although crossing that border was monitored so that was one route he wouldn't use.

The escape options open to Carter seemed endless to Robert, he would need a lucky break on a par with winning the lottery if he managed to track down, let alone arrest Carter. Robert asked if the French police could saturate the Chartres area today and each of the five areas he had highlighted on the next four days. They might just hit the target. If Carter realised or spotted the increased police presence, he might just panic or make a mistake at some point. Robert wasn't really hopeful, his hundred mile targets were little more than a guess, a hunch nothing more. But he had no idea just how accurate he was, Robert had guessed Carter's whole escape plan, in fact he had added things that Carter would have readily adopted, had he thought of them. Robert was far more imaginative than Carter and had their roles been reversed, Robert would have easily outsmarted Carter.

All that Robert had got wrong was the timing. Carter was behind him not in front. The paint job on the van had taken all day and he was miles adrift. Had Robert thought about it, he would have seen that Carter would have holed up somewhere, he hadn't even reached Chartres. They were on each other's doorsteps, but a day adrift. For once Robert had overlooked the obvious.

CHAPTER 74

Carter was pleased with the van and his new sleeping bag had enabled him to sleep in comfort at last. Knowing that most of France would be looking for him, he thought he would have to be very careful, although the odds were very much with him at the moment. Plugging the sat nav in, he looked at possible routes down to the Dordogne. There were plenty of them and he was lost for choice, he had to find a route that didn't wander all over France, he felt that it shouldn't be too obvious, just reasonably go in the general direction. Choosing his destination he plotted his route, but had no intention of following it, just the general gist of it. It would keep him going in the right direction more than anything. Travelling at night would be a bit too suspicious, especially on country lanes, so he chose late afternoons and evenings. The van was now green not white so it would pass many of the basic checks.

Right from Dreux, Chartres was almost impossible to avoid, there were few small roads he could take, and it didn't help that the countryside was as flat as a pancake. The twin towers of the cathedral were visible for miles. Traffic was always heavy around the city as six major roads and the A11 motorway all converge on Chartres. Carter took a chance and just joined the stream of cars heading in his direction. It was a short run into Chateaudun, again there was no real back road so he stayed on the N10. However, once past the town there was an excellent small road straight into Blois and the Forest Domanale de Beulogne, that he could hide out in. With all the time in the world now, he could stop off at little villages and buy food and drink, and then pull up in a parking area and almost have a picnic, knowing that he was so far off the beaten track as to be pretty safe.

Bergerac was to be his destination he decided, so close to Robert's plans, but so far away, he was too far to the east by choosing Cahors. Of course Carter would make it to the south of France, it would have been a monumental piece of bad luck had he not. The forest offered him a lot of hiding places but there was an annoying aspect to the area, it was littered with lakes and mosquitoes, which meant he spent the night in the van rather than outside. It was stiflingly hot in the van as the windows had to stay up. In the end Carter could stand it no longer and started up the van to find a better site.

It was short drive to Loches which had a small but ideal forest to the north of the town. It meant driving in the dark which was dangerous as people would wonder what he was doing in the forest at that time of night. It was a chance he had to take. Finding a back road, he pulled up and threw a few branches over the van. The sleeping bag was thrown on the ground and he used the kitbag as a pillow. Unsettled by the change of plans, he dreamt again that night. It was hot that night and his brain started to think he was back in the desert as he slept. Dreading seeing the dead soldier again, he shouted out and woke up in a cold sweat.

Dear God, he thought, I need to get some sleep, can't risk being tired when driving. Going back to the van, Carter found a bottle of scotch and took several large swigs. It would help him sleep. It had the desired effect but it didn't stop him dreaming. Back came the desert, the explosion, the face, the blood, the accusation, the panic and the screams. Carter was sitting up inside the van, laying on his bag. Looking down at his hand, he was shaking. That bloody dream, it always came back to haunt him, shatter his peace, it wouldn't leave him, made him cry out in fear. Carter needed a breathing space and got out of the van and sat down close to it.

The scream that night had been heard by a hunter out in forest hunting boar. They were bloody nuisance, eating his crops, knocking down his fences, but they were great eating. With his gun held at the ready, the hunter approached the van to see what the noise had been all about. Was it an attack, a rape? Did it matter? He would deal with it. As the hunter approached, Carter heard a twig snap and instinctly rolled out of sight behind the front of the van. Peering under the vehicle he could see the hunter's feet and then the barrel of a gun prod inside the van at his empty sleeping bag. Carter felt around him and managed to find a fallen branch. Gripping it tightly, he crept around to the open door and leapt at the intruder. Carter took him completely by surprise and smashed the hunter in the face with the branch. He beat him again and again until his head was bloody pulp.

'Sod it,' said Carter, 'Why was this bastard trying to kill me.' looking down at the bloody figure, he smiled and gave the body a hefty kick. He threw the hunter's gun in the van along with his sleeping bag. Jumping in the van, Carter left the body where he fell and reversed the van back down the forest track. Knowing he had to put at least fifty miles between the attack and where ever he could hide tonight. South, just go south he thought, somewhere will look right. Giving the map and the sat nav a quick glance, he could see there were forests around

Limoges and it was far enough away to be safe. Get out fast, punch it in the sat nav, go direct, take the risk for once.

The trouble was that meant using the A20, he couldn't do that, luckily the old road ran alongside the motorway and he managed to get on that instead. 'Soon be safe,' he muttered to himself, 'Soon be safe.' Back in the forest amongst the mess of Carter's camp, the hunter stirred, he managed to reach for his mobile and dial for help, he left the phone on so it would send his co-ordinates to his rescuers. The ambulance eventually found him, and because the injuries were caused by an attack, and not an accident, a gendarme came to. It would be some time before the hunter would be able to scribble a jumbled description of his attacker, an attacker who was driving a green 2CV van. A green van with a racing bike in the back, he reported to his superiors. They should be on the lookout for the van. The gendarme had no idea what he had just reported but it would make someone smile in the morning.

CHAPTER 75

Because the attack was so unusual, it was investigated immediately by the police. At the site, fingerprints were found on several items and cross checked. There was almost joy in the police HQ when Carter's prints came up as a match. The police looked at the report and the evidence from the hunter and then instantly contacted Robert for his reaction. It was one of surprise and satisfaction, that turned to pleasure. 'It's green, it's bloody green, we've been looking for a white van and he's painted it. And green, how many green 2CV vans are out there, not many I bet. Prat, he has undone all his hard work hiding from us. He's also been using forests as cover, so that is where we are going to concentrate on, can we get any military to help with searches of the forests, know it's asking a lot but we could do with some extra manpower.' He paused for a moment.

'We know where he was yesterday, he will have fled the area in a bit of a panic, he wouldn't have been expecting to be hunted at gun point, he doesn't know it was an accidental encounter. And he will hole up in another forest, he has no real option has he? If he is still going south, that is where he will be. But just where?' 'After Limoges, the countryside becomes very hilly and wooded. That would be a good starting point,' said Robert's liaison officer, 'But it's close on five hundred km away, we can't get there quickly.'

'We can with a helicopter, get one organised please, I'm sure the police have one for traffic duties I can borrow. Can you inform the Limoges police what to look out for and tell them I am on the way to help co-ordination.'

Robert started to gather his notes whilst watching out of the corner of his eye to make sure it was all happening. Much to his amazement there were no objections to his request and a military helicopter was provided, simply because of its greater range, and with absolutely no problems. The Limoges police were happy to have Robert on board, they had several officers who spoke English to help. Two hours later Robert was on the ground and organising another helicopter trip.

Robert knew he was right, he had to be in this area, but how to find him? What Robert had suggested was a helicopter fitted with a thermal imagining camera, something that could locate a hot human or an even hotter green van. It was his best bet by far. The police had worked out the most logical routes from Blois to Limoges using minor roads and had the helicopter refuelled for an intensive search programme. Robert co-ordinated the ground search and then sat with the pilot to work backwards from Limoges airport back to Loches. It was a huge area but the helicopter would be flying at two hundred kph which would hugely reduce the time spent in the air and hopefully just be used to direct the ground forces as they encircled Carter.

Robert knew Carter was trapped, he had given away his MO, they knew what he was driving and they had a pretty good idea of where he was heading. Police were converging from both directions, one force combing the roads from Loches, the other being co-ordinated by Robert from Limoges. We've got you now, Robert thought to himself as he belted in and put the headphones on. The pilot had already been briefed on

263

the search area to be covered. Robert had the map divided up into search areas and was eager to start. After all the pre-flight checks had been completed they were in the air and heading north to the first forest area in minutes. He was looking for the green van and then any heat source in the trees. 'He has to be here somewhere,' said Robert to no one in particular. 'Must find him, must find him.'

There was one small problem. Carter having fled from the forest, simply headed south in panic because he wasn't thinking, he was reacting. Pulling over after a few miles, Carter realised he would be heading straight into a trap, it would be easy to outguess him on the route now. The route south was the obvious route the police would think he would take. It must be avoided at all costs. In the end he decided to go west, towards Angouleme, short of going back on himself, it was the only other option. There were no easy routes except the departmental roads and he found himself zigzagging down country roads which wasted so much time. It meant that he wasn't distancing himself quickly enough.

There was also nowhere to hide, the countryside was open, there were no towns to hide in even. There were no woods until Chinon, that wasn't really far enough away, only about fifteen miles away, but it would have to do. Carter couldn't risk going into town, but he needed to get the van off the road. Robert was scanning the forest, he had covered big chunks of it, there were no obvious heat images, every now and then he would pick up groups of people walking but no vehicles that fitted the bill and no single people. It was frustrating to say the least. But Robert knew he must be there, somewhere. By now Carter had found the old road into Chinon and the forest. Picking a track, he drove as far up as he could and put the van under a tree out of sight.

There was a helicopter buzzing about in the distance, but it was a military one, nothing to do with him he thought. The bike was removed from the back of the van for Carter to go into town. Taking the hidden money from the van, just in case, Carter peddled off into town for supplies and hopefully news on what was happening around him, hoping that his face wasn't all over the papers still.

CHAPTER 76

Watching Robert hunt down Carter, the pilot could see the frustration on his face grow, as the search area grew ever smaller. Search teams were radioing in negative reports all afternoon and it was becoming obvious to Robert that Carter wasn't in the area, and he couldn't understand how he had got away. They had the resources to make sure he didn't escape. But in the end Robert had to admit they were getting nowhere. Carter simply wasn't there. The trail had gone cold, again. When the fuel started to get low, Robert ordered the helicopter back to Limoges where it was refuelled and sent back to base.

Robert reported back to police HQ and said he would be staying in Limoges and co-ordinating the search from there for the next few days.

La Maison Blanche in the centre of Limoges served as his base for the next two days. Nothing was ever heard of Carter in that time, and Robert was resigned to the fact that somehow Carter had escaped. God knows how. Looking at the map he admitted he had got it wrong. Carter hadn't gone south, he hadn't stayed in Loches, he hadn't taken the routes south on the motorways, he would have been spotted for sure.

Would he have taken the chance to go west, it was very empty and open, where were the forests? There was nothing between Loches and the coast, just a small wood at Chinon. Was it worth searching? Explaining his thoughts over the phone, he convinced the local police that a search might be worthwhile. They did as they were asked, and the van was found late that afternoon, prints taken off it convinced everyone it was Carter's. Sod it, thought Robert, where was he, why Chinon? Looking closer, he realised it had a railway running through it.

Carter had also realised this, and he and the bike were on a train, they had a two day start on Robert. Carter had come to the conclusion that the van had become a liability, it was easily spotted, he had to hide it every night which cut down his options. Sooner or later they would figure that out. There had to be a better way to get to the South of France and the railway had provided it. It was so obvious, safe and quick. Even if he was on CCTV they would have a hell of a job chasing him, as he used minor stations to change to different lines. Carter had crossed all over the countryside from major town to another, just to confuse matters. Everything of value was in his backpack, including the money. Eventually he arrived at Bergerac station, now where?

Carter stepped out into the bright sunshine, it was blinding. He would go east, it was where the tourists go. There were gites and B&Bs everywhere, but what he was looking for was a rundown house that was obviously English, almost certainly owned by an elderly couple who had come to France to live out the dream in the sunshine. Now in their twilight years they had the option of returning to Britain, or living where they were, but in gentile ruin. Someone who needed help.

Carter was on his beloved bike and heading for Issigeac, which was far enough off the beaten track to be a good hunting ground. It took him well over five hours to find a likely victim. A faded sign outside the run down house said vacancies, in English. I'm not surprised, thought Carter, this place has seen better days. Perfect, looks promising, a nursing home in need of help. Walking up the drive to the house, he was met by a lady well into her sixties, she had a bunch of carrots in her hand, freshly picked from the vegetable patch where a lawn would have been some years back.

'Saw the sign. You've still got some rooms spare hopefully,' Carter said. She nodded. He wasn't surprised, he would have been amazed if she had any guests. 'I'm looking round for somewhere to stay for a few weeks while I have a cycling holiday. That possible?' 'Got plenty of rooms,' she answered in English, 'Don't have many residents now, too much competition.' 'Can I come in, wouldn't mind a look round if that's OK,' he asked. 'Of course it is, but you won't find anything too special, all a bit basic now, can't afford to do the place up now that David has gone.' Carter followed the old woman and stepped into the kitchen. It all looked very run down. 'David?' he asked.

'My husband, he died last year, left a lot of debt and a lot of repairs he didn't sort out, I'm finding it hard to cope. We cashed in our pensions and bought this place but he couldn't cope with it, and I ended up doing it on my own, and failed. As the place gets more and more run down, the less people want to stay here, vicious circle. You are the first visitor for over six months. Carter grinned, 'Any chance of a coffee, I think I might be able to lend you a hand here.'

A coffee was made and they got into a long conversation about the woes of the old couple. David had been in ill health for several years, drunk a lot, and run up debts just to exacerbate the situation. When he died, she was left with the gite and little else. She wasn't able to maintain it and it lost visitors because it now looked such a mess. That was her only source of income, and it was all downhill from that point.

'Are the rooms still OK?' asked Carter, 'I could do with kipping down, been a long day,' She led the way to what was once a grand room, it was dusty and needed a good airing. There was no bedding on the ornate bed frame. Carter helped her find sheets, pillows and a duvet to make the room resemble somewhere he could stay. 'Now that's an improvement,' and he threw his bag on the bed. 'OK I'm bloody hungry, where can I get some food around here?' he grinned her again. She laughed, 'Silly question. If you are going to stay, then I better feed you. Come into the kitchen, we need to talk, you said you could help, let's see how.' Thirty minutes later Carter's plan fell neatly into place.

CHAPTER 77

Robert was packing. There was no way he could trap Carter now, he had no idea where he had gone. Handing over the case to the French investigators was painful, and all he could do was ask them to look out for Carter, admitting he couldn't even help with his final destination. Because there were no ID or passport checks or even borders, people could move freely from one country to another. It was a hopeless situation for Robert, Carter was free to roam over the entire continent. Sure there was a European Arrest Warrant out for Carter but the chances it would be executed were slim. Robert somehow doubted it would ever be used now. Disappointed didn't come close to how Robert felt, he had been so sure he would catch Carter.

Going home would be an admission of failure, admission he had lost one of his key officers for nothing. But he had nothing to offer, no ideas, nowhere to go, but back home. The plane from Limoges would take him back. Back to a dingy office where he could shut out the world and hope people had short memories about this case. Jaeger had no family, she hadn't married, her family were long gone, and she would fade from memory as well.

Robert had one duty to perform for her, her eulogy at her funeral the following week. It would be performed with all the usual honour guard ceremony and pomp. Everyone would be sad, tears would be shed and then they would go home thinking what a bastard he was, sending her out on her own, in pursuit of a dangerous criminal, a murderer. The thought of his boring office would be almost pleasurable compared with his lonely existence at home. He would phone his mother, explain everything, yes he was back now. But he wished he wasn't, which was the exact opposite of Carter who had found a new home.

CHAPTER 78

Carter lay in bed, the room still smelt musty but it was comfortable, he had a full stomach, he was safe, in hiding, somewhere the police would never think of looking for him. Carter slept the sleep of the dead that night, without dreams. A deal had been agreed with Barbara, he had discovered her name after a few glasses of wine. It was an arrangement that suited them both down to the ground. She would provide him with somewhere to live and feed him, he would renovate the gite and her house, and help her get the place up and running again, he could do that easily. The next morning they were both up early, there was a splendid breakfast on the table and they discussed what he need to do to keep his side of the bargain. They agreed before the outside of the building was renovated, the inside would need sorting, something to show off to customers.

That was fairly easy, there were four internal guest rooms and he was in one of them. The real money came from the external buildings which were let out to couples. Carter looked at the buildings, bugger there was a lot of work to do on those, and he told her so, don't even think about those until next year. She was disappointed and thought he was reneging on the deal. Carter stopped her and pulled a notepad off the shelf and started to write a list of everything that needed doing. The house was in a bit of a state and he listed everything that he could see was wrong with it, or at least what needed to be done to make it at least liveable in again.

Then the grounds, then the external buildings, he did a quick calculation on the costs and showed it to Barbara, her face fell. 'I haven't a hope in hell of finding that sort of money,' she said. 'Have you got anything? Because this is going to cost' said Carter. 'Anything at all?' 'Not much' she said through her tears. Disappearing into another room she came back with a cardboard box a few minutes later, which she emptied out onto the table. 'These are my savings, all that is left after David's debts, not much is it.'

Carter was stunned, there was a lot of spare change, lots of small euro notes, nothing over a twenty, and he estimated there was just a few hundred euros spread across the table. 'That is going to just about going to buy the paint,' he said sarcastically. 'Just how on earth did you think you were going to repair this house?'

'I still get my UK pension every month and I sell vegetables in the market every Saturday, which keeps me going, it's all I've got now,' she replied. Carter didn't know whether to laugh or cry. She was in a desperate state, but she provided a safe haven, think man, you have a way out here, just be careful. 'Right we have to do a deal. I need somewhere to live out here, you need an income. You obviously thought you could earn something through me, but you need a lot more guests. I'll put money into this place, but I want a legal share in exchange minus my cost of living. At your age you can't run this forever, if you get this up and running, and I put money in, you sell it as a going concern, buy a nice little house and we split the profit - agreed?'

She thought for a minute 'OK, I like the idea, I'll get the place valued as it stands, you repair it, we get it revalued, split the profits and I retire. Until then, I house and feed you at cost not at the going rate. Aren't people going to think it's odd, you doing all this?' he said. 'Welcome to your second cousin Barbara, tell them I'm your only family, and I've come to help you retire and improve my inheritance.' She laughed and nodded an OK. 'Welcome to the family son,' and she gave him a huge bear hug.

Carter smiled, he knew he was safe for now, he could live here for years if he wanted to, he wasn't sure just yet. There was a lot more to life than gites, but it would certainly do for now. Looking at the list in front of him, he changed his mind on the order of completing the repairs. The roof needed tile repairs and the guttering putting back. Easy, but they took him two days. Barbara was delighted. She stopped going to the market to sell the vegetables, they were eating them now.

Carter found Barbara had an old Volvo estate and he used it to go into Bergerac to buy DIY materials, paint and new linen for the house. The car was battered, but it worked and it didn't raise any eyebrows, it was a typical peasant farm vehicle. Carter in the meantime had attacked the garden, trimmed everything in sight, moved the vegetable patch to the rear of the garden now it was clear, and sowed the front lawn so that it would be just grass again. The place began to look good again. Carter started to strip the other guest rooms and repair them before painting and papering them. He even made Barbara a new sign saying rooms available, and much to her surprise, travellers started to use the house on a B&B basis. Carter let his room and moved to the gites. That gave her a bit more revenue to start on the outbuildings. He kept out of sight during the visits, just in case, and worked on the gites, away from the main house.

Carter would often strip down to just shorts in the hot weather and he enjoyed working dressed like that. He knew Barbara liked him strutting around the property stripped down and it didn't come as much of a surprise to find she made a fuss of him. Sometimes it would be a casual touch, a more than lingering brush past, hands on his shoulders when she stood behind him at the table. There were plenty of coy smiles, and one night after a shower he just walked into her room naked and hugged her before kissing her gently.

'You can always repay me this way. I think you could do with a man around the house again,' he said. And she agreed, with a laugh, it was a pleasant way to do business. Carter made love very gently that night, but he discovered she had a good appetite, obviously having missed that part of her life since the death of her husband. It was not unusual for her to creep up behind him when he was painting something, hold him from behind and slowly reach down inside his shorts. Carter didn't get much painting done when she was in this mood, but he didn't complain. It just took him a bit longer to finish anything, and it made her immensely happy that Carter still found her attractive. He didn't especially, but he had a good libido now and never refused a free screw. It suited them both. Love and sex, different motivation but the same end result.

The house was finished, but the outbuildings were a different matter, they needed a lot of work and Carter knew he was taking on a building project that would take him months to complete. The season was coming to an end, so any work would not exclude any passing trade. As the season drew to a close so the B&B customers dropped off, and they relied solely on Carter's money to do the repairs. She increased her demands on him, and he would often find he had to have sex before he got around to repairing anything. Not that he minded, and winter meant they had more time for other things without tourists interrupting. The roofs were eventually repaired, then the windows and doors renovated to make the structures weather proof if nothing else. The money from his accounts was draining fast which worried him, but as a safeguard he kept all the receipts for his materials, just in case. But Barbara had kept her word and had the property revalued, and even drawn up an agreement between them. Carter had to use his own name which was dangerous, but he had no option, all his accounts were in his English name. After all this time Carter hoped his name wouldn't ring any bells. Working through the winter he brought the two gites back to life, as well as Barbara. Perfect for the new season.

CHAPTER 79

Robert was utterly depressed and defeated when he had returned to work, months earlier. Sitting behind his desk, in a closed office, he still couldn't quite believe Jaeger was dead, and he felt immensely guilty. Robert became an isolated figure in his department. When he had returned to England, he had performed at Jaeger's funeral, but the press also attended the ceremony. They ran stories on the needless death of the officer, questioned the policy of sending her to France with no back up, and started a campaign against her bosses, in particular Robert. That destroyed his reputation and he found he was handling lower grade cases than he had before her death.

The case against Carter was downgraded to pending, but not closed. The French police kept in touch to prove they were still looking, but the reports became less and less frequent until in the autumn they stopped. His superiors suggested, not too subtly that he might consider early retirement, he refused to even think about this. They tried a new angle and said he should take a medical and then take a holiday to recover from the shock. After the medical he was diagnosed with clinical depression and was put on a compulsory three month sick leave and asked to consider early retirement again. Robert understood they were obviously trying to ditch him, it was all PR, a damage limitation job and he would play them at their own game.

Agreeing to sick leave, he went home, and closed it down, phoned his mother to tell her what was happening, and to make sure she had support from her friends and neighbours. Sitting down in front of his laptop, Robert thought where to go. Somewhere to recover, but his brain had other thoughts, he found he was looking at Cahor and the surrounding districts. Local airports? He smiled, all booked for tomorrow.

CHAPTER 80

Autumn was really taking a hold on the French countryside, it was getting colder, the leaves were changing colour, but Carter didn't mind. His work was almost complete on the gite but he had used a mass of his cash. Barbara was delighted and had put the property up for sale so he could get a return for his effort and she could retire and not worry about money again. It had gone from dereliction to a proper business, but also gone were the tourists, the potential buyers who would pick up the dream of living in the sunshine in France. For so many people it would remain a dream, they wouldn't take the plunge, wouldn't spend their money, wouldn't join the dream. The property was added to a local agent's website and they just waited.

It suited them both really. Both would miss each other's company when the property was sold. In a way they were both happy for the status quo to remain stable for the present. There were no takers, the weather turned and the tourists departed. It was quiet. The markets closed down and all they could do was out wait the winter, if nothing else they had a source of income, a viable business, it would sell, eventually.

But Barbara was showing her age in the cold weather, and her worries caused by her late husband had done nothing to help her past ailments. She didn't always have great health and often took to her bed where Carter would nurse her. Barbara often just needed to rest, it was as if she simply ran out of energy and Carter would send her to bed. Their sex life came to a halt and he knew he had seen the best of that arrangement. He wasn't a bad cook and could make a decent soup which she enjoyed and could cope with, when she was ill. Knocking on her door, he would present her with a tray, soup, a glass of wine, fresh bread and a smile when she wasn't feeling up to much. Suddenly she didn't look quite so young. Recently the bouts of illness had grown more frequent and she began to refuse food.

OK he thought, not everyone wants to eat when they are feeling poorly, but often she couldn't keep food down at all. Carter summoned the doctor who looked worried after examining Barbara. He shook his head at Carter. 'This is bad, sorry but she has liver cancer, it's terminal, she doesn't have much time I'm afraid.' That hit Carter like a sledgehammer. 'Have you told her? How long has she got?' was all he could think of asking. 'Days, possibly a week, a month at the outside.' the doctor replied. Carter could see his life unravelling again.

Turning to Barbara, 'Sorry love,' was all he could say and he held her hand gently. Carter had watched people die in combat, but this was different. Barbara just wasted away, she found it hard to move sometimes, she seemed to evaporate before his eyes and soon became only a shadow of the wonderful lady he had known. She died eight days later, she wouldn't go into a hospital but preferred to die at home, her home was where she was happiest. Somewhere she could see the beautiful countryside she loved. It was not an easy death, but during the last two days, Barbara was sedated so she would feel no pain, and she died in Carter's arms in the early hours of the morning a week later. He wept for her, she was possibly the only person who had ever shown him any love, and he would miss her.

Carter didn't understand the legal process of dealing with her death in France, and the matter was handed over to her lawyer to contend with. There was no will and all Carter could do was register his stake in the property and wait. After her funeral in the local church, he had her cremated as she had asked, and her ashes were scattered in the garden. Carter was visibly upset at this. The law demanded that a search was made for a next of kin, which was easier said than done. There were no children and Barbara was an only child. There would be cousins, other family members somewhere in the UK, but it would take a long time to find them, and then agree on what to do with the property.

Carter was told by the solicitor that he could continue to live there until everything was sorted, and an agreement was made between all parties. His safe haven was gone, along with his money, what the hell did he do next. His act of charity had backfired on him and he was left with almost nothing and nowhere to go. Carter had no idea that things were going to get a lot more complicated and dangerous for him in the next few days. Two people were converging on his home, he wouldn't know either of them, but they would turn his life upside down.

CHAPTER 81

Christine Fowler looked at the letter again, she didn't quite believe it. It stated she was the only known relative of one Barbara Simpson who had recently passed away in France. Consequently her property and any goods therein were now her property. However there was an outstanding charge on the house to pay for work that had recently been carried out on the said property. There are existing instructions to sell the property as a going concern to the highest bidder, but I await your advice on this matter as the new owner.

There was a photograph of the property, directions, and a phone number of the office with the correspondence. Christine phoned the number and talked to the lawyer for close on an hour. She said she would love to see the property, particularly as she had never heard of, let alone met her great aunt, and she needed to at least sort through her possessions before the property was sold. There was a definite possibility she might want to retain the property and pay off the outstanding bills. If it was as nice as it looked, she might want to follow in her aunt's footsteps and move there and live her dream for her.

There was holiday owing from work and Christine decided to take it and pay a visit to this wonderful mystery property. It would seem the gods had smiled on her after all this time. There was a regional airport at Bergerac she could fly to and she was able to rent a car as she booked her flight for the following day. The lawyer would meet her at the house where they could discuss the future of the property, and how to proceed with the sale or not. Carter wanted nothing to do with the sale of the property and informed the lawyer he would not be present when Christine arrived. His possessions were packed ready to go, he was under no illusion his time there was very limited, he might ask to stay on as caretaker until the property was sold and his money returned, but that was as far as he was prepared to go.

Time was short and he wanted to move further south before winter set in. Spain was calling. His stay in France was over and he felt it was time for a change, now Barbara had gone. By coincidence Robert had landed at Agen some days earlier and was enjoying the area as a tourist in this hire car. Cahor proved a great base and he loved the black wines. But after a week most of the sights had been covered along the Lot, St Cirq, even Figeac, as he headed towards the Dordogne and the famous gorges.

Robert half-heartedly wanted to contribute to catching Carter and he kept contact with his office just in case there were any developments. Knowing he had taken the wrong decisions earlier, still prayed on his mind. There were plenty of places to stay, the countryside was fabulous, the people friendly, the food superb and the wine excellent. There was a feeling of calmness returning to Robert's mind, but there was always a nagging doubt that he could have done more, he could have caught Carter, and Jaeger should not have died the way she did.

As he drove nearer and nearer to Bergerac, he had no idea that Carter was a stone's throw from him, but the he wasn't looking for Carter, he was thinking about his own future. Could he cope with going back? Could he cope with retiring? There was a feeling he would retire into an empty existence, just what was the point of that. Would he just be playing a waiting game with the inevitable, now wouldn't that be a wonderful thought. There was no family except his elderly mother, no interests or hobbies, he wasn't even a decent gardener, but he was enjoying travelling. That might be an option, sell up and travel.

Just like Christine. She had left her boring job in UK and was enjoying the French countryside. It was only a short drive to her aunt's house, and the lawyer was already there with the deeds and the keys. Christine fell in love with the house immediately, she couldn't sell it and she told him so. 'What about this building bill. Can you arrange a meeting with Mr Rogers?'

'He's in the out building now, but is still upset about Barbara's death. He is acting as unpaid caretaker at the moment but wants to move to Spain with the repair money Barbara promised to pay back when the property was sold,' the lawyer replied. She was aghast, 'I can't sell this, it was my great aunt's dream, it's beautiful and it's mine apart from the building bill. I want to move here, I can sell my house in England and repay him, what is outstanding?' The bills were handed over and there was a sharp intake of breath when they were handed over. Christine looked at them in disbelief. 'Really? Jesus, this is an enormous amount. What did he do, rebuild the property?'

'As far as I can gather from Barbara, that is not far from the truth. It's all legal, I kept all the bills as Mr Rogers purchased the materials. He lived here in exchange for the work he did and paid for his keep. He worked hard and as you can see, he did an excellent job. They became very close friends and I believe he would have liked to retire here as well. He says he has used nearly all his own money and now circumstances have changed he needs to move on and find a new home. I don't think he will talk to you, he just wants his money back, I have his account details and the money can be transferred at any point. It doesn't have to be immediately, it can be done over a period of months, so long as you agree on a plan to complete within the year.'

'I would have to sell my house in England to repay the bills and that might take up to a year, so this won't be quick. I need to discuss this with him, you say he is in the guest house? I at least want to thank him for looking after my great aunt,' she answered and stomped off before the lawyer could stop her. Carter was in the small gite, his bags packed by the door, ready to throw in Barbara's old Volvo, the bike already loaded. Christine threw open the door catching Carter by surprise. Christine just stood there looking at Carter in disbelief. 'You, Jesus I know you. You've been all over the papers, you are the murderer they have been hunting!'

She turned to run and scream for help but Carter was too quick for her. Leaping over the bags, he grabbed her from behind, pinning her against the wall. Carter whispered in her ear 'Say a word, utter just one word, scream or shout, and it will be the last thing you will do. Understand? Just who do you think I am?' Carter didn't really need an answer, his cover was blown and it left him in a bloody impossible position.

'You're that guy the UK and French police have been chasing, a shooting in Dieppe, a police woman killed and you've killed in England as well. I've seen your photo in the papers. You are wanted all over Europe.' Carter held her tight against the wall, he could feel her shaking. 'Don't kill me,' she pleaded. 'I won't say anything, I promise, you looked after my aunt, I wanted to say thank you, that's all. I can't sell this place, it's beautiful.' she started to cry. 'Don't kill me, please don't.'

Carter pulled her head back by her hair and slammed her head against the wall as hard as he could. Such was the impact that her face dented the plaster board and she was knocked out cold. Carter calmly picked up his bags, threw them in the Volvo and went in to see the lawyer as if nothing had happened. 'She's looking around the grounds, might be some time, so I wouldn't bother waiting. I'm off, you know where to send the money, bye.' Christine wasn't found for several hours, and couldn't believe she was still alive. She told the solicitor what had happened, he brought in the police and her new neighbours came round to see what the fuss was about.

Her story was all over the papers the next day. 'Escape from death' read Robert, he couldn't believe what he was reading. Carter's face stared out from the front page, mocking him again. He had been hiding just down the road!!!

CHAPTER 82

The headline was certainly eye catching, his French wasn't that great so he only got part of the story, but he recognised Carter's photo immediately. 'Bugger me, he's done it again. hiding out under our bloody noses again, and no one noticed, no one recognised him. Robert managed the gist of the story, but asked one of the hotel staff to help him out with the rest of the story. It was incredible, Carter had hidden in plain view all this time. Robert was on the phone to his office immediately, he explained everything that had happened, where Carter had been, and where he was.

'I'm going to the Bergerac police, get on to them now as I'm travelling, we have a wonderful chance of catching him again.' 'But boss all this happened yesterday, he could be bloody miles away by now,' was the reply at the other end of the phone. Suddenly a dose of reality hit Robert squarely between the eyes. Yes of course, he will be on the run, with a day's head start. So close thought Robert, so bloody close, again. It didn't matter, he was so close to putting things straight once more, the need for revenge was so very powerful still. It simply took over his life, it would overrule everything, every sane thought he had in his body. Hunting time, Robert thought as he jumped in the car. Looking at his map, he thought Spain is still the obvious choice. His mobile was located and he phoned the car hire company. 'Hi, Robert Steel, can I drop this car off at the Bergerac office, I need to catch a plane. I can? Fine.'

Robert phoned his office again. 'Spain' he said, 'He is going to try and get across to Morocco. I just know he is, can we warn the Spanish police?' His office said they would do their best. Robert managed to arrange a private flight to Gibraltar. There was a big smile on his face now. 'Got you, you bastard. I'm ahead of you now, I know where you are going and I'm going to be there to greet you. The plane left two hours later with a very happy policeman aboard.

In the meantime Carter was well inside Spain and in the middle of Madrid when the Volvo overheated and broke down. The road system in Madrid was a nightmare, he had never seen so many roads merging so illogically. Motorways came at him from the left as well as the right. Driving slowly so he didn't get lost, didn't agree with the old car, and he had to escape off a slip road as steam issued from under the bonnet. Carter had no idea if the Volvo was repairable or it was simply protesting at the way it had been driven for the last two days.

Nobody knew he had Barbara's car so it didn't matter which roads he used, and he had hammered the old vehicle as if the devil was after him. It was motorway on and off down as far as Biarritz, where he pulled over to rest. The car had been full of petrol when he started, it needed topping up now. Looking at his meagre pile of cash, he realised he needed to do something about it. Hotels were out for a start, petrol and food were essential. The motorway over the Pyrenees was almost impossible to avoid from Biarritz and he ended up on it whether we wanted to or not. There seemed to be a toll booth every couple of miles which was proving very bloody expensive. Sod that woman, she had Barbara's house and most of his money he thought. That would have to be put right at some time in the future.

High above him Robert was gloating at how he was going stop Carter and arrest him before he escaped to Africa and freedom. Carter was looking at his ancient car thinking Morocco would just have to wait for a while. There was no real plan of action plotted out, he had just fled. There was no way of knowing how easy it was going to be to get over the Med and lose himself on the other side. Had they realised this was where he would be heading? Was it another rash decision he would regret? He couldn't think of a better plan at the moment. Did he look for a few local villains on route, do a bit of heavy work, it shouldn't be too hard to find someone who needed a bit of muscle from an outsider like him.

Be careful old son he thought, you've been recognised once, don't go doing it again. Be bloody careful and know your customer before you start working for the wrong people. The car had stopped steaming and he gently limped off the main road into a much quieter back road where he could catch a bit of sleep. It was not to be, the bloody dreams were back because of the stress he was under, and he found himself struggling with the dead infantryman in his dreams. In the early hours of the morning he drove out of Madrid slowly to find a secluded lay by to try and sleep.

Robert had already landed, hired another car and lay in wait for his prey. He would have him this time, not realising a piece of Scandinavian engineering had cocked up his timing. The Spanish border from Gibraltar took ages to cross, but it didn't matter, he had all the time in the world. It would enable him to suss out the port and ferry facilities, see how easy it would be to reconnoitre the area. Did he make this an official issue? He emailed a request through to his office for a copy of the

European Arrest Warrant as a starting point, along with copies of Carter's photographs. Robert thought this would have to be official, the Spanish police would have to know what he was doing there, and he badly needed their help.

Carter was also thinking to himself. Morocco would enable him to contact groups who needed fighters. Carter needed to fight again. It was the only thing he was really good at. Europe was at peace, the Middle East too far away, and he didn't trust either Iran or Iraq. Syria was far too unstable and he was white and Christian, he would be a target if he wasn't careful. No, stick to North Africa for the moment. OK, money was a bloody problem, he hadn't got too much of it at the moment. That would be a problem to solve in the morning.

There was a bottle of Scotch somewhere in one of his bags, it would help him sleep. It didn't, and the dreams came back to haunt him. But no one heard him scream, he was on his own in the middle of nowhere, and he had to cope in his solitude. In the morning he was tired through lack of sleep and hung over because of the Scotch. Bad combination to say the least. Breakfast would have to be obtained on the move, he was sure there would be places to pull in somewhere down the road, but it didn't look too hopeful from where he was standing.

In contrast Robert had enjoyed a comfortable hotel room, he too hadn't had too much sleep, he was excited like a schoolboy about to receive a treat, but he had the advantage over Carter of knowing what his plan of action was going to be. Plus he had a bloody good breakfast to finish off. There had been a lot of emails going back and forth from his office and the hotel took his phone and conveniently printed them out for Robert. They were handed over before he managed to finish coffee, it brought a smile to his face, especially as his office who had been in touch with the Spanish police. They were only too pleased to help catch Carter. Robert even had a list of contacts with the local force. Wiping his hands on the serviette, he thought to himself, you are now outnumbered and surrounded. It was now very much a waiting game for both men.

Robert was in hiding in the port, but Carter was still pulled over at the side of the road wondering if he was about end his freedom by not thinking properly. For Robert it was vital he trap Carter, bring him to justice, get revenge for Jaeger. He knew that he must be patient, not make assumptions, look at the options Carter might take, and have his own options ready to cope with them, and any change of plan Carter might take. For Carter, he was wondering if his luck was about to run out, had he made it obvious where he was going and what he was going to do. If he hadn't, the police weren't going to use too many brain cells figuring out where he was heading - Africa, and that meant just one place, as there was only one crossing point to Africa. They would have that well covered. No, he needed to pause, rethink, re-plan, hide, then escape.

The Volvo slowly pulled in at a small roadside cafe a few miles down the road, where they were selling fruit outside. Carter enjoyed a large coffee in the cafe and took a wrap outside to sit in the sun where he could think properly. When everything had been going so well, his luck had disappeared and he had lost his money. That would definitely be recovered at some later date, that was his money and he would never survive without it. But its recovery would have to wait and even then, he might never recover it.

He knew he would spend the rest of his life looking over his shoulder if he remained in Europe, he would have to escape. His options would be limited. Africa would be the obvious choice, easy to get to and opportunities to fight again. There was the US or Canada but they would be difficult to get in and what would he do there? The same would apply to Australia and New Zealand. All of them would be hard to gain entry to with his present documents and ID. It had been good luck getting to Europe and he had found the perfect host with Barbara. That had been ideal but the chances of finding that situation again were very slim.

Spain offered a lot of possibilities he could exploit for the time being. The holiday season was over, the students had gone back to university so there were opportunities on the coast where the ex-pats hang out, an extra pair of hands would be appreciated. Could he change his appearance again and blend in for a year before escaping to Africa when no one was looking. It would have to be somewhere close to the ferry. The map came out again. Costa Del Sol would do nicely he thought.

The fruit sellers were doing a roaring trade selling melons and Carter went over a brought one. The Moroccan neatly sliced the melon in half and Carter commented on his skill with the knife. 'Yes I do carvings for the tourists, work in the kitchens, I do shaves, take off your beard?' came the reply. For the next half an hour Carter sat patiently whilst he had his head and face shaved amongst the melons. His moustache was retained and Carter admired his new look in the tiny hand held mirror the Moroccan held out for him. 'Perfect' said Carter. 'Just right for my next job.'

The Volvo was filled with water, the map was consulted and Carter was away once more. It would take him all day to reach

Malaga where he hoped to find somewhere to crash out and at least have a drink before starting life all over again. Leaving behind the dry plains of central Spain, Carter started to see green olive trees growing up the hills, vines and eventually he saw the sea. Mission accomplished he thought, now for a drink. An hour later he was sitting in a bar a couple of streets away from the Mediterranean.

Robert had spent a fruitless day scanning passengers in the port, looking for anyone who might look like Carter. The guy had so many different guises that he thought he recognised a couple of innocent travellers and had them stopped to check their details. They were all set free much to his disappointment. In the end Robert realised he was possibly a day or two early, Carter hadn't arrived yet, but he would come, he knew it. This would be the only place he was likely to catch him. Robert had no idea how he would arrive, on foot, bike, in a car? There was no record of what he was driving if anything. Robert did not know about Barbara's car simply because no one had reported it missing. Nothing. Leaving details of Carter and all the photos plus the Dutchman's identity behind, Robert admitted defeat for the day and went back to his hotel where he checked in with his office. No new information or sightings. OK, too early, Carter will be there tomorrow he thought, and he would be up bright and early to see the first travellers away in the morning.

Carter wouldn't be there, he was enjoying a late night lager in a seedy bar in Malaga. Choosing where to drink had been a bit of a challenge, he wanted a rough bar, somewhere a bit of trouble might happen. His lager lasted a long time, he didn't want to be pissed when he picked a fight later. Opening hours seemed to be pretty flexible and it wasn't until the owner decided to throw everyone out after one am so he could get some sleep, that the disagreements began.

A couple of guys insisted that the bar was closed too early and they needed another drink before facing the joys of home. They became abusive, then angry and tried to become violent before Carter stepped in. A well-aimed punch laid one of the guys out in seconds, the other put up a bit of a fight before Carter managed to bodily throw him out of the door. The first drunk was dragged out of the door and dumped in the street as well. Carter closed the door and drew a couple of bolts to make sure they stayed out. He returned to the bar and finished his lager, nodding to the barman. 'Is it always as annoying as that?' he said. 'No, it's usually worse than that' came the scouse reply. 'You know how to handle yourself, need a job,' he joked. 'Actually yes,' said Carter. He wasn't sure if this was serious or just a joke to end the evening. 'You serious?' 'Definitely. I don't have anyone else to run this place and I could do with a bit of help as most of the other bars have closed down at the end of the season, this is when I get a lot of my business, but it's bloody tiring. Mike's the name.' A hand was held out and Carter shook it.

Another lager was poured which led to a scotch chaser. They spoke for another hour before Carter said he needed to find somewhere to kip down for the night. 'You will be lucky at this time of night. There's a sofa upstairs you can use for the night as a thank you for sorting those two out.' 'Appreciate that,' Carter replied, 'Can I get my bag and take up that offer?' Ten minutes later Carter found his luck had really changed again. He might well go to Africa, but wanted to see how things panned out here first. His plan had worked perfectly, he had a new home and possibly a job, fingers crossed. The bar had a flat above with a sofa in the living room. It wasn't that comfortable, but it would do, especially after all that drink. There were no dreams that night.

Robert wasn't sleeping, he was on tenterhooks, Carter must show tomorrow, the next day at worse.

Little did he know that Carter had no intention of coming, well not for a long time, he had changed direction, and he wasn't going to miss this opportunity, it might lead to all sorts of good things. But Carter was playing a dangerous game. The Costa del Crime wasn't as safe as it was in the 70s and 80s when British crooks began retiring to Spain, because it had no extradition treaty with the UK then. Carter realised this had all changed but there was still a fairly strong criminal fraternity amongst the ex-pats. But knowing he was fairly safe from the British police was offset by Operation Captura run by the Spanish police. They arrested close to a hundred British criminals a year, and he needed to keep a low profile to stay under the police radar. He would have to do the same in Spain as he did in France and immerse himself in Spanish life, lose himself in their culture.

There was another risky but interesting aspect to the Costa del Crime, as it had links to North Africa and South America to enable criminals to smuggle drugs, a popular past time with the more violent criminals from Britain. Carter knew gangs often played out their feuds in Spain, he might be able to get some work from these people, you never knew. As Carter would be working on slowly and quietly building up his reputation, Robert was wondering what was going to happen to his. Five days had been wasted checking the ferry, and it was slowly becoming apparent that Carter was not going to cross over to Morocco.

Every day he filed a negative report on sightings, and every day his office said much the same in return. Robert was so sure that Carter would go to Africa. He had banked on it, but he was wrong, again. There was a little of his enforced sabbatical left before he had to return to England and face the music. Despite his best efforts, he had consistently failed to apprehend Carter. There would be no glorious return with the capture of a master criminal to his name. There would only be a form waiting, asking him to take early retirement. Yeah right, thanks.

Dreading this, Robert sat with his own map spread over the breakfast table, he could only guess where Carter had gone. Spain was easily as big as France and the people were crammed into a few huge cities, and all along the coast. Finding a single individual was going to be bloody hard work. Robert had already tapped into the intelligence forces that ran Operation Captura, but they had heard nothing new and they had a huge network of informants, plus an equally huge database which he was allowed access to.

Robert knew this was going to be down to gut feeling - not that had been useful so far, but it was all he had at the moment. There were plenty of 'old lags' in the area, some he actually knew and several he was convinced had committed crimes in the UK but had never been charged. These were the old style robbers, not the violent gang leaders of today. He put out a few feelers to the Spanish police with a suggestion he would like to talk to a couple of 'friendly' criminals who would keep their ears to the ground and help out, either for a small fee or immunity from prosecution provided they don't take part in any criminal activity now. They were the trusted but invisible informants.

An unmarked police car rolled up to his hotel in the afternoon after Robert had received a call from the Operation Captura officers that morning. The driver collected Robert and proceeded to drive along the coast.

'There are some friendly criminals out here who we tolerate. They provide intelligence on the violent criminals who rock the boat or smuggle in drugs. We all despise them but it is a huge business worth millions. Breaking them is close to impossible. It sometimes descends into violence, violence is bad for business, it frightens the tourists away, and tourists are what keep this country alive. So we have a mutual respect for each other. They provide a collection of whispers, we put them together to make a case, the violence goes away and everyone has a quiet life.'

'It works in our country as well,' said Robert. 'Let's see what they can offer on Carter.' Robert and the Spanish officer pulled up at the villa on the outskirts of Malaga. A well tanned, well built man in his late 50s met them. There was a long leggy blonde in the background who provided drinks alongside the pool at the rear of the house, out of sight, before disappearing into a bedroom. All three talked for a long time, and Robert explained he needed help tracking down Carter. Favours were asked and granted with a promise of hundreds of pairs of eyes watching out for Carter. Contacts were exchanged with a promise of a constant update on the situation. Robert knew this was as much as he could do for the moment, and he reluctantly returned to his hotel.

Packing ready for leaving in the morning, Robert made one

last call into his office to say he would be flying back in the morning. He would have a weekend of peace and come in on Monday to face the music. His office acknowledged that fact, and said he should do a briefing when he got back to bring everyone up to speed. Robert thought this was good idea and said he would sort his notes over the weekend ready for everyone. It was impossible to enjoy a drink in the bar that night, and he went up disappointed at the failure to settle this once and for all. Carter would turn up eventually he thought, or he would disappear off the face of the earth to be discovered in a shallow grave, years in the future. Robert quietly smiled at that thought. His flight back was uneventful and he landed at Gatwick full of anxiety and apprehension of the meeting on Monday. Two trains and a taxi later saw him standing in front of his cold dark house. It was starting to drizzle. The case was dropped off inside the door and he picked up the phone. 'Hello mother, I'm back now, how are you?'

CHAPTER 83

Carter fitted into his new home, Mike was delighted to have another pair of hands. The arrangement was remarkably similar to Barbara's and it worked for both of them. Carter looked suitably sinister behind the bar in his new guise, and there was very little trouble. People enjoyed coming there and Carter started to pick up little snippets of information, names were mentioned in conversations. Taking it all in, he mentioned them to Mike one evening. Who were these people? 'Couple of names there I wouldn't mix with old son,' he said 'Nasty, nasty family, very violent, people disappear with them'.

Carter remembered the name, remembered the face in the bar and looked forward to meeting up with this character again. Could be a bit of work on the side for him, and he didn't mind what it was, so long as it paid. He had his board and keep, all he could drink in the evening and a small wage, so he could manage but without the house money he was stuck behind the bar for the time being. So he served behind the bar, kept the peace and kept out of trouble, until opportunity arose.

The face who knew the family with the nasty habits reappeared a couple of days later and Carter made a point of chatting with him through the evening. A couple of drinks became doubles and the man's tongue became much looser than it should have. Carter told him he was ex forces, had done a bit of heavy work on the side, and he might be interested in a bit of contract work as a freelancer, but he didn't know anyone in town.

The 'face' had a name, Pillippe Santos, who was getting very friendly and very talkative now, 'I might be able to help you there,' he said tapping the side of his nose. Pillippe wasn't seen for a couple of days after that, but he returned late one evening carrying a small parcel. 'Got a minute, and a private room we could talk in? he said. Looking around, Carter nodded to the small office behind the bar. The parcel was handed over and Carter unwrapped it. It was a nine mm automatic pistol and clip of shells.

'Are you all mouth, or were you serious the other night,' Pillippe said. 'Met people like you before, lots of stories, lots of gob and no balls,' He grinned at Carter, it was an evil sarcastic grin and was about to take the gun back and rewrap it. Carter looked at him, and in an instant grabbed him by the throat pulling him towards him, as he did so he lowered his head and head butted him hard enough to break his nose. The gun was grabbed and pointed at the downed figure. 'You ever say that again and I will use this on you. You will be number four, understand?'

The man struggled up, blood pouring from the split across his nose. Carter threw a towel at him to stop the bleeding. 'What do you need doing? Nothing could be written it was agreed, Carter had to memorise everything about the victim, when, how and most importantly who. 'I presume I can charge a fee for this?' said Carter slipping the clip into the gun, he swung the gun round to point it at Pillippe. 'Fucking right you can,' and a small manila package was thrown at him. 'A thousand now, a thousand when it's done. Now let's see if you really do have the balls to do the job. If you don't, I will be there, your life will be one of terror. I will be out there and you will have to look behind you every time you go out.'

'I suggest you leave now, don't ever threaten me again. I prefer we work together but you really don't want to make an enemy of me, you really don't,' scowled Carter. They both went back into the bar, the Phillippe left leaving Carter to ponder what he had walked into. This was a dirty job, but he had killed before, both in the army and since. It wasn't new to him, this was more calculated, he would become a paid killer, just not in uniform. The victim was scum and the world would be a better place without him. It was a job to be completed within the next two weeks and Carter needed to recce the area and pick the killing field. Do this right he thought, and it might lead to a bit more work and some decent cash on top.

CHAPTER 84

Robert wasn't looking forward to the debriefing. When he got to the office he saw that the audience included two senior officers as well as his own team. This looks bloody ominous he thought. Standing in front of the briefing board, which was covered in photos of Carter, his victims and now details from France. Carefully placing his file on the desk beside him, Robert withdrew a single piece of paper. Looking up at his audience he could see they were desperate to see what he was going to say. Robert regarded many of them as friends, certainly trusted officers, people he could depend on, people he would support, he only hoped they would do the same for him. A voice from the back of the room shouted out 'Good to have you back boss' and the room erupted with a round of applause, much to the pleasure of Robert who smiled at his reception. A glance at his superiors told a different story.

'Thank you gentlemen, that was much appreciated, but I feel I have failed. We discovered the identity of our sex attacker and who murdered the Maidstone girl. That was bloody good work by you all. We tracked him all over the country despite him changing his appearance several times and came within hours of catching him at Dover. That was sheer old style leg work and I'm proud of the effort you all put in. Carter managed to kill twice more before he escaped to France. We know how he did it, and we nearly out smarted him there. DS Jaeger went to France to assist the police there when they had him cornered. But by taking the matter into her own hands she was killed and Carter escaped again. She had no idea he was armed, but should have assumed he was. It was a mistake, but she was a bloody courageous officer and we all miss her. I have nothing but praise for her, she nearly succeeded in something I haven't been able to do.'

There was a pause to gauge reaction, complete silence as they wanted to see where this was going. Was he going to resign? 'I took over the case and pooled every resource into tracking him down, But France is simply too big to cover and I'm afraid Carter avoided my efforts to capture him. He went to ground, using the same ploy in France as he did here in the UK. It was only a piece of luck that someone recognised him that we knew where he was. Unfortunately he managed to get away before the alarm was raised. We know he wants to go to Spain and ultimately cross over to Morocco, possibly to join up with some dissident group and offer his military services to them. We also know he has lost most of the money he stole or embezzled in the UK, so he must have found employment somewhere. I think I prevented his crossing to Africa with the increased surveillance I put in place. I was hoping he would try for an immediate escape to Africa, but I think he realised that was too obvious. He is trapped in Spain. The Spanish police have been brilliant and thrown all their resources behind finding Carter. I am in constant contact with the Spanish police. The net is closing in on Carter. The man makes mistakes, but he is just so bloody lucky. Just how he has managed to escape is unbelievable, but his luck will run out, he will be caught, he will stand trial here. This case is still very much open. I promise you that. I'll see him brought to justice and I'll do it for Jaeger.'

There was silence in the room as Robert gathered up his papers and strode to his office followed by the two senior officers. The door was closed. Inquisition time he thought. 'Well that was a nice speech Robert,' said one. 'Just how do you propose to catch Carter now?' 'You will have a full report on your desk in the morning with everything I have put in place with the Spanish police,' answered Robert. A form was dropped on his desk by the other officer. 'You haven't completed the early retirement form.' 'I think you know where that can be stuck,' came the response. 'Now if you don't mind I have a job to do.' As they left, Robert breathed a sigh of relief, 'Well old son, you've got away with it for the moment, but as you said, you have a job to do.'

CHAPTER 85

The old Volvo had been cruising around the town and out into the countryside for several days. Carter was making sure he knew the ground well, he was good at his fieldwork. He was the only one who would do the choosing of the place, time and method, and it had to be right. The victim's villa was gated, had high walls, CCTV, and was almost certainly guarded, that was a difficult target area, a no, no, as far as Carter was concerned. The target ran an operational office which he had checked out earlier, the same situation seemed to be in place there. Another place to avoid. According to Pillippe the guy often clubbed and socialised, but he was surrounded by minders or in a crowded place.

The guy didn't get out of the car when he came back to the villa, the gates were automatically opened by remote control. His office was in the centre of town which would draw too much attention, and he would almost certainly be seen, so the obvious target areas would be when he was clubbing or eating out, which he did several times a week. His real weak spot was that he worked to a routine, ran on clockwork. An ambush seemed to be the logical option. A walk by would be the safest method.

Carter chose the day, the time and the location with little difficulty. The nightclub was the easiest. It was on the edge of town, had a car park at the back, so it would be reasonably isolated and he would have a reason to be walking there. Friday was chosen, he would be lying in wait, out of sight around the corner where he could observe the victim's car arriving. There was no sign of nerves on the day, Carter had done his usual bar routines and arranged to have the evening off for once, he had said he was seeing a hot bird and taking her out to see if he could get any further. This raised a good laugh in the bar and he was wished good luck for the night.

Carter was half an hour early and sat in the car smoking a cigarette. Dead on time the victim's car rolled up. The minder got out first and looked around and then stuck his head back inside the car to say everything was OK, and they walked towards the rear door of the club. Carter was already out of the car and close behind the pair, his hand on the gun, ready for action. The minder's jacket flapped open and Carter could see he was armed as well. Carter approached carefully as if to pass by. In the same moment he hit the minder in the head as hard as he could with the gun butt, and turned on the victim. The pistol was raised in his hand, cocked and ready. There was no sign of nerves from Carter and the victim stood in shock as Carter fired into his chest, and he crumpled to the ground. Calmly he fired three more bullets into the body, the last one into the head, a definite killing shot.

The minder was coming to and trying to struggle to one knee and was in the process of drawing his gun. Carter fired into one leg and then hit him as hard as he could with the gun. He fell to the ground unconscious. It seemed no one had seen or heard the shooting and Carter calmly walked out onto the street and around the block to the old car, and drove slowly away. Carter didn't go straight home, he went cruising and eventually for a drink. It was well past midnight when he went back into the bar. 'Well how did you get on,' he was asked. 'Yeah definitely scored there,' he grinned and he went to make up the sofa bed and hide the gun.

Carter slept well, he had no dreams, he had done his job, done it well and got away with it. He was looking forward to the second manila envelope, and with luck a little more work. The gun was cleaned, wiped down and hidden. The results of his handiwork wouldn't be known until the morning.

Mike looked at the morning paper in disbelief. 'Damn, another shooting, what's the matter with these people, this is going to drive people away. Stupid bastards will kill the tourism trade as well as each other.' He threw the paper down in disgust, Carter casually picked it up but it was in Spanish and he had no idea what the story said. 'What happened?' asked Carter. 'Spanish drug runner got shot and killed last night. An ambush, bodyguard shot, police are interviewing him to get a description of the shooter.' 'Is this some sort of gang vendetta?' asked Carter. 'Yeah, been going on for years, this killing is a bit different, sounds more professional, from what I've read. This will start it all over again. Be a few more killings I reckon. Whatever you do don't get mixed up with that mess.'

Carter shook his head, 'Not a chance mate, this suits me down to the ground, business is good, free board and keep, and I get the pick of the ladies when they bother coming in.' 'Well you did alright the other night.' They both laughed. Business continued with customers dribbling in during the day and increasing during the evening. The turnover was good as there was no competition. Hope it continues thought Carter. A week later Phillippe reappeared, and an identical envelope was passed over to Carter. 'About bloody time,' he muttered.

'Well you did a half decent job, but you should have finished off the bodyguard, they have your description now and you look pretty distinctive. There will be a few more people looking for you now after what you've done. Won't take them long to track you down. But do you want another job before you go?' This threw Carter into a quandary. His look was distinctive, he would have to change that again. And another job, was it pushing his luck, especially as they had his description.

'Tell me about it, but it better be better paid than the last one. I did realise who that guy was. I've taken out one of the opposition, a big shot by all accounts. Think I was short changed then.' The target was discussed during the evening whenever a drink was ordered. Carter thought this one was far more dangerous and it would command a much bigger fee. There was a real chance he wouldn't be able to work in the area after this contract. 'I'll do it.' He said. 'But in my time and in my way.' 'Don't take too long, I'll be back in two days. You know who he is, do your research and let me know if it's possible.'

The next day Carter took off the moustache, ditched the glasses and purchased a baseball cap for a bit of a change, with luck is disguise or change of appearance might fool a few people. His excuse to Mike was the girlfriend didn't like the facial hair and she thought he needed a younger look. When he wasn't busy in the mornings, Carter took the aging Volvo out to do his research. This target was much harder to hit, it would take a lot of planning. The opportunities for a clean kill were very small. Again it would be a walk by hit and there was a good chance he would get injured in the process, even killed for his trouble. Was it worth it? These are drug runners he thought, who would miss them, Yes, he would take the contract. The big disadvantage was the location of the victim, right in the heart of town. It was bloody hard to observe the target if nothing else. The car was too noticeable and he left it in a nearby resident's bay for a short time. When he returned, there was a bloody parking ticket on the screen. He screwed it up and threw it in the gutter. All I need he thought. Who cared, not my car.

CHAPTER 86

When the parking ticket was picked up it was obvious it was not going to be paid because it was on a foreign vehicle who thought they could get away with not paying the fine, the authorities simply tracked the registered owner and reissued the ticket. The new ticket landed on Christine's doormat a few days later, but addressed to her great aunt. She had no idea what it was about and took the ticket to her lawyer, as he dealt with all her aunt's business. It only took a few minutes for him to realise Carter had stolen the aunt's car. The lawyer had forgotten Barbara even owned it. Christine didn't even know of its existence, and certainly not that Carter had stolen it. The lawyer phoned the department in Spain and explained the situation and asked them not to pursue the matter which they agreed to do, especially when he explained the reason why.

The lawyer smiled at Christine and he picked up the phone again. 'This will cheer someone else up', he said. Speaking to the police at Bergerac he explained about the car, the ticket and the obvious fact that they now knew Carter's location, or his general location at least. Emails and phone calls went back and forth between the Spanish and French police. There was real excitement that there was a lead to Carter once again. The call to Robert in England came as a bolt out of the blue. Robert couldn't believe Carter had made a simple mistake, a bloody parking ticket of all things, ha, ha, ha. His laughing brought several of his team into his office. There were tears running down his face from laughing so much. 'A bloody parking ticket,' he laughed. 'A bloody parking ticket. We've got him, but we are going to be careful this time. We need to track him down from this, find the car and we find him. I'm going to let this sink in and then I'll be packing my bags again.'

But Robert had to consider how to play this. Did he barge in and try and take charge of the situation or sit back and hope the authorities in Spain could catch him. His own record so far hadn't exactly been very successful, and as much as he wanted to jump on a plane, he knew he shouldn't. The Spanish police now knew which town to look in. They knew the car to look out for. They had photos of Carter's many guises. It would just be a matter of time. The net must be closing in on Carter soon, he thought. Robert fretted on what to do. There was no real option, stay out of it, let others do the leg work, be there when he was captured. Nothing more, that would suffice, he would be in charge when Carter was handed over. Early retirement, not a chance, he had waited for this moment of glory, and he could bask in it when Carter was jailed.

Robert was receiving regular reports back from Spain, they had patrols out looking for the car, once found they could stake it out and wait. Today however, they would be unlucky, Carter was in the car and he was miles away looking at a cartel boss's house and wondering how to kill him. This was a hard one, the target was well guarded, his office was also his home. He worked completely randomly, rarely went out and was almost impossible to get to. Carter's earlier assassination had made him even more careful. The house wasn't fortified, it just had high walls, no CCTV to draw attention to it, Carter was pleased at that. A more direct approach was needed to flush this target out. Five gallons of petrol proved to be the solution.

At four in the morning, Carter climbed over the garden wall, that was easy for someone used to army assault courses. Keeping to the shadows, he didn't think anyone would be too awake at this time in the morning. Carter poured the petrol all over the rear of the house, and under the door in the dark, leaving the half full can on the door step. A lighted cigarette thrown from a safe distance away, set the petrol alight. Carter had already phoned the fire brigade and they would be faced with a wall of flame when they arrived. Carter was in the car at the front of the house, waiting. In the distance he could hear sirens. Amazingly there was no response from inside the house despite the mass of flames, and Carter wondered how deeply someone could sleep and not be aware of the fire.

Just as the fire engines turned into the road, there was shouting from inside the house and the front door opened. The petrol can exploded and flew into the air trailing burning petrol behind it. A woman ran out in a panic, and Carter ran across to her, calming and directing her to safety. Another person emerged and Carter did the same to them, he was helping people escape, gaining their trust. Fire crew were everywhere now, hoses were being rolled out and Carter was still helping people out of the building, but there was no sign of the target. He went over to the sheltering occupants. 'Anyone else in there?' They nodded, 'How many?'

'Two' they said, and Carter did his mock hero entry into the house to find them, they were still in the passageway downstairs where he thought they would be hiding. They knew the fire was deliberate and wouldn't move. Carter franticly waved them outside, they still didn't move, he waved them out again, just as part of the roof fell in. That made so much noise Carter knew he had got it right. Drawing his gun he grinned at them before they realised he was the assassin. They didn't move as he shot them both without anyone outside hearing the shots. Giving it a few moments he backed out of the house with his arm shielding his face. Turning to face the people he had rescued he shrugged his shoulders and said he couldn't find them, he ran to the leading fire engine and gestured desperately to the crew that there were still two people inside. They rushed in as Carter quietly slipped away.

Carter had done a perfect job and no one would suspect it was murder until the bodies were closely examined. Driving to the sea, he parked up in the dark, peeled off his clothes and dived in. That would clear the smell of smoke. There were clean shorts and a T-shirt in the Volvo, his old clothes went in the bin. The drive home took about 20 minutes and he parked in a public car park a couple of streets away, as it was a resident only parking zone where the bar was situated. Carter crept in and collapsed on the sofa bed. A voice from the bedroom shouted 'You score mate?' 'Too right mate,' came the reply. 'Twice'. He could hear the laughter in the next room. Carter slept well, no dreams, his violent side had been quenched, his brain was happy.

At the scene of the fire, the authorities were kept busy. The roof had completely fallen in obscuring the two bodies. They wouldn't be discovered until the morning and their murder hidden for days. The Spanish police however, had been both busy and efficient, but it would take the police another two days to find the Volvo. Because it was in such a public place, it had a tracker attached rather than put it under surveillance, just in case the police were spotted watching it. It would help find out where the car and Carter were going and where he was hiding. They waited for it to move again, and this time they would be ready to pounce, but from the comfort of an office. That evening, Phillippe came into the bar. Again they chatted over a few drinks, and a fat envelope was passed to Carter discreetly which he pushed under the counter.

'You did a good job on those guys. But they know they are being hunted and taken out. They have no idea who and why, and you don't want to know the reason behind that vendetta. Do you fancy one last job before you take a breather and lie low for a while?' 'Depends' replied Carter, 'Tell me more.' The pair talked on and off for hours over quite a few drinks. Carter had to serve throughout the evening so not to make it obvious he was paying Pillippe too much attention.

But all the time Carter was thinking, was it worth the risk of the final job for now? This would be far more dangerous and would almost certainly provoke reprisals. He would have to move after the job, his luck just wouldn't hold that long. Carter was unaware his luck had already been compromised and he was riding it now. His day off wasn't for another two days so it was impossible to do any real research until then. His mornings were spent on the beach after the cleaning chores and he would return in time to open up for the lunchtime drinkers. The police assumed Carter wouldn't have left the Volvo too far away from where he was hiding and were distributing posters of Carter, and a few other miscreants, whilst visiting every caretaker, bar and shop in the area. They had mixed the posters just so they didn't pre warn Carter they were looking just for him. Carter missed them by minutes when they visited Mike's bar. Luckily Mike hadn't really taken much notice of the posters, and certainly hadn't spotted the one with Carter emblazoned across it.

When Carter did get a day off, he went off to do his research for the last contract. Well that was the plan. When he arrived to collect the Volvo it had a flat rear nearside tyre. He kicked it in frustration. 'Shit, that's all I bloody well need,' he muttered to himself and stomped off back to the bar. 'Any chance of borrowing the jeep Mike? I've got a flat,' he said. Mike nodded and threw him the keys. 'Leave your keys here I'll get the garage to come over and change it, is it in the public car park?' said Mike. 'Yeah, thanks' Carter replied as he left. 'Ask them to check the rear brakes while they are about it, please.' There was little time to sort this job he thought, better make a good job if I'm about leave the country and his mind raced ahead to how he might escape and start a new life in Africa.

CHAPTER 87

Robert was bloody annoyed at the phone call. The phone was slammed down and he stomped out to the incident board. Staring at it in the hope it might give him some inspiration.

'Damn it,' he eventually uttered to himself. 'So bloody close again and they screw it up.' 'What's up boss? his assistant asked 'What's the problem?' 'Carter's car was fitted with a tracker, we all thought that was a great idea. When it moved the Spanish police picked it up quickly and did a raid when it stopped. The Volvo was in a bloody garage having its bloody brakes sorted! Carter wasn't driving it, now he will have been warned and he isn't going to be driving anywhere.'

Carter was definitely warned and was already well ahead of Robert. When the police surrounded the garage, the garage had phoned the bar to ask why the police were so interested in Carter's car, and Mike had immediately phoned Carter in turn to warn him the police were on the scene. 'Nothing to do with drugs is it?' he was asked. 'No think there is a problem with the ownership papers from the old lady who gave me the car before she died. Some mix up I presume. I've got the papers at the bar I'll pop back and try and sort this, sorry to get you mixed up in this, sure it can be resolved easily.' 'OK, bring the motor back will you,' said Mike, and thought nothing more about it.

Carter hadn't even started his journey and was back at the bar within minutes. It would be a race against the police who were still questioning the garage owner about the ownership of the Volvo and trying to extract an address for Carter. Luckily the mechanic feigned ignorance and said he was asked to repair the car by phone and the owner would pay him when he returned, and he wasn't sure where he lived. Carter raced into the bar, ran upstairs to collect the two packs of money, he then stuffed his few possessions in a small bag, which included the guns, and left quickly, but not before taking Mike's driving licence from his wallet.

Although there was a car hire company in town and Carter would have no trouble hiring a car until the weekend using Mike's licence, that means of escape would be too obvious. Carter took the tourist bus into Seville instead, and then changed onto the train to Madrid, arriving in the early evening. Perfect timing as far as Carter was concerned. A plan had been forming in his mind during the journey, and a phone call was made to confirm why he was on this route and had taken this option. There was a smile on his face when he found his assumption was correct. He was going north again, not south and certainly not Morocco, there was some unfinished business to sort out.

As night fell he spotted a cheap hotel, used Mike's licence as ID and paid in cash. There was an equally cheap restaurant attached to the hotel and he ate reasonably well, but certainly drank too much that night. The bedroom was hot, and hadn't been cleaned too well but he was too tired to care. His nemesis returned that night to plague him, and he was exhausted the next morning when he grabbed a couple of rolls and plenty of black coffee before taking on the next step of his plan.

There was no problem finding a local car hire company and using Mike's ID, Carter took possession of a cheap Seat for his journey. The hire car was absolutely hammered on route to make sure he got across the French border quickly. He still had a long way to go even then, and didn't arrive at his final destination until nearly dark, but he drove past it to find another cheap hotel away from his target. Again Mike's ID was used and a room booked in his name. Walking into town he found a bar that served food and repeated the previous night's performance, but with more drink. A lot more drink.

Again his dreams kept him awake but he didn't mind so much, he could plan his visit to Ms Christine Fowler carefully and slowly. Carter knew he had to observe her gite very carefully and make sure she was the only occupant before making his move. Eventually he dozed off and managed a few hours' sleep before waking at six am. His head spun and he felt sick. All the coffee in the room was drunk before he went downstairs to see if he could get a breakfast of sorts, and more black coffee. There was a lot to plan today before a night visit to get his money back.

The phone call the previous day had been to the estate agents in town, simply to ask if Barbara's gite was still up for sale, he explained he had seen it during the summer, and he now had the opportunity to purchase it. The agent explained he was sorry, but a relative had decided to live there, in fact he knew she had sold up in Britain and moved into the house permanently. 'Sorry about that, can I help you with any other property?' but the question fell on deaf ears, the line was dead and all he could hear was the dialling tone.

Absolutely perfect thought Carter, I'd made a guess and been proved right. The Seat drove along the road next to Barbara's gite, Carter could see there was only one car on the drive, it all looked quiet, and he couldn't see any other visitors. Half a mile up the road was a foot path he knew would lead back to the gite. The road was wide enough to run the car over the verge and off the road. No one would pay it any attention. Carter slipped away and walked back towards the gite. There was plenty of undergrowth to hide in and Carter continued walking until he was out of sight before doubling back and hiding. The hand gun was in his pocket and ready to use.

CHAPTER 88

Robert had the update from the Spanish police earlier in the day. They had tracked Carter back to the bar through the mechanic's mobile number. Mike admitted he put Carter up for a while and was using him as his bar keeper after settling a fight some weeks earlier. Yes he'd popped in early, but it was his day off and he was probably down on the beach somewhere eyeing up the local talent. Give him a couple of hours and he would turn up hopefully. The police sat and waited. The posters the police had circulated had also caught the eye of one of the victims of the fire rescue, and she alerted them to the fact that Carter had rescued her and several other people from the house. He was definitely identified as being at the location. Up until then the police hadn't released the fact that there were two victims who hadn't been killed by the fire, but had been shot and then left to burn. They did not want to exacerbate the situation of damaging the tourist trade with tales of drug gang executions.

However, they had already matched the bullets forensically to the killing in the car park and had a description of Carter from the bodyguard. Suddenly everything dropped into place and Carter became the primary target of a nationwide manhunt. Mike had no idea he had been sheltering a murderer, he just said he could handle himself and was useful around the place.

Their real problem the police had, was the fact that Carter had fled again, they had no idea where he was, where he was likely to flee to, or what he was driving now as the Volvo had been impounded, the chase had ground to a halt again. This had all been explained to Robert over the phone. Time for some intuition thought Robert. Carter had money now from the two contracts, or he assumed he had, and he would need transport to escape, but where was he going to go now? Africa seemed wrong somehow, think man, think.

Spain would be too hot for him now. There was a European Arrest Warrant out for him as well. But now Carter had been implicated in three drug related murders on top of that. Spain would be out of the question now, and with no way to use the ports, so was Morocco now. He would inform the port police to keep a fresh look out for Carter regardless, he couldn't make assumptions, this had to be done logically, he had to cover every base, there had to be no holes in his strategy, no mistakes. Carter had to get out of Spain, how was he going to do it? Hire a car? Robert had thought of that but nothing had been taken out locally, all the names had been cross checked, no he hadn't used the obvious route out, must have been the train. CCTV revealed nothing. Robert had got it right, he just hadn't looked far enough, his policeman's brain wasn't imaginative enough. So where the hell would be go? Back to France? No, he would be bloody mad to go there, far too well known already, and the police would be on the lookout for him. And hadn't he lost all his money there, and that would be galling for him. Again Robert informed the Bergerac police of his fears. Just in case. Don't take any chances.

Carter had a liking for hiding amongst ex pats, so were there any gullible colonies? Tuscany was the obvious choice, the Balearics? The latter wasn't much of a choice because of the small nature of the islands, too easy to trap him there.

Greece? Cyprus was a good option, especially the Turkish side, certainly worth a look at. Would he go into mainland Europe? He certainly could, but where would he go? What would be his reason to go and where would he hide? Robert had a feeling he would use his knowledge of the English to gain their trust and lose himself amongst the crowds again. Carter was conditioned by the army, he didn't plan, he reacted, He was street wise and just bloody lucky, so far.

CHAPTER 89

Carter was getting stiff, he had been laying in the under-growth for hours watching Christine. She seemed to have no interest in life other than getting suntanned. She had peeled off her bikini top and stayed out until sunset, when she went in the house still topless, to prepare a meal. Carter could hear pans and plates being nosily used. Carter didn't move until it was dark, the house was poorly lit he noticed, possibly only by candles, so he wouldn't be seen. Sliding carefully and silently out of his hiding place, Carter slipped around the garden until he was standing outside the back door. Christine hadn't seen or heard him, and he managed to silently stand at the end of the table without her even noticing.

Sensing something, she looked up and screamed, dropping her plate in the process. 'Don't bother screaming, there isn't anyone for miles. Just shut your bloody face, I want my money, you are living in the house I paid for. I built this for Barbara, she didn't have two pennies to rub together, but she was kind to me and I helped her. But you wanted it all, you could have kept quiet and paid me, but you didn't, and now I want what's mine.' She grabbed a carving knife off the table and waved it threateningly at Carter, but he just laughed her.

'Dear, I did years of unarmed combat in the army, I'd have that off you in a second, now put it down. You and I need to talk, and do some business. I know you have sold up and moved here, so you have lots of money floating about, and I'm going to get mine out of you now. I think that's fair and you get to keep the house with your money, not mine. Switch your computer on, you are going to transfer my share over the internet. Then I will go and you won't see me again, ever.' Carter smiled at her, 'Computer on now, please.'

Christine did as she was told, Carter was her worst nightmare, and he was here in her house. She had assumed, along with every policeman she had spoken to, that he had fled to Spain. Backing into her small study, whilst facing him all the time, Christine switched on the computer. Punching in her password she opened up her on line bank account. Carter told her his account and how much he wanted transferring. 'That's more than all your bills,' she was brave enough to say. 'Well you shouldn't have been so greedy, I've added a bit of interest for my trouble and enough to cover my travel expenses. I can ask you to transfer everything but I want what's mine only, I think that is fair,' he smiled at her.

Leaning over her shoulder he grabbed a breast and rubbed her nipple until became hard. She didn't dare refuse his advance. After a few minutes the transfer went through, and Carter checked it had been transferred using his own phone, which he immediately switched off so it couldn't be traced. 'There, that was easy wasn't it, I'll go now and you won't ever see me again. I promise.' She looked relieved at his statement, but didn't believe him. 'Are you happy with that arrangement? Eh?' he asked. She just nodded.

'Good then I'll be off. But you know I want something more from you, a bit of interest before I go. Stand up, turn around and face the computer. Carter kicked the chair away. His hands reached out and pulled her bikini bottoms down. Pushing her head down so it rested on the desk, he put one hand firmly on her back whilst the other spread her legs apart. He started to rub her public hair before inserting fingers into her vagina. He continued to push his fingers in and out before whispering in her ear, 'Think I'm owed this,' before pushing his penis deep inside her. She flinched but made no further movement after that, this was a one sided act of enjoyment. When Carter climaxed, he grabbed her neck hard and swung the gun butt down on her skull, knocking her unconscious. He withdrew and smiled at the prone figure sprawled across the table.

'Silly girl to think I could be trusted, and you did try and double cross me, this serves you right. Call it Karma.' Carter proceeded to electronically empty the rest of her account into his. 'Well you won't be needing it will you,' he smiled as he looked at the screen, 'That's better.' Carter then went around the house looking for anything flammable. Whatever he found was thrown over the furniture in every room, 'That should make a nice bonfire. Sorry Barbara, I can't let anyone take this house, if I can't have it, then no one can. You understand, don't you. And you wouldn't want this greedy cow to have it. I certainly don't.'

Beginning in the bedroom he started a blaze using his lighter. Every room got the same treatment. Taking the laptop with him so it could be disposed of later, in a river far away, Carter stood outside and watched the fire take hold. When he was convinced the conflagration would totally destroy the house he calmly walked back to the hire car, with the computer under his arm. The car would have to be dumped now, but he would use it for the time being to get as far away as possible.

There was no point in going south, back to Spain or remaining in France. So where next? It didn't really matter, he had his money again, and hers, plus the contract money. Not really thinking what he was going to do, he just headed east to see where it would lead. Toulouse sounded good. It would have good rail links and he could sit down, transfer all the money into different accounts for future use. Hide it all.

The fire wasn't reported for hours, simply because there weren't any neighbours for miles around. When the fire brigade finally arrived, the house was little more than a smouldering wreck. The roof had caved in and only two walls were still standing. Christine's remains were eventually found the next morning when the forensics team investigated. The fractured skull was obvious even then, and the police were immediately informed. It was a deliberate arson attack, coupled with a murder. The local police had just received a warning from Robert earlier and were going to go out that morning to warn Christine to be careful, as Carter was on the loose again. Like Robert, they hadn't thought Carter would be daring enough to go back to the gite.

An email explaining what had happened reached Robert after lunch and he read it with horror. 'Poor bloody girl, I thought she wasn't safe, but never dreamed Carter would come back, and certainly not kill her. And what for? Revenge, money, both possibly,' he said to himself. 'Now where he bloody hell has he gone? I can only think it will be one of the options I thought of earlier. But that is a bloody big area to cover. God where do you start on this one.'

Carter hadn't moved very far at all, he was in a decent hotel in Toulouse thinking about his future and just where to go next. A big decision that would take him to heaven or hell. Robert was in his own hell, Carter could go just about anywhere, what hope in hell had be got of catching him? Carter was thinking hard now, he was sitting in the dining room of the Hôtel Croix Baragnon, right in the centre of town. It hadn't taken him long to drive to Toulouse and the hotel suited his needs down to the ground. For once he had slept well and the dreams hadn't occurred that night, his blood lust was sated and his brain happy.

Breakfast was very good and he was studying a tourist map he had purchased that morning. He had left the hire car in the station car park and it was unlikely it would be discovered for days. The town had great rail links and he could go just about anywhere in Europe with ease. There were obvious choices, Tuscany being top of the list, but he could imagine the police in England thinking, where would he go next? They would discount both France and Spain as he was too well known there and look for him in pastures new, Italy, Croatia, Greece, even Turkey. They were logical creatures so let's get them looking in the wrong places for a start. The car being in the station car park would make them guess I had got on the train and gone east. So let's comply with the obvious. After walking to the station, Carter purchased a ticket to Monaco and got on the train an hour later, after making sure he was standing next to the station CCTV. However, he had no intention of going to the coast, and got off at Carcassonne. To the south was one of his favourite wine areas, Corbieres, should be able to find work on the farms there. Failing that, he was close to the coast and the hotels, they always needed an extra pair of hands. Carcassone proved to be a delight for Carter, an ancient town, cheap hotels and after asking around, he found the perfect hiding place.

Carter took a completely different course, he became a

volunteer. In return for volunteering to help renovate historic sites, he got free food and lodgings. No one would think of looking for him here. Right on the doorstep again. It was utterly out of character for him, but it would suit him down to the ground until the end of the season, and then he would think what to do then and only then. In the mean time this was safe, unless anyone recognised him and he would make a joke of it, and say the photos looked like him, but no, he had a doppelganger.

Most of the volunteers were students who wouldn't be interested in international criminals, he hoped. Carter would keep a low profile and keep to himself. Somehow, he would obtain a new identity, it hadn't been too hard so far, he was sure he could do it again. The restoration organisers had only been too happy to see a fresh pair of hands. They showed Carter where he could sleep and offered him a simple meal for the evening and a locker to put his bag in, which he happily took.

There was a single room with a sleeping bag and pillow on the basic bed, a chair in the corner, and not a lot else. They would wake him at seven thirty and expect him on site at eight thirty to begin at nine. There would be a break on site and food would be brought there. They would finish at six pm and go back for an evening meal, by the way did he have any special skills or was he happy to act as a labourer? Carter said he could turn his hand to most things and would be happy to try just about anything they wanted done. No further questions were asked and Carter hid away again, out of sight, hopefully out of mind. The heat would die down and he could get on with his life again. You know I might even get to Italy one day, he thought.

CHAPTER 90

The hire car was being assessed by the police. It had been broken into, the CD player stolen and several of the windows smashed. It was proving hard to move because the tyres had also been let down. Eventually it was hauled onto the back of a breakdown truck and taken to the town council workshops before trying to try track down the owner. That proved a little easier as there was a hire company sticker in the rear window. They were in turn phoned and told to collect their property along with paying the costs of the recovery.

Two days later when the car was returned, Michael received a summons and large invoice for not returning the car and the insurance excess for the damage. When he refused to pay anything, the police were involved and Mike had several CNP officers in his bar. They said he had hired the car, his licence was used as ID and the car stolen and wrecked. If he didn't pay, the officers would arrest him. There were several heated phone calls between him and the hire company before Mike convinced them his licence had been stolen, and used as ID. The finger was squarely pointed at Carter once more, and reports were filed that would mean the man hunt was on again. The report took a day to filter down to Robert, who was overjoyed.

'He's made a mistake again, knew he would. The car has given away his location, he should have destroyed it, pushed it in a lake, burnt it out. Now we know where he is heading or at least we know where to start looking where he left off.'

Robert was on the phone to the police at Toulouse to verify

what they had. The hotel had been tracked down, again using Mike's ID. But where he had gone from there was a mystery. The police had assumed he had either hired another car or left by public transport. One thing they did have on their side was times and dates of his stay in the city. They investigated the railway station and came up trumps and identified Carter from the CCTCV recordings.

'We have a clear identification of Carter from the recording tapes,' said the voice at the end of the line. 'Absolutely no question, he made no attempt to hide, he was in clear view for some time. We have shown his picture to the staff and one of them remembered him, because he purchased a ticket right through to Monaco.'

'Monaco?' said Robert in surprise. 'Without doubt. It looks as if he was thinking of going to Italy.' 'So why stop at Monaco? Doesn't make sense, this is a little too obvious. I don't like this, it's a little too easy unless he wanted us to know where he was going and wanted to laugh in our faces. But he's not that stupid, is he? Were you able to check the CCTV at Monaco? said Robert hopefully. 'We knew you would request that, and we have checked. There is no sign of him, and we have checked for several days after, just in case. He must have got off the train before then, we are checking that possibility and will let you know if we find anything.' 'Thank you, that is much appreciated, keep in touch,' and Robert put the phone down and punched the air in triumph.

'Got you, I knew you'd make a mistake, thought you were so clever didn't you. The net is closing again and you are not going to escape now, I'm coming for you and you will pay for what you have done.' Robert felt like packing a bag and flying out, but he knew he wasn't ready for that just yet. Instead he sat in front of the computer and put up maps of the area. What were the obvious towns to start on? Carter had almost certainly gone to ground in the countryside somewhere, Farms and vineyards would be the first place to start, then hotels, gites, the list was endless.

Robert knew he was being far too optimistic, it was a huge area they were contemplating to search, but there was an easy way to put the fear of God into Carter and make life uncomfortable for him at the same time. Robert had many 'friends' in the media and often slipped them a story to get a little extra publicity on a case he was getting stuck on. The newspaper or TV station concocted a story along the lines he wanted, this was printed or screened, which gave Robert a second chance to speak about the case. The added publicity often jogged people's memories or gave the informers something to do. It was an added weapon for him to use. Especially if money was involved. Robert had already ascertained that a reward would be offered for information leading to the arrest of Carter.

Robert intended to try it out on Carter. He wrote a long piece of background material so that the media had something to work on. Included were the murder in Maidstone, Tracey's drowning and the drug running and murder in Dover. The killing of Jaeger in France was highly featured, including the kidnapping of the shop keeper in Dieppe and the shooting of the drugs contact. The information went on to talk about the three contract murders in Spain and the connection to drugs again, and finally the ruthless killing of Christine and the fire and destruction of the gite in France. Robert said the police knew he was heading towards Italy and possibly points further east, but that he was hiding close to Toulouse, possibly on a farm, vineyard or hotel. All the known photos and disguises of Carter were included in his 'press release'.

Robert had made a huge deal out of the fact that Carter was a ruthless criminal who would use murder to escape. The story featured heavily in England in the Sunday papers who knew a good story when they saw it. Their counterparts in Europe picked up the story and flooded the media and TV with the shock revelation Carter was back in France, and killing again.

CHAPTER 91

Carter was unaware all this was going on behind his back. He had other things on his mind. Standing in front of him was a used cross country motor bike. It was also road legal which is what Carter really needed. One of the big problems with a car was it prevented him using the motorways as there were tolls, ANPR cameras and the inability to get off the road if he was being chased. This however, gave him a whole new flexible ability to get about, and get away if needed. Having lost his bike fleeing from Spain, Carter had been looking for another form of transport. Cars had proved too easy to track, but this new solution looked perfect, and he rode it back to his temporary home.

The restoration work around the city had been going well, he had managed to keep a low profile and was once again changing his appearance, his hair was longer and the beard was coming along nicely. They liked his work and it provided food and shelter which was exactly what he needed. But he had no idea Robert was about to drop a bombshell on his peaceful life.

It took a while for English papers to reach the south of France and they were usually a couple of days behind their release in England. A Sunday paper wasn't a luxury Carter would often treat himself to, so he missed his face being splashed all over the inside of all the tabloids eager to fill their pages with sensational articles. There were few English left in the area at this time of year, so the demand for English papers was low. However, the French papers picked up on the story, perhaps not with such vigour as the English ones, but certainly with enough coverage to make Carter shudder when he saw his face plastered all over le Figaro and Le Monde when he went into town on his way to the restoration project. Somebody has it in for me he thought, time for a move again. In fact he had also been identified on site by one of his co-workers, but by the time they went looking for him, Carter had cleared out his locker, packed everything in his backpack and was already on the road heading for safety.

Using the motorway he made good time to the coast where he turned south to Perpignan which was close to the Spanish border. Stopping in the town he purchased a small two-man tent, food and drink from a supermarket and set off again to the seaside town of Argles, where he holed up on a small campsite near the beach. It was out of the way and in the opposite direction to the one they would expect him to take. He would be safe for the time being. No one knew he was travelling by bike, he hadn't taken it to the restoration site, it remained at his hut, so they had no way of knowing how he was travelling.

The tent was erected, the cold food unwrapped and eaten straight from the packets but washed down with the best part of a bottle of Languedoc. The red wine was heavy, fruity and had the desired effect, he was already tired, and the wine ensured he slept well, he didn't dream, his mind was on other things, escape being at the top of his priorities. The next morning he rode into town and picked up more food and a pocket atlas of France. That would be studied in depth to see if there was an alternative escape route or some safe destination that the police wouldn't think about.

Walking down to the gritty beach, Carter ate and drank his fill before examining the atlas. Did he go back to Spain, he was close enough to go back over the border easily, but he would have to be very careful and eventually someone would spot him or he would make a mistake somewhere. Somewhere where he wasn't known would be the obvious solution. A new country. Italy came to mind but they were bound to chase him there. Further afield? Greece, Turkey? It was a bloody shame his route to north Africa had been blocked, he liked the sound of Morocco. But it was a stable country, he would stand out like a sore thumb if he tried to use his skills as a soldier. Returning to study the maps, he spotted something he hadn't even thought about before. Algeria. There were plenty of ferries out of Marseilles to Corsica, Sardinia, Italy and a 20 hour service to Algiers. Bloody perfect!

There was plenty of unsettled arguments in the African countries bordering the Med, he was bound to find some useful work there. Carter lay back on the beach and thought about his options. It was too dangerous to stay where he was, in fact most of Europe would be closed to him soon. No, time for pastures new, he went back to his tent and slept. His mind was at ease for once, even the dead didn't disturb his dreams for once. It was already plotting the escape route and a new life. Carter smiled in his sleep. The next morning he sat in the clubhouse plugged in the laptop and joined the free wi-fi to research Algeria to see if there might be enough of an opening for his skills to be put to use. What he read didn't encourage him much. Years of turmoil seemed to have resolved themselves, and although there was still unrest, the military seemed to rule the roost, and likely would do for a long time yet. The other disquieting factor was the introduction of Russian military companies such as Wagner, who would make his arrival less than welcome. Libya was another hot spot but it would be Muslim fighting Muslim for the control of the oil. The more he looked at it, the more unlikely Africa would be of use to him and his skills. His research did however throw up some interesting facts in that British, German and American companies were recruiting mercenaries in these countries. That might be worth looking into.

CHAPTER 92

Robert knew his plan was working, not quite as expected, but working all the same. The news of Carter working on a safe site in France was encouraging. It proved he had out guessed Carter, and that a manhunt using the media, did work. Carter had obviously got wind that he was being hunted, and he was lucky again to have escaped before the authorities could get to the scene. But only by the skin of his teeth this time. Robert was slowly closing down his alternative routes of escape, and putting pressure on him. The story route had worked, and the chance to do a follow up press piece was quickly seized upon and released to the French media. Again they splashed Carter's face all over the TV and papers, sooner or later someone would spot him and hopefully he would be caught napping. The story ran over a couple of days, more to pad out the editorial than anything. It was sensationalist and easy editorial that could use no end of photographs, maps and images of burnt out residences, bars, victims and the like.

Because of his hideous crimes, Carter became something of a celebratory in France, the press loved the fact that he was English, evil and the brilliant French police force were hunting him down, and they expected to catch him soon. It took on a surreal 'Day of the Jackal' approach all of its own. In fact the French authorities had absolutely no idea where Carter was at that precise time, they knew where he had been, they knew where he had worked, they had a good description of him from his co-workers, but they had no idea where he had gone, what his mode of transport was, nor where he was heading. They were hoping the publicity would smoke Carter out, that someone would recognise him, or he would be spotted.

Again it proved to be a simple phone call that alerted the police to Carter's location, or at least how to start to look for him. The sale of the bike prompted the seller to phone in its details to the newspaper. A reporter was sent instantly to interview the man and pictures of the ex-owner appeared in the paper the next morning. To do justice to the man, he did have the courtesy to inform the police as well. That information was distributed to every police force in south west France.

Carter didn't see it until the day after. Picking up the paper, he paid for it and walked very quickly out of the shop before anyone recognised him. Donning his helmet so he couldn't be seen, he rode away feeling much safer back on his bike. In his back pack was everything he really needed and he thought it better not to go back to the site and pick up his tent. That would be easy to replace, and he had plenty of money. Swearing under his breath, 'Bugger, this changes everything, no way can I stay in France,' he said as he mounted the bike.

As he left the camp site he turned south and headed for Spain. 'Last place they would expect me to go. Have to completely re-plan what I was going to do. Who cares, they haven't got a clue where I am or where I'm going,' he said to himself. Little did he know that his whereabouts had been phoned in by the previous bike owner, several people in the village and a couple from the campsite who had all recognised him and were keen to stake a claim to the reward offered. The chase was on again. But Spain was very close and the Spanish police surely wouldn't be looking for him after all this time. Would they?

First stop would be Barcelona, it was big enough to lose himself in and he was convinced the police would think he was going to Africa or Italy, not back into the most dangerous place he could think of. As he roared off his mind racing, Carter couldn't think where he was really heading. The road went to Figueres, which was almost impossible to miss, but after that he could take the coast road rather the AP7, scenic if nothing else, but harder to monitor. The town was famous for being Dali's birthplace and he would have loved to explore it but it would have to wait until he was safe again. After passing through Figueres he took the coast road into Barcelona, reaching it after a couple of hours. Riding into the centre of the city he found the docks were a lot nearer than he thought. Just out of curiosity he wondered what countries he could reach from there. He was amazed to find that in just twenty hours he could be in Rome. Now that really would throw them off his trail.

Carter wanted to see just one thing in Barcelona before he left, the Familia Sagrada. It dominated the city skyline and he had heard people rave about it. There was no point in being on the run all the time, you had to stop, and when you did, it would be a shame to waste an opportunity to see something world renowned. Being a good tourist he went inside and couldn't believe his eyes. The interior was beyond stunning. He was not artistic or religious but this place was something else. Possibly the most beautiful building he had ever been inside. The roof looked like something out of a fairy tale and the huge stained glass windows threw rainbows across the floor. It took him nearly two hours to fully take in the total effect of the wonderful architecture before his survival instinct kicked in and he realised he needed to board the ferry.

The bike took him to the ferry port and he purchased his ticket just an hour before it sailed, that was pure good timing. The ferry had a decent restaurant and bar and he enjoyed a slap up meal and a decent bottle of wine before curling up on a vacant seat. The ship was far bigger than he expected and there were few people making the crossing. There was a lot of space and quiet areas where he wouldn't be disturbed. Rome here we come, and up yours coppers. There was no way they would think of looking for him in Italy, his decision to go on the ferry was totally on the spur of the moment, totally out of character, and nothing short of brilliant, he was safe again. Carter slept for a good deal of the twenty hour crossing and only awoke when people started to move about hoping that breakfast was about to be served.

Joining the queue he managed to put together a decent meal which he washed down with a lot of coffee. Even then there was still a long way to go and he didn't arrive in port until early evening. Disembarking he found he was still a long way west of Rome and he decided to find a cheap hotel in Civitavecchia before deciding where to go next. There were plenty to choose from, and picked one with a secure parking area and a bar next door. Perfect, life was looking good again. Another meal, another bottle of wine, a quiet room and a decent bed proved ideal. There were no dreams and he slept like the dead.

CHAPTER 93

'Absolutely nothing' said Robert, 'Absolutely bloody nothing. He has gone to ground again, but where this time? We know where he was hiding, we know what he looks like again, we know he is on a bike now, we know the number, make and colour of that. So why can't we find him?' Looking down at the report Robert realised he had been close again, but all he had achieved was to flush Carter out.

Earlier, the French police had swooped on the campsite, found the empty tent with the newspaper inside. Carter had seen the publicity and obviously fled in a hurry. But where? Robert read through the report again, the publicity had worked, he had been recognised by several people, that proved he was getting careless and thought he was safe and didn't need to hide. The only downside was the publicity had pre-warned Carter he was being hunted very successfully, and that people were on the lookout for him again. Robert wouldn't use that tactic again, he needed to think like Carter did, use a lot of animal cunning now.

Several hours later another email announced that had picked up Carter's trail again. An ANPC camera had tracked him crossing the border into Spain and another CCTV had spotted him in Figueres. They hadn't found any trace of him after that. Robert thought, that's bloody clever, going back into Spain, if it wasn't for the Big Brother cameras, he would never have guessed Carter would have taken the chance of going back to Spain. Carter was chancing it for sure. Was he being clever or panicked?

But was he going to hide there? Had he got a bolt hole? Was this a red herring yet again, and was he going to double back into France? Both countries were looking for him now. Spain would be very difficult for him, especially now they had a specific search area. Robert looked at the map again. Why Spain, had Carter been careless with the cameras, or did he want to be spotted? There was a good chance it was a deliberate ploy, and he would cross back in to France at some point. Robert couldn't work out if he was acting in pure survival mode or planning something. Robert realised that Barcelona was not that far away from where Carter was last spotted, was it worth putting out an APB there? No harm in that, just a lot of hard work for the Spanish police again.

Sure enough three hours later, another email came back from Spain with a report that Carter had been picked up on the city CCTV and was definitely in Barcelona. They hadn't found any traffic records of him leaving, and they were now engaged in a city wide search for the bike. So close but Robert could only pace the office waiting for further news, but nothing else came that night, and he decided to eventually go home and get some rest. Tiredness overcame him when he stepped through the door. It was cold inside, and he found he had nothing in the house to even make a decent sandwich with. Bugger.

There was a pub at the end of the road that would knock him up a snack, but when he got there, they had closed the food section as it was so late. Going home again he picked up his car for the short drive to the supermarket. Pushing the trolley around in a dream, he cherry picked anything that was easy to eat, as he couldn't be asked to cook anything at this time of night. Cooked chicken portions, ham slices, bread and a few tins went into the trolley. It looked sad in the bottom of the trolley, so he picked up some microwave meals to join them. These were the sort of thing his mother bought in M&S. Was he getting old, and taking the easy way out of nourishing himself.

Paying for them, he piled everything on the front seat of the car as he resented paying twenty pence for a bag, even if it was environmentally friendly. Back in the sad house he threw one of the instant dinners in the microwave whilst he poured a large scotch. Minutes later the timer went off, but he was already sound asleep. The scotch beside him untouched. When he awoke, he realised he was still hungry but couldn't face the now cold instant meal he found in the microwave. Coffee and cereals would have to do this morning. Looking at the scotch, he found it tempting, but put it back on the kitchen worktop ready for the evening. He didn't want to start drinking first thing in the morning, far too many of his colleagues had gone down that route, and didn't want to go downhill to being a drunk, just yet.

It was only when he got to the station that he found he was still wearing yesterday's clothes and he felt crumpled and disorganised. Life was catching up with him and he would have to make an excuse and get back home to change later. There was an email on his desk that Carter had been recorded boarding the ferry yesterday, he was now in Rome somewhere. 'Bastard,' he shouted out loud in his office, 'Bastard, bastard, bastard. He's running circles around all of us again. Do we have any contacts with the Italian police,' he shouted at his startled staff in the CID room. 'If not, find someone quickly, he has a day's march on us again.' Storming out of his office he went home, changed, had a coffee to gather his thoughts and then went back to plan how to catch Carter in a completely new country. Carter had taken Robert completely by surprise, thinking he had him hemmed in and close to capture, had proved completely inaccurate.

Robert simply hadn't considered the possibility of Carter going back to Spain for a start, and then to be completely out manoeuvred by using the ferry to escape, was utterly frustrating. He hadn't out guessed Carter at all, simply moved him into territory where he wasn't known. Carter had the run of a completely new country now. OK, they knew he was heading for Rome, it was always full of visitors and tourists, he would be close to impossible to track down there, but he would move on eventually, but where? Robert almost felt like tossing a coin to make a decision. Instead he took out a large scale map of Italy kept in the office. Rome was very central, would he stay there? Unlikely. North or south? North, if he went south it would trap him, the only escape routes would be via ferry to Sardinia or Corsica.

North then, it was logical.

Carter thought the opposite and had headed south and ignored Rome altogether. Too obvious thought Carter, need to think things out, go to ground for a short while to make sure he hadn't been followed and that his tracks had been covered. France and Spain were too hot for him now. North Africa still appealed to him, but the chances of fighting there were risky. If he was going to be a mercenary it would have to be through one of the big security companies. Not sure he liked that but worth some research and an email of two when things calmed down.

The pocket guide to Italy he had purchased on the ferry was

in his pocket. He had studied it on the long sea trip and had picked out several places he wanted visit, although that made him feel like a tourist. That didn't worry him, it was easy to lose himself in a big town rather than a village. There was cash in his pocket and he could book himself into all sorts of cheap chain hotels using the business accounts he had set up, with nothing that could be traced to him.

Naples would be his first major stop over, a bit of a long ride but he could find somewhere closer to overnight and investigate the town at his leisure later on. Naples was about two hundred and fifty km from Rome, an easy ride but the roads were limiting for him. If he avoided the motorways there was a coast road he could use that would avoid Latina and Caserta and take him into Naples. Carter didn't need a map to find Naples, Vesuvius stood out for miles. It dominated the town from every angle and was very prominent from the old town around the docks. What amazed him were the number of houses built on the slopes of the volcano, what were these people thinking?

Rather than stay in the town, he intended to stay in the port at Salerno that would give him a chance to try out the bike around the Amalfi coast road. Can't be a tourist he thought to himself as he opened up the bike above Sorrento. The sea to his right was the most incredible blue and he could see Capri in the distance, home of the rich and famous, but he didn't care about them, this was all about him. It wasn't the fastest of bikes but the ride along the twisting narrow road down into Amalfi was brilliant and a couple of times he had to take evasive action to avoid the compact tourist buses that also travelled on the road at speed. It didn't take long to reach the town and he pulled into the car park facing the entrance to the town. The place was swarming with people, which he hated, but it suited him fine today.

It was almost a parody of everything he thought was wrong about the tourist trade, and he had to chuckle at the number of shops selling plates with Amalfi emblazoned all over them, a throwback to the sixties. Subtlety wasn't one of their strong points, nor was good taste. Finding a bar he sat down and enjoyed a blonde beer whilst people watching. It was tempting to look for a cheap hotel in the town but he thought it would be safer to travel on to the port, less obvious place to stay. Carter had no idea what to expect in Salerno, he just knew it had plenty of links to the islands in the Med, which would be useful in an emergency, but he thought he had done enough to throw any police chase off for quite a while. It was a short journey to the port. It provided one surprise which delighted his military back ground, there was a museum dedicated to the Allied landings in nineteen forty three.

The landings were the second largest after D Day with a thousand ships and two hundred thousand soldiers, and he was intrigued. It was a piece of history he knew very little about and he spent an age in the museum watching actual film of the landings.

Eventually he left to find a cheap hotel. The town was a delight and much better than he imagined. Roman ruins, a medieval castle, cathedral and excellent seafront took him by surprise. The town was full of B&Bs and he had no trouble finding a place to stay. Life was being good to Carter for once. Yes, he was on the run, but that wouldn't last for ever. Sooner or later the police would forget about him and his crimes would fade into the record books. All he had to do was keep his head down. But for how long? When he went to ground in France it had worked beautifully, but not so well in Spain. He was in the lap of the gods it seemed. In his heart he thought that eventually his luck would run out, but if he played his cards right, that might be years away, he just had to make sure that was the case, but how?

Carter wasn't known in Italy so he had no qualms about talking to people he met in the bars in town. Most were Brits who had settled in the area and regarded it as home. The area was more peaceful than Naples, and nowhere near as expensive as the Almalfi area. The occasional drink purchased for an expat brought a plethora of information about the area, it's people, customs and any opportunities that might be exploited. It seemed that it was pretty safe place to live and the only crime people worried about was bribery and corruption, but that was true across all of Italy.

Carter discovered that there were a lot of holiday lets in the area but as the season closed in, many of them closed up for winter. The big problem there was it left the properties vulnerable to break ins. One guy Carter spoke to said many of the properties now had house sitters to guard against that eventuality. His ears pricked up. This was an opportunity to lose himself in full view once again, this would do nicely. It was obvious that he couldn't provide that service in that particular region. Chances were he might well have been spotted or tracked there. There was a definite need to move to another area, just for his own peace of mind. Eventually his description would filter into Italy and this chap might well remember him and say how interested he was in house sitting. No, it would have to be further afield. His attempts to find a good hiding place would have to be made further north now.

During his stay in the town, Carter changed his lodgings several times before deciding he had enough information to try and find a suitable house to take under his wing. So where do most of the tourists go, Rome, Florence, Sienna, Pisa? Carter decided Rome was out, but the mountains and hills around Sienna had plenty of villas. Why not start there.

Carter met up with his contact on several occasions to see how to he could become a glorified housekeeper. Google of course provided the answer, there were no end of agencies that looked for guardians. Carter looked through a lot of sites and picked a couple of the more down market ones, knowing the checks wouldn't be quite so deep. Using his bar contact to translate, Carter managed to phone one of the agencies who seemed to deal in remote properties. There was a need for a reference and passport details before they would employ him. Carter explained this to his drinking partner who happily supplied an excellent reference by email, but only after he had been well fed and watered during the evening. 'Always happy to help a fellow Brit,' he smiled.

'All set then' he said thanking his co-conspirator. A bottle was left on the table as a thank you, and Carter asked him to keep their chat a secret as he had some people he owed money to, that he wanted to avoid. This was greeted with a knowing nod and a shake of hands. Carter packed up his belongings one last time and got on his bike to try his luck, he had a feeling this could be his lucky day. Arrezo it was then, a large villa with an out building he could use as his own. Up in the hills about five km away and totally isolated from the main town.

Details of where to find the agency were messaged to his phone and Carter replied he would be there in two days to pick up the keys. It was close to three hundred km away and he need to keep to the minor roads again. The road to Avellino and Benevento took him clear of Naples, he took the mountain road to the ancient towns of Campobasso and Isernia. After that it was a long quiet run into L'Aquila. Quiet and L'Aquila didn't quite go together and the town had suffered a major earthquake some years earlier, destroying many of the historic buildings in the process. However, because of this it didn't have the huge numbers of tourists other Italian cities suffered from, and as it was only about ninty minutes away from Rome, they tended to divert to the somewhat calmer city. It would make the ideal overnight stop. As usual Carter chose a minor hotel on the outskirts of town and paid in cash.

In the morning he was away quickly and took the road to Perugia close to where he was collecting the agency keys. He found the city quite amazing with stairs and escalators within the city walls, somewhere to investigate at his leisure in the future, but for now he had to get out of sight, The twisting road to Arezzo was enjoyable on the bike, and Carter thought he would look forward to racing here. The interview at the agency was a formality, and he collected the keys and directions after a short talk on what was required of him, and how to get to the villa. After all the paperwork was completed, he compiled a small stock of food which was added to his back pack, including a decent bottle of scotch. The villa was described as remote and so it proved. As he left Arezzo and headed for Florence, he was diverted onto smaller and smaller side roads until he ended up on a track leading to the house.

Checking the main building and convincing himself that it was secure, he made himself comfortable in the small holiday villa next door, which was to be his home for the foreseeable future.

This was the life, he thought to himself. I could be very comfortable here and get paid into the deal. The only drawback was there was no town close by, he would have to rely on picking up supplies from a few small shops in the local villages. Carter wasn't so sure this would be a good idea as he would soon become known there. Still that was a minor problem, he would investigate that at his leisure another day. There were enough provisions safely tucked away in the house to last him for a while. The holiday home was basic but comfortable and as the night set in Carter realised just how remote the place was, he couldn't see another light for miles, he was on his own up here. The bike was hidden away in a barn and chained up securely. The main villa was checked again and Carter returned to his temporary home. There was a TV but it was all Italian, German and French stations. Eventually he found the BBC News Channel, but he soon got bored with that, returning to subtitled American series where he could just about make out the plot lines, even if it was badly overdubbed in Italian. It was a good start to his new adventure, and Carter knew he was safe for now.

CHAPTER 94

Robert was frustrated. Again he had absolutely no idea where Carter was. Italy was as small an area he could pin Carter down to. The tracking system has not clicked into place quite so effectively in Italy as it had in France and Spain, and Robert had no real idea of where Carter was hiding. The only lead he had would be through the bike. It was French registered, but that wouldn't be a problem, people crossed the borders between countries so easily, and it wouldn't look out of place in Italy. An APB was issued and Robert asked the Italian police to keep a close look out for the bike or any hint of Carter. There were of course CCTV cameras on the motorways but if Carter was on any of the tapes, they had long been erased by now. This was a serious dead end for Robert.

In the days that followed here was no sign of Carter, or the bike, and Robert was once again tempted to issue an appeal to help track him down, but thought there must be better ways of spreading the story, without tipping off Carter with a big manhunt. Robert had many press contacts in the UK and wondered if any of them had contacts with Italian magazines or knew a press journalist who might be interested in an exclusive story. Feelers were extended and one of his contacts came back with a name to say an Italian magazine would be very interested to publish an in depth story on Carter, and how the chase had ended up in his country. Deja vu thought Robert. Robert started the long process of collating all the information on the case again so that he could have everything ready for a meeting he had set up for later in the week. The story had to be sensationalist, but that wasn't Robert's job, he would just present the facts and let the journalist polish it into a story. It was a long shot but worth a try. To hunt Carter, he just needed a starting point and this might just provide one.

When Robert met up with the journalist in London, he handed the file over. The journalist said he worked freelance for Chi and had sounded them out on a story particularly concerning the death of Jaeger, the drowning of Tracey, and narrow escape of his Australian lover, the drug killings. In fact it had sex, drugs and crime all rolled into one, made it a wonderful story, and he was sure it could be made into a wonderful article. Robert asked if the source could be kept secret for the moment, in return, if and when Carter was finally brought to justice, he would personally do a follow up article praising the magazine in helping catch the criminal. There was a well frequented magazine website that could also be exploited.

During a coffee, the two discussed how to maximise exposure over a protracted period. It was decided to put tasters out on the web and the magazine, to tempt readers into looking forward to a tasty true sexy, murder story. Robert was sure this man could do the job well. Italians always loved drama and this story could be blown up into something quite huge. Robert jokingly said it would make a good film and he should investigate that possibility. Although he laughed at the idea, Robert saw the journalist's eyes light up. 'That is a brilliant idea, my friend. Even if Carter escapes and is never found, this would make a wonderful film. I can see it now. A definite Hollywood blockbuster.' Then he too burst into laughter. 'We will leave that for the future, in the meantime, I will write up the tasters to tempt a few readers and then send you the draft to make sure I have everything correct. Not that would worry me too much if I haven't. Italian magazines don't have too much of a reputation on that front.'

Coffee was finished and the men shook hands and left, Robert turned around and shouted back 'Don't forget, anonymous!' There was dismissive and flippant wave of the hand from the journalist who didn't even turn around.

CHAPTER 95

Carter wasn't worried about being found, this hiding place was so remote he hadn't seen a soul since he arrived. There was absolutely no one about and he had to go into the villages to see anyone, or into Sienna or Arrezo to meet anyone. His appearance was again changing, the beard was growing back but at the moment he just looked rather unshaven. That would become a nicely sculptured beard eventually, and he wouldn't look too out of place in Italy.

Carter enjoyed the solitude but it could be slightly unnerving and on more than one occasion he went out to investigate strange noises, but found nothing. One night he heard scuffling noises outside and went to investigate, only to be confronted by a boar and a herd of small piglets all rooting about in the remains of the veg patch. Carter had to laugh, he had been scared of the 'pigs' in the UK to find the real ones in Italy had only made him jump, and were easily shooed away.

Chuckling to himself on the way back to his little house, Carter thought he must explore the area a bit more, he would go stir crazy up here on his own. But that night a large scotch helped him sleep, and in the morning he was on the bike and heading into Arezzo to enjoy life a little. By lunch time he had filled the backpack with Chianti, fresh bread, all sorts of meats and sausages from the market and was looking for a quiet spot for lunch. The town was full of bars and small restaurants, and he had no trouble finding somewhere.

It was still sunny at this time of the year and he sat outside admiring the beautiful Italian women who seemed to be everywhere in this town. Carter missed sex, it was nothing to do with love or commitment, it was a pure animal act and he needed it. Now he was working properly he was definitely on the lookout for a likely partner. Was he going to get lucky today or go without? Ordering a wine to go with his meal he couldn't help notice the waitress had been looking at him, as he in turn, looked at the passing women. When she returned with his wine she commented in perfect English, but with a wonderful Italian twang. 'You like Italian women?' It was intended as a humorous comment, but Carter detected a note of longing behind it.

Carter was somewhat taken aback, he hadn't thought he would be approached. 'Of course,' he replied, 'Who wouldn't, I think they are all beautiful, must be the pasta, gives them wonderful curves.' She laughed, 'And me, do I have wonderful curves?' 'Oh yes, and in all the right places too,' he replied. 'Right answer,' she laughed and returned to the kitchen, smiling all the time.

Carter knew he was onto a good thing and watched her all afternoon as she flirted with not just him but all the customers. Every time she came out from the kitchen, she smiled at him, and he smiled back. By the time he had several glasses of wine she had paid his table rather more attention than it should have done. By late afternoon, the lunch diners had gone and she came and sat down at his table and poured herself a glass from his bottle. Her apron came off, and she smiled at him. 'What you said earlier, was that just flattery to put me in a good mood, or do you find me attractive as well. I am not as pretty or a young as the girls you have been watching,' and she pouted at him provocatively.

Carter knew he was onto a good thing if he played this slowly and gently, she would be like putty in his hands. He reached across the table and gently took her hand, 'You are not as young as they perhaps, but you are just as pretty, and with far more experience of the joys of life I would think. I love experienced women. But I don't even know your name. 'Sophia.' and she actually blushed in response. There was no second guessing where this was leading, and it would be by mutual consent by the feel of it.

'When do you finish, because I would like you to show me the wonders of the town Sophia. Would that be permissible?' 'I have just finished. Maria does the evening shift, I am free now if you would like to walk around a little.' Carter smiled at her, she was begging to be added to his list of conquests, he was going to really enjoy Italy he thought.

The evening went well, she was comfortable with Carter and showed him around the town. She had taken him from the commercial centre up to the cathedral perched on an incline at the top of the town. It started with holding hands to an arm around a shoulder to one around her waist to draw her closer. At the cathedral they were passionately kissing and Carter knew she would be his, don't waste the moment, act fast. Perfect thought Carter, as his bike was parked around the corner, would he be up to the act. 'Come with me I want to show you my home, I will cook for you this evening if you want.' 'That should be amusing, the English are not renowned for their cooking,' she laughed at him. 'But I do a great breakfast', he grinned.

The intent was there now, and he had issued an obvious

invitation to stay the night. She smiled at Carter, 'Why not, but I cook for you tonight, deal?' 'Deal, my bike is just around the corner'. She grinned again and took the backpack from him as she snuggled up behind him in the passenger seat. Minutes later they were roaring up the mountain road to the villa. She held him tightly, but her hands wandered constantly, which encouraged him no end but made it hard to concentrate. When they arrived, they didn't bother with food for a long time, clothes were starting to be discarded almost as soon as they got through the front door.

Carter wasn't wrong, she certainly was experienced and she also knew what she wanted. As he pulled off his T-shirt, she had already unzipped him and had her hands inside his pants. She pushed him backwards over the arm of the sofa and fell on top of him. Her clothes soon followed and she dictated the position as she straddled him, allowing him to slip inside her. She pushed against his chest whilst moving her hips slowly until she climaxed with a low 'yessss,' in just a few minutes. Sitting upright now, Carter realised she hadn't finished and she continued to rub her vagina against him. Sex with this one is going to be bloody good, bordering on the sublime he thought as she came again. This was going to be a long night he thought.

Several hours later she stood naked in front of the cooker preparing a meal from the strange collection of food he had picked up earlier in the day. Carter crept up behind her, reaching around to grasp her breasts. 'Turn it down a little please, so it won't burn,' he whispered as he pulled her hips back toward him. Reaching down he guided himself into her and she pushed back onto him. 'Dinner can wait,' she said. It wasn't eaten until very late that night.

CHAPTER 96

The article didn't go into publication for several weeks, by which time Robert had established a good relationship with the Italian police. They were briefed on Carter, his MO, description and the fact he had gone to ground somewhere in Italy. The only real clue they had was the bike and an ABP was circulated to all units to watch out for the French registered bike. Hotels and any likely places he might stay, were regularly checked but to no avail.

When the article did get printed, there were numerous reports of Carter, mostly erroneous. There were a couple of sightings that made sense from hotels and Robert was able to use them to try and track his movements. They were incomplete but indicated he had gone south first and the come back into the central region. There was no trace for several weeks and he hadn't crossed north by any major route as he hadn't been spotted by the ANPR cameras. The police assumed he was somewhere in Tuscany or close by. The area had an enormous ex pat population and they started a systematic search of British owned farms, vineyards, hotels and B&Bs but with no success.

Robert was beginning to suspect Carter had escaped once again in some new guise. Or he had gone to ground in some form he wouldn't be able to second guess. Either way it was frustrating and Robert had to fall back on the fact that Carter might make some sort of mistake or he would let his guard down and be spotted. It was going to be a waiting game. Until there was proof Carter was in a specific area, he had to run the case from his office in the UK. Not very satisfactory, and all very long distance. Back to a bloody waiting game again, all very cat and mouse, but the cat nearly always got the mouse in the end.

CHAPTER 97

Carter was woken the next morning by a sharp jab in the ribs. There was a fresh coffee thrust under his nose and Sophia smiled at him from the end of the bed. 'I have to go to work soon and you promised me breakfast, remember? I'll need you to drop me back into town for work.' Carter was feeling horny but she rebuffed him saying, 'We don't have time for that this morning 'I'm afraid, and I'm hungry!' Carter couldn't quite rustle up a full English from the odds and ends he purchased the day before, but over another cup of coffee it didn't matter, they enjoyed each other's company before biking into Arrezo.

'Get me a crash helmet and pick me up at the same time tonight,' she shouted at him as she rushed into the cafe. Carter had no intention of moving and sat down at the nearest table to await Sophia's arrival so he could order a coffee and admire the talent again, just to wind her up a little. She was not amused to find him at the table, but brought him his coffee, threatening to tip the next one in his lap if he was still admiring other ladies when she came back. A lady scorned, he thought to himself. The coffee was drunk and he left in search of a second crash helmet to avoid being pulled over by the police.

There were plenty of other cafes in the town and Carter spent his time sitting at these, admiring a different selection of nubile young ladies. If he had pulled once, he could do it again he thought with some contempt. Sauntering slowly back to her cafe, he was deliberately late. She was also playing it cool and had sat at one of the tables with a glass of wine. The half empty bottle was placed in the centre. There was no second glass. Carter didn't say a word but merely drew up the second chair and sat down.

Placing the new crash helmet on the table he reached for her glass only to receive a withering look from Sophia. 'Don't,' she said, if you want a glass, go and get a glass from the kitchen.' 'That's your job,' he laughed at her. 'No, if we are a partnership, then we do things together. I am not your servant. I bought the wine, if you want a glass, get your own,' and she starred at him in defiance. 'OK, I will but you are mine tonight, so be prepared,' and he left for the bar, grinning all the way.

The bottle was soon demolished and Carter said, 'Do you want another, which means I shouldn't drive, or do we go back to the villa now and continue where we left of last night?'

'I have an apartment here if you want to stay, and we can have that second bottle,' she coyly announced. The glasses were refilled, and then refilled a second time. They were both rather the worse for wear when they fell into her apartment. There was plenty of drunken fondling and kissing, clothes were removed, but he found he couldn't perform. Sophia tried her hardest to get a repeat performance of the previous night, but without success.

Carter was devastated and retreated under the duvet. She joined him and cuddled up to console. 'Sorry too much wine, shouldn't have drunk so much, I'm sorry,' he muttered. He had failed again and he turned away. This wasn't what he wanted at all. But sleep and too much wine overtook him within minutes. It was hot and it prompted memories of the desert to enter his brain. The heat, the dust, the smells, the attack, the noise, the explosion, and finally the blood and gore as the solder next to him disintegrated. Carter shouted as he thrashed about in the bed. Screams rang out.

'Dio mio!' Sophia shouted in his ear. She desperately shook him over and over again until he woke sweating from his nightmare. 'Must get away,' he shouted back at her, his eyes glazed, Carter had no idea where he was, it was all strange, he was somewhere alien, he didn't understand anything. Pushing Sophia aside, he stood up and held his head in his hands.

'Dio mio!' she repeated, 'What devil are you? What happened? Are you possessed?'

Carter just looked at her, he was confused and distressed, 'It was a nightmare, a bad dream of something that happened to me. I nearly died and someone was killed because of my mistake. He haunts me in my dreams, he doesn't leave me in peace, ever.' Collapsing back onto the bed, he broke down in tears, 'I killed him, I killed him, I killed him. It was all my fault and I can't do anything about it. He comes back to remind me what I have done to him.' Sophia didn't know how to react. There was a madness in this man. Was she safe with this lunatic? Would he hurt her, she really didn't know.

'I'll go, I must go, get away,' he said frantically. Sophia watched helplessly as he grabbed up his clothes and fled the apartment. She heard him slam the door downstairs and watched him from the apartment window as he ran up the road, pulling on his T-shirt as he went. Disappearing around the corner Carter made a bee line for his bike. He thought he wasn't too drunk to ride it, but he was certainly way over the legal limit. Unlocking his helmet off the bike's pannier, he jammed it on and went to move off just as he caught sight of the police car in his mirror. Fuck, too late, they have seen me and I can't risk being questioned, he thought as he roared off.

As he did so, the road was immediately illuminated by red and blue lights of the chasing police car, but Carter had a good start on the car and he left them standing. Unfortunately it didn't last long, and he under estimated the sharpness of the next corner and ended up lying flat on the road, winded. The police car disgorged its two occupants who grabbed Carter, and left him standing helpless and shaken, while he gathered his thoughts on how to avoid being arrested. If he was taken into custody, he was doomed. The police handled him roughly, which Carter resented, and he instinctly reacted, fighting back with his army training coming into play. The police were just local officers, they had no idea how to handle an ex-army unarmed combat expert. Amazingly even drunk, he managed to head butt and then push one officer over, and immediately swung around to punch the other in the face. That was enough to floor him and Carter turned his attention to the officer who had been pushed down, he was reaching for his gun and Carter knew he had to be disarmed quickly. A well aimed kick saw the gun fly into space and another kick to the face rendered him unconscious. The gun was recovered and Carter shot through both front tyres of their car to make sure he wasn't followed. The gun was dropped without thinking, that was all he needed it for, just enough to delay them. There was going to be trouble now, and he had to put some real distance between himself and the police quickly. The two officers were still prone on the ground, when Carter remounted his bike clumsily and rode off to the holiday villa to hide. His hands were shaking and he had trouble controlling the bike around the tight bends. The lights on the bike were switched off, so anyone following him had no real idea of the direction he was taking, dangerous but effective.

It was a good fifteen miles up to the villa but he made it in record time. The bike was hidden in an outbuilding behind straw bales, a cover thrown over it and general farm rubbish piled in front. Scurrying off inside the building, the lights weren't switched on in the villa, as he had to make sure the building looked deserted and locked up for the season, if anyone came looking for him. His hands were still shaking as he locked up, and he poured a large scotch to help him calm down as soon as he sat down. What a stupid fucking mess he had made of that.

Back in town there were crowds and police cars everywhere, descriptions were being radioed in from the two hapless officers, the gun had been recovered and bagged, and a man hunt started. Sophia had left her apartment and joined the crowds to find out what had happened. She had heard the gun shots and feared the worse. When she heard it was a drunk on a motorbike who had assaulted two policemen and run off, she knew instantly in her heart, that it was Carter. What had she got herself into? Did she inform the police, did she say what he was like that evening, would he come back, and was she in danger. She was utterly confused, she needed to help him, he was so troubled. She decided she was the one to save him. Would he have gone back to the villa? Where else would he go? If he wasn't there, what did she do?

She was relieved to hear that no one had been killed despite the gun shots, just a few dented egos from the police officers, who although they outnumbered him, had been out fought and somehow let the madman escape. Slowly the crowd dispersed, the police cars went back to the station, leaving just the forensic team on the scene. Sophia went back to her apartment, she would search for him in the morning, it was too obvious to go out into the mountains now.

She spent a restless few hours in the apartment, eventually leaving about 6am when she could stand it no longer. She couldn't pace the floor in the apartment any more. There were few hours before she had to start work and during that time she needed to make contact with Carter, if she could. There was an ancient Fiat five hundred owned by the cafe that was used for deliveries, that she had access to. That could be used to go to the villa and hopefully speak to Carter. If he had fled, she would have to come clean and tell the police what she knew. The Fiat started after a couple of false starts and she drove away in a cloud of exhaust fumes.

The car strained at the hills and she knew it wouldn't make the steep track that led to the villa. That would have to be walked. If he was watching, he would see her approach. The Fiat was parked on the roadside close to the villa track. There were plenty of places where you could pull over without attracting attention. Walking up the gravel track there was no sign of life. A walk around the building did not entice Carter out. She called his name to no avail. Disappointed she went back to her car, assuming he had now fled. When she opened the door, Carter slid into the other front seat. 'Drive,' he said, 'Anywhere but here. Go!' Startled by his appearance, she did just that, and headed off on the road to Sienna.

'Do you have your mobile with you?' She nodded. 'Phone the cafe, tell them you had an emergency call from a family member in Sienna and you have borrowed the car and you are having trouble with it. As a consequence you won't be in today, can Maria cover for you and you will swap rotas with her later. Don't do it yet, let's get to Sienna and I'll talk to you properly. I'm in trouble and I need to think how to hide.' Carter lapsed back into silence and sat brooding until they arrived in the town, entering through one of the city walls. They parked up, found a cafe and ordered coffees.

'You will have guessed it was me who had the argument with the police, they will be hunting for me after I fired off those couple of shots. I have nowhere to go and I need to hide until the heat dies down,' said Carter. 'There is my apartment we could use, you could hide there but you need to change your appearance dramatically. I think I can help there,' she grinned at him.

A trip around the town saw his head shaved, his clothes totally changed, glasses and some theatrical make up purchased, they would do a dry run that evening to make sure it worked. Returning to Arrezzo, Carter noted there were no extra police cars on the road, was he safe? Were there any police sniffing around the villa, was the bike safely hidden? He asked for the car to pull in so he could check, for his own sanity if nothing else. Sophia took him a little further down the road this time and Carter jumped out and scrambled up the bank. Fifteen minutes later he was back, satisfied he hadn't been investigated and the villa was off the police radar. Sooner or later the search would spread to the villa and he would be discovered because he had stupidly used his name on all the paperwork. He needed to avoid that possibility, and he was already formulating plans to avoid capture. When they arrived back in Arrezzo, she gave him her keys, parked the Fiat and went to make her apologies to the cafe owner. She did not get back to the apartment until after midnight to find Carter with a false moustache. She laughed but admitted it suited him and changed his whole look. She said that he really shouldn't go out until after dark.

Carter relaxed but knew he was a fugitive and he had no idea how to avoid being constantly on the run. There had to be a long term solution, but in the short term he had to avoid arrest and he knew eventually he would have to leave the area for pastures new. One day he would just up and leave Sophia, Arezzo and Italy, and hide somewhere else. Although they were both tired, sex resumed as normal and they both slept like babies that night. Carter was at ease for the moment, he would hide here and try and explain things in the morning.

There was a promise that he would stay in the apartment during the day and meet up with Sophia in the evening. They would check on the villa every day but use the car, not the bike. That should buy them some time. Carter wouldn't have slept so peacefully if he knew he had left a vital clue behind during the attack. That clue was about to cause him a lot of grief.

CHAPTER 98

The police gun had been examined for prints and the forensic team couldn't believe their luck. Carter's prints were on the gun. The computer files immediately identified his prints and an alert was issued and four police forces were contacted with the news. The Italian police took immediate action and put out a national alert. They also had a good description of the bike from the officers. That bike could well be his downfall and they would keep a very real eye out for it.

When the email arrived on Robert's computer, he had to read it twice. Not only did it confirm Carter was still in Italy, they had him in a specific town or its surroundings. All the roads out of Arezzo had traffic cameras, they tracked Carter out of the town but couldn't find him arriving anywhere else. 'Got him,' shouted Robert and he phoned the contact number on the email. After half an hour Robert had agreed a policy with the Italian team and sat back to see if there would be any further developments.

Robert was back on the computer, this would be a long day he thought. Maps were brought up on screen, the area between Arezzo and Sienna looked fairly barren. There was no town of any size, but lots of small villages just off the beaten track. 'He has to be in that area somewhere, has to be!' Robert muttered to himself. It was tempting to fly out and join in but judging by his previous attempts to help, he wouldn't make a lot of difference, and he sat down to study the maps again.

'Where is that bloody bike, find that and we find him,' he said, again to no one in particular. Robert spent the next hour sending emails to Italy with suggestions he thought might help, but he was sure that they had it all under control. They needed to narrow the search area down to a much smaller area. Eliminate where he wasn't, what was left had to be his hiding place.

CHAPTER 99

Sophia was up early so she could go off to her job, she would have something to eat at the cafe. Carter was still in bed and she warned him not to go out during the day. If he wanted to venture out, it had to be in disguise and only in the evening. They would meet up after her shift. Carter knew he would go stir crazy if he spent all his time locked up in the apartment. After an hour he decided that was enough and he needed to get out. Donning his disguise he put on his 'local' clothes and slipped out.

There was little point in strolling around the town, that was asking for trouble, he had to get back to the villa and get his bike. That would have to be smuggled in, or hidden up outside of town. It was very recognisable, so hiding it would be the better of the options. There was now the small problem of getting back to the villa. It was fifteen miles away, he could walk it just about in the time needed to meet up with Sophia later but it would be a tight. It was worth the risk because there were plenty of police about, the bike definitely didn't come back to town then, he would hide it somewhere. The bike was important, he had to be mobile, it had to somewhere handy, not fifteen miles away. Sophia would have to brought into his plans somehow he realised. If she didn't want to play ball, she would have to be left behind, her decision.

Whatever! He started to walk out on the Sienna road, his hand out, thumbing a lift. It was a rare sight now and few drivers took notice but one kind soul took pity on him, and gave him a lift after twenty minutes of walking. Carter managed to get through to the driver he was staying with friends but his car had broken down, it was being fixed by his friend. Pointing out where he needed to be dropped, Carter thanked the driver and set off up the gravel track. The villa was still locked up and secure. No one seemed to have disturbed it. His belongings, money, passports and clothes were packed up and hauled out to the bike. The bales were removed, all the farm tools put back and the bike wheeled out. His kit was packed and the bike started up.

There was plenty of time to get back to Arezzo but he needed one thing, a big groundsheet or cover to disguise the bike. DIY wasn't something the Italians have much of a taste for so he ended up looking for an agricultural supplier. Driving round the local villages he found just what he was looking for, and purchased a large heavy duty cover and a couple of large expanding straps to keep the cover in place.

Aware that every policeman in the area would be looking for him, Carter took as many tracks and small roads as he could back to the apartment. The town was quiet at this time of the day and he wheeled the bike into a small back road, covered it after removing his kit and strapped it up. It looked innocuous enough. Slinging his possessions over his shoulder he made his way back to the apartment and hid his bag under the bed. It was close enough to the end of Sophia's shift for him to be able to slip out of the apartment and slowly walk round to her cafe.

Feeling safe now, he went to a table that gave him a good view of the court yard and an escape route if needed. It took Sophia a few minutes to realise he was sitting outside. She didn't acknowledge him but simply took a coffee over to him. Carter

371

made it last as long as he could, ordered another and waited for Sophia to finish her shift.

Eventually she cleared up, walked out and discreetly signalled him to follow. So far, so good, he thought to himself, no one had recognised or challenged him, and he made it back to the apartment without incident. 'There are police everywhere,' she said. 'They are definitely out to get you. What made you take off like that. I thought the devil had possessed you. You knew you were not fit to ride the bike, why didn't you just sit down somewhere and sober up. Oh no, you had to ride off, the macho man and to assault two policemen, shoot up their car and ride off. You are a moron. You frightened me and now you are a wanted man, and I will be jailed if they ever find I have sheltered you.'

'I panicked, the rest was to make sure I didn't get arrested,' he answered. She scowled at him, 'All you would have got was a warning or a fine.' 'Not as simple as that, I got into trouble in Spain and there is a warrant out for me. I would have gone to jail,' he replied. She looked at him in horror, 'What did you do?'

'I killed someone! It was an accident but the police don't think so. I got into a fight, the other guy fell and hit his head, but they think it was deliberate. I'm on the run.' Sophia didn't know what to do. She feared for her life now and backed away from him. 'You need to go,' she screamed at him. 'Calm down, I'm going to go but I want you to come with me,' he said.

'You must be joking. Why would I go with you?' She was becoming very agitated and Carter need to calm her down and get her on side as quickly as possible. 'All that is behind me, things will calm down soon. I want you to come away with me for a short while, until things calm down at least. You have holiday owing, make the excuse you need to take care of a sick relative or something. I have money, a lot of money, we can go where we want, do what we want, escape. You are stuck in a dead-end job, going nowhere, just existing, and you are not getting any younger, nor am I. Just think about it for a while. This is your chance to escape. Go somewhere new, start again.'

'How much money? And how can I trust you,' she sneered at him.

'Enough to buy a house easily, and more,' he said. 'And you can't, but what have you got to lose. We fit together bloody well, in more ways than one,' and he laughed.

'Where?' she said somewhat startled at his outburst. 'Perugia. Fantastic city, easy to hide, lay low for a month, come back, pack up and find a tropical island, our paradise where no one will find us. How does that sound? You have nothing here, all of is this is rented. You have nothing to make you stay. No family, no money and few friends. What have you got to lose? Nothing!' Sophia calmed down, she was listening. She didn't believe Carter at all, she needed a guarantee from him. 'Will you give me my own money? I have never had my own money. Do this and I will go. When?'

'Tonight. The bike is a couple of roads away, I have my kit from the villa. Pack a bag with enough clothes for a couple of nights and we will buy you something nice in Perugia.' She didn't ask how he had got to the villa, or how he had got the bike back to Arezzo. It didn't matter now. She wanted to escape. Do it tonight, why the hell not? If it went wrong, what had she lost? Try it, she could always come back. A few minutes was all it took to knock up a quick meal, which was quickly followed by packing just a few things that would fit into the panier on the bike.

They crept out of the apartment, carrying a bag each, to the hidden bike. It was quickly uncovered and the cover folded for future use. The bike should be disguised where ever it was taken. Making sure that there were no squad cars in sight, they mounted the bike and gently rode off down as many side streets as possible before joining the main road to Perugia. The motorway could be avoided for most of the journey, the final approach around the lake would be recorded, so Carter again switched off the bike's lights until he could take the twisting road into the city. Once into the Palazzo dei Priori, Carter chose a small hotel, hiding the bike down a narrow side street close to an Irish pub. They booked in and chose a room at the back of the hotel. It was quiet and they would get some rest before deciding what to do next.

'Let's stay here for a couple of days to sort things out. You have a proper passport I need to do something about mine,' Carter said. 'I could use a bit of help to sort out some false papers, no idea where I could source them, have to make some subtle enquiries I suppose. I have some contacts in Spain, and person who might want to do some business with me again. I still have his number.'

Carter spent the rest of the evening phoning. At first he didn't get much of a reception, but as money was discussed, the listener at the other end became more receptive. They would need some passport photos of Carter and gave him a PO account address they could be sent to. Payment would be in cash and in person at a pre-arranged point outside of town, rather than a public place. It wasn't going to be cheap, but it was his only chance of a long term escape mechanism being put in place. With everything actioned, they both relaxed and decided to try out on the town and get something to drink. Carter was convinced he had it all sorted now. The police had no idea where he was, he had money, he had a partner who believed in him, and now he had an escape plan finally that would work, he just had got to wait for his new ID and they could be away. The Caribbean seemed to be a great idea, it didn't have to be a British Island either. Beginning to sound good, he thought.

CHAPTER 100

For the previous three days, the police in Arezzo had combed through the town, whilst other units had checked through outlaying house, farms and villas.

Eventually they came across the villa Carter was meant to have been guarding, it had been broken into and ransacked. Obviously the thieves had enjoyed the peace and tranquillity of the area and had made a thorough job of taking everything of value and wrecking the rest. The owner was contacted, who informed them that an agency man was supposed to be guarding the property. Once they were contacted, Carter's name came into the frame again. Forensics confirmed his prints were all over the villa along with a lot of other people's. Sophia's also appeared and she was on the police records for minor misdemeanours regarding tax fraud, a favourite Italian past time.

They had a direct link between Carter and Sophia. Her records gave an address in Arezzo which was duly investigated. Now the police knew they had the right person, as Carter's prints were all over her apartment. It was apparent they had fled the scene some time before, and the police would have to spread their search area wider again. All of this was emailed to Robert who was going back into frustrated mode again. 'Always so bloody close, but not close enough. He has a three day lead on us again, he could be anywhere by now, He's probably not even in Italy.'

However, all Robert could do was wait for further news and hopefully a break through somewhere down the line. No, that was too much for him, he had a gut feeling this would be Carter's final confrontation. He had to be on the scene. There was still some holiday owing and he booked himself out for a couple of days so he could catch a flight out in the morning.

There was no local airport, so a hire car would be necessary from Pisa. That evening by pure luck, the traffic police had a reported incident of an unlit bike being ridden around Perugia earlier in the week. It registered with the traffic team that it matched the description of an unlit bike leaving Arezzo after the attack. When a further alert went out to look out for a French registered bike, possibly with two passengers, they thought this sounded too much of a coincidence and examined tapes of the motorway cameras earlier in the week. There were several possibilities, but one three nights ago fitted perfectly. There was a good chance they were now in Perugia. Certainly worth putting the local police on alert to check hotels and boarding houses in the city.

Carter had received a message on his mobile, the ID was complete and ready. The contact didn't want to meet in Perguria but close by at Assisi the following evening. Carter agreed and said he would bring the money. Carter explained to Sophia what had happened, and he was going to collect the papers the following day. 'I will come with you, we can leave all this, leave the bike and go to Rome on the train. They won't be expecting that. If we leave the room as if we are coming back, if it is inspected they will think we are still in the city. From Rome we can fly anywhere before going to the Caribbean, cover our tracks very efficiently.' Sophia intended to be with Carter when he collected the passport, otherwise he could easily escape without her, and she had no intention of letting him do that. Carter was her future and she intended to hold on to him. Carter looked around the room, there was nothing of value there, she could replace her clothes easily enough. Actually it wasn't a bad idea, why not? All they really wanted was the backpack, the new documents and they could be away very easily. It was a long ride to Rome and he preferred the train to the bike.

Robert had managed to fly to Pisa, hire a car and was on the long journey south past Sienna. In Arrezo he stopped and introduced himself to the police and explained he had been chasing Carter since the murders in England. They in turn gave him an introduction to the police in Perugia. After an hour Robert arrived exhausted but was actually welcomed by the police there. Far from a hindrance, they thought he might help them search for Carter, they also thought if it went wrong they could blame Robert for interfering. It was a win, win situation for them. A blaze of glory if it worked, and a scape goat if it didn't.

Robert would be in one of the squad cars as they investigated the city. That would put him in direct contact of control in Perugia. Unbeknown to Robert, Carter had just left Perugia, they had abandoned the hotel room, retrieved the bike and were heading to Assisi. Robert was back in the middle of the town and asked which areas had been searched. He said that Carter seemed to favour small hotels and B&Bs, and they should concentrate on these first. An hour and a half later they found the room Carter and Sophia had taken, and with the help of the owner, gained an entry. It looked as if they had gone out for a meal or a drink, until they questioned the maid who said they had crash helmets with them and a back pack. They were definitely not in the building. The mention of the crash helmets immediately rang alarm bells with Robert. 'They are on the move, send an ABP out to all cars that they have only recently left Perugia and will be close by to the city.

'Going to get you now son,' he muttered to himself and he ordered the car to the north side of the city hoping he could catch him on the motorway. He also asked if the traffic could be monitored, especially on the motorways and received a confirmation that was already being done. The net was closing in, but Carter had no idea that he was being hunted. Everything had worked out fine. The meeting went without a hitch, he was now Edwarde Baptiste, a French engineer, which would very helpful if they settled on any of the French Caribbean islands. Carter had a couple of celebratory drinks, which Sophia didn't approve of, but allowed him under the circumstances.

Money was exchanged, the courier went his way and the bike was started to carry them to Rome. Carter said he would leave the bike at the station, complete with keys, to enable it to be easily stolen. It would no doubt be driven all over the countryside in a wild goose chase, and help divert where they were really heading. Road blocks were already in place around the city with the cars careful hidden out of sight. Carter passed one on his way back to Perugia and was instantly recognised. His position was radioed ahead with the spotter car in silent pursuit some two hundred metres behind. As the bike approached the city, one of the other police cars suddenly pulled out in front of Carter, blocking the road.

Carter swerved but hit the police car in the bonnet, swinging the bike around into the driver's door. The impact threw him on to the bonnet of the car, but Sophia wasn't so lucky, she hit the door and fell off the bike unconscious and badly injured. Her body prevented the door being opened which gave Carter a chance to pull the bike away. It was still running and he jumped on it and sped off leaving Sophia behind.

It seemed incredibly callous to the police but Carter didn't think like that, this was survival and nothing else. The bike needed to be ditched and he needed to get the train to Rome as he had planned. Whatever he did, he needed to get through Perugia, out the other side and get away. Perfect bike country he thought, bloody awkward for the chasing cars. Robert had heard all the radio messages which were being translated for him in the car. 'He's coming back into the city because he knows we can block him to the north, he has a plan, he knows how to escape, take us back to the centre for the moment, we can be directed from there,' said Robert. Within minutes they were back in the main square and patrolling round hoping to hear a report of a sighting or even see him themselves. Cat and mouse, though Robert and now we are about to pounce. One of the cars had spotted Carter now and confirmed he was heading back into the city at high speed. Robert was waiting.

CHAPTER 101

'There he is, there he is,' shouted Robert pointing up the street. 'Up there, that street, there!' The patrol car immediately skidded to a halt and reversed to a point it could hand brake turn up the side street after Carter. 'Radio it in, we may need help to corner him,' shouted Robert. The co-driver was in immediate and constant radio contact with the Italian police HQ, giving their position every few seconds.

Carter was on his beloved motor bike and riding for all he was worth down the narrow streets, but the patrol car was still catching up with him far too quickly, the driver was motoring like a maniac. Carter knew the bike was his only hope of avoiding the police, it had got him out of trouble earlier that evening and it was his only hope of avoiding them now. They had blockaded him very effectively then but he had managed to escape by the skin of his teeth because the bike was so manoeuvrable.

He had the advantage now, in that the medieval roads in the old town were so narrow it was hard for the car to follow safely. Or so he thought, there were several load bangs behind him which he thought were gun shots until he realised they were parked car wing mirrors being smashed off. So they weren't going to drive safely, they were just going to catch him regardless of the consequences. They were very intent in catching him, and any second, the car would ram him, knocking him off his bike so they could eventually arrest him, and make sure he spent the rest of his life behind bars. It had been a long chase, but he wasn't finished yet.

Carter did a dangerous skid almost coming to a halt in the process to be able to skitter down an alley, which completely threw the patrol car off his track. He heard the car scream to a halt, the driver yelling in frustration, which made him laugh. Carter knew he was going to make it now, he had thrown them off and he had a clear head start on the police car.

In the valley below he saw the train he was originally hoping to catch, he wouldn't be able to do that now, the chase had taken too long, but an idea came into his brain, dangerous but he could do it, if he dare do it, it was playing a giant game of chicken. The passageway emptied out onto the main road which led to the station, he accelerated as fast as humanly possible to race the train to the crossing. If he could get there before the police car, he could get away and hide again and pick up the train at a later date. Behind him he could hear the patrol car, it had found a way around the town, and was now on the same road as he was.

The crossing was just four hundred yards away, the half barriers were down and the train nearly there. It was going to be close and that bloody car was nearly upon him, that just made him race harder. 'Can we get to him before the crossing, he mustn't get across,' shouted Robert.

The driver said he is never going to beat the train to the crossing, we've got him trapped. Robert could see the train was fast bearing down on the crossing, but so was Carter, there were just yards separating them. The bike might just get across the crossing in front of the train with only nanoseconds to spare. Robert couldn't believe he was even going to attempt it, but then what had he got to lose. Carter put one last effort into avoiding the train, he switched lanes at the last second to get a clear run on the side of the road without a barrier. The chasing car was almost alongside him. They were all going to be killed, there was no way they could get across in front of the train.

'Don't' was all Robert could think of shouting as Carter cleared the crossing less than half a second in front of the train. The patrol car slammed on its brakes, turning sideways on to the crossing, it slid under the barrier and there was a shower of sparks as the train hit the car and ripped off the whole side. All the occupants instinctly threw themselves across the car as the airbags went off with a deafening bang. The car was pushed back out onto the road and Robert couldn't quite believe he was still alive, and Christ, Carter had avoided capture. Again. Struggling out of the wrecked vehicle he used his mobile to explain what had happened, and to arrange a tow truck and transport back. So bloody close again.

CHAPTER 102

Here is the 10 o'clock news. And we turn to Italy for breaking news. It has just been confirmed that Carter Rogers, the notorious murderer and drug runner has been killed in Italy. He was apparently being chased by a patrol car when he attempted to cross in front of a train on an automated crossing. Police say he safely crossed in front of the train only to be hit and killed by a train travelling in the opposite direction.

The news faded into another article and Robert smiled, it had all happened in front of him a few hours before. Switching the hotel TV off, he swallowed the last of his scotch and settled down for the night. Tomorrow he would return to England, he might even get welcomed as something of a hero after bringing the Carter case to finality, although not quite in the fashion he had intended.

At least Carter didn't get put away to then be released for good behaviour at some point in the future. Carter was dead, this was what he really wanted, Carter was gone and good riddance. So much for early retirement, they could stick that, there was still life left in him, and he smiled at that thought. I got him for you, Katrina, I got him at last. You can rest in peace now.

THE END